Rivalry

Rivalry

Marina Martindale

Good Oak
Press, LLC

Good Oak Press, LLC
P.O. Box 51244
Denton, Texas 76206-1244

Editor: Cynthia Roedig
Proofreader: Leslie Skarecky
Cover Illustration: Wes Lowe
Cover Design: Good Oak Press, LLC
Typesetting: Good Oak Press, LLC
ISBN: 979-8987051498

Acknowledgments

Thank you to the team who helped me create Rivalry. Cynthia my editor, Cynthia Roedig, my proofreader, Leslie Skarecky, and Wes Lowe, for another outstanding cover illustration.

To Dan:

ᓭ ONE ᓯ

JENNA WINTERS WATCHED her clients' faces as she finished her presentation. All three appeared to be deep in thought. Oscar Shelton and his family were commercial real estate developers in the Denver area. Their latest project was a luxury resort and spa called The Shelton Inn at The Denver Tech Center. While they had been clients of Salisbury and Norton Architects for many years, it was Jenna's first time working with them. Focusing her gaze on Oscar, his eyes seemed to soften and a hint of a smile came over his face.

"Interesting," he finally said, "and you brought up a very good point. While the waterfall fountain would have created a nice ambience between the lobby and the atrium, I agree with your concerns about the expense of the additional plumbing, along with the maintenance costs, and I too like the idea of using more interior landscaping in the atrium."

"I agree," said Oscar's son, Chris. "I also think we're about ready to start the next phase."

"I'm not." There was a hint of anger in the young woman's voice. "I wanted the waterfall fountain."

"Apparently my daughter-in-law disagrees," said Oscar, "so the three of us will have to discuss the matter further." He turned his attention to the black man seated next to Jenna. Chad Runyon was the project architect.

"We'll start working on the other changes you suggested," said Chad.

"Good, because I want to break ground this spring. Thank you, Chad, and the rest of your team as well. I like the changes you've made so far, and I look forward to our next meeting."

As the meeting broke up, Chad escorted the Sheltons to the elevator. Jenna, along with the two other architects, Mitch Harper and Jim Langly, were waiting in his office when he returned.

"Nice presentations, everyone." He cleared a small stack of blueprints off his desk and took his seat. "It's always nice to see the clients happy, and you were right about the fountain, Jenna. It was way too much."

"I'm glad you had my back," said Jenna, "because I didn't know what to expect."

"Oscar and his son are good clients. I worked with them on a couple of office buildings, back when Ian was their project architect. They know what works and what doesn't; although, I'm not so sure about this latest daughter-in-law. She's wife number three for Chris, and I've not worked with her before."

"Then I guess we'll have to wait and see what happens, and I'm afraid Ian was before my time."

"I remember him," said Mitch. "I worked with him on a few projects as well."

"You would have liked him," said Chad. "He mentored me when I first came onboard, and I inherited his office after he left. He's now an architecture professor in Arizona."

They turned their attention to the drawings while Jenna and the others took notes on their tablets. CeCe Wood, another interior designer, greeted Jenna with a smile when she returned to her desk.

"So, how did it go?" she asked.

"It went well."

"I take it they liked your suggestions for the lobby."

"They did. At least the old man did."

"Good, because he's the one whose opinion counts. He also has a thing for blondes. Or so I hear."

"Say what?"

"Hey, I'm just messing with you." CeCe had a mischievous look on her face. "I hear his wife used to come to the meetings too, back in the day. She apparently had blonde hair, but I don't think she wore it long like you do."

"Then I guess I'll take it as a compliment, although being a redhead must take you off the hook entirely." Jenna turned her attention to her computer and noticed the time on the screen. "I don't know where the day went. I didn't realize it had gotten so late."

"It sure has, and thank goodness it's Friday. So, do you and Ken have any plans for the weekend?"

"We're supposed to go to a big family wedding tomorrow night."

"Yeah, I heard about the wedding, but you don't seem to be too excited about it."

Jenna shrugged. "I guess I'm just not big on going to weddings."

"Everything okay with you two?"

"We're fine, CeCe. I know you've known Ken since high school. I also know you have high hopes, but we've only been seeing one another a few months."

"I know, and I was about to say you may find this wedding a little more interesting. Apparently, there's a rift of some kind in Ken's family. It goes way back and had something to do with his grandfather having a falling out with one of his sisters, back when they were younger. From what Ken tells me, all the uncles, aunts, and cousins from both sides of the feud will be there. Hopefully, there won't be any big brawls."

"Will his grandfather, and the sister in question, be there?" asked Jenna.

"Ken's grandfather passed away a few years ago. I don't know if the sister is still around or not. If so, she would be quite elderly by now."

"Well, it's unfortunate when these things happen, but with one, maybe both, being gone, I doubt it'd be much of an issue anymore." Jenna shut down her computer and gathered up her coat and purse. "See you Monday."

Jenna took the elevator down to the parking garage and slipped behind the wheel of her gray Camry. She checked her text messages while she waited for the car to warm up. Ken was with one of his friends at a sports bar called O'Malley's Grill. She was welcome to join them if she wished. She quickly typed a reply.

"Thanks for the invite, but I have things to take care of if we're doing the wedding tomorrow night."

His reply came a moment later. *"I understand. See you tomorrow. I'll pick you up at five."*

Jenna felt relieved as she drove out of the parking garage. After a quick stop at nearby deli, she went straight home. It had been a long, stressful day. She looked forward to a quiet evening and long, hot soak in the tub.

* * *

Ken read his message and put his phone away. "Jenna can't make it, so it looks like it's just us guys tonight. Let's order some burgers, and we can watch the game."

"Or the scenery." His friend nodded toward two women standing next to the bar. "Check out the blonde in the red sweater, and brunette in the navy-blue dress standing next to her. Wanna try your luck?"

"Well, of course I do, Greg. Anytime. The one in the blue dress looks hot. So, what do you have in mind?"

"Just wait and see, Kenny boy," he said with a smirk. The two women were scanning the room, looking for a place to sit, but all of the tables were occupied. Greg caught the blonde's eye and motioned for her and her friend to come to their table.

"Are you sure you don't mind if we join you?" she asked.

"Not at all. We have plenty of room." He extended his hand as he and Ken introduced themselves. Ken pulled back one of the empty chairs and helped the other woman out of her coat.

"The name's Jeri." She gave him a sultry smile as she sat down and smoothed out her dress. "And this is my friend, Erin. Her boss just gave her a much-deserved raise, so she suggested we go out and celebrate."

"Congratulations on the raise," said Ken, "and what about you, Jeri?"

"I'm afraid I didn't get a raise."

He couldn't resist flirting back. "You didn't? Then I'm sorry to hear it. So, what do you do that you're not getting paid enough for?"

"I'm an office manager for a restaurant supply company. I'm also a part-time student. I'm working on my MBA."

"Good for you. I'm a number cruncher myself. I work with a CPA firm. It's me and two other accountants. So, why don't we buy you dinner to celebrate Erin's raise, and to help make up for you not getting one."

"Are you sure?"

"Of course, I'm sure. It's our treat." Ken flagged down their server and ordered cheeseburgers for Jeri and himself while Greg and Erin opted for a taco platter and a Caesar salad. As they enjoyed their meal, Ken realized he and Jeri had the same sense of humor. They also loved sports, although Jeri was more of a Packers fan than a Broncos fan.

"You're kidding," said Ken.

"My dad was a die-hard Green Bay fan. It was the only team we watched when I was a kid."

"Well then, I guess we'll have to take you ladies to some Broncos games."

"I'd love to. Anytime," said Jeri.

"What about you, Erin?" asked Greg.

"We'll see."

The conversation shifted to other topics. The more Ken talked with Jeri, the more he felt drawn to her. Erin, however, was less talkative than the others and appeared to be somewhat standoffish.

"Thanks for dinner, guys," said Jeri as she pushed her plate away. "It was delicious."

"I'm glad you liked it," said Ken.

"I enjoyed the company too. You know, Ken, I could sit here and talk with you all night."

"Me too, but what would people say?"

As their server gathered up their empty plates, Ken reached for his wallet and discreetly gave her one of his cards.

"All kidding aside," he quietly said, "I'd really would like for the two of us to get together again. Soon."

"Me too. I'm writing my personal cell number on the back of mine." Ken gave her a wink as he put her card in his wallet.

"In the meantime, can we buy you ladies a cup of coffee?"

Jeri turned her attention to Erin, who seemed ill at ease as she gave Jeri a pleading look. "While we would love to stay and have coffee with you, I'm afraid we'll have to take a raincheck."

"Gotcha," Ken said under his breath. "So, I'll call you. Soon. I really mean it."

"Thanks. I look forward to hearing from you." Jeri turned her attention back to Erin, who looked relieved as she grabbed her purse. Ken helped Jeri with her coat and gave her a warm hug before she and Erin stepped away.

"Well, I'm glad one of us had a good time," said Greg. "I was hoping she'd be quick and easy, but she turned out to be about as exciting as a plate of warmed-over mashed potatoes. So, what about you? Will you be hooking up with her later? Or are you worried about Jenna finding out?"

"Nah. Jenna's a real sweetheart, but things are starting to wind down, although she's still a lot of fun in the sack. So, before we part company for good, I want us to do a few more horizontal mambos for the road." He looked at Jeri's card and smiled. "But if it means anything to you, I'll definitely be following up with this one."

❧TWO❧

JENNA RUMMAGED through her closet and asked herself a question out loud. "So, what do you wear to a wedding you would just as soon not attend, with a guy you're no longer interested in seeing?" She pulled out a simple, long-sleeved black dress. "It certainly suits the mood, but I'm not sure if wearing black to a wedding would be in good taste. Then again, do I really care if Ken likes it or not?"

She tossed the dress onto her bed, along with a red jacket. Completing the ensemble was a pair of black cone-heel boots and a long, gold chain necklace. Satisfied with her outfit, she hopped in the shower. Ken arrived as she was putting on her earrings. He greeted her with his usual kiss.

"Nice outfit," he said. "So, are you ready to go?"

"I think so. Let me get my coat."

Ken helped her with her coat and walked her out to his black Chevy Blazer. The late afternoon sun was dipping low and the temperature was dropping. Jenna shivered underneath her coat as she sat down in the passenger seat and waited for Ken to fire up the engine.

"My parents couldn't make it to the wedding," he said. "They're still on their cruise, and my sister went back to college, but there'll be plenty of other family there. Exactly who, I don't know. Many of them are relatives I don't know and don't care to know."

"Really? How come?"

"It's kind of a long story, but I'll try to keep it brief. My grandfather was a well-respected physician here in Denver. He had a younger sister, named Marjorie, who went off to college in Arizona, and soon became engaged to a man my grandfather didn't think was suitable."

"And why wasn't he suitable?"

6

"He wasn't a student. He was an aircraft mechanic. I'm not exactly sure how they met."

"So, what's wrong with an aircraft mechanic?" asked Jenna. "You know my father is an airline pilot, and they depend on their mechanics to keep flying safe."

"I understand, but you're missing the point."

"Okay. Then what was the point?"

"He was working class." There was a hint of disdain Ken's voice. "He came from a farm family in Nebraska."

"Why would his family have even mattered?"

"It mattered because my grandfather's family came from old money, and a farm boy turned grease monkey wasn't an acceptable choice for a husband, but she married him anyway. So, my grandfather pretty much wrote her off. Fortunately, she and her husband stayed in Arizona. We still saw one another at the obligatory weddings and funerals, but we didn't socialize. We stayed in our respective corners."

"Now that's cold," said Jenna. Ken responded with a shrug and went on with his story.

"From time-to-time we'd hear stories about Marjorie. Apparently, the farm boy did well. He eventually became the head honcho at a Cadillac dealership in Phoenix."

"I see. So did your grandfather ever change his mind?"

"No, he did not. My grandfather had another sister. Her name is Carolyn. She was never involved in their dispute. The bride is Aunt Carolyn's granddaughter, but I don't know if Marjorie and her family will be there or not."

Ken went silent and they soon drove into a church parking lot. The late winter air felt much colder when Jenna stepped out of the Blazer. The sanctuary was nearly full when they came inside. She felt relieved to be seated in the back. As they waited for the ceremony to begin, she focused her attention on the building itself. It was a typical Protestant church with oak pews and high vaulted ceilings with dark wooden beams. Big stained-glass windows lined the outer walls.

The minister soon stepped up to the altar, along with the groom and his four attendants. The organist began playing, and four bridesmaids, wearing black dresses with white bodices, made their way up the aisle. Taking their places at the altar, Jenna felt more at ease in her black and red outfit. Everyone rose to their feet as the bride and her father made their entrance and slowly walked up the aisle. She looked stunning in her ornate white satin gown and cathedral-length veil.

During the ceremony, Ken only seemed interested in trying to figure out who else was there. The reception would take place at a nearby hotel, where a sit-down dinner would be served. Hopefully, they would call it a night once the meal was over and the wedding cake was cut. On the way home, she would tell him she was ready to end the relationship. With any luck, he would feel as relieved as she was.

The wedding party was all smiles when they came back down the aisle and took their places in the narthex to greet their guests. Jenna gave the bride a warm smile as Ken introduced them, but she sighed in silent relief once they were in the parking lot.

* * *

The huge ballroom where the reception would take place was filled with elegantly set tables. A small wooden dancefloor had been placed off to the side, and a band was setting up next to it. A portable bar stood near the dancefloor. As Ken signed the guestbook someone checked off their names and they were escorted to their table. A green poker chip had been placed at one setting to indicate someone had ordered the pasta. Ken seemed displeased as he helped her out of her coat.

"I still don't understand why you didn't you get the chicken cordon bleu like everyone else," he said.

"I already told you. Swiss cheese gives me really bad heartburn."

Before Ken could respond another group arrived at their table. His face lit up as he greeted them with a happy smile.

"Uncle Walter, it's good to see you." He gave his uncle and aunt a big hug and greeted the rest of the group with handshakes. He was especially happy to see Joey, one of his cousins. He appeared to be the same age as Ken, and they both had the same dark hair and blue eyes.

"So, where are Uncle Ed and Aunt Leslie?" asked Ken.

"They're coming," said Walter. "They should be here any minute."

Ken introduced everyone to Jenna, telling her how he and Joey had grown up together and were more like brothers than cousins. His other uncle and aunt soon arrived, along with their children and a young grandchild. They were seated at the next table, and before long Ken was involved in their conversations. Jenna felt awkward as they chatted among themselves.

"I think I'll get a soda," she finally said. "Can I get you anything, Ken?"

"I'm good." He quickly turned his attention back to his family.

The room was filling up as Jenna took her place in line at the bar. Waiting her turn, she watched an elegantly dressed elderly woman in a wheelchair. She appeared to be good spirits as she engaged with other guests who greeted her with warm hugs and affectionate kisses. No doubt she was the grandmother of the bride.

"You're next," said the man standing behind her.

Jenna looked over her shoulder and found herself face-to-face with a sandy-haired man. "Sorry. I guess I wasn't paying attention."

"It's quite all right," he said. Stepping up to the bar, she ordered a Dr. Pepper and quickly stepped off to the side. The sandy haired man soon joined her.

"So which part of the clan are you from?' he asked.

"None," she said. "I'm here with a friend. His name is Ken Frank."

"I see." He suddenly looked a little awkward. "Then he would be one of the Jennings. Dr. Walter, his grandfather, had a daughter named Annie, who married a man named Patrick Frank."

"Ken mentioned something the other day about his grandfather being a doctor, but I'd not met any of his family until tonight." She stopped and extended her hand. "By the way, the name's Jenna. Jenna Winters."

"Nice to meet you, Jenna. I'm Andrew Grayson, but my friends all call me Drew. So, what do you do when you're not attending fancy weddings?"

"I'm an interior designer. I work for an architecture firm here in town."

"How interesting. I'm a civil engineer. I work for a firm in Dallas. I make sure the building doesn't fall down."

"Well, there you are," said another voice. The woman in the wheelchair, along with her caretaker, greeted Jenna with a smile. "I see you're getting acquainted with my grandson, so I thought I'd stop by and say hello before the bride and groom get here." She extended her hand. "And who might you be?"

"I'm Jenna Winters. I was just telling your grandson I'm an interior designer."

"Really." The old woman seemed pleased. "When I was younger, I thought about becoming an interior decorator, but then I ended up meeting my late husband, and that was that." A sad look came over her face, but she quickly shook it off and gave her grandson a smile.

"You know, Drew, I think that maybe after dinner, you should spend some time getting to know this lady better. I think the two of you might like one another."

"We'll see, Grandma. Ms. Winters is here with other friends."

The bride's father walked up to the band and asked to borrow a microphone. The bride and groom were on their way, and he asked the guests to please take their seats. Jenna excused herself and hurried back to her table as the wedding party made their entrance. Ken barely acknowledged her when she took her seat. He was still busy talking with his cousins. Listening to their conversation, she realized they would be staying long after dinner was over. The waitstaff began serving the salads while the bride's father, and the groom's father, toasted the happy couple. Once they were done, Ken and Joey picked up where they left off while the rest of Ken's family talked among themselves. Jenna sat in silence and pretended to be interested in their conversations. The main course arrived a few minutes later.

"What are you? A vegan or something?" Walter's wife loudly asked as the server set Jenna's entrée down. Suddenly, everyone's eyes were on her.

"No, I'm not a vegan," said Jenna. "My mother used to make pasta primavera when I was growing up, and I've always been fond of it."

The other woman seemed unimpressed. "We're not big on pasta. I suppose it's okay if you like cheap, comfort food, but we prefer to eat healthier."

Jenna was about to ask if a piece of chicken rolled up in ham and cheese and fried in breadcrumbs actually was actually healthier, but Walter jumped in before she had the chance.

"Now, now, Theresa." He quickly turned his attention to Jenna. "We do, on occasion, have lasagna or stuffed manicotti. Our personal chef has some wonderful Italian recipes which we really do enjoy. We just don't eat it very often."

"And neither do I," Jenna said firmly. One of Ken's cousins jumped in and quickly changed the subject. Jenna turned her attention back to her meal, hoping to enjoy the rest of it in peace. Once she finished, she grabbed her purse and stood from her chair.

"If you'll excuse me, I'll be right back."

Ken gave her a stern look. "And while you're away, we would appreciate it very much if you would avoid talking to the woman in the wheelchair."

"What are you talking about? Isn't this her granddaughter's wedding?"

"She isn't Aunt Carolyn." Ken pointed out another table. "Aunt Carolyn is sitting over there, in the peach-colored dress."

Jenna looked in the direction Ken had indicated. It was her first time seeing the white-haired woman in the peach dress.

"I'm sorry. I thought the lady in the wheelchair was your great aunt."

"Technically, she is," said Walter. "However, she married a man my father didn't approve of, and she did so out of spite. Her actions were an embarrassment to the family, and we too consider her an outsider. However, we understand Aunt Carolyn feels differently."

Jenna was stunned. The disagreement between Ken's grandfather and his sister had been passed down two generations, and perhaps a third. Looking at their faces, she realized each one was as arrogant and condescending as their grandfather had been.

"Sorry to hear it," she said, "but I just spent the past week working with a difficult client who thought she was the center of the universe, and I'm afraid the stress has finally caught up with me, because I feel a migraine coming on."

"Great," said Ken. "So, what do you want me to do?"

"Nothing," she said. "I don't want to spoil your evening, so I'll take Uber home. Then I'm going straight to bed." She looked at the others as she grabbed her coat. "Goodnight, everyone. I enjoyed meeting all of you. Sorry I couldn't stay longer."

She excused herself and hurried out to the lobby, relieved Ken hadn't tried to follow her. Putting on her coat, she quickly stepped outside. It felt good to breathe fresh air, even on frigid winter night. Her Uber driver would pick her up in approximately seven minutes. Once she arrived home, she changed into her sweats and called her mother. She too thought Jenna had done the right thing.

"People like Ken and his family are toxic," she said, "and toxic people can do a lot of damage. He was also becoming much too critical of you, and I'm greatly relieved you decided to end it with him."

"Me too. When I first met him, I really thought he was someone special, but once he became so demanding I started having second thoughts. Now I'm looking forward to having more girls' night outs. I just hope CeCe understands."

"I don't see why she wouldn't. She introduced you to a friend, and instead of it being one date, it lasted nearly four months. That's a pretty good outcome if you ask me."

A man's voice called out in the background. "Claire, where's the—"

"I already told you, Nick. Second drawer to the left of the stove." She turned her attention back to Jenna. "Your father may be able to fly an Airbus from one coast to the other, but when he's home he simply can't function without me."

"There you go, sounding like an old, married couple again."

"Because we are an old married couple, and a happily married couple I might add. I love your father as much as I did the day I married him, which is what I want for you as well. I'm sorry it didn't work out with Ken, but at least you were able to see him for what he was before you made a serious commitment."

After they ended their call Jenna made herself a cup of hot cocoa. Curling up in front of the TV she channel-surfed until she stumbled on an old episode of *The Golden Girls*. As she thought it over, she realized it would be best not to say anything she might regret later. Before going to bed, she typed a short text message.

"Feeling better and calling it a night. I want you to know I've enjoyed hanging out with you, but the time has come for me to say goodbye and wish you the best."

He replied a few minutes later. *"Thanks for coming to the wedding. Sorry my aunt upset you. I'd really like to make it up to you, so how about going to dinner someplace special tomorrow night?"*

Jenna took a deep breath before she started typing. *"Thanks, but no. I really have enjoyed being with you, but it's run its course and we both know it. I sincerely hope your next one is a keeper."*

Jenna waited a few minutes before setting her phone down. Part of her felt a little sad, but most of her felt relieved.

* * *

Ken tossed his phone down with a sigh. Jenna had ended it, thanks to his aunt. Ken liked being in control, and he wasn't accustomed to being dumped. He would have to deal with Jenna later. For the moment he wanted to focus his attention on Jeri. Grabbing his phone, he sent her a text message, asking her if she would be interested in joining him for Sunday brunch.

❧THREE❧

JENNA GRITTED HER teeth as she stepped out of the elevator. No doubt CeCe would expect a long-winded explanation about why she had ended it with Ken. Taking off her coat, she booted up her computer and went to the break room to grab a cup of coffee. A disappointed looking CeCe was waiting when she returned.

"I spoke to Ken yesterday. He said you've decided to go your separate ways. So, what happened?"

"Nothing happened. It was simply time for us to move on."

"Are you sure? Sometimes it takes people awhile to figure out they found the right one. It may take months, even years."

"I genuinely liked Ken when we first met, but as I got to know him better, I realized we weren't as compatible as I thought, but it's okay. We still enjoyed one another's company, and we had some fun times together. There are no hard feelings, and we wished each other well. I also appreciate my married friends taking the time to introduce me to people they know, so thank you once again. I used to do the same thing, back when I was married to Arthur."

"Really? I didn't think you guys weren't married very long."

"We weren't. The marriage only lasted about a year." Jenna smiled at the memory. "We were both eighteen and thought we knew everything, but what we didn't know was that the person you're madly in love with at eighteen isn't necessarily the same person you're in love with when you're twenty. At least we were smart enough not to start a family, and another good thing came of it."

"Which was?"

"I got a job at a furniture store, and soon realized I wanted to be an interior designer. Fortunately, my parents didn't spend my college fund, so I was able to go back to school the following year."

Jenna excused herself and returned to her desk. Logging into her computer, she found a message from Chad. He wanted her to stop by his office so they could go over more of the changes on the Shelton project. To her relief, CeCe was busy on the phone when she left.

* * *

Jenna spent the next few weekends socializing with friends, but times had changed. Most of her friends had either gotten married or were otherwise involved in a serious relationship. Stacy, her best friend since high school, was still single, but a new man had recently come into her life as well. Jenna was starting to feel as if she were the lone spinster in the group. Arriving at work one morning, CeCe told her about Ken's new girlfriend.

"Her name is Jeri, and he seems quite smitten with her."

"That's nice," said Jenna, not knowing what else to say.

"Are you okay? You seem a little jealous."

"No, I'm not jealous. I'm just a little surprised, that's all. I suppose we don't think about our exes moving on. Must be an ego thing. Anyway, I'm genuinely happy for him, and please tell him I wish him the best."

"Of course. You're sure you're okay?"

"I'm fine." Jenna turned her attention to her computer. "Besides, I need to get ready for the next meeting with the Sheltons."

"Oh, is it today?"

"Yep. One o'clock this afternoon. We're in the home stretch, at least for the design phase."

"Then I won't keep you."

Jenna worked through lunch, wanting to be sure everything was ready for her upcoming presentation. She felt a nervous flutter in her stomach as she stepped into the elevator. Chad was busy with some last-minute details when she arrived at his office.

"Ready to go?" he asked.

"I think so. How about you?"

"I'm getting there, but first I want to give you a heads-up."

"About what?"

A serious look came over his face. "Apparently, Chris' wife is a real princess. You know the type. They've never heard the word no in their entire lives, and they absolutely positively have to have everything their way, otherwise they'll turn into Medusa and make you wish you really could be turned into stone. Apparently, she's still insisting on having a waterfall fountain in the area between the lobby and the atrium."

"Lovely," said Jenna, "but I thought Oscar told her no."

"He did, and his word is final. However, she won't let go of it, and I want you to be prepared, just in case she throws a tantrum."

Chad's phone rang. The Sheltons had arrived. He hurried out to greet them while Jenna joined Mitch and Jim in the conference room. Oscar and Chris greeted her with handshakes, but Chris' wife, Michelle, stood off to the side and refused to acknowledge her. Once everyone took their seats, Chad made his presentation. Jenna was up next. Oscar nodded in approval as she spoke, while an angry-looking Michelle scowled at her.

"So, are there any questions?" asked Jenna.

"Yes. I have a question." Michelle's eyes turned into narrow slits. "Where the hell is the waterfall fountain? Did I not make myself clear to you the last time? I said I wanted to keep the fountain."

"I know you did," said Jenna. "However, your father-in-law told me he doesn't want it."

Oscar immediately spoke up. "Jenna, would you mind showing her how much the fountain would cost?"

"Not at all." Jenna opened a file on her tablet and jotted the information down on a slip of paper. "Here's the estimate I presented at our last meeting. It includes the cost for the additional plumbing, along with the labor and other expenses, including the yearly upkeep."

She handed the paper to Oscar. He looked it over before passing it onto Michelle. "Tell you what," he said. "If you really want a waterfall fountain, I'll be more than happy to include it, as long as you agree to pay for it."

Michelle responded with another angry scowl. Chad immediately spoke up.

"Hang on a second. I just remembered something. Jenna knows an artist who does sculpture, so why don't we ask her to talk to him? He can probably create something to suggest a waterfall, but without the expense of the plumbing or the upkeep."

For the moment, Jenna was speechless. Oscar, however, latched onto the idea.

"Hmm...now there's a thought. I certainly wouldn't object to having some original artwork in the lobby. What about you, Michelle?"

Her face looked calmer, but she had no smile. "Maybe, but I'd have to see it first."

Chad looked relieved. "Okay, then. We'll have Jenna contact her friend and see what he can come up with."

"Of course." Jenna gave Chad an uneasy smile, and the meeting soon adjourned. Chad took their visitors back down to the lobby, and Jenna was anxiously waiting in his office when he returned.

"Is there anything wrong?" he asked.

"Hopefully not. The friend you told them about was actually one of my college art instructors. I haven't had any contact with him in a decade."

"All right." For a moment Chad appeared to be in deep thought. "Okay, now I remember you telling me that, but he's still there, isn't he?"

"No, he isn't. He wasn't a professor. He was a grad student working as a teaching assistant. I took a drawing class from him at the beginning of my freshman year. He graduated the following semester."

"I see." Chad shifted awkwardly in his chair. "Well, in that case, I guess you'll have to Google him. If he's not around any longer, you'll have to visit some art galleries and see what you can find."

"Okay. Let me see what I can do."

CeCe gave Jenna a strange look when she returned to her desk. "Uh-oh. Did something happen at the meeting."

"Yeah, you could say that."

"So don't leave me in suspense."

"As expected, Oscar's daughter-in-law threw her little tantrum. Then Chad told the Sheltons I knew someone who could create a sculpture for them, and as he did, my heart sank."

"Really? How come?"

"I haven't seen or spoken to the artist in years, and I have no idea where he is now. In the meantime, everyone, including the daughter-in-law, is all excited about having a custom-made piece of art."

"So? Google local artists and see what names comes up. For all you know, your friend may not be in the area anymore." She studied Jenna's face more closely. "Wait a minute. There's more to the story, isn't there?"

"Bill was more than just teacher. I considered him a mentor, and we became good friends."

"Nothing wrong with that, but there's still more, isn't there?"

"It was right after my divorce. I fell head over heels in love with him, but he of course never knew it. I was really hoping we'd stay in touch after he graduated, but he wasn't interested. His wife had passed away a couple years before, and he was still grieving the loss."

"I see." CeCe appeared to be in deep thought. "You know, two years isn't very long when you've lost a spouse, and it's entirely possible that he could be married to someone else by now. You're also contacting him for professional reasons, assuming he's still around, and since nothing happened between you, I don't think you have anything to worry about. I'm sure he'd be happy to hear from you."

"Hopefully, you're right."

Jenna went to her desk and typed Bill's name in the search bar. The results appeared a few seconds later. To her surprise, he was still in Denver, and was now a professor at a local community college. She clicked on a few links and found his contact form. Taking a deep breath, she hoped for the best as she hit the send button. An email response arrived a few hours later. Bill did private commissions and would be happy to do the project.

I guess this means we've gone full circle, with the pupil giving the teacher an assignment. I've thought about you over the years, so I'd like to invite you, and your spouse or significant other, over for dinner Saturday night. Nothing fancy, just pizza, and we can talk more about the project.

She smiled as she typed her reply. *My significant other has moved on to greener pastures, so it'll just be you and me.*

He replied a minute later. *Sorry to hear it, but I look forward to seeing you.*

Jenna smiled to herself as she shut down her computer and grabbed her sweater. As she hurried out, she gave CeCe a thumbs up.

❧FOUR❧

JENNA LAID BOTH outfits on the bed, still unable to decide which one to wear. Not having seen Bill for many years, she wanted to look her best without being overdressed. Her cream-colored cotton dress was perfect for early spring. It came with a pink belt, three quarter length sleeves, and a full skirt which came down to the mid-calf. It was simple and comfortable with a v-neck bodice, making it sexy but not overly suggestive.

Her other option was a less revealing navy-blue pantsuit. While more businesslike, it was also too formal for a casual dinner at someone's home. Taking a deep breath, she hung the pantsuit back in the closet. Thirty minutes later she grabbed her bags and hurried out. Her phone guided her to Bill's home, which, to her surprise, was within a mile of her own. Her hands were shaking as she rang the bell. The door opened a few seconds later.

Bill looked much the same as she remembered, although his wavy brown hair now had a slight touch of gray, and he wore a pair of gold-wire glasses. He greeted her with a lingering embrace and invited her inside.

"I'm afraid I don't have a maid," he said, "although I somehow manage to keep the dishes washed and take out the trash."

"It's fine Bill, really."

"So, how are you?"

"I'm good," said Jenna. "I have a job I really like, and I still keep a sketchbook. Sometimes on weekends I'll go to places like Sterne Park and do some sketching, just for fun."

"I'm happy to hear it. You were certainly one of my more talented students, and I'm happy you found a profession where you can use your drawing skills."

"You taught me well. So, what about you?"

"I finally gave up my day job after I got my master's degree, and I started teaching at Foothills Community College. There was enough money left in Mary Beth's insurance policy to put Connor through college as well. He went to Colorado State in Fort Collins and majored in business, and he now works for a healthcare company in Florida."

"I guess he would be all grown up by now," said Jenna.

"He certainly is. In the meantime, I'm renting an artist studio in a renovated hotel, which is where I create my bigger sculptures, although I don't spend much time there during the winter months. It has an old furnace which has seen better days, so for the moment I'm working on smaller projects. Here, let me show you."

He led her down the hallway to one of the bedrooms, where photography lights and a white backdrop had been set up. A computer and a large flatbed scanner sat on top of a long folding table. Pulling up an extra chair, he told Jenna to take a seat. He sat down next to her and clicked on the mouse. A photo of a nude man and woman, facing each other in a dancelike pose, filled the screen.

"Lately, I've been playing around with wood reliefs," he said. "I start by photographing the model, or, in this case, models, in front of the backdrop."

"I take it they know one another."

"They certainly do. Josh and Stephanie are a husband and wife who do art modeling on the side."

"I see."

"It costs a lot of money to put kids through college. Josh is also a hell of a painter. We're both with the same art gallery, which is how I came to know him." He clicked on the screen, and an intricate pencil sketch appeared.

"I then create the background. For this piece, I want the tree branches to mimic the models' movement. From there I scan it into the computer, layer in the models, and print out the pattern. I do the carving out in the backyard shed. This is a work in progress. Here's a photo of what I've done so far."

"My goodness." Jenna was amazed as the image filled the screen. "It's a beautiful piece of wood, and such close attention to the detail in the hands and faces. This will be stunning once it's finished."

"Thanks. I'm hoping it will be as well." He clicked on the mouse and another nude photo of Stephanie appeared. She was laying on her side with her head propped on her elbow. "I plan on creating a life-like bronze from this photo. I'm just waiting for the weather to get a little warmer so I won't have to depend as much on that rickety old furnace. I keep hoping the landlord will get around to replacing it one of these days."

Jenna reached into her tote bag for her laptop. Once it was ready, she gave Bill a virtual tour of the Shelton's new hotel and spa.

"I see what you mean," he said. "There should be a focal point of some kind in the space between the lobby and the atrium, and you're right. A fountain would be way too much. You said the interior landscaping was all native flora. Correct?"

"Yes."

"Got it. Would you mind sending me some renderings?"

"Consider it done. I'll email them to you in a few minutes."

"Good," said Bill. "So, while you're doing that, I'll order us some pizza, because I'm starving."

"Me too."

"Does pepperoni and bell pepper sound okay?"

"Sure does."

As they waited for the pizza to arrive, Bill mentioned something else he was thinking of trying.

"Have you ever heard of body painting?" he asked.

"Is that where the artist paints a design on the model's body?"

"Exactly. The model is a human canvas. Some artists will paint several models and photograph them together to create an optical illusion, such as a lizard or a frog. I love working in three-dimensional media, and it's something I've not tried before, so it would be fun to see what I can come up with."

Jenna tried to suppress a giggle.

"What's so funny?" he asked.

"Well, being as you've brought it up, I sorta have some body art myself."

"What do you mean?" He studied her face more closely. "Wait a minute. Are you saying you got a tattoo?"

"I sure did. A few years ago."

Bill looked intrigued. "Well, don't just sit there. Tell me the whole story."

"Okay, okay. One Saturday night, my best friend Stacy; you remember me telling you about her, don't you?"

"Of course, I remember."

"We were hanging out together and we got bored. It was getting late, but we still wanted to find something interesting to do, so we hopped in her car and started driving. A few minutes later we came upon a tattoo parlor. It was open twenty-four hours, and she dared me to get a tattoo. I said I would, but only if she agreed to get one with me."

"So, I take it she agreed."

"She did. So, there was a guy working there by himself. I thought he looked pretty hot. He had long blond hair with a dark blond mustache and beard, and he was a real sweetheart. As we were looking through some tattoo patterns, trying to decide what to get, he offers us some rose hip tea. That's when I had an aha moment and decided I would have a rose tattooed on my hip."

"I see, and what did Stacy get?"

"A butterfly on her bum."

Bill started laughing. "Indeed. I'll bet she gets some interesting comments from the men in her life."

"I'm sure she does, although she's never mentioned any of them to me."

"Good for her. Thanks to social media, too many people are sharing too much personal information about themselves. I respect those who are more discreet. So, what else have you been up to since I last saw you?"

"I got my degree in interior design. I also took as many business courses as I could. At one point I thought about going into advertising, but like you, I prefer working three dimensionally."

"Then you made the right choice. I noticed how enthusiastic you were when you were showing me the hotel lobby, and I'm glad it worked out for you. Sometimes people finish their degrees, only to discover they don't like their career choices once they start working."

"It happens. So, what about you?" she asked.

"It's a mixed bag with me. I honestly enjoy teaching, but creating art is my life's passion. I also had a son to raise, so I never had the option of moving into a loft and living a Bohemian lifestyle, but it's okay. I love being a dad, and I wouldn't trade my son for anything. Sometimes teaching interferes with my art, but not too often, and I really do enjoy working with young people. I especially love hearing from former students who've become successful."

"I see. So how many other former students have you heard from?"

"A few have friended me on Facebook, but so far, you're the only one who's contacted me directly. You're also the first to hire me for a commission."

"Actually, the firm I work for is hiring you. I'm just the go-between."

"In that case, I stand corrected," he said with a wink. He started to say something else, but the doorbell interrupted him. The pizza had arrived. Taking their seats at the kitchen table, they immediately dug in, making small talk over their meal. Afterwards, Bill cleared the table and stashed the leftover pizza in the refrigerator.

"You know," he said, "I just can't get your tattoo off my mind. I still can't believe you did that. You never struck me as the impulsive type."

"Most of the time I'm not. However, Stacy is known for occasionally getting wild ideas. Usually, I can talk her out of it. This time I couldn't, and once I saw the guy doing the tattoos, well…"

"So, did he ask you out?"

"No, he didn't. Turned out he was married. He said his wife was a nurse, and they both worked the night shift."

"Oh, well. So, have any other interesting men come into your life?"

"A few," said Jenna, "although most of the time it didn't go beyond the first date. A few became platonic friends, like we did, but they eventually moved on. There was one who I really hoped would make a commitment, but he didn't feel the same about me, and in hindsight, I'm glad he didn't."

"Really? So why is that?"

"He was close to his parents, which, at the time, I thought was a good thing. Later on, I realized he was a Mama's boy, so it wouldn't have worked."

"I remember you were close to your parents as well."

"I was and I still am."

"I take it they're doing well."

"They are. Dad is still flying. He'll retire next year, and they're talking about buying an RV and exploring the back roads."

"Which is something I'd like to do myself someday." He took two wine glasses from the cupboard. "I have a nice, late harvest zinfandel, if you'd like to try some. It's a really nice dessert wine. I also baked a black forest pie."

Jenna raised her brow. "You did? I seem to recall you talking about how kitchen challenged you were."

"Okay, so it was a frozen pie, but I still baked it earlier today. I also had to adapt to being a single dad, and I learned many of my mother's recipes. Sometimes it took a few tries to get it right, but thankfully, my mother was only a phone call away."

"Then I'd love to stay for dessert."

Bill cut the pie and poured the wine. Jenna swirled it in her glass and took a whiff. "It has a really nice bouquet."

"I see you've learned about fine wine."

"I have. So, how is your mother and the rest of your family?"

"My mother is doing well. So is David, my brother, and his family, but we lost Dad a few years ago."

"Oh, no. I'm so sorry."

"Thanks. It was kind of a fluke. He'd come down with a really bad case of the flu. Mom kept wanting to take him to the emergency room, but he refused. He kept saying he'd be better in another day or two, only he wasn't getting any better. Finally, he gave in, and when they got to the ER, they immediately put him in the ICU. Unfortunately, it was too late. He had developed pneumonia, and he passed away the following day."

"How awful. I am so sorry."

"It came as a shock to all of us. It was especially hard on Connor. He was still coping with the loss of his mother, and he'd been close to his grandfather as well. He was in high school when it happened, and for a time he thought about going to medical school, but once he looked into it further, he changed his mind."

"I thought you said he was a healthcare worker."

"He works for a healthcare company," said Bill. "However, he doesn't work with patients. He works in healthcare administration. His department oversees the company's revenue and operating expenses."

"Sounds interesting."

"He's always been good with numbers, and he makes damn good money too. He wants to buy a house someday, but first he wants to save up enough to make a substantial down payment."

"Sounds like he's a smart kid who knows the value of money."

"I made sure of it," said Bill. "So, as I mentioned in my email, I've thought about you over the years, and I was delighted to finally hear from you. It also sounded like you're not seeing anyone at the moment."

"No, not at the moment."

"You've always been special to me, but because of the student-teacher relationship, I had to keep a proper distance. Obviously, things have changed since then, and I now consider you a peer. So, if it's okay with you, I'd like to spend some time with you and get the know the new you."

"Well of course it's okay. I'd like to spend some time with you as well."

"Then we'll have to get together again, sometime soon. In the meantime, I have some ideas popping through my head for your project, and I want to do some quick sketches while they're fresh in my mind. So, as soon as we're done with dessert, we'll call it a night."

Jenna soon grabbed her sweater and Bill walked her out to her car. "I see you have nice set of wheels."

"I bought it about six months ago. It's the first new car I've ever had."

"Which means you're making a good living, and I'm glad I was able to help you get where you are now." He gave her a hug, and sweet, gentle kiss. "Good night, Jenna. It's good having you back." He gave her another long squeeze and waved goodbye as she drove away.

৶FIVE৶

BILL SIGHED IN frustration as he stared at his blank sketch pad. He was trying to come up with other ideas for Jenna's project, but his creative mind had completely shut down. All he could do was think about her and wonder why fate had brought her back into his life. There was something truly special about Jenna. He had been drawn to her from the moment she first stepped into his classroom. Sipping his morning coffee, he allowed his mind wander.

Was it possible to have more than one soulmate? Some people thought so. Over the past twenty-four hours he had read many online articles talking about different kinds of soulmates, and their purposes in people's lives, but the more he read, the more confused he felt. What he needed to do was to stop thinking and get back to work. Perhaps spending time on a different project might help. He refilled his coffee mug and went out to the shed.

He gave the wood relief a closer look while he waited for the shed to warm up. The model's faces had come out perfectly. Rubbing them with his finger, he thought about the photo shoot with Josh and Stephanie. They had a genuine love for one another. It came through in the photo, and he had captured it in the carving. He also knew Josh was well into his thirties when he met Stephanie, which proved your soulmate didn't necessarily come into your life when you were in your teens or twenties.

"Or maybe I'm still overthinking things," he said out loud with a sigh. Picking up a chisel, he went to work, carefully and methodically chipping out tiny pieces of wood as more of the image came to life. His phone beeped as he worked. Connor had sent him a text message.

"Just saying hi and wondering if spring has arrived in Denver. I wore my usual polo shirt to work, just like I do every day."

"You little smart ass," said Bill. He quickly typed his reply. *"It's getting warmer during the day, but you still need a sweater at night. Have a good day. Love, Dad."* He reached for his coffee as he put his phone down, only to discover it had gotten cold. The morning was going by faster than he realized, and he to teach a class that afternoon. Switching off the heaters, he hurried back to the house.

* * *

CeCe greeted Jenna with her usual Monday morning smile. "So how was your weekend? Did you meet up with your friend?"

"I sure did," said Jenna. "He agreed a waterfall fountain would be way too much, so he'll see if he can up with something more suitable, which means I now get to be the go between for him and the princess."

"Good luck on that one."

"No kidding. I may need to invest in a flameproof suit."

"Probably a good idea. So did anything else interesting happen?" As usual, CeCe was fishing for more information.

"He's happy I became an interior designer, and I'm excited to be working with him again." Jenna turned her attention to her computer. There was more to be done on the Shelton hotel than just the lobby.

Bill emailed two preliminary sketches a few days later. The first was a bighorn sheep. It would certainly complement the native plants in the interior landscaping. His other sketch was an abstract group of curves, suggesting a flowing river. Each sketch included the measurements for the final piece. Both would be big enough to create an interesting focal point without interfering with the traffic flow to and from the lobby. Jenna printed them out and showed them to CeCe, who seemed genuinely impressed.

"You said this guy was good, but I didn't realize he was this good. I may want to talk to him about my project."

"Awesome. If you'll hang on a second, I'll get his card." She quickly grabbed one from her desk drawer and handed it to CeCe.

"Willis Angus Haskell," said CeCe. "Good name for an artist, but I can understand why he goes by Bill. I see he's with the Garrison Gallery. I've worked with them before."

"Check out his website. He works in different media."

CeCe quickly punched it up on her computer. "Impressive. I see what you mean about his work. He's very talented."

"He is indeed. I really meant it when I said he's one of the people who helped get me where I am today."

CeCe clicked on the About Us page. A recent photo of Bill, standing next to one of his bronze pieces, appeared above his bio. An odd look came over her face. "Hmm…he looks a little older than I expected."

"What do you mean?" asked Jenna.

"I know you said he was a grad student when you first met him, so I naturally assumed he would have been a few years older than you, probably in his mid-twenties or so. However, he looks like he's in his late thirties or early forties."

"He's in his mid-forties."

"I see, and you're twenty-nine, which makes him almost twenty years older than you."

Jenna was becoming uncomfortable with the conversation. "We're sixteen years apart, which is the same age difference one of my friends has with her younger sister, although I've never really thought about it that much. I considered him a mentor, and we became good friends. And just so you know, my father and I have a good relationship, so I wasn't looking for a daddy figure."

"Okay, okay. You don't need to get all huffy about it. I was just commenting about the age difference. Most twenty-somethings usually don't have friends in their forties, but I get it. He was someone you deeply admired. What I meant to say is he is indeed very talented, and I'm glad the two of you had a chance to reconnect."

"Sorry, CeCe," said Jenna. "I didn't mean to overreact either, and now that I have the sketches, I need to forward them to Oscar and the princess. I'm just hoping she won't reply with some scathing email about why she hates them."

"I understand, but Oscar is the one writing the checks, not her. From what I hear, he has a genuine appreciation for fine art."

Jenna returned to her desk and composed her email. An hour later she had a response. Oscar liked both pieces, but preferred the sketch suggesting the river. His daughter-in-law preferred it as well, and he was happy they finally had something they could agree on. Feeling relieved, she quickly composed an email to Bill.

The clients have agreed to your fee. They want the second sketch.

His reply came a few hours later. *Good choice. It's my favorite as well, and it was the closest I could come to a waterfall fountain. I'd like to take you to dinner to celebrate. Busy tomorrow night?*

She smiled as she typed her reply. *Sure am. My old drawing instructor is taking me to dinner.*

His response came a minute later. *Who are you calling old? I'm a happy middle-aged man. I'll be at your place at six.*

ᔇSIX

JENNA GREETED BILL with a smile as she invited him inside. "Nice place," he said. "I can certainly tell you're an interior designer. Your home looks like something from a magazine."

The living room had light-colored wood flooring, a built-in fireplace with a red brick surround, and beige colored walls, giving it a warm, cozy feel. A blue-gray sectional sofa faced an oak entertainment center, which contained a large flat screen TV along with an impressive antique collection. Framed modern artwork hung on the other walls.

"Thanks," said Jenna. "It took a while for me to find everything. I hate the cheap, particle board junk you find in so many furniture stores, so my mother and I went to a lot of estate sales. The coffee and end tables are mid-twentieth century modern."

"A classic style, and some of your art glass reminds me of sculptures I've made."

"Have you ever worked with glass?"

"A little, but not much. I prefer working in other mediums, and speaking of which, I've finished the wood relief. Let me show you." A look of pride came over his face as he handed Jenna his phone.

"Well, I'll be," she said. "It came together perfectly, and the figures look incredibly lifelike. So where will it go now?"

"It'll be included in my show at Garrison's, this coming July."

"Good to know, and I almost forgot. One of my co-workers, Cecelia Wood, will be calling you soon. I showed her your website, and she has a client who may be interested in one of your bronze figurines."

"Thanks for the referral, but please have her call Garrison's. They're my official dealer." He stopped to look at his watch. "I think we've had enough shop talk for now. I'm getting hungry, and we have more to catch up on."

He took her to a nearby Chinese restaurant, where they took turns sampling items from each other's plates. Afterwards they returned to Jenna's house, and Bill spotted a domino set on the kitchen table.

"So, what's this?" he asked.

"I vividly recall a conversation we once had. Something came up about dominos, and I talked about how Stacy always gave me a hard time whenever I beat her. Then you said you could, and I quote, 'beat both of us with one hand tied behind your back.' So, I think the time has come to see just how good you are."

Bill feigned his innocence. "Did I say that? I don't seem to recall."

"Can I get you anything to drink before we start?"

"A beer would be great, if you have some."

"Sure do."

"No, no, stay there," he said. "I can get it. You need to get the dominos ready. Would you like a beer as well?"

"Actually, I think I'll have a soda instead."

"Coming right up." He grabbed a Diet Dr. Pepper and a can of Coors for himself. "So, before we start, would you like to make the game more interesting by making some kind of wager?"

"You mean you want me to take your money away from you?"

He gave her a look. "Careful now. They say pride comes before the fall."

"We'll let whichever one of us wins decide." Jenna had a glimmer in her eye as she opened the game with the double three. Bill added the three-four.

"Hmm…Looks like I scored on that one."

"You did, but the game's not over yet."

"I know it isn't." Bill won the first three rounds. Jenna won the fourth, but Bill scored a big win in the fifth. Afterwards she was unable to catch up with him.

"Well, well, well," he said gloatingly. "I won the game, fair and square."

"I know you did. So, what do you intended to take?"

"My time." He gave her a long, passionate kiss. "Goodnight, my dear. We both have to go to work in the morning, but I'll be back. Doing anything Friday night?"

"Not a thing."

"Do you like Italian?"

"I love it."

"Then I'll pick you up at five thirty, and we'll head straight over to Vito and Gianna's. As long as we're there by six we should be ahead of the big dinner rush. Then we can go back over to my place and hang out for a while. Maybe watch a movie, or perhaps play another round of dominos."

* * *

Bill was parked at the curb when Jenna arrived home. She quickly put her car in the garage and hopped into his red Ford Explorer. He raised his brow as he watched her fasten her seatbelt. "I really like your outfit," he said. "The gray ruffled blouse looks stunning and professional at the same time."

"Thanks. We work with well-to-do clientele, so we're required to look professional, but come the weekend, it's blue jeans and t-shirts."

Another party was waiting ahead of them when they arrived at the restaurant, but they were seated a short time later. Bill ordered two glasses of merlot and an antipasto. He raised his glass when their wine arrived. "Here's to old friends and new beginnings."

"Here, here," said Jenna. They took a sip and began discussing their week.

"The Sheltons really are excited about the sculpture," said Jenna. "I have to keep reminding them it won't be ready until this fall, when we have our grand opening."

"And when will that be?"

"It was originally planned for mid-September, but now it's looking more like mid to late October. These things always take longer than expected."

"Good to know. I plan to start working on it after the semester ends." Bill talked about some of his other projects over the main course. "So, as you can see, I have a lot to get done. My show at Garrisons will be at the end of July, and while it may sound like it's a long way off, I actually don't have a lot of wiggle room."

"Believe me, I know," said Jenna. "I've had clients who thought all I had to do was snap my fingers and poof. It was done. You can imagine the looks on their faces when I told them no, it doesn't work that way."

Bill pushed his half-eaten plate of lasagna aside. "I keep forgetting how big their portions are, so let's get some to-go boxes."

"Good idea. I wonder if leftover chicken parmesan would make a good breakfast?"

"I don't see why it wouldn't, although cold pizza is definitely the best."

They reminisced about old times on the ride to his place, and he offered her a soft drink when they arrived. "I got you some Diet Dr. Pepper," he said.

"Thanks. I'd love one."

He set the soda on the table and told her to take a seat. "So, about the dominos rematch," he said. "I've looked everywhere, but somewhere along the line my dominos have disappeared. I'm afraid it comes with the territory of having kids. I do, however, have a poker set, and only a few of the chips are missing. So, would you be up for playing a friendly game of poker instead?"

"Sure. I like poker, too."

He stepped away, returning a moment later with the poker set. "You know, I keep thinking about your tattoo. I still can't believe you did that."

"Well, I did."

"I know you did, and I would love to see it sometime."

"You would?" Jenna couldn't resist teasing him. "So how exactly do you plan on accomplishing this?"

He gave her a playful look. "I was thinking we could play five-card draw, winner take all. If I win, I get to see the tattoo. If you win, you get to have a good laugh at a silly old man."

"Think you can beat me at poker, do you? My friends all tell me I'm a card shark. And just so you know, you're not a silly old man. You're a sexy, middle-aged man who's still in his prime."

"I don't know about still being in my prime. I turn forty-six in August." He took a deck of cards from the case. "I also happen to be a very good poker player, too, as you're about to find out, Ms. Card Shark. So, here are the rules. We each get the same amount of chips, but no buying more later on. The first one to go belly up loses."

"Sounds good, and I'm so sure I'll win I'll even let you deal first."

"We'll see." Bill carefully counted out the poker chips and shuffled the deck. Dealing the first hand, he drew one card, while Jenna drew three. He then placed his bet.

"See you and raise you," said Jenna.

"I'll call. So, let's see what you've got."

She quickly laid her cards on the table. "Pair of nines," she said smugly.

"Nice hand." He nonchalantly set his cards down. "However, I have a pair of jacks, and a pair of sixes."

"Okay, so you got lucky this time."

"Don't temp fate." Bill shuffled the cards and dealt the next hand. Jenna won the next three games, then his luck started changing. He smiled as he raked in another big pot. "They say poker chips have no home."

Jenna looked him in the eye. "They also say not to count your chickens before they hatch, although I need to take a short break. I've been in these heels all day, and my feet are letting me know it."

Bill suddenly looked concerned. "Are your feet hurting you?"

"They're not hurting, but they feel a little tired. I usually change into my slippers as soon as I get home."

"Then let me see what I can do. I'll be back in a minute." He quickly stepped away, returning a minute later with a pair of white cotton socks. Jenna eagerly kicked off her shoes and put the socks on.

"We may as well give you a nice foot rub while we're at it," said Bill. "It'll make them feel better, and would you like another Dr. Pepper?"

"No thanks. I've had enough caffeine for the day, so I'll have a glass of ice water instead."

"Coming right up."

Bill brought her a glass of ice water, along with one for himself. As he took his seat, he motioned for her to placed her foot on his lap. As he massaged her foot, she leaned back in her chair and closed her eyes. "This feels heavenly. I'm on my feet for much of the day, running back and forth, doing this and that. If it were up to me, I'd wear sneakers, but upper brass wouldn't approve."

"I understand," said Bill. "The college has a dress code for faculty, but thankfully it's business casual. No way could I handle wearing a suit and tie every day. So, how are you feeling now?"

"Much better. "

As he massaged her foot he realized he was becoming aroused. Taking a deep breath, he tried to ignore what was happening. "You women put up with a lot. I remember how you always took pride in your appearance. You even made blue jeans and t-shirts look classy."

"Must be the way I was raised. My mother was a stylish dresser." She took a deep breath and sighed in contentment as she switched legs and put her other foot in his lap. "I'm so relaxed right now I could fall asleep in my chair."

"Now, now. We don't need you falling out and hurting yourself."

"I guess that wouldn't be much fun, would it? So, let's get back to the game." Jenna sat up and looked at Bill. "Are you okay?" she asked.

Feeling the urge to panic, he had to think quickly. "I'm fine. I was just remembering something from when I knew you before. Nothing serious. So, where were we? Oh, now I remember. I just won another big pot."

"Well, don't get too attached to it, because I intend to win it back."

"We'll have to see about that." Bill dealt the next hand. They placed their bets, and he decided to raise the stakes. "See you and raise you," he said.

"I raise." Jenna added another chip.

"I call. So how many cards do you need?"

"Just one," she said.

"I'll take two." He gave her another card and took two for himself. "I'll bet three." He pushed his chips into the pot. Jenna only had four chips left.

"See you and raise you," she said.

"Are you sure you want to do that?"

"Positive."

"Okay." He added four more chips to the pot and put his cards on the table. "I have three of a kind. All tens."

Jenna shifted uncomfortably in her chair. "Dang. I was really hoping I could scare you off."

"I don't scare easily. So, let's see your hand."

"You know, if I'd gotten what I wanted, I would have beaten you. I was going for a flush, but it didn't happen." She set her cards down. There were four hearts, along with the seven of clubs.

"Well look at that," Bill said gleefully. "Once again, Lady Luck is on my side, because I won fair and square, twice in a row. So, you know what happens next, don't you?"

"I know. You get to see the tattoo, although it would be awkward for me to show it to you in a pencil skirt. Do you have a robe, or a long t-shirt I could borrow?"

"Sure do. Wait right here." He stepped away, returning a moment later with a blue bathrobe. Jenna grabbed it and hurried off to the bathroom, while Bill anxiously waited for her return.

* * *

Jenna felt the tension in the air as she hurried down the hallway. Having seen the intense look in Bill's eyes while he was rubbing her feet, she knew they about to take their relationship to the next level. Once they did, there would be no turning back. As she removed her skirt and undergarments, she was grateful to have chosen the blouse she was wearing. With any luck, both of them would feel calmer once he saw the tattoo. She took a breath and put on Bill's robe, securely tying it around her waist. Returning to the kitchen table, she pulled the robe back and carefully revealed the tattoo.

"So, what do you think?" she asked.

"I'm not sure," said Bill. "The artist did an amazing job. However, I still can't believe you did this."

"I made sure it was in a spot where it could easily be concealed. The only time anyone would see it would see would be if I were wearing a high cut bathing suit or a bikini. However, I don't have a pool or a hot tub, so I have no need for a swimsuit."

"Jenna Winters, I'm shocked. Shocked, I tell you. What would happen if I were to take you on a beach vacation? We'd have to go to a nude beach." Both felt the tension once again. The intense look in Bill's eyes returned as Jenna's face turned red.

"Hey, I was only teasing," he said.

"I know you were."

His eyes bore into hers. "You do know you've always been a bit problematic for me."

"What do you mean?"

"I was drawn to you from the moment I first laid eyes on you, but back then you were strictly off limits. I couldn't even invite you out for a cup of coffee, because if the wrong person saw us together, I might have had some serious explaining to do, and I wasn't about to risk losing my job. I was always grateful whenever you stopped by my office to chat, but even then, I had to be careful not to say too much. I thought about giving you my personal email address after I graduated, but then I changed my mind. I had a son to raise, and I thought you'd be better off with someone who had less baggage."

"You were special to me as well," said Jenna. "I really was disappointed that you never asked me out, but I also knew your wife hadn't been gone very long."

"No, she wasn't. It was another reason why I decided not to pursue you. So, imagine my surprise when you contacted me about the sculpture. As I said before, I've thought about you a lot over the years, and I'm very much enchanted by the woman you've become. You will always be near and dear to me, and I would be very grateful if you would allow me the honor of making love to you."

She looked into his eyes. "I've wanted to make love to you as well. I just wasn't sure if you wanted to."

"I've wanted to make love to you since the first night we got back together, but it would have been too soon. However, I think we're both ready now." He wrapped his arms around her and kissed her, running his hands down her back and squeezing her rump.

"You naughty girl," he said teasingly. "You're not wearing any panties, are you?"

"I had to take them off so you could see the tattoo."

"I see. So, what else did you take off?" He untied the robe and slowly pulled it open revealing her blouse. Its long shirttails covered her hips and upper thighs.

"Now that looks sexy." He ran his hands over her hips and down her thighs as he kissed her once again.

"I think we should go make ourselves more comfortable," he softly said. Jenna remained silent as he took her hand and led her down the hallway to the master bedroom. Once inside, he helped her out of the robe, giving her another long, passionate kiss as he squeezed her bare backside. Jenna moaned at his touch.

"You like that?" he asked.

"I sure do." She slowly unbuttoned her blouse. Underneath was a lacy pink bra. Bill grinned with approval.

"I see you like fancy underwear, but at the moment I think it's a little too dressy."

He unhooked her bra and gazed at her naked body. "You are so incredibly beautiful," he said. "More beautiful than I ever imagined."

He gently swept a lock of her hair away from her face and caressed her breasts. Running his hand down her body, Jenna softly moaned as he began stroking her. Turning down the covers, he waited for her to settle in the bed. Once she was comfortable, he laid his glasses on the nightstand and took his clothes off. Lying down next to her, he began rubbing her belly.

"I'm still thinking of experimenting with body painting," he said, "and I'd like to paint some roses on other parts of you."

Jenna felt her face flush. "We'll see."

He kissed her breast and lightly brushed her other nipple. Kissing her other breast, he rubbed her belly and slowly worked his way down.

"Every inch of you is beautiful."

He began massaging her. Jenna squirmed and moaned in delight at the sweet sensation. She began pleasing him in return. He, too, groaned in contentment.

"Oh, baby… You are so amazing. I have to have you. Right now."

He climbed on top of her. She let out a loud gasp as he entered her. Wrapping herself around him, she squeezed him as tight as she could. As they began their dance, her moans turned into grunts, growing higher in pitch as he picked up the pace. Her cries grew louder and she felt as if she were about to burst. Unable to hold back any longer, she let herself go. Bill reached his own release as she writhed in ecstasy. He, too, cried out in pleasure as she felt him moving deep within her. As they came back down, he laid his head on her chest while she gently stroked his hair.

"That was incredible," he finally said. "I haven't experienced anything like it in a long, long, time."

Jenna continued to stroke his hair in contentment as they silently held one another. It felt good to finally be in his bed.

❧SEVEN❧

BILL AND JENNA were overjoyed to have found one another again, and they reveled in their newfound relationship. One night, while relaxing in front of the TV, Bill asked a question Jenna wasn't expecting.

"I've been wondering something."

"Wondering what?" she asked.

He nodded toward the TV. "Here we are, laughing at this young woman who, no matter what she does, always ends up with the wrong guy. It got me to thinking about you. Did you ever find the right guy? And if so, why aren't you together?"

"Well, at the time I married Arthur, I truly thought he was my one and only."

"I see. So, what happened?"

"I guess you could say we outgrew one another. We were sixteen when we first met, and we thought we'd be in love forever, so we got secretly engaged."

"Secretly engaged?"

"He asked me to marry him," said Jenna. "I said yes, but we didn't tell anyone. We knew our parents wouldn't approve, so we made our own plans."

"So, what kind of plans did you make?"

"We decided to get part time jobs so we could start saving money. By the time we graduated, we'd saved up enough to rent a one-room apartment. We signed a lease the day after we graduated, and the following day we told our parents we were moving out. We just didn't tell them we were moving into the same apartment. We hit the thrift stores the next day. We found a set of TV trays and an air mattress, along with some sheets and dishes. Then, as soon as we unpacked everything, we changed our clothes drove downtown. We were married a few hours later, and we went home and honeymooned on the air mattress. We planned on taking a big trip later on, when we had more money."

"Alright, so what happened next?" asked Bill.

"We told our families we'd gotten married the following day. To say they were surprised would be an understatement. My mother was especially upset. She'd always dreamed of me having a big wedding someday, so she didn't take it very well."

"Neither would I, had Connor run off and gotten married right after high school."

"And knowing what I know now, it wouldn't go over well with me either. However, at the time, we thought we'd planned it out perfectly. Arthur soon found a job as a short-order cook, while I started working at a furniture store."

"What about college?" he asked. "Were either of you taking any classes?"

"No. We planned on going to school online, when we could afford it, but at the time neither of us were making much money. What little remained in our savings accounts quickly evaporated, and as reality set in, the romance wore off. We both realized we'd made a terrible mistake, but we didn't want to admit it to our parents, so we hung in there for as long as we could. Then Arthur became friends with one of the managers where he worked. She was in her thirties and divorced, and he soon became her boy toy. As soon as I found out about it, I filed for divorce and moved back in with my parents. I started college the following August, which is when I met you."

"I remember you telling me you'd been married before, but you never said much about it, and I had no idea he'd cheated on you."

"I really did love him, and it took me a long time to get over what he did. Even now, I sometimes wonder if he was my soulmate. If he was, we met at the wrong time."

"Have you thought about looking him up?" asked Bill.

"I already have. I found him on Facebook. He's now a sous chef at a swanky restaurant in Cherry Creek. He's also married to someone else. They even have a little boy who looks a lot like his dad." Her eyes turned misty. "If only we'd been patient and waited until we finished college, like our parents told us to do, it would have been me, and not her."

Bill's voice was firm. "You don't know that. Once you started college your interests may have changed, and you would have met a lot of new people. I also think you did what you did because deep down, you both knew you weren't meant to be for the long term, and you thought you could change your destiny. Arthur was your first love, but he wasn't your soulmate. So now I'm curious. Is Winters your married name?"

"No. My married name was Holt. I took my maiden name back when we divorced."

"Now just so you know, I, too, fell madly in love with someone when I was twenty. Her name was Julia. I wanted to marry her, but she ended it before I could ask. Like you, it hit me really hard, but then I met Mary Beth a few months later. There are no words to describe the difference between her and Julia. We completed each other." His mood abruptly turned sad and his eyes also turned misty. "Nor are there words to describe the pain I felt when I lost her, and it's a pain I'll live with for the rest of my life."

"Are you okay?" she asked.

"I'm fine. I'm just having a moment." He took a deep breath and shrugged it off. "I'm also glad we reconnected. You make me feel ten years younger."

"I do?"

"You certainly do, you little vixen."

❧EIGHT❧

JENNA RECEIVED AN unexpected text message from Ken a few days later. She was stunned when she read it.

"I hear you're seeing an old friend, and I'm surprised to hear my successor is almost old enough to be your father. I'm not trying to tell you how live your life, but I still care about you, and I would hate to see you widowed at a young age."

Obviously, CeCe had told Ken about Bill, and she needed to set her boundaries with him. Taking a deep breath, she carefully typed her response.

"Thank you for your concern, but since we're no longer seeing one another, you needn't worry about me. CeCe says you've found someone new and you're happy with her. I'm sincerely happy for you as well and I wish you both the very best."

She hit the send button and tossed her phone on the coffee table as she tried to concentrate on the program she was watching. Afterwards, she watched the ten o'clock news. While feeling more relaxed, she nonetheless had a difficult time falling asleep. Her morning alarm rang much too early, adding to her sour mood when she came to work. As usual, she had arrived before CeCe. Grabbing her morning coffee, she booted up her computer and checked her email. The delay with the carpeting for the Shelton hotel had finally been resolved. At least she had something to be grateful for. CeCe showed up as she opened her next email.

"So, how are you doing today?" asked CeCe.

"Not so great."

"Why? What happened? You look upset about something."

Not wanting others to overhear, Jenna lowered her voice. "I got a rather interesting text message from Ken last night. He said he was

38

surprised to hear his so-called successor was nearly old enough to be my father. So, what was that about?"

CeCe looked guilty as she desperately tried to backpedal. "What are you talking about? I don't understand."

"I haven't heard from Ken in months. Then, out of the blue, he sends me a text message questioning my friendship with Bill, which, for the record, is none of his business. I thanked him for his concern and reminded him we're no longer an item. He apparently got the message, because he never responded. So, do you mind telling me how he got this information? Because he sure didn't get it from me."

CeCe tried a different approach. "Okay. Now that I think about it, I seem to recall Ken asking me how you were doing, but it was some time ago. I simply told him you were doing fine, and you were working on a project with an old friend."

"I see. So, did you by chance tell him anything else?"

"Not that I can recall."

Jenna's voice remained low. "I see, but it still doesn't explain how Ken would have known Bill is considerably older than me. Nor does it explain why he would be concerned about my possibly becoming a widow at a young age. As I've said all along, Bill and I are good friends, nothing more."

"Jenna, I'm truly sorry this happened. I really am. I may have mentioned something in passing about you and Bill being old friends from way back, and you were enjoying working with him again, but I most certainly never implied anything about the two of you being an item, much less ever saying anything about you marrying him someday."

Jenna knew CeCe wasn't telling her the whole story, but it wasn't the time to force the issue.

"All right, then please allow me to set the record straight. I may be single and unattached for the moment, but it doesn't mean I'm desperately looking for a husband, because I'm not. If I should happen to meet someone I like, I'll go out with him, assuming he asks me, but whatever happens between us stays between us. If we were to become engaged, then I promise that after my parents, you'll be the first to know."

CeCe looked Jenna in the eye. "I understand, and believe me, I never intended to pry into your personal life. Most of the time I'm just trying to make friendly conversation. I also consider you a friend, and I honestly want you to find someone who can truly make you happy, which is why I introduced you to Ken in the first place."

"I know you did, and I appreciate it."

"You're welcome. So, with that being said, if I'm ever asking too many personal questions, or if I should say anything else to make you feel uncomfortable, just let me know and I'll shut up. In the meantime, I'm going to have a little talk with Ken myself. I think his actions were over the top as well. So, are we still friends?"

Finally, Jenna's tone softened. "Yes, we're still friends."

"Good. I'm glad we got everything out in the open. Now if you'll excuse me, I have a client presentation later today."

"Of course, and good luck with it." Jenna turned her attention back to her project, but she couldn't shake the nagging feeling she hadn't heard the last from Ken.

* * *

Ken wadded up his food wrappers and checked his watch. He had a few more minutes before his lunch break ended, so he grabbed his phone to check his messages. To his surprise, he had an urgent text from CeCe.

"I got the third-degree from Jenna when I arrived at work this morning. What were you thinking by sending her a text about the guy she's seeing now?"

He sent her a quick reply. *"Sorry, CeCe. It's a guy thing. We don't like hearing about an ex moving on."*

She responded a minute later. *"Why would it bother you? You told me yourself you were getting ready to end it with her, so how is her seeing someone else affecting you?"*

He pursed his lips as he typed. *"Because I wasn't quite ready to end it, but then, thanks to my aunt, she beat me to it."*

"Sorry it happened, but if you were going to end it anyway then it really doesn't matter who ended it first. Time to move on."

CeCe was missing the point, so he tried to phrase it differently. *"I still consider her a friend. I don't want to see her in a situation which could end badly for her."*

He grabbed his phone and was walking back to his office when it beeped again. He muttered an expletive under his breath.

"Anything wrong, Ken?" asked one of his coworkers.

"I'm fine. It's just CeCe, going on about nothing, like she always does." He hurried into his office and took a seat. This time CeCe had asked him about Jeri. He quickly pounded out a response.

"Jeri is fine. We're doing great."

"I'm glad you've moved on. So, stop bothering Jenna."

Ken was becoming annoyed with the conversation. He would stop bothering Jenna when he was good and ready. For the moment, however, he needed to put his phone away and turn his attention to the folders on his desk.

❧NINE❧

JENNA GRABBED HER phone when she heard the text alert. Bill had arrived. Opening the front door, she saw a U-Haul truck parked at the curb. Bill hopped out as she approached.

"Anything wrong?" she asked.

"Not at all. I just want to show you something." He took her behind the truck and opened the cargo doors. Inside were several large crates, carefully secured into place. "As you can see, everything has been loaded safe and sound. The sculpture for the hotel lobby is toward the back, along with the one of Miss Stephanie, and several others."

"I can't wait to see them," said Jenna, "and thanks for the invite. I've never been to an art foundry before."

"You're welcome. I thought it might be a good excuse for a Saturday morning outing." He opened the passenger door and waited until Jenna was safely inside the truck. They were soon on the Interstate, heading south to Colorado Springs, but Bill seemed unusually quiet as they drove.

"It's been really good having you back," he finally said. "I've really enjoyed the past few months."

"It's been good having you back as well, although I have a feeling there's more to it."

"I'm afraid there is."

Jenna felt her stomach drop as Bill took a deep breath and sighed. "I guess I've come down with a bad case of mid-life crisis, because I'm starting to feel stuck. I love my teaching job, but they want me to put in more hours. If I give them what they want, I won't have enough time to create my art. I'm also paying rent for studio space which is virtually unusable during the winter months. On top of that, I really miss Connor. It's been lonely not having my son close by. He and I have been talking it over for some time now, and after much discussion, I've decided to move to Florida."

"I see," said a stunned Jenna.

"Now just so you know, I won't be leaving right away. I still have my show at Garrison's in July, but I won't be starting any new projects because I need to get my house ready to sell. I've already talked to a real estate agent, and I've applied for a teaching position at a college in Fort Meyers, which is where Connor lives. I'm leaving right after my show. I just wanted you to be prepared."

Jenna struggled to hide her emotions. "Then I guess we'll have to find a place to store the Shelton piece. We still have a long way to go before the hotel construction is complete."

"I already planned on having it delivered to my studio. It'll be safe there. The building has a state-of-the-art security system. I can also arrange to have it delivered to the hotel later on. My lease expires at the end of November, so please let me know if there's any changes for the grand opening date."

"The grand opening is still set for late September. At least for now," said Jenna. "First thing Monday morning I'll start the paperwork so Salisbury and Norton can cover the storage costs. You have enough to worry about."

"Thank you. I appreciate it."

"You're welcome, and I'm sorry you won't be there for the grand opening."

"I am too, but I'll be there in spirit. So, what about the rest? Are you okay with this?"

Once again, Jenna had to hide her true feelings. "You'll always be very near and dear to me, and I'm going to miss having you around. You also said you have no intention of ever marrying again. In fact, I doubt you'd even live with someone full time."

"Probably not. I enjoy female companionship, but I have no desire to live with anyone fulltime. Connor tells me there are plenty of attractive widows in Florida, and it'll be nice finding people who understand what it's like to lose a soulmate. I also want you to know that even if I weren't leaving, I would have set you free once your project was complete. You need to find your special someone, and lately I've had a feeling that my being here is preventing him from coming into your life."

"But as you've said, many times, we're just good friends. So, if another man had come along and asked me out, I would have gone out with him."

"I know you would've. I'm just saying I have a feeling your soulmate will be here very soon, and my being in such close proximity could create some unwanted complications."

"I understand."

"I make no claim of being psychic," said Bill, "but my hunches are usually right. So have you met anyone lately who's piqued your interest at least a little?"

"No, not lately."

"Well, all I can tell you is once I'm in Florida, your life is going to change."

"Then I guess time will tell." Jenna silently fought back the tears as her mind flashed back to another sunny spring day nearly ten years before. It was the end of the semester. Bill was graduating, and he was telling her goodbye.

"You okay?" he asked.

"Yeah, I'm fine. I'm just a little tired. Busy week at the office."

"I understand. Final exams are coming up next week, so it's been a hectic time for me as well." Their exit came up a few miles later. Bill drove several blocks through an industrial area before turning onto a side street and into a warehouse complex. Driving up to the main building, he rolled down the window waited briefly until a man in coveralls came out and extended his hand. Bill quickly introduced him as Ron, the foundry owner.

"Go around to the back," said Ron. "I'll meet you in the loading zone."

Bill slowly drove behind the building. Ron stood in front of a big metal door with two other men. Within minutes all of the crates had been carefully unloaded and opened. Bill gave the items a close inspection. All were made of dark gray clay, but one piece had somehow gotten a small gash. He quickly grabbed his repair kit, and within minutes the damage was completely gone.

"Oh wow, look at this." Jenna was staring at a large, abstract clay sculpture.

"Do you like it?" asked Bill.

"I sure do. It really does suggest a flowing river. Do you mind if I take a few photos for the client?"

"If you'll give me your phone, I'll take one of you standing next to it. Then they can see the scale."

"Good idea. So why didn't I think of it?"

Bill shrugged his shoulders as Jenna handed him her phone. Once he was done, Ron invited them inside and gave them tour of the foundry. It was similar to a steel mill, but on a much smaller scale. The last stop was a room where the patina was painted onto the finished sculpture. Ron then led them into his office and offered them some bottled water.

"My goodness," said Jenna. "I had no idea there were so many steps involved in creating a bronze statue. All that mold making and casting and recasting."

"It's a bit of an undertaking," said Ron, "but we have it down to a science." He turned his attention back to Bill. Jenna's piece would be delivered to Bill's studio. Everything else would go to the art gallery. Like Jenna, Ron was sorry to hear Bill was leaving, but he wished him the best in Florida as they shook hands. Bill remained silent until they were back inside the U-Haul.

"So, what did you think?" he asked.

"It was interesting," said Jenna, "and thanks for taking the photos. I'll email them to the Sheltons on Monday. Then it's onto the next phase with the project. Visiting the job site and making sure the flooring and fixtures are what I asked for."

"How interesting, and who knows? Your soulmate might be some buffed out construction worker." Jenna gave him an odd look but Bill remained nonplussed. "Hey, I'm just saying you'll probably find him when you least expect it. It's how these things usually happen."

They stopped for lunch at a Denny's, and afterwards they took a backroad home to Denver. Once they arrived, Bill dropped her off without suggesting they spend the rest of the weekend together. Jenna felt disappointed when she came inside. Checking her phone, she found an urgent text message from Stacy. She had sent it two hours earlier and wanted Jenna to call her as soon as possible. Jenna immediately placed the call and Stacy quickly answered.

"What's up?" asked Jenna.

"You know, Bo, the new guy I've been seeing?"

"Yeah, what about him?"

"Turns out he's married."

"Say what?" Jenna plopped herself down on the sofa with a hard thump.

"I noticed things weren't adding up, so last night I called him out on it. He finally admitted he has a wife and a two-year-old kid. So, after calling him a few names you can't say in polite company, I asked him what the hell was he thinking?"

"And what was his explanation?"

"He said his wife, quote, 'put on a few too many pounds' after their daughter was born, and he's tired of all the domestic drudgery."

"What a jerk," said Jenna.

"Which is way more polite than some of the names I called him. So, I told him to get the hell out and never contact me again. He grabbed his things and left in a hurry."

"I'm so sorry. Stacy."

"Me too. I thought he was single, and I sure as hell didn't set out to be a homewrecker."

"I know you didn't, but to your credit, you started asking questions once you realized things were out of kilter, so don't go beating yourself up. I have a feeling he's done this sort of thing before."

"I'm sure he has, but how do you trust someone after something like this?"

"It isn't easy. I guess you have to take more time getting to know them."

"No doubt," said Stacy. "So has this ever happened to you?"

"Good question, and I'm honestly not sure. You know me. Most of the time it never goes beyond the first date, but I do pay close attention to what they say and how they say it. If I get any kind of a weird vibe, I move on."

"So, how's it going with Bill?"

"Not so good."

"Why? What happened?"

"I just found out he's moving to Florida."

"I am so sorry," said Stacy. "I know you were hoping he'd come around this time, and I was really rooting for the two of you as well. So, how are you feeling? And be honest about it."

"I'm crushed. I love him as much today as I did back then. Maybe more."

"So why won't you tell him how you really feel?"

"Because he refuses to let go of his late wife. I know they were soulmates, but moving on with someone else doesn't mean you're replacing them. I could no more take her place than he could take Arthur's place, but somehow, he's convinced himself that loving me, and making a commitment to me, means he's being disloyal to her."

"Losing his wife must have been devastating," said Stacy, "especially at a young age, and being left with a child to raise on his own. I can see why he might be a little gun shy about marrying again."

"So, what do I do?"

"I wish I had the answer, but I don't. So why don't we go do something fun and see if we can get our minds off this stuff for a while. I'll pick you up around six? We'll go grab a burger somewhere, and then we'll figure out something else after that."

"Sounds like a plan," said Jenna, "as long as we don't end up at another tattoo parlor."

"You are such a spoilsport."

❧TEN❧

BILL SPENT THE next few weeks getting his house ready to sell. He packed up his photography room and woodshop and repainted some of the rooms. He then had the carpets cleaned. His hard work paid off and he soon had an offer. His next task was to decide what to keep and what to leave behind. Going through the closets, he was amazed at how much he had accumulated. He had a big yard sale and donated what was left to a local charity. In the meantime, Jenna's completed sculpture had arrived safely at his studio. He invited her to join him when he packed up his remaining belongings. Her eyes popped when as she saw the sculpture.

"It's absolutely beautiful. The Sheltons will love it, and I'm sorry you won't be at the grand opening."

"I am too. Perhaps you could stream it to me on your phone."

"I'd be happy to, and again, I can't thank you enough."

"My pleasure, and I'm glad we were able to reconnect again."

"Me too." As Jenna snapped photos of the sculpture, Bill gathered up more of his personal items and added them to a half-filled moving box.

"Can I help you with anything?" she asked.

"Thanks, but no. I've just about got it." He wadded up some packing paper and stuffed it inside the box. Once it was sealed, he grabbed the broom. Jenna stepped aside as he swept up the floor and took out the last load of trash. A sad look came over his face when he returned.

"I had a really good run here, despite the old furnace."

"How long were you here?" she asked.

"Six years, and it feels sad to walk out the door for the very last time."

"Have you found a studio in Florida?"

"Not yet. I'm still looking for a gallery to represent me. So far one has expressed an interest, but I want to visit a few more before I make a final decision. After that, I'll look for some studio space, and as sad as I feel about leaving, I'm also looking forward to opening up shop in Florida." He removed a key from his keyring and handed it to her.

"This is now, officially, your baby. Be sure to return the key to the landlord when they pick up the sculpture."

"Of course."

"Then I guess we're good to go. I need to stop by the gallery to make sure they have everything ready for tomorrow night, and we'll grab a burger when I'm done. Then tomorrow night, after my opening, I'm taking you someplace really special."

"Come to think of it, I don't think I've ever seen you in a suit."

"Because you haven't," he said. "I only have one suit, and I only wear it once or twice a year. The rest of the time it's blue jeans or sweats. I'm just not a fashion maven. So, if you'll do me a favor and grab the broom, I'll get the box, and we're out of here."

* * *

Jenna did a double take when she opened her front door. "Well, look at you," she said. "You look like the CEO of a big company."

"Now don't go saying nasty things like that," Bill said jokingly. "I'm having a hard enough time as it is with this tie choking me." He looked her up and down. "You, on the other hand, look amazing. I love your white dress. I seem to recall you wearing it once before."

"No doubt you do. I wanted to go full circle." Grabbing her purse, she hurried outside. A white Chevy Malibu waited at the curb.

"Where's your Explorer?" she asked.

"On a trailer, hitched behind the rental truck. We'll Uber it tonight." He opened the back door, patiently waiting as she slid across the seat. He sat down next to her, but said little as they rode to the gallery. When they arrived, Jenna looked at the exhibit while Bill talked with the gallery owners. The woodcarving of the two models was displayed on a wall, along with several others. The bronze pieces were all proudly displayed and beautifully lit. Bill brought her a glass of white wine as the first patrons arrived.

"I need to work the crowd," he said, "so feel free to mingle, and for all we know, your soulmate may be here tonight." An older couple approached him and asked him a question. As they stepped away Jenna strolled around the gallery. Before long she spotted a familiar face. CeCe had arrived, along with her husband, John.

"I see you made it," said Jenna.

"I made a point of it. I want to see more of his work, and I'm sorry to hear this is his last show in Denver."

"I'm afraid so, but let me show you around."

Bill stopped by as CeCe was admiring one of his smaller bronze pieces. Jenna quickly introduced them. As they shook hands CeCe asked him a few questions about his work, which he was more than happy to answer.

"What a charming man," she said once he left. "I'd say you were lucky to have him as a teacher."

"I think so, too, although I'm really going to miss him."

"I'm sure you will, but you could always go visit him in Florida."

"No," said Jenna. "He seems to think someone new is about to come into my life, and he doesn't want to do anything to interfere. Bill was always a bit eccentric, in his own way."

"Maybe so, but he has a point. Sometimes a close friendship with someone of the opposite sex can scare off a new prospect. I also think he's right about someone new coming along. It's been months since you and Ken parted company. Someone is bound to come along, sooner or later."

"So, they tell me, and speaking of Ken, how is he doing these days?"

"He's doing well, and he's still with Jeri. You haven't had any more problems with him, have you?"

"Nope. Just the one text message."

CeCe excused herself to look at some other artwork, but before she and her husband left, they purchased the small bronze figurine. Once they were gone, Jenna continued to mingle with the crowd. She answered people's questions whenever she could, and she introduced Bill to a few serious buyers. The show ended at precisely eight o'clock. As promised, Bill took her to dinner at a five-star restaurant in Cherry Creek, but it would be a bittersweet evening. Returning to Jenna's house, she made him a nightcap and they sat on the sofa and talked for hours. Finally, he looked at his watch and stifled a yawn.

"I need to go," he said. "It's getting late, and I've set my alarm for five a.m. I want to be on the road before the rush hour traffic."

"Would you like to stay here tonight?"

He gave her a sad smile as he gently touched her hand. "I appreciate the invitation, but no. It would only make it that much harder in the morning." He grabbed his phone and tapped on the Uber app. His ride would pick him up in less than three minutes. He wrapped his arms around her and held her tight.

"Before I go, I want you to know something. If I were to have married again, it would have been you. So, what I want now is for you to find someone who'll love you the same way I loved Mary Beth."

He gave her a lingering kiss. "And with that, my dear, I'll be on my way." He gave her another long kiss and a sweet, parting smile. "Until we meet again." He hurried out and closed the door behind him. Jenna cried as she locked it, knowing she would never see him again.

❧ELEVEN ❧

CHAD PARKED alongside the chain-link fence and looked at Jenna as he shut down the engine. "Are you ready?" he asked.

"I think so." She picked up her tablet and hopped out of Chad's Subaru. The Shelton hotel construction was nearly complete, and they were there to give their clients a tour. Chad's phone rang as they walked toward the building.

"Hang on," he said. "It's my assistant." Jenna stood by as he took the call. He was only on the line for a moment, and he gave her a smile as he disconnected. "I have good news. The princess won't be coming after all. It'll just be Oscar and Chris. They should be here in about twenty minutes."

"Which is certainly a relief," said Jenna. "We're not ready to install the sculpture yet, and I didn't want to have to explain to her, for the umpteenth time, that it's perfectly safe where it's being stored. Did they say why she isn't coming?"

"Nope, but I'm guessing it's because she didn't want to get her shoes dirty."

"No doubt," Jenna said with a chuckle.

As they came inside the building a man in a hard hat and coveralls greeted them. "How's it going, Harvey?" asked Chad.

"So far, so good," he said. As the two men talked Jenna opened a file on her tablet and gave the lobby a closer look. Once she finished taking notes, she took the elevator to the top floor to inspect the completed suites. They were freshly painted and the flooring had been installed to her satisfaction. All that was needed was the furnishings, which would soon be delivered. After taking a few more notes she took the elevator down to the other floors. Some of the guestrooms were being painted.

49

Others were waiting for the flooring to be installed, but most were ready to be furnished. Returning to the lobby, she found Chad and Harvey inspecting the front desk.

"How are the upper floors?" asked Chad.

"They're looking good, and so far, I'm pleased," she said. "However, I just found out that the big chandelier for the lobby is still on backorder."

"And when will it get here?"

"I'm not sure. I'll call them as soon as we get back to the office. We could go with the brass chandelier if we absolutely had to, but I want it in bronze."

"Don't worry, Ms. Winters," said Harvey. "We can always switch it out later."

"I know we can, but I want to keep the costs down as much possible."

"Which we very much appreciate," said another voice. Oscar and his son had arrived. Chad quickly introduced them to Harvey, and they all hopped into the elevator together. After a complete tour of the building, they returned to the lobby.

"I'd say we're making good progress, Chad," said Oscar. "Chris and I would also like to take you and Jenna to lunch so we can discuss the items I was asking about."

"Of course, but first Jenna and I need to go over a few things with Harvey, so we'll join you as soon as we're done. Where would you like to meet?"

"Vito and Gianna's."

"Sounds good. We'll see you there in about thirty minutes."

* * *

Jenna did a double-take as she and Chad approached the restaurant entrance. The chalkboard by the door said the day's lunch special was pasta primavera.

"Is something wrong?" asked Chad.

"No, nothing's wrong. I was just remembering a wedding reception I went to this past winter. Someone at my table was giving me a lot of grief because I'd ordered pasta primavera instead of the chicken cordon bleu everyone else was having. She made a big to-do about me possibly being vegan."

"Good grief." Chad opened the door and waited for her to step inside. Oscar quickly spotted them and motioned for them to join them at their table. Their server soon arrived, once again telling them about the daily special. He then asked Jenna what she wanted to have.

"Go ahead and take their orders. I'm still trying to decide." To her surprise, all three men ordered the special. Chad spoke up as the waiter turned his attention back to Jenna.

"Don't worry, Jenna. No one here is going to judge you."

"In that case, I'll have the special, with chicken." As the server stepped away, Jenna told Oscar and Chris about her experience with Ken's aunt at the wedding reception. "So, after telling her it was one of my favorite foods when I was growing up, I got a big lecture about pasta being cheap peasant food. Talk about being arrogant. Sheesh."

"Well, if you're a peasant, then so are we," said Oscar. "My mother was an Italian American, so I grew up eating all kinds of Italian dishes, which is why I suggested this place. The décor may be out of date, but they come the closest to my mother's cooking, and like you, I adored my mother's pasta primavera. So, did your boyfriend stick up for you?"

"No, he did not, which is one of the reasons why he's no longer my boyfriend."

"Good for you. When you get to be my age, you realize life is too short to be wasted on people who don't appreciate you. To that end, I would like to thank you for all your hard work on our new hotel, and I'm sincerely looking forward to working with you again in the future."

"Thank you, Oscar. I look forward to working with you, and your son, as well."

"Here, here," said Chad. They raised their iced tea glasses and took a sip. Afterwards, the conversation turned to the grand opening festivities. Jenna reached for her phone and showed the others the photos of the sculpture.

"It's a beautiful piece," said Oscar. "I'm also sorry to hear the artist has left town."

"I am too," said Jenna, "although I'm told some of his work is still available at Garrison's Gallery."

"Then Chris and I will make a point of stopping there on our way home. We may want to include more of it in the atrium."

* * *

"So how did the tour with the clients go?" asked CeCe.

"In a word, fantastic," said Jenna. "The hotel looks really good, and with the exception of the lobby chandelier, everything is pretty much on schedule."

"Is the chandelier still on backorder?"

"It is, so I'm going to make a quick phone call." Jenna looked up the number and dialed. After punching several buttons, and a brief hold, a live person came on the line. It took several minutes for the woman to find Jenna's order, and after going back and forth they finally ended the call.

"So, what did they say?" asked CeCe.

"They said it'll be shipped next week."

"Of course it will, and I just won the lottery. So did you cover your rear end and order the brass one, just in case?"

"Yep. It'll be here Friday."

"Good job," said CeCe.

"Thanks, and now it's onward and upward. I need to shift gears and update a couple of things before I run up to the conference room. It's time to meet with the client for the next project. We're designing a new branch for a local bank."

"Still working with Chad?"

"I sure am. He even asked for me personally." Jenna quickly finished up her business and hurried to the elevator. She soon found an anxious Chad trying to open a file on the conference room computer, but it wasn't loading.

"What happened?" she asked.

"The computer has decided to throw a hissy fit."

"That's not good."

"No, it isn't," said Chad. "As you know, we're working with a committee on the bank project. Two of them have just arrived and are waiting downstairs while the others are on their way. In the meantime, I can't get the files to open. I've tried everything I can think of, including scanning the computer for viruses, but so far nothing's working. I guess I'll have to reboot it. So would you mind getting the two who are waiting downstairs?"

"Not at all," said Jenna. "I'll be back in a couple of minutes."

"Thanks. I owe you one."

Jenna rushed out to the elevator and took it down to the ground floor. Two middle-aged men in business suits were waiting in the reception area. To her relief, the computer was up and running when she brought their guests to the conference room. Mitch arrived a moment later, and the phone rang as they exchanged greetings. The remaining clients had arrived. Chad quickly stepped out as Mitch and Jenna made small talk with the two men. Chad soon returned, bringing two other men, and a woman, with him. They too appeared to be in their forties, and all wore expensive suits. As they took their seats, Chad began the presentation.

A rendering of the new bank building appeared on the screen. As Chad and Mitch talked, they showed their clients detailed drawings of the floor plan, along with a few other exterior renderings, which they both explained in detail. Then it was Jenna's turn. The first slide was a computer illustration of a lobby with wainscot paneling on mint green walls.

"These days we do most of our banking online," she said. "If we go to the bank in person, it's oftentimes because we have business which can only be taken care of face-to-face. This can be stressful, so rather than add to the tension with bright lights and stark white walls, I'm suggesting a warmer, more inviting interior with a classic design and softer lighting to help the customer feel more at ease." She watched the clients as she talked. They seemed to like her ideas.

"Interesting," said one of the executives. "So, what do you think, Rob?"

"The interior is certainly warm and inviting and I like the classic style, but I think it would look better with light gray walls instead green."

"We can certainly do that," said Jenna.

"Then I guess we've solved one problem, but there are a number of other things I'm not so sure about."

Jenna returned to her seat as he asked Chad and Mitch a few hard questions. Once he was satisfied with their answers, another client spoke up. It was obvious that some on the committee didn't agree with everything they had seen, while others were quite happy and didn't want as many changes. It took more than an hour for them to find middle ground.

"It looks like we have our work cut out for us," said Chad. "So, as soon as you're ready, I'll walk you out to the elevator."

As Chad escorted their clients out, Mitch and Jenna made their way to his office. A harried looking Chad arrived a few minutes later.

"The first presentation can be a bit of a nail biter," he said, "but holy guacamole. This was more like the battle of overinflated egos. Let's just hope it doesn't turn out to be the project from hell."

"I hope not," said Jenna, "but I watched Mr. Richardson closely whenever the two of you were talking. I got the distinct impression it's his first time overseeing this kind of a project, despite his claims to the contrary, and the rest of them saw it too."

"I had that feeling as well," said Mitch.

"He may change his tune once we run the numbers for all the changes he wants," said Chad.

"Assuming he's still on the committee," said Jenna.

"One can only hope. In the meantime, the Shelton project is wrapping up, and I'm really looking forward to the upcoming grand opening festivities. I'm sorry your friend who made the sculpture won't be there. Hopefully things will go well for him in Florida."

"They were, the last I heard. He'd made an offer on a house that was about a ten-minute drive from where his son lives."

"Close, but not too close, which is where I hope to be someday myself. I love my kids, but I'm sure looking forward to the day when they're all out on their own."

It was late in the day when Jenna finally returned to her desk. As usual, CeCe was full of questions. "So how was it?" she asked.

"To be honest, I'm not sure where to begin," said Jenna. "It's one of those corporate projects where we're working with a committee, and we have someone who may be difficult to deal with."

"Those projects sometimes start out a little rough, but it tends gets better once the things are underway. Chad's also known for having good people skills."

"He certainly does. He's much more patient than I am."

"I'm with you. Sometimes I have to stop and count to ten."

Jenna checked the time. It was four forty-two. "I'm going to finish up a couple of things and sneak out of here a little early. It's been a long, hectic day."

"I know it has, and don't worry. I won't tell anyone."

✨TWELVE✨

STACY'S THIRTIETH birthday had arrived. She wanted to celebrate with a weekend camping trip. Her blue Nissan Rouge was fully loaded when she came to pick up Jenna. After tossing in Jenna's bag, along with a few more blankets, they were on their way to Rocky Mountain National Park. Stacy was excited about the trip, but Jenna wasn't so sure. Once inside the park, Jenna clinched her teeth as Stacy drove. The curvy mountain roads had no guardrail, and Stacy was having trouble finding the campground.

"Relax," she said. "It's all good. According to my GPS, it'll be coming up in about another quarter mile. My bad for making a wrong turn back there, but at least I got to stop and take some photos, and I'm having fun with my new camera."

"I know you are," said Jenna. "It really is a beautiful day and the fall colors are stunning. I'm just not looking forward to freezing my buns off tonight,"

"You are such a wuss." The mock exacerbation resonated in Stacy's voice. "Sorry you didn't have a proper sleeping bag, but I brought along some extra blankets as well, so you should be fine. I also seem to recall you saying you loved to go camping when you were a kid."

"Sure, I did. When I was nine and my parents sent me to summer camp. When you're a kid everything's an adventure, and you can sleep just about anywhere."

"So, look at it this way. It's an opportunity for you to reexperience a happy part of your childhood." Stacy pointed out something on the side of the road. "Here we go. I see the campground. It's coming up on the left." She turned into the entrance and slowly drove around.

"So far so good," said Stacy. "It looks like there's only one other group here, and we'll be on the other side so we'll have some breathing room. And looky there. Each spot has a picnic table, and a nice, level place for a tent."

"I'll help you pitch the tent," said Jenna. "Did you remember to bring the tarps?"

"Sure did, and look over there. They even have a bathroom, so you should be good to go."

"It's more like a porta potty. The sign back there said the regular bathrooms are closed for the season. I'm also wondering if the water might be shut off for the winter."

"I have no idea, so I brought along plenty of extra water, just in case. Don't worry. I thought of everything."

Jenna helped Stacy unload her truck and they began pitching the tent. Stacy stepped off to the side when Jenna carefully staked it down.

"There we go." Jenna handed the hammer back to Stacy. "It's all weatherproofed and secure. So did you want to do anymore hiking?"

"A little." Stacy twisted her blonde ponytail into a bun as she spoke. "We're getting into the time of day when we'll start getting some nice lights and shadows. I'll toss some sandwiches in our backpacks and we'll get going."

Jenna grabbed her phone and snapped a photo of their campsite, but she frowned when she opened her Instagram app. "That's weird. I'm having trouble getting a signal."

"Because there isn't any," said Stacy. "There's no Internet or cell phone service out here. It's all Mother Nature."

"No worries. I was just asking."

"Turning thirty is a big milestone, and I wanted to go camping so I could unplug for a little while. My parents used to talk about how when they were kids, people went to the great outdoors to get away from the phone and the RV. Nowadays we take our technology with us everywhere we go, and I think we may be doing ourselves more harm than good. There are times when we need peace and quiet."

Stacy grabbed her backpack and the two women headed out. As they trekked further into the wilderness, Jenna realized her friend was right. The scent of the trees, and the sound of chirping birds, felt soothing to her soul. As they were walking, something caught Stacy's eye, and she motioned to Jenna to join her.

"Come look at the view from over here."

"Wow, that's amazing," said Jenna. "It's like you can see the whole world from here."

"Funny how I've lived in Colorado since I was ten, and you've been here your whole life, yet we take it all this beauty for granted."

"They say familiarity breeds contempt, and you certainly have a point about the need to unplug. We get so wrapped up in our jobs and the whole having to make a living mindset that I think we sometimes forget how to live."

They sat down and silently took in their surroundings as they enjoyed their lunch. Afterwards they continued their hike, making frequent stops to take in the scenery. Finally, Stacy looked at her watch. "It's getting later than I thought, and we need to start making our way back to the campground. I brought some meal pouches we can cook in a skillet. Would you prefer lasagna or chicken and dumplings?"

"My, my, how fancy are we?" Jenna said smugly. "And here I thought we might have to shoot a bear or something."

"Nope, but since you brought it up, maybe we can do a birthday hunting trip next year."

"Let's wait and see first," said Jenna. "A lot can happen in a year. For now, lasagna sounds great. You know I love Italian food."

"There you go, being a spoiled brat again."

Upon returning to the campground Stacy lit the camp stove, and the scent of garlic and oregano filled the air. Afterwards Jenna presented Stacy with a small birthday cake, and they settled in their tent. Huddling underneath their blankets, Stacy began wondering what the future might have in store for her.

"My grandmother called me this morning to wish me a happy birthday, and while she said it in a tactful way, she thinks I'm an old maid because I'm thirty and not married yet. So, am I an old maid?"

"I don't think so," said Jenna. "Perhaps in her time you may have been, but things are different now. Women go to college, and many of us want to get our careers off the ground before we even think about getting married and having kids."

"I know, but our biological clocks are still ticking. If I want to have a healthy baby someday then I really shouldn't put it off until I'm thirty-five or forty."

"I'd like to have a kid or two myself. Bill talking about his son really brought it close to home for me, but lately my prospects for finding someone to have them with haven't been so good."

"It's a shame he was so adamant about not getting married again. I really thought the two of you made a great couple, even if he was a bit older than you."

"I thought we did too." Jenna paused for a moment and sighed. "Right before he left, he finally admitted that if he were to have married again, it would have been me, and you know how much I would have wanted to have kids with him."

"I know, Jenna. I'm so sorry it didn't work out."

"Me too, although he still thinks I'll find my soulmate soon."

"Really. So, have you met anyone new?"

"Nope."

"Me neither. So, what's wrong with us?"

"Nothing," said Jenna. "We just haven't found the right ones yet. I guess it takes longer for some people."

"I suppose it does." Stacy went quiet for a moment. "For what it's worth, I'm glad you ended it with Ken."

"Why do you say that?"

"Granted, I only met him a couple of times, but I didn't like his vibe. He struck me as a narcissist."

"Well, it turned out he was pretty arrogant."

"Yeah, I remember you telling me about what happened at the wedding."

"And he's now someone else's problem," said Jenna. "According to our mutual friend, he started seeing her right after we went our separate ways. Apparently, he's pretty taken with her, although I think I told you about the text message he sent me later on."

"You sure did," said Stacy. "So did CeCe take care of it?"

"I believe she did. I haven't heard a peep out of him since."

"Good to know, but if it were me, I'd be really careful about what I say to CeCe. From what you tell me, she strikes me as the type who likes to stick their nose into other people's business. You need to set your boundaries straight with her as well."

☙THIRTEEN☙

JENNA UNLOCKED the door and the two men stepped inside. As she pointed to the sculpture, one of the men gave her a smile.

"I remember this," he said, "and I thought this place looked familiar. I helped deliver it. Ron said the artist's name was Bill Haskell."

"He was the artist. This used to be his studio."

"Did something happen to him?"

"No, nothing happened to him," said Jenna. "He moved to Florida a few months ago."

"That's right. I remember Ron saying something about it too. Don't worry. We'll get it loaded, and we'll meet you at the Shelton Inn."

"Thanks, Phil. I'll be there as soon as I can. When you get there, ask for Harvey Cruz. He's the construction superintendent, and he knows where the sculpture goes."

"Gotcha. Go get the dolly, Tom, and let's get it back into the crate." His assistant hurried out, and they were soon ready to load the sculpture into the truck. And older looking Asian woman arrived as they wheeled the big crate out the door.

"I'm looking for Ms. Winters," she said.

"I'm Ms. Winters, and you must be Sally Chang. Nice to finally meet you in person." The two women shook hands and Sally inspected the studio, making notes on her clipboard.

"Well, I see he left the place clean, which I really appreciate. Not all the artists do, you know. So do you have the key?"

"Right here." Jenna took it from her keyring, and Sally eagerly grabbed it from her. After filling out the rest of paperwork, she tore off the top sheet and handed it to Jenna, along with a check, made out to Bill.

"Here's his deposit money," she said. "He didn't leave me a forwarding address, so please be sure he gets it."

"Of course." Jenna took her leave, but she felt profoundly sad once she got into her car. The studio was Bill's last tie with Denver. Once he received the check, he would have no reason to return.

"Don't go there," she sternly said. "You have work to do, and come to think of it, I don't have his mailing address either. Guess it'll have to wait until after the grand opening."

A landscaping crew was hard at work when Jenna arrived at the hotel. The delivery truck was parked in front and the cargo doors were open. The lobby was bustling with activity when she came inside. The staff was busy getting the hotel ready to open while the construction crew was putting on the final touches. Jenna hurried toward the atrium, where the two men were carefully dismantling the crate. Phil greeted her with another smile.

"You're timing is perfect, Ms. Winters. So, is this where you want us to put it?"

Jenna quickly pointed out the spot. "It goes right here."

"Do you need the dolly?" asked Harvey.

"No, we can lift it," said Phil. "It only has to go a couple of feet. Are you ready Tom?" Phil counted to three. The two men carefully lifted the sculpture, and gently set it down as Jenna gave them a thumbs up with a big smile.

"That's perfect," she said. Taking out her phone, she snapped a few photos and sent them to Bill. No doubt he would be relieved to know the sculpture was safe in its permanent home.

"It really does look nice," said Harvey, "and if you'll come with me, Ms. Winters, I want to show you something else." He walked her to the lobby and pointed to the big chandelier, hanging from the ceiling. Once again, a big smile broke out across her face.

"I don't believe it," she said. "It finally came. So, when did it get here?"

"A few hours ago. We left the brass chandelier in its box and we were going to wait until the very last minute to hang it, but as you can see, the bronze one has arrived."

"Thank goodness. So, where's the brass chandelier?"

"I put it in one of the storage rooms while I wait for your instructions."

"I'll take care of it in the morning," said Jenna. "In the meantime, you not only made my day, you've made my entire week."

"Thanks, but I'm just doing my job." Harvey stepped away and Jenna ventured into the atrium. The restaurant space, along with two store spaces, had been leased, and the employees were busy setting up shop. One tenant was a novelty clothing store called Katie's. The other was a hotel convenience store selling snacks, souvenirs, and other items people sometimes forget to pack. The new restaurant was called Sam's Place. Once again, Jenna felt sad as she walked out to her car. The Shelton Inn had been one of her favorite projects, and she was sorry to see it come to an end. She started up her car and checked her phone. So far Bill had not responded to her message. No doubt he was out enjoying his new surroundings in Florida.

* * *

The next day seemed slower than normal. As the hours dragged by even CeCe seemed quieter than usual. Chad was making progress with the design changes for the bank building. With any luck, they would soon start the construction phase. Hopefully, their next client would be more pleasant to work with. It was late afternoon when Jenna finally went out to her car. She returned a few minutes later with a hanging bag.

"So, what do we have here?" asked CeCe.

"Something for the big grand opening tonight. Hopefully, it'll go with my shoes."

"I don't see why it wouldn't. You're wearing basic black pumps."

"Then I guess we'll find out soon enough." Jenna hurried off to the ladies' room, returning a few minutes later in an elegant mauve colored cocktail dress with a matching jacket. CeCe smiled in approval.

"Well, look at you," she said. "What a gorgeous outfit."

"Thanks. It belongs to my mother. She bought it for a cousin's wedding, and she was kind enough to let me borrow it."

"Then you two must wear the same size."

"We do. Word has it the Sheltons have invited a lot of VIPs to the grand opening, and I wasn't sure if any of my outfits would be dressy enough. Anyway, I need to run. I told them I'd be there no later than four-thirty."

"Hang on a second." CeCe quickly took her phone from her purse. "I want to take a picture of you before you go."

"Okay, but make it fast."

CeCe snapped a few photos and Jenna hurried out. The front parking lot was filling up when she arrived at the hotel. Walking up the entrance, she spotted Chad, donned in a three-piece pin-striped suit. He was busy chatting with someone on the phone, and he motioned to Jenna to wait as he wrapped up his conversation. From what Jenna could hear, it sounded like he was talking to someone at an art gallery. He soon ended the call and greeted her with a smile.

"CeCe sent me a photo of you in your outfit," he said, "and it looks very nice."

"Thanks. She has a flair for fashion design, as well as interior design. Did you know she studied both when she was in school?"

"No, I did not. So, are you ready?"

"Let's do it."

Chad extended his arm and escorted her inside. The lobby was packed with people enjoying complimentary champagne and hors d'oeuvres. Walking toward the atrium, she saw several people admiring the sculpture. No doubt Bill would be pleased. She would have to take more photos to send to him later. As she made her way into the atrium, she watched people admiring the interior landscaping. Two of Bill's smaller sculptures had been incorporated into the atrium, and a few people were admiring them as well. She sent photos she had taken the night before to Bill, but he had only given her a lukewarm response, which wasn't like him. Hopefully, things were going well in Florida. As she continued her stroll around the atrium, she realized she was hungry.

Sam's Place was open, and they had set up tables in the atrium with finger sandwiches and veggie dip. Jenna helped herself to a small plate of fresh vegetables and watched the crowd as she enjoyed her snack. Once she finished, she strolled around the atrium and slowly worked her way back to the lobby.

A man in a business suit was standing next to Bill's sculpture. He appeared to have some art expertise as he pointed out different aspects of the piece, but his back was turned toward her. As she walked past him, he reached out and grabbed her by the hand.

"You'll have to thank this lady, too," he said. "She's the one who commissioned it."

An astonished Jenna looked up, not believing her eyes. She found herself at a loss for words as the people he was talking to walked away. It took her a moment to find her voice.

"What on earth are you doing here?" she asked.

"Well, at the moment, I'm talking to people about my art."

"I know that. So, when did you get back into town?"

His mood turned more serious. "The day before yesterday. The reason I didn't tell you is because I wanted it to be a surprise."

"Oh, I'm surprised all right."

For a moment Bill looked uncertain, so Jenna tried to reassure him. "It's okay. I'm surprised in a good way. So, what happened?"

"Things didn't work out in Florida. I'll fill you in on the details later."

"Is everything okay?"

"It will be, and we're both doing better now that we're back."

"We?" she asked.

"I brought Connor with me. It's kind of a long story, but don't worry. We're both okay." He wrapped his arms around her and gave her a squeeze. "In the meantime, it's good to see you. Chad forwarded me the photo of your outfit, so I knew it was you walking by, and you are truly a sight to behold. However, it looks like someone else wants to talk to you."

Oscar and Chris, along with Michelle, were all smiles as they approached Jenna. Once again Oscar sincerely thanked her as he shook her hand, while Michelle stood in awe when she was introduced to Bill.

"You really helped us avoid a big family brawl," said Oscar. "Chris and I love your art, and we definitely want to put more of it in our other buildings as well."

"I appreciate the compliment," said Bill, "and I'm happy to know I helped keep the peace in your family. However, I'm in between galleries at the moment, but as soon as I find new representation, I'll let Jenna know, and she can pass the information along to you."

"Which we would very much appreciate," said Oscar, "and again, thank you for creating this wonderful piece of art."

Oscar and his family stepped away and Jenna gave Bill and inquisitive look.

"I called Garrison's as soon as I got back," he said. "Turns out they've brought in a new artist whose work is similar to mine, and while they would have loved to have me back, they're only able represent a limited number of artists. Fortunately, your boss may have a solution. Apparently, his predecessor's wife is part owner of another gallery here in town, and Chad called them a little while ago. They would like to meet with me."

"I'm glad," said Jenna. "He was out front, talking to them on the phone, when I arrived."

Bill checked his watch. "So how much longer do you have to be here? I'd like to take you to dinner. Somewhere quiet, where we can talk."

"I have a better idea. Why don't you meet me at my place? We'll order some pizza, and I can change into something more comfortable. I borrowed this outfit from my mother, and I would just as soon not risk spilling anything on it."

"Good idea. I'll stop at the hotel and change as well."

"Then let me say goodnight to a few people, and you can walk me to my car."

✋FOURTEEN✌

JENNA HURRIED HOME and changed into her sweats. Bill arrived in his usual jeans and sweatshirt and greeted her with a lingering hug and a warm, passionate kiss.

"It feels good to be out of that suit," he said. "I've worn it twice in the past few months, which is way too often for my taste."

"It looked like you were wearing a different tie this time."

"I always knew there was something special about you, and you're right. I was wearing a different tie. I have a small, and I mean very small, tie collection."

"Okay, I'll bite. How many ties do you have?"

"Three," he proudly said. "Although one is a Christmas tie. It's red with snowmen printed on it. The college always wanted me to attend their holiday parties, and speaking of which; I contacted them before I left Florida. We were able to reach an agreement on the additional hours, so I got my teaching job back. I'll be starting in January, which means I'm off the hook for any Christmas parties this year."

"I'm sure you must be relieved."

"It helped."

Jenna offered him something to drink, and they sat down at the table. Once again, the mood turned serious.

"So, where to begin," he said with a sigh. "I arrived in Florida without any issues, and for the first few weeks everything was fine. I found a house I liked. Unfortunately, it failed the inspection, and the lender backed out."

"Bummer, and I'm sorry it happened. So where were you staying?"

"At an extended stay hotel. It was like a small, efficiency apartment. I didn't want to impose on Connor."

"Of course."

"Two days after the house fell though, everything suddenly turned upside down. As you know, Connor was working for a healthcare management company. One of their properties was a physical therapy clinic, and they had a young lady working there as an office manager. She booked the appointments and billed the insurance companies, and, unbeknownst to everyone, she was also embezzling a huge sum of money. We're talking hundreds of thousands of dollars."

Jenna's jaw dropped. "You're joking," she said.

"I wish I were," said Bill. "Connor noticed the numbers weren't right, and he wanted to investigate it further. So, he stopped by and had a talk with the young woman. He was trying to determine if she was making honest mistakes, or if there was something else going on. He said she acted very defensive and never gave him a straight answer to any of his questions. He also noticed the clinic manager was acting strange as well. When he returned to his office, he discussed the matter with his supervisor. She contacted the higher ups, as was company policy. The lady in question was arrested a short time later, and she's looking at some serious jail time."

"Sounds to me like he did the right thing," said Jenna. "He also gave her the benefit of the doubt until he was sure she had done something wrong."

"Connor has always been fair minded. Unfortunately, someone decided to take revenge. The following morning an anonymous source told the media that the woman in question had once accused Connor of sexual harassment, but the company had covered it up. Of course, it never happened, and there was no evidence to back it up. Connor had never met the woman until the morning he interviewed her, but as soon as the story broke, he was put on administrative leave with pay while they conducted an internal investigation. In the meantime, the media went wild."

"Do they know who tipped them off?" asked Jenna.

"It had to have been an insider. We're pretty sure it was the clinic manager, but so far it hasn't been proven. A police detective showed up at Connor's apartment the day after the story broke, but I wouldn't let him to talk to my son without an attorney being present. He was soon cleared of any wrongdoing, but by then the damage was done. His picture had been plastered all over the media, and even though the reports all stated he hadn't been charged, making someone look guilty is apparently good for ratings."

"I'm afraid it is," said Jenna.

"Once he was officially exonerated, we both decided it would be best to come back to Colorado, but I made sure I found a damn good attorney before we left. Connor wants to file a civil case against his former employer. They knew, for a fact, that another employee had tipped off the media without their knowledge or consent, yet they chose to remain silent and allow Connor to became the scapegoat. Their only concern was protecting their corporate image."

"Sounds like someone may have given them some bad advice."

"Maybe so, but Connor's reputation was seriously damaged because of what happened, and he deserves compensation for the harm it caused."

"I agree. So, how's he doing now?

"Much better," said Bill. "One of his buddies was in between roommates, so Connor is staying with him. He also started sending out resumes before we left Florida. He's anxious to get back to work and put it all behind him. His old employer said not to worry, they'd give him a good recommendation, but with all that has happened, I'm not so sure we can trust them."

"And rightly so. I hope he finds something soon."

"I'm sure he will. Connor's a good worker, and there's always a need somewhere for someone with his skills."

The pizzas arrived a few minutes later. Over the meal Bill asked Jenna about her camping trip with Stacy.

"It was an adventure, all right."

"You know, I somehow can't picture you roughing it in the great outdoors. You've always struck me as the city type."

"And believe me, I much prefer the amenities of modern life. Things like plumbing, heating, and electricity, but I also think it would be nice to have a little cabin in the woods, or a house on the beach."

"Airbnb, my dear," he said. "All the pleasure, but none of the maintenance."

"Then I'll have to look into it. So, what about you?"

"I'm in a bit of a holding pattern for the moment. I'd been living in my house for over twenty years, so I had a lot of equity in it, and with the house in Florida falling through, all the money is still in the bank. I also have a job, but you could say I'm on leave at the moment, so I'm hoping to find a lender willing to work with me. But to answer your question, I'm in another extended stay hotel for now."

"You may be in luck," said Jenna. "CeCe's husband works for a bank. Maybe he can help you. I'll talk to her tomorrow, and speaking of money, I have something for you." She opened her purse and presented him with his check.

"So, what did you think of Sally?" he asked.

"I'm not sure. She's quite a character."

"She is indeed."

"She called me after we took over the lease," said Jenna. "She wanted me to help her find a new furnace, so I got her a good deal. She said it has to be installed before she can look for a new tenant."

"Do you know if she's found anyone?"

"I don't think she has. She wanted to wait until after the sculpture was gone before she replaced it. Salisbury also paid the remainder of the lease, just in case something happened and we had to push back the grand opening date, so you're good through the end of November."

"That's a relief. I'll call her first thing in the morning to let her know I'm renewing. I'll also reimburse your boss for November."

The conversation turned to Jenna's latest work project, and some of Bill's ideas for new artwork. "I'm working on some sketches," he said. "I want to get a good head start, before the spring semester begins. And while I wish I could stay longer, Connor sent me a text earlier today, asking me to stop by on my way back to the hotel. I'd like to make it up to you Friday night. I can either take you to dinner, or we can order in."

"I'd love for us to get together, but you probably need to watch your spending until your new job starts, so maybe I could treat you to a homecooked dinner."

"You could," he said, "as long as I bring the groceries."

"You're on, so I'll see you Friday night." Jenna walked him to the door, and he smoothed her hair away from her face.

"Be sure to get a good night's sleep Thursday night, because I'll be keeping you busy until the wee hours on Saturday morning."

"You naughty boy you."

He gave her a long, lingering kiss. "It's good to be home. See you Friday."

Jenna tidied up the kitchen after he left. Afterwards she checked her messages. To her surprise, she had a new text message from Ken. It had come an hour before.

"CeCe sent me a photo of your outfit, and you look fabulous. Glad your project went well. Jeri and I are doing fine. Hope you're doing well too."

This time he made a point of respecting her boundaries. Jenna debated with herself about sending him a reply, but decided it would be best if she didn't.

* * *

Connor was relieved to see his father's face when he opened the door. "C'mon in, Dad. Caleb is out for the evening, so it's just the two of us, and we can talk in private."

"So, what happened?"

Connor handed his father an envelope. The return address was from a law firm in Fort Meyers. "This arrived today. It's a copy of the letter my attorney got from their attorney. Not only are they denying any wrongdoing, they're now saying I was fired for insubordination, which is a load of crap, and they know it. We now have the documentation to prove Angela called Devon right after she was released, and that Devon emailed the media from his computer at the clinic."

Bill motioned toward the sofa. "Let's sit down, and I'll explain what happened."

"Okay, but first I should ask if you'd like something to drink."

"I'm fine, so let's talk."

Connor sat down and nervously ran his fingers though his dark wavy hair. His father gave him a reassuring look.

"Back when your mother was still with us," said Bill, "she used to talk about the games lawyers play. She said everyone would start out beating their chest, as if to say they were the biggest, baddest attorney since F. Lee Bailey.

"Who's F. Lee Bailey?" asked Connor.

Bill gave his son another look. "He was a very famous lawyer. You'll have to look him up. Anyway, according to your mother, the other party always starts out denying any wrongdoing, so those first few letters back and forth can get downright ugly, but it's all BS and everyone knows it. It's simply part of the game. They're trying to intimidate you so you'll give up and go away, but she said once you make it clear that you're not going anywhere, they'll oftentimes want to settle out of court. You need to relax and let your attorney do his job. It may take some time, but the law is on your side. You didn't do anything wrong."

"Other than doing the job I was hired to do."

"I understand. I also have a hunch Devon knows more than he's admitting."

"Which is entirely possible," said Connor. "Apparently there've been rumors about him and Angela being romantically involved, which wouldn't be good for him, being as he's also married. We also believe Angela may have blackmailed him into making up the story for the media."

"Which is entirely possible, but the longer this goes on, the worse it looks for your ex-employer, so they'll eventually want to settle and make it all go away."

"I hope you're right, Dad, but in the meantime, it sucks."

"I know it does. So how are things going with Kelsey?"

Connor's mood instantly changed. "They're going great. This coming Thursday will be her last day at work, and she'll be here in about two weeks."

"And where will she be living?"

"Probably the same hotel where you are until we can find a place to rent. Then, once I find a job, I'll start putting money away for a house." For the first time, Connor smiled. "I still can't believe I fell for a brunette. I've always had a thing for blondes."

"What was that?"

"You okay, Dad?"

"I'm good."

"Anything I should know about?"

"Not at this time, but if there is, you'll be the first to know."

"Okay," Connor said tentatively. "So, moving on to some other good news. I've gotten a couple of bites. One is from a software company. The other, interestingly enough, is Southern Memorial Hospital. They're local and independently owned."

"Sounds like things are looking up. So, which of the two would you be the most interested in working for?"

"The software company."

"I see," said Bill.

"They're both mid-level management positions, and I plan on interviewing with both. If the hospital offers me a job I'll take it, but of course there's no guarantee I'll get either one, so I'm still looking. I have enough in the bank to live on for about three months, but I'm hoping to find something sooner. I'm also hoping what happened in Florida won't be an issue here."

"It won't," Bill said firmly. "You were cleared of any wrongdoing, and you have the documentation to back it up. You'd also be telling the truth if you said you left is because the old man wanted to go back to Colorado, and you wanted to be closer to family."

Once again, Connor smiled. "Oh, you mean I can blame it on you?"

"You could, and it wouldn't be the first time you blamed your problems on me."

Connor tried to feign his innocence. "Now when did I ever do that?"

"Too many times to count," said Bill, "but at least you're starting to sound more like yourself."

"I know. I'm trying not to let it all get to me, but it still feels surreal."

"I'm sure it does, but you're handling it well. We live in a crazy would where bad things happen to good people."

"I know," said Connor, "and I miss Mom too, but I'm not a kid anymore. I have my own life, and hopefully Kelsey and I will have a family of our own someday. Then you'll have grandchildren to spoil."

"You might want to think about buying her a ring before you buy the house, but let's not do the grandpa thing just yet, okay?"

"No worries, Dad. I'm not in any big hurry, but come to think of it, you were younger than me when I was born."

"I was," said Bill. "Your mother was older than me, and we didn't want to wait too long to start a family."

"I know. So, tell me more about the blonde."

"It's like I said before. If and when the time comes, you'll be the first to know. In the meantime, November is coming, and the first big cold front of the season arrives on Friday. We need to get you some winter clothes."

"I know, but I hate going shopping, so I'll see what I can find online. I also hung onto all my ski gear, so I have a heavy-duty winter jacket. Maybe we can go to the storage locker tomorrow and get it."

"We certainly can," said Bill. "So, text me when you're ready, and we'll hang out afterwards and go grab a bite somewhere."

⊱FIFTEEN⊰

CECE HAD FALLEN behind on her project, so she arrived earlier than usual. Jenna walked in a short time later, greeting her with a bright smile. "Well, look at you," said CeCe. "You must have gotten a raise for all your hard work on the Shelton Inn. You're positively glowing."

"Come to think of it, a raise would be nice," said Jenna.

"I gather the opening went well."

"It did. The restaurant is officially open with a limited menu, and the famous sculpture looks fabulous in its new home. The Sheltons were very pleased."

"Yeah, but there's more to it. I hear an old friend is back in town."

"He is."

"So, when is he going back to Florida?"

"He's not."

CeCe looked surprised. "He's not? So, what happened?"

"Apparently, things didn't go as planned," said Jenna. "Fortunately, he hadn't purchased a home yet, so he and his son decided to come back to Denver, which is where John comes in. Bill got his old job back, but he won't start until January, so for the moment he's staying in a hotel. He also has the means to make a substantial down payment, so can John work with him?"

"I'm sure he can. Do you have his number?"

"No, I don't."

"Then let me take care of it right now." CeCe took one of John's business cards from her desk and snapped a photo of it with her phone. "I'm sending this to your phone. Then you can send it on to Bill."

"Thanks, CeCe."

70

"So, is he still with Garrison's? I'd like to use more of his work for future projects."

"No," said Jenna. "Garrison's brought in a new artist, but another gallery has expressed an interest. As soon as I know more, I'll let you know. I also got a text from him a little while ago. He was able to get his old studio back, complete with a new furnace. He'll be back in business once the new furnace is installed."

"Good to know. I take it he still does private commissions."

"He does. In the meantime, I'm hoping to be done with my end of the bank project by Friday. With any luck, I won't have to deal with them directly once construction begins. Funny how the Sheltons were such great clients to work with, and this new bunch is so awful."

"It happens," said CeCe. "You may recall me working on a school awhile back. Talk about a bureaucracy. Good gravy, Marie. So many rules and regulations and every little thing had to be approved by the committee. Sheesh."

As Jenna booted up her computer, CeCe picked up her phone and began typing a message.

* * *

Ken looked up when he heard his phone beep. CeCe had sent him a text message. Glancing at his phone, it appeared to be brief.

Jenna's ecstatic. Her old friend came back from Florida.

He sighed as he pushed his phone away and tried to go back to work, but the idea of Jenna having another man in her life irked him. Wanting to find out more, he reached for his phone and typed.

"I thought you said they were just friends."

CeCe quickly responded. *"They are, so far as I know. How's Jeri?"*

"She's fine. Thanks for the update and we'll talk later." He set his phone down and once again tried to get back to work, but his mind kept wandering. While he still enjoyed Jeri's company, the chase was over. They had settled into a comfortable, but boring, routine, and he missed the excitement of the chase. Therefore, he would have to find a way to entice Jenna away from his rival without Jeri finding out. Hopefully, she would be as much fun in bed as she was before.

* * *

Jenna stopped by CeCe's desk a few hours later. "My mother sent me a text earlier today. She and my dad want to see the hotel, so we're going there for lunch. They just got here, and I'd like to introduce them to you."

"I'd be honored."

Jenna hurried out to the elevator, returning a few minutes later with her parents.

"My gosh," said CeCe. "You and you mother look so much alike. Other than her hair being shorter than yours, the two of you could pass for twins."

"You're very kind," said Claire. "Jenna's told us a lot about you, so I'm happy to finally meet you in person."

"As am I," said CeCe. "So, enjoy your lunch. My husband and I plan on going there this weekend."

Jenna waited until they were safely inside the elevator before asking the inevitable question. "So, what did you think?"

"I'm not sure," said Claire. "She seems friendly enough, at least on the outside, but I'm getting a not so good vibe about her. If it were me, I would keep her at arm's length."

The elevator stopped on the fourth floor. Two other people stepped inside. Jenna and her parents remained silent as they rode down to the parking garage.

"I'll drive," Jenna said once they stepped out.

"No, we'll drive," Nick firmly said. "But first, we need to get your mother's dress."

"Thank you again for letting me borrow it. It was a big hit and everyone loved it. I'll get it and meet you in the visitors' parking lot."

Jenna felt like a kid again as she road in the back of her father's Mercedes. Her parents were genuinely impressed when they stepped inside the hotel lobby.

"I guess hanging onto your college fund was a good idea after all," Nick said light heartedly.

"You did a fabulous job," said Claire. "I'll always remember the dollhouse you had when you were little. You'd spend hours moving the furniture around. Everything had to be just right."

As they strolled through the lobby, Jenna showed them the sculpture. "And if you'll follow me, I'll show you the atrium." Her parents were in awe as she walked them around. Afterwards, she took them to Sam's Place. The dining room featured tan colored faux brick walls with hanging tiffany lights and large picture windows. A built-in oak bar stood at the far end of the room. The hostess escorted them to a table next to one of the windows.

"I'm afraid I can't take the credit for this," said Jenna. "All I did was plan the space. The tenant did the rest."

"And they certainly did a good job," said Claire. "I love the contemporary décor." She turned to her husband. "You know, Nick, we may want to do our New Year's Eve staycation here, assuming you're not working over the holiday."

"We'll see."

Their server soon arrived, but after he left, the conversation soon took a different turn.

"So, you mentioned something in your text message about Bill being here last night," said Claire.

"He was," said Jenna. "It was a complete surprise. He came back to Denver a few days ago. Things didn't work out in Florida as he had hoped."

"Really? So, what happened?"

"It's kind of a long story. First the sale on his new house fell through. Then his son ran into trouble with his job."

"What sort of trouble?" asked Nick.

"I'm afraid I don't know all the details."

Nick looked concerned as Jenna filled him in on what had happened with Connor. "Unfortunately," said Jenna, "all the bad publicity had tarnished his reputation, so they decided to come back to Denver so he could have a fresh start."

"It's becoming a serious problem," said Nick. "At one time, those kinds of things would blow over and soon be forgotten. But now, thanks to the Internet and social media, it's out there forever. They were wise to hire an attorney and take legal action."

"And what about you and Bill?" asked Claire.

"We're still good friends."

"So, I gathered," said Claire, "but there's a history there. At the time you were still reeling from Arthur, and he was still grieving the loss of his wife."

"I know, but we've both come a long way since then, and just so you know; if I were to meet someone else, I'd go out with them, but Bill will always be someone special."

"I understand. I'm just saying I don't want to see you getting hurt."

"I know, Mom, and neither do I. Nor am I expecting any kind of commitment, but hypothetically speaking, let's say it did get serious. Would you and Dad be okay with it?"

"He's been teaching at the college for years," said Nick, "which means he's stable, and it sounds like he's a good father to his son. However, there is a significant age difference."

"I know there is, although he's quite a bit younger than you and Mom, which means he isn't old enough to be my father."

Nick tried to suppress a smile. "I understand. So how old is he?"

"He just turned forty-six," said Jenna. "He celebrated his birthday while he was in Florida."

"Okay, so there's a sixteen-year age difference. I'm not saying that in itself is a bad thing. There are other couples out there with similar age differences who seem to be quite happy. However, statistically speaking, women live longer than men, so if you were to marry him, chances are you'd be widowed at a relatively young age."

"Yes, I know. Ken sent me a text message saying the very same thing."

"When was this?" asked Claire.

"It was before Bill went to Florida, and yes, I reminded him that we are no longer an item, and whoever I'm seeing is none of his concern."

"Which was wise," said Nick, "but at the same time I'm also a little concerned. Has he been stalking you?"

Jenna's voice was firm. "No, he has not. It was a one-time thing. He did, however, send me a text last night. CeCe really liked Mom's dress, so she took a photo with her phone, which she apparently sent onto him. He complimented me on the dress and congratulated me on the hotel completion. That was it."

"Did you respond?"

"No. He has another girlfriend, and they've been together for some time now. I don't want to be the cause of any kind of misunderstanding between the two of them."

"Which you again were wise to do," said Claire, "but it also confirms my suspicions about CeCe. She's a gossip."

"She can be, at times," said Jenna.

"As I already told you, I'd be really careful of her. You don't socialize with her outside the office, do you?"

"No, Mom, I don't. We're coworkers and nothing more, although she did come to Bill's recent show at the art gallery."

"She did?"

"It's okay. She was looking for artwork for one of her clients. She also had her husband with her. They stayed long enough to find a piece they liked, and then they left."

"But even if she were there for a legitimate reason, I'm still not comfortable with it. Call it a mother's intuition, but I still have a bad feeling about her. She comes across as the type who likes to stir the pot, so you need to watch your back."

৶SIXTEEN৵

CECE GRABBED HER sweater and hurried out to the elevator. Once outside, she crossed the street and entered Megan's Diner. Ken was already seated in one of the booths.

"I forgot how good their coffee is," he said. "I wish they sold it online." He looked at her more closely. "So, what's up? You look happy about something."

"It's been an interesting morning. Jenna's parents stopped by a little while ago, and she introduced them to me. They were going to lunch at Sam's Place. It's a new gourmet restaurant at The Shelton Inn."

Ken raised his brow. "Lucky you. I never had the opportunity to meet them. So, what are they like?"

"They're good people. Her dad's an airline pilot, and her mother used to be a flight attendant. Jenna borrowed the dress she was wearing last night from her mother. The reason they stopped by was so her mother could pick it up."

"From what I hear, The Shelton Inn is quite a place."

"It is. Jenna did an amazing job. John and I are going there Saturday night to check it out for ourselves. Maybe you and Jeri could join us."

"We'd love to," said Ken.

CeCe grabbed her phone and started punching buttons. "Then I'm adding two more to our table."

"Thanks. So, tell me more about Jenna's friend being back from Florida."

"From what I gather, she didn't know he was back until she ran into him last night. She said she also introduced him to the Sheltons, and they were thrilled to meet him. Apparently, the sculpture was a big hit. I'm looking forward to seeing it for myself."

"So how close are he and Jenna?"

"She says they're good friends and nothing more. Sorry if I may have said anything to give you the wrong impression."

They turned their attention to their menus, and a server soon stopped by to take their order. Once she left, Ken resumed the conversation.

"So, getting back to Jenna. She may not be giving you the entire story concerning her relationship with her friend. Is she by chance seeing anyone else?"

"Not that I'm aware of. She did, however, make the point, not so long ago, saying if she were to meet someone she liked she would go out with them, and if anything happened, I'd be the first to know, but she said it sarcastically."

"Because she knows we're friends, and she doesn't want word getting back to me."

"Maybe so," said CeCe, "but as I've also pointed out before, you were getting ready to end it with her anyway, so whatever she does or doesn't do no longer matters. Still, I wish both of you had given it a chance. Sometimes people grow on you over time."

"Sometimes they do," said Ken, "and for what it's worth, I'm starting to wonder if I did the right thing, you know, letting her go without a fight."

"What do you mean? Did something happen between you and Jeri?"

"No, Jeri and I are fine. However, Jenna ended things a little too soon. I planned on seeing her a few more times, you know, just to be sure I was doing the right thing by letting her go."

"I'm sorry to hear it. You know I care deeply about both of you, but I also think you and Jeri are a good match as well. From everything you've told me, it sounds like you have more in common with her than you did with Jenna."

"Don't worry. I have no intention of letting Jeri go, but we're not ready to make a commitment either. At least not yet."

CeCe rolled her eyes. "Oh, c'mon, Ken. Who are you trying to kid? She's twenty-seven and you're thirty-one. A lot of women her age are already married or otherwise spoken for. I'm not saying you have to buy her a ring right this second. I'm simply saying don't wait too long. Other men are going to find her attractive too, and I'd hate to see you lose out because someone else came along."

"If it's meant to be it'll happen. Meantime, I'm still curious about Jenna's friend. Like I said, I still care about her, and I don't want to see her end up with the wrong guy. So can you tell me anything more about him?"

"He had a show a few weeks ago at Garrison's Art Gallery."

"I know he did," said Ken. "You've mentioned it before."

"Jenna introduced him to John and me while we were there. He's a charming man, and I can understand why they're good friends."

"I understand, and you know I like art too. At least some art. So, what's his name? I'd like to look him up."

"Willis Haskell, but Jenna calls him Bill."

Ken made a note on his phone. "Thanks. I'll have to check him out later. So, what else can you tell me about him?"

"According to Jenna, he also teaches part time at one of the colleges."

"Which one?"

"I don't remember, but I can ask her."

"No, it's okay," Ken quickly said. "I was just curious. It's no big deal."

"Okay, then I'll sum it up by saying he seems to be a good guy, and I understand why she's happy they reconnected. I also know you would like to remain friends with her, so my advice to you would be to respect her boundaries."

"I know. You've already told me."

It was time for CeCe to change the subject. "So, how are your folks doing these days?"

"They're doing well." The conversation turned to different topics, and after their meal they argued over who would pick up the tab.

"I already told you. Put your debit card away," Ken said sternly. "I'm the one who suggested we meet for lunch, so it's my treat. Next time we'll go Dutch. Fair enough?"

"Okay, fair enough."

He dropped his card on the table. Their server quickly came and snatched it up. "So do you have time for another cup of coffee?" he asked.

"I wish I did, but I'm coming up on a deadline, so I'll see you and Jeri this coming Saturday."

Ken helped her with her sweater, and she hurried out the door. He smiled to himself as he sipped his coffee and made more notes on his phone. CeCe had given him more than enough information to suggest Jenna and Bill were more than just friends, and he wasn't about to allow her to replace him. Swallowing down the last of his coffee, he grabbed his phone and hurried out.

❧SEVENTEEN❧

BILL AWOKE TO daylight streaming around the window curtains, but it didn't seem to be as bright this morning. Perhaps he had woken up too early. He checked his watch. It was his normal wakeup time. Rolling out of bed, he went to take a shower. Afterwards, he made himself a fresh cup of coffee.

Bill missed his coffee maker. The one in his hotel room only made one cup at a time, and he always enjoyed a second cup. Sometimes a third. Filling his Styrofoam cup, he opened the drapes. The view was hardly spectacular. His room looked into a small parking lot behind a neighboring building. The morning sky, however, looked dark and foreboding. A cold front was moving in. At least he had gotten Connor's ski jacket from the storage locker, along with his own winter coat.

Connor seemed to be doing better. The software company had contacted him for an interview, and he would meet with them the following week. He had also applied for a position at another company. Bringing him back to Colorado had been the right thing to do, but at the same time, Bill's own life was on hold. While grateful to have his old teaching job back, he was anxious to get back to the business of creating art. The new furnace for his studio had been ordered, but the installers were booked solid until the following week. He was also waiting for Jenna's boss to send him the information about the other art gallery, but so far Bill hadn't heard from him. Taking another swig of coffee, it suddenly occurred to him.

"Well, duh," he said out loud. "Maybe he sent you an email instead of a text."

He picked up his phone and opened his email. Scrolling through the messages, he found Chad's email. Sorenson's Fine Art would be happy to talk with him. All he had to do was call them at his convenience and make an appointment with someone named Paul Taylor. He clicked the link to their website. Not only was it an impressive gallery, it was closer to his studio than Garrison's was. They were open from ten to six, giving him plenty of time to microwave a frozen breakfast and run a few errands.

He quickly placed the call when he returned. The woman who answered the phone sounded familiar, but he couldn't quite place her. She scheduled an appointment for him to meet with Paul Taylor at two-thirty that afternoon.

* * *

Bill did a double take when he stepped inside the gallery. "I thought I recognized your voice on the phone. How are you, Stephanie?"

"I'm doing great." She stood from her desk and greeted him with a warm hug. "Josh and the kids are doing well too. Leia is all excited about being in an upcoming Halloween play at school, while Logan is getting into everything."

"Yeah, kids his age do that, but don't worry. He'll outgrow it."

"Hopefully sooner rather than later. Meantime Josh saw the wood relief you did of the two of us. He said it looked amazing. I'm told there was a small bronze statue of me as well, but being a busy mom, I just didn't get the chance to see them before they sold."

Bill handed her a card. "Don't worry. They're on my website, and as soon as I find a new place, I want to do another photo session with the two of you."

"We'd love to, so give us a call when you're ready, and I'm sorry it didn't work out for you in Florida."

"Stuff happens, but at least I got to spend some time on the beach while I was there, and the people in Florida were wonderful. I definitely want to go back and visit sometime, but for now my son and I are happy to be back in Colorado."

Paul soon emerged from his office and escorted Bill to the conference room, but Stephanie was away from her desk when he left.

* * *

Jenna's eyes popped when she opened her door. "Good heavens. Let me brush all those snowflakes off you. So, did you buy the whole store?"

"I left a few things on the shelves, but not much." Bill set the grocery bags on the kitchen counter and tossed his coat and backpack onto the sectional sofa. Returning to the kitchen, he took a fresh bouquet from one of the bags.

"For you, my dear," he said with a kiss.

"Gosh, I don't know what to say, other than thank you."

"You're welcome. I'm guessing it's been a long time since anyone's given you flowers."

"I certainly has. In fact, I can't even remember the last time, and they're beautiful. Let me see if I can find a suitable vase for them. I know I have one around here somewhere."

As Jenna searched for something to put the flowers in, Bill began unloading the other grocery bags. She returned a moment later with simple white ceramic vase and filled it with water.

"Stacy gave this to me," she said. "I think it was for my birthday, two years ago." She popped the flowers into the vase and quickly arranged them. Once she was satisfied, she set them on the table as a centerpiece.

"I figured we had better things to do than spend a lot of time cooking," said Bill, "so I got us a rotisserie chicken, along with potatoes and gravy, and a few deli salads. I also brought brownies and whipped cream for dessert."

Jenna started opening the food containers. "Yum! You got my favorite. I love broccoli salad."

"But wait. There's more. We don't want to forget about breakfast, do we? I make a pretty mean Denver omelet, so I brought all the fixings, along with some blueberry muffins, although I almost forgot the most important thing." He reached into the last bag, taking out a bottle of chenin blanc.

"I don't know what to say," said Jenna. "This was supposed to be your welcome home party. I was going to fix a nice dinner for you."

"You don't have to say anything my dear. Just enjoy."

Jenna stepped away to set the table while Bill carved the chicken and tossed the potatoes and gravy into the microwave. As he carried their plates to the table, Jenna lit some candles and turned out the lights.

"There, that's more like it." She took her seat, and they raised their glasses to toast his homecoming.

"I guess Florida didn't work out for a reason," he said. "As beautiful as the beaches were, it just wasn't the same without you being there. So, I'm hoping that maybe we can go back and visit someday, but definitely not during spring break."

"I'd love to, and I agree about spring break. Maybe we can go at the end of the semester."

"Then we'll have to look into it. So, how was your week?"

"Not bad," she said. "I finished up my end of a project for a difficult client. In the meantime, nothing new has come across my desk, so I'm doing busywork projects. You know, reorganizing my desk, that sort of thing."

"Then it sounds like your week was similar to mine. So do you do your own independent projects?"

"You mean like moonlighting?"

"Yes."

"Sometimes," said Jenna. "I don't work with architects outside the firm, but if someone is interested in redoing their home or office, I'll work with them as a consultant, but it's by referral only. I don't market my services."

"Really? So, would you by chance be interested in helping someone find a house?"

"Maybe," she said playfully. "It depends on who the someone is."

He gave her a wink. "He's a really nice guy, who's sorta new in town."

"Uh-huh. So have you started looking yet?"

"A little, online. I was waiting for your friend's husband to confirm my preapproval for a mortgage, and I got his email earlier today. It's supposed to snow tomorrow, but it'll clear up on Sunday, so I have an appointment with my agent at one o'clock Sunday afternoon, weather permitting."

"Then I'd love to go with you."

As Jenna carried the dirty dishes to the sink, Bill went to take a closer look at the fireplace. Jenna came back to the living room a moment later.

"It's gas," she said. "The logs are fake."

"I know, but it needs something else. Do you have any extra blankets? We could put one on the floor and have dessert in front of the fire."

"What a great idea." She stepped away to get a blanket. When she returned Bill unfolded it and spread it across the floor. After smoothing it out, he returned to the kitchen, where Jenna was busy rinsing the dishes. He walked up behind her and wrapped his arms around her waist, giving her a firm squeeze.

"I really have missed you. More than I thought I would."

"Me too."

"So did you meet anyone while I was away?"

"Nope."

"Not even some buffed-out carpenter at the job site?"

"Nope." She tried not to laugh, but Bill caught on.

"Interesting. You're not into the buffed-out type. So, what about the skinny carpenters? Did you notice any of them?"

"Nope. I didn't notice any of them either."

"Really? So were you even looking for another guy?"

"No, I wasn't."

"Why not?"

"Because I didn't have time," she said. "I really was busy with work. So, what about you? Were you seeing anyone in Florida?"

"I was working with a real estate agent named Amy, who was helping me find a house. She was about fifty, although she looked a lot younger. She was also a widow. Her husband passed away a couple years ago. They were married twenty-seven years and had three kids."

"I'm sorry to hear it. So, were you dating her?"

"I planned on asking her out, but I was going to wait until after I'd closed on a house. We did, however, have lunch together one day while we were house hunting, and during the conversation something came up that was, well…unexpected."

"How so?"

Bill took a deep breath and sighed. "Somehow, we got into a discussion about life after losing a spouse. She said that moving on after they're gone doesn't mean you forget about them, because you can never forget them. She also told me she was seeing someone, and it was getting pretty serious. I asked her if they planned on getting married. She said they were."

"I see."

"So, I told her about Mary Beth, and how I wasn't going to remarry, because she could never be replaced. Amy then told me, quite matter-of-factly, that I was missing the point entirely."

"Really?"

"So, I asked her what she meant. She responded by asking me if I loved my son. I told her of course I love my son. Then she asked what would have happened if Mary Beth and I had had other children. Would I have loved Connor any less? Then it hit me. I said of course not. I would have loved all my kids the same, and I immediately changed the subject."

Jenna quickly turned around. "So, what are you trying to tell me?"

"What I'm saying," said Bill, "is while I'm not making any promises, I am willing to take things one day at a time and see where we go." Once again, he wanted to change the subject. He put his hands on her breasts and gave them a squeeze.

"Those feel really nice and I'd love to play with them for a little while. So, shall we make ourselves comfortable by the fire?"

"What about dessert?"

"Later." He took her by the hand and walked her into the living room. "Once again, we seem to be overdressed for the occasion, so let me help you get a little more casual." He unzipped her dress, tossing it, along with the rest of her clothing, off to the side. She groaned in contentment as he kissed her breasts.

"Why don't you go relax in front of the fire? I'll come join you in a minute."

Jenna sat down on the blanket while Bill removed his glasses and tore off his clothes. Sitting down next to her, he gently brushed her hip.

"I still can't get over your tattoo. It's sexier than hell, and it really turns me on." He began kissing her breasts, and as they made love, Bill let himself go, feeling a passion he hadn't felt in years. When it was over, they cuddled together in front of the fire.

"How are you feeling?" he asked.

"Amazing. And how are you feeling?"

"The same, but don't get too comfortable."

"Why not?" she asked.

"Because we're going to take a shower together, and then we'll have dessert. At least the first round of dessert."

"What do you mean?"

"We'll have the brownies and whipped cream. Then, I'm putting some whipped cream on other things."

Jenna's eyes popped. "Are you serious?"

Her face flushed. "No, I'm afraid I haven't."

"Well then, I guess there's a first time for everything. I really meant it when I told you I'll be keeping you up until the wee hours of the morning. Then, tomorrow morning, guess what we're doing right after breakfast?"

"I'm afraid to ask. Were you by chance eating a lot of raw oysters while you were in Florida?"

He looked her in the eyes. "As a matter of fact, I was. It's supposed to stop snowing tomorrow night, so I'm taking you back to Vito and Gianna's. Afterwards we'll come back here, and I'll be your Italian stallion."

Jenna burst out laughing.

"What's so funny?" he asked. "I really am part Italian you know."

✎EIGHTEEN✐

KEN PARKED NEAR the hotel entrance and cautiously stepped out of the Blazer. "Better watch your step," he said. "Most of the snow has melted, and it's starting to ice over."

"Thanks for the warning," said Jeri. "With this icy weather, I'm surprised your friends didn't cancel."

"We're used to it."

"I know, but I've only been here a couple of years, so I'm not used to it yet." She shivered underneath her coat as they walked up to the front door. To her relief, it opened automatically, and they hurried into the warmer air inside. Stepping into the lobby, Jeri stopped for a moment to take it all in.

"So, your old girlfriend designed all of this?"

"She works for the architects who designed the hotel, and CeCe said it was one of her projects."

Jeri felt unsure of herself as she took in her surroundings. She knew Ken's old girlfriend had been an interior designer, but she didn't realize Jenna had done anything so grand. They walked through the lobby and Ken abruptly stopped in front of a large sculpture.

"What are you doing?" she asked.

"I want to see the sculpture CeCe was telling me about. The artist is an old friend of Jenna's." He looked closer at the plaque. "It's called, The River of Life, and the artist is one Willis Angus Haskell."

"That's nice." The conversation was making Jeri feel uncomfortable. "So, what about your friends? I'm sure they must be waiting for us."

"We'll be there in a minute. I just want to take a closer look, after having heard so much about it. So, what do you think?"

"To be honest, I'm not sure. I've never really been into art. No doubt there are people out there who may find it interesting, or even see

84

some sort of hidden meaning behind it. To me it's just a bunch of curvy lines that don't mean a thing. I guess I don't understand the significance."

Ken agreed, much to her relief. "I feel the same as you, but be forewarned. CeCe is seriously into art, and she thinks this guy is marvelous."

"To each their own." Finally, Jeri was starting to feel surer of herself. "So, if she starts talking about how wonderful this guy is, I'll just smile and change the subject."

"You got it." Ken gave her hand a squeeze as they walked into the atrium, but Jeri was once again caught off guard as she took in the high ceiling and lush interior landscaping.

"So, what do you think?" asked Ken.

"I'll give her credit for knowing her stuff. It sort of reminds me of a cathedral."

"She is indeed very talented, although she really wasn't the best choice for me as a girlfriend. As you can plainly see, we lived in two entirely different worlds. Then there was the night I brought her to my cousin's wedding."

"I remember you telling me about it. You said she really embarrassed you, leaving early and all."

"She sure did."

"I'm sorry she embarrassed you, but I'm not sorry it didn't work out with her, because her loss is my gain. Those creative types are known for being overly emotional, while we practical people are much more down to earth."

"Exactly." Ken took her hand and they made their way to the restaurant. A big smile came over her face as they approached the entrance.

"I had a feeling we were going to Sam's Place. Everything in there, from the ranges to the dishes, came from my employer."

"Really? So have you invoiced them?"

"I have."

"How much did it cost?"

"Sorry, I can't tell you."

"Have they paid you yet?"

She chuckled. "You know I can't tell you that either."

"Okay. So did you at least tell them you know a good CPA?"

"What am I going to do with you?"

He discreetly patted her rump. "You already know what to do with me, so hold that thought for later."

"You're insatiable."

Stepping through the doorway, Ken told the hostess they were meeting another party.

"Of course," she said. "Right this way." CeCe looked up and greeted them with a smile as they came up to her table. Ken greeted his friend with a hug and pulled out the chair directly across from CeCe. As Jeri took her seat, Ken made the introductions.

"I'm glad to finally meet you in person." CeCe extended her hand to Jeri as Ken sat down next to her. "I've heard so much about you."

"And I've heard a lot about you as well." Jeri glanced around the room, wondering if perhaps Jenna had decorated it as well. "Ken was telling me about Jenna on the way here. As I told him, she's very talented, but I too had a role in making this place happen, although it may not be quite as glamourous."

"Really?" CeCe looked surprised. "So, what exactly did you do?"

"Ken may have told you I work for a restaurant supply company. We provide just about everything a restaurant owner needs, with the exception of the chefs and waitstaff."

"Then I certainly am impressed,"

"Ken may have also told you I'm working on my MBA. I'll complete it at the end of the year."

"Yes, he did tell me you were going to school part time."

A server stopped by to take their drink orders. Ken suggested he and Jeri order a half carafe of their favorite cabernet sauvignon. John immediately spoke up and said to make it a full carafe with four glasses. Once it was delivered, they toasted to good friends.

"So, CeCe, what more can you tell me about Willis Angus Haskell?" asked Ken.

CeCe looked confused. "Willis Angus? Oh, you mean Bill? Jenna's friend who created the big sculpture by the lobby."

"Yes. So, what do you know about him?"

"He's a very talented artist, as you already saw. Not only did he do the piece in the lobby, but some of his other sculptures are scattered around the atrium. The Sheltons really love his work."

"Sounds like it. So, what else can you tell me about him?"

"Ken, you brought this up the other day, and I've already told you all I know. I recently purchased one of his smaller pieces for a client, and while I was there Jenna introduced us. He's a very intelligent, very articulate man, and I can certainly understand her being friends with him. They've known each other for a long time."

Once again, Jeri felt uncomfortable. "Ken showed me the sculpture when we came in, but I'm afraid I don't know much about art."

"Neither do I," said John. "So, tell me more about your plans after you finish your MBA."

"I'm hoping my boss will give me a promotion once I graduate. I enjoy working for the company, and the outside salespeople earn sizable commissions. Of course, there's no guarantee it'll happen, so I'm sending out resumes to other companies as well."

"Would you consider working for a bank?"

"You bet I would."

John took one of his cards from his wallet and wrote something on the back. "Here's the website where you can apply online, and please mention that we've met. While I can't guarantee that knowing a senior loan officer will get you an interview, I know it wouldn't hurt either."

"No, it wouldn't," said Jeri. "I'll fill out an application first thing tomorrow morning, and thank you."

"So, what are your plans for the rest of the weekend?" asked CeCe.

"Nothing spectacular," said Jeri. "I have my usual Sunday date with my washer and dust mop. I'm really looking forward to the time when I can afford a maid."

"Jenna says the same thing," said CeCe. Once again, Ken seized the opportunity to question her about Jenna and Bill's relationship.

"Are you sure Jenna's never mentioned anything else about Bill in passing?"

"It's like I said before. She doesn't say much, and while she was sorry it didn't work out for him in Florida, I can tell she's happy to have him back in Denver."

"So, you're saying they could be more than friends."

"I honestly couldn't tell you if they are or not. She doesn't volunteer any information."

Their server arrived before Ken could ask another question. Once he left, Jeri changed the subject. Over the meal, CeCe talked about a project she was working on.

"Granted, it's not anything as lavish as this, but even the smallest projects are important to someone, so I do my best for each client, regardless of their budget.

"Which is as it should be," said Jeri.

John checked his watch and flagged down their server. "It's getting late, and CeCe and I have plans for tomorrow."

Jeri felt relieved once the bill was paid, and she remained gracious as she told John and CeCe goodnight.

"I really enjoyed meeting you." CeCe gave Jeri a big hug as she said goodnight. "I also hope to see you again. Soon."

"Me too." Jeri was all smiles when they left, but her mood changed once she climbed into the Blazer.

"So why all the questions about you ex and her friend?" she bluntly asked.

"It's not what you think. I'm not interested in getting her back. However, I still care about her as a person, and I think she can do better."

"All right, but it sounds to me like she and CeCe have a good rapport, and I'm sure she has other friends too."

"It's okay, Jeri. You don't need to get all jealous. Like I said, I'm not trying to get her back, and I'm sorry you got the wrong impression." He gave her a soft, gentle kiss. "I'm taking you home, and when we get there, we're going to kiss and make up."

❧NINETEEN❧

THE FIRST SNOWSTORM of the season had passed. Sunday morning was bright and sunny with warming temperatures. After a leisurely brunch at a nearby diner, it was time for Bill to meet with the real estate agent. Don Parker was a fiftyish-looking man with a receding hairline and black horn-rimmed glasses. After introducing him to Jenna, Don told Bill he had found several listings for him to consider. Three were in Littleton. The fourth was in Highlands Ranch.

"They're all similar to your old home," said Don. "Unfortunately, none have storage sheds, but they all have roughly the same square footage."

"What about the back yards?" asked Bill.

"I'm not sure. However, they're all on decent sized lots, so you should have plenty of room for another shed."

"Good, because I'd rather not have wood dust in the house."

"They're also older homes. You said you were looking for more of a fixer-upper, and they could all use a little TLC. Nothing major. They just need a little fresh paint, and perhaps some new flooring."

"Then let's go take a look," said Bill.

Don led them out the back door, where his white Suburban waited. Bill passed on first two houses. One had an old roof, while the other needed new appliances. He perked up as they drove past a strip mall.

"There's my old King Sooper's," he said.

"The house is within a quarter mile of your old home." Don turned left at the traffic light, and onto a side road two blocks later.

"I'm somewhat familiar this subdivision," said Bill. "It was built a few years after Mary Beth and I bought our house. I think it may have even been the same builder."

"It was." Don turned onto another side road and into a cul-de-sac. A For Sale sign stood in front of a single-story brick house with slate gray trim.

"There's a nice big flower garden in the front yard," said Don, "although it's dormant this time of year."

"Hopefully, they planted perennials. I'm not big on gardening."

"Gotcha covered," said Jenna. "I've been known to have a green thumb."

They hurried up the walkway, waiting patiently as Don unlocked the front door. Inside was a nicely furnished living room.

"Looks like the carpet has seen better days," said Bill.

"It's undoubtedly the original," said Jenna. "I recommend replacing it with wood vinyl planking."

"I had the same thought."

The kitchen had been upgraded with newer appliances and ceramic tile flooring, but the cabinets needed attention. After inspecting the bedrooms, Don took them down to the basement.

"Finally, a finished basement." Bill's face lit up as he took a closer look. "The last one we saw looked like something out of a slasher movie. This one has good lighting too, which is another plus, but the old vinyl floor is completely shot. It'll have to be replaced with wood vinyl as well. Then I can set up a photography studio."

"I thought you did sculpture," said Don.

"I do, but many of my projects start with a live model. Combining my home office with a photo studio, like I did before, just wasn't working. It was way too cramped." Bill looked at Jenna.

"I put all of Mary Beth's belongings in the basement and closed it off, but Connor insisted I donate it to charity before I moved to Florida. What few items I kept can go in a closet."

"And speaking of storage, take a look at this." Don opened a side door, revealing a large utility room with storage shelves.

"Now that's handy." As Bill walked around the room, they heard a loud meow. A calico cat had ventured down the stairs and started rubbing against Jenna's legs.

"You're such a pretty kitty. So where did you come from?" As she petted the cat, Don pointed out a litter box in the far corner.

"Apparently, we've invaded someone's personal space," he said.

Jenna's phone beeped. Someone had sent her a text message. She grimaced when she saw who sent it.

"Everything okay?" asked Bill.

"It's all good. It's just a text message from my friend, Nora. She can be a real drama diva at times. She wants to know if anyone's interested in doing an early girl's night out tonight."

"You can go if you'd like," said Bill. "Connor and I usually get together on Sunday nights."

Jenna silently sighed in relief. "I'll get back with her later. Right now, I'm focused on you. What do you think about the house?"

"So far it's a winner."

"I'm happy to hear it," said Don.

Bill took another look around the basement. Once he was satisfied, they went back upstairs. Don opened a sliding glass door which led to the backyard. It included a wood deck and two large cottonwood trees. The trees would provide plenty of shade once their leaves returned, helping to cool the house during the summer. There was also plenty of room for a storage shed.

"They've obviously taken good care of the place," said Jenna. "I really don't see anything wrong, other than normal wear and tear. So, what do you think?"

"The kitchen is definitely bigger than what I had before," said Bill. "The bedrooms look a little bigger too."

"You've got about a hundred more square feet than you had in your old house," said Don.

"Which I would consider a plus." Bill looked at Don. "You said the owners have been here for twelve years. Do you know why they're selling?"

"The owner is a single mom. According to her agent, her youngest child went off to college this past August, and she wants to downsize to a duplex or a condo."

"Makes sense."

"So did you want to head over to Highlands Ranch look at the last house?" asked Don.

"Nope. Let's go back to your office and make her an offer."

* * *

Bill signed and initialed the last of the paperwork. "Anything else?" he asked.

"Nope. We're all done, for now," said Don. "I'll send it to the seller's agent. You've made a fair and reasonable offer, and from what I'm told, she's anxious to sell. I'll let you know the minute I hear back."

The two men shook hands. It had been a long but productive afternoon. Bill squeezed Jenna's hand as they walked out to the parking lot.

"I'm feeling pretty optimistic about my offer," he said. "Let's just hope this one passes the inspection."

"I don't think you have anything to worry about," said Jenna. "Remember, I have a trained eye. I didn't see any cracks or other irregularities to suggest a potential problem, and it appears to be in good repair. So why did your house in Florida fail the inspection?"

"There was a major problem with the foundation."

"That'll do it."

"But in hindsight, it worked out for the best. I admit I was looking forward to not having to deal with the ice and snow anymore, but had I been under contract when everything fell apart with Connor, we wouldn't have had the option of coming back here so he could have a fresh start."

"Then I guess it happened for a reason."

"I think so too. You know, I really am proud of him. He's handled it like a trooper, while a lot of other people would have fallen apart. Conner was a still a boy when we lost his mother, and being single dad wasn't easy, but I guess I somehow managed. If Mary Beth were here, she would be just as proud of him as I am."

Jenna felt her stomach drop. She was still competing against Bill's deceased wife, and it was a competition she could never win. Bill remained silent for the rest of the drive, but he seemed more like himself once they arrived at her house. He began gathering his belongings and stuffing them into his backpack.

"I'm going to miss you," he said.

"I'm going to miss you too, but you're welcome to stay here until your house closes. No sense spending money on a hotel suite if you don't have too."

"I appreciate the thought, but let's see what happens with the house first. If she accepts my offer, I may camp out in my studio until the deal closes. I've stayed overnight there before."

"I see." Jenna tried to hide her disappointment as Bill put the rest of his belongings in the backpack and zipped it shut.

"I'm going to get out of your hair for a while, but don't worry. I'll be back." He wrapped his arms around her and kissed her. "That was nice. Let's do again." His next kiss lasted longer.

"So, what time is Conner expecting you?" asked Jenna.

"In about twenty minutes."

"Then I guess I'll see you later." She walked him to the front door, and he reminded her to lock it as he stepped outside.

❧TWENTY❧

JENNA STOOD BY the front window and discreetly waited as Bill's Explorer drove away. Once it was gone, she marched back to the kitchen and grabbed her phone. While she hated being less the honest with Bill, she didn't want to involve him in her problems. Opening the app, Ken's text message reappeared.

"Had dinner last night at Sam's Place. I must say I'm impressed. You did an outstanding job, and you made me feel very proud. I also saw the famous sculpture. By the way, we're still friends, so you don't need to ghost me."

"Calm down, Jenna," she said to herself outload. "He may be an arrogant, pompous ass, but don't let him get to you. You don't want to do anything you'll regret later." Gritting her teeth, she sat down on the sofa and began typing.

"I'm glad you liked the hotel, and I'm happy you and your girlfriend enjoyed Sam's. Now that you're seeing someone else, I don't think it's appropriate for us to stay in touch. I wish both of you the best."

She hit the send button and tossed the phone on the coffee table, hoping this time Ken would finally get the message. As she felt her body relax, she realized she was hungry, so she made herself a ham sandwich. Afterwards, she started her laundry and grabbed a dust rag. Once her housecleaning chores were complete, she opened a can of Diet Dr. Pepper and took a well-earned break of the sofa. She soon noticed she had a new text message. Picking up her phone, she stared in disbelief. Ken had sent her a response.

"You have nothing to worry about. Jeri and I are nowhere close to making a commitment so we're both free to see other people. She's out with of her girlfriends tonight, and I'd love to see you, so let's meet for coffee somewhere and catch up."

Jenna checked the time. It was six fifty-two. Ken had sent his message at four-seventeen. "Sorry I missed you Ken," she said out loud, "but I was busy scrubbing toilets, so I guess today just isn't your day." She punched up her mother's number, and as she was telling her about Bill's offer on the house an incoming call interrupted her. To her dismay, Ken was calling.

"Sorry, Mom. I have to take this call. Then I need to pop something in the microwave."

"I understand, and I'm glad you had a good weekend. I'm also keeping my fingers crossed for Bill."

"Me too. Love you and tell Dad I said hi."

She touched the button and answered Ken's call with a snarl in her voice. "Alright, so what's going on?"

"Nothing," he said, brushing her off. "I just wanted to say I really was impressed with the Shelton Inn, and I have a whole new appreciation for what you do. I'm also sorry things ended the way they did. My aunt can be real bitch when she wants to be, but she's also Joey's mother, and I've learned it's best to just ignore her when she gets in one of her moods. I was going to apologize for what happened on the way home, but I never got the chance. By the time I left, you'd already sent your message."

"It's okay, Ken. You have nothing to apologize for. I was honestly ready to—"

"Why don't we discuss this in person. Have you eaten yet?"

"No, I haven't, but I'd really—"

"Then why don't I buy you dinner, to make up for what happened."

"Sorry, but I just popped something in the microwave. Like I said, I've had a long day, and I'm beat."

"Are you sure? Because it's my treat. We'll go someplace really casual where we can sit and talk. Afterwards I promise I'll bring you straight home and be on my way."

Jenna's voice remained firm. "Thank you, but no."

"Okay, I won't force the issue. We can talk on the phone if you prefer. As I said in my message, I was really amazed at the new Shelton Inn. According to CeCe, it was your project."

"It was. My parents, and my other friends, were impressed with it as well."

"So, tell me about your other friends."

"There's really not much to tell. You met Stacy, and we have a mutual friend in CeCe. My other friends are women I went to college with."

"Oh c'mon, Jenna. You don't need to play dumb with me. I know all about your friend, Willis Haskell, although CeCe says he goes by Bill."

"Really." Her voice turned edgy. "So how much do you know about him?"

"I know he's the old friend you reconnected with to do that sculpture for the lobby, which I saw, by the way. I also know he's the same guy who's considerably older than you. And while I don't mean to offend you, I'm just not into art, so I didn't get the significance of it."

Her tone became more condescending. "Well, that's the thing about art, Ken. Sometimes the idea is for the viewer to interpret it in their own way, as was the case here."

"Really? Then I guess it was interesting."

"I'll let him know, and now you know everything about what I've been up to since we parted company. So, I'll say goodnight, and I honestly hope it works out with your new girlfriend. From what I hear, the two of you are a good match."

"And as I said, we haven't made a commitment, nor are we living together. We're both free to see other people if we wish. In fact, as we're speaking, she and her friend are at a bar watching a Broncos game. They're both good looking women, and you know there's bound to be more men there than women, so who's to say she's not giving her phone number to some other guy as we speak, or even taking him home with her?"

"If she does, it's between you and her."

"I know, but the point is I wasn't ready to end things with you, and I've been second guessing myself ever since. I'm not asking you to take me back, but since you're not seeing anyone, there's no reason why we couldn't meet somewhere for coffee or a drink."

"Thank you, but I'd rather not. I've moved on, and you need to move on as well."

Ken started to say something else, but Jenna disconnected the call. "Good grief, Ken. What part of the word no are you not getting? Well, I know one way to fix the problem, once and for all." She tapped on her phone and blocked his number. "I don't know why I didn't think of this before, but at least it's done now. I'm also blocking your email address while I'm at it."

❧TWENTY-ONE❧

CONNOR OFFERED HIS dad a beer when he came inside the apartment. Caleb and another young man were watching the Broncos game. Three extra-large pizza boxes were strewn across the coffee table. A few slices remained in each. Connor told him to take a seat in a well-worn chair.

"What's the score?" asked Bill.

"The Broncos are up by three," said Caleb. "There's only three minutes left to go in the fourth quarter, so help yourself to some pizza."

Connor brought his dad a can of Coors as Bill grabbed a slice of pepperoni. All eyes were on the screen as the other team punted the ball. Once the Broncos had possession they worked their way back down the field, scoring a nail-biting touchdown in the final seconds of the game.

"Good game," said Bill. "Sorry I wasn't able to get here sooner. I was out house hunting."

"You were?" said Connor. "Did you find anything?"

"I think so." As Bill and Connor were talking, Caleb and his friend grabbed their coats.

"I need to make a beer run," said Caleb. "Do you need anything?"

"I'm good," said Connor.

Caleb and his friend hurried out, and the conversation took a more serious tone. "How's the job hunt going?" asked Bill.

"It's going," said Connor. "I was hoping to get the job with the software company, but they went with someone else. In the meantime, I'm still waiting for an interview with the hospital. They're still interested, but so far, they haven't scheduled an interview. Apparently, the person I need to talk to is out of town. Then this morning I applied with two other companies. One does property management. The other is another software company."

"Be nice if you could get onboard with the hospital."

"I know, but right now it's up in the air. Meantime the property management job sounds interesting, although it doesn't pay as well as the others."

"At least you're in a position where you don't have to take the first thing that comes along. How's Kelsey doing?"

Connor was suddenly all smiles. "She'll be here a week from today, if not sooner, and I already found us an apartment. She's been sending out resumes as well, so hopefully she'll find something soon. Then things will finally be back to normal. So, tell me about the house."

"It's about a quarter mile from where you grew up. Similar floorplan and the same builder. Jenna didn't see anything structurally wrong with it, which came as a big relief after what happened in Florida."

"Jenna?"

Bill immediately realized his mistake. "She's a friend, who also happens to be an interior designer."

"So, she's the one who commissioned the sculpture."

"Yes."

"Interesting. I keep meaning to go check it out. Maybe we go can grab a beer at Sam's Place next week."

"We can do that."

"I take it she's the blonde."

"What?"

"Oh, c'mon, Dad, you don't need to play games. You mentioned something about a blonde last week, but then you changed the subject."

"I did?"

"I'm going to get straight to the point," said Connor. "You were a terrific husband to Mom, but she's been gone a long time. I admit I was glad you stayed single while I was growing up, because back then I wasn't ready for you marry someone else. And just so you know, I was fully aware that you were seeing other women, even though you never let on. I also knew the reason I did sleep overs at Uncle Dave and Aunt Melanie's house wasn't just so I could spend time with my cousins. It was because you were spending time with your lady friends."

"I see. So did it bother you?"

"A little. At first. I didn't like the idea of my mother being replaced, so I talked to Uncle Dave about it. He kept reassuring me no one could ever take Mom's place. As I got older, I realized he was right."

"After we lost your mother, I decided I would never marry again, so I was never serious with any of them."

"Friends with benefits. Nothing wrong with that."

"Whether they were or not wasn't your concern," Bill said sternly.

"I know, Dad. What I'm trying to say is that was then and this is now. Mom would have never expected you to spend the rest of your life alone. To be honest, I think it would be nice if you did find someone, and frankly, I'd feel relieved if you were to marry again. Then I wouldn't have to worry about you. So, tell me more about the blonde."

"Later." Bill checked his watch. "I imagine Caleb and his friend will be back soon, and I'm ready to head out. I've had a busy day, and I'm ready to call it a night. No doubt you have a busy week ahead of you as well."

"They say the hardest job is finding a job."

"It can be, and I almost forgot to ask. Anything new from your attorney?"

"Not a thing," said Connor.

"These things take time, so no news is good news. So with that, I'll say goodnight, and next time I'll bring the pizza." Bill hugged his son goodnight and hurried out, chastising himself for letting Jenna's name slip out.

* * *

CeCe looked up from her computer and greeted Jenna with a smile. "You certainly look happy this morning. So how was your weekend?"

"Fantastic," said Jenna. "Bill and I are all caught up on everything. So, what about you? Did you make it to Sam's Place?"

"We did, and kudos to you. The Shelton Inn is magnificent. You did a stellar job, and I for one think you deserve a big raise."

"Thanks." Jenna excused herself and started walking toward her desk.

"I also I invited Ken and Jeri to join us."

Jenna quickly spun around. "You did? And what did you think of her?"

"I like her. Everything Ken said about her made it sound like they were a good match, and meeting her in person confirmed it. They even look alike. She has long, dark hair, the same shade as his. Then, when I hugged him goodnight, I told him he'd be a fool to let her go."

"Do you think he'll follow through and marry her?"

"Hopefully, he will, but who knows?"

Jenna considered telling CeCe about Ken calling her, but thought better of it. She hurried back to her desk and booted up her computer. Checking her messages, she found a memo informing her of a staff meeting in the conference room at ten o'clock. No doubt a new job had come in. She looked forward to starting her next project. In the meantime, she wanted to grab some coffee, and she stopped at CeCe's desk on her way to the break room.

"Know anything about any new projects?" she asked.

"None I'm aware of. Why do you ask?"

"I just got a notice about a meeting in the conference room in about an hour."

"It's the first I've heard about it, and you may be right about a new project coming in. I'm still working on my current one and didn't get the memo. You'll have to fill me in when you get back."

The breakroom was empty when Jenna filled her mug, but one of the newer architects came in as she set the carafe down. "Did you by chance get a notice about the staff meeting this morning?" he asked.

"I sure did," said Jenna. "I guess a new project has come in."

"No, nothing new has come in. At least none I'm aware of, but I know two other people who got the same memo, and we've all been on board for less than three years. The holidays are coming up, and we all have kids, so we're hoping it's not bad news."

"Then I hope it's not bad news either." Jenna hurried out, but CeCe saw the worried look on her face.

"Is everything okay?" she asked.

"I don't know," said Jenna. "I just bumped into someone who said no new projects have come in."

"Which doesn't mean a thing. Maybe they're letting you know you're a contender for Employee of the Year for your work on the Shelton Inn."

Jenna instantly felt relieved. "Hmm…I'll bet your right. Funny how our minds work. When something unexpected happens, we always assume the worse."

"Probably goes back to the cave man days. You know, fight or flight."

Jenna returned to her desk and caught up on her email, but she couldn't shake her bad feeling about the meeting. Several other staff members were anxiously waiting when she came into the conference room, and she felt the tension in the air as she took her seat. Marcy Morgan, the HR manager, arrived a few minutes later, along with her assistant, who carried a small stack of envelopes. Jenna's heart sank as they took their seats.

"Thank you for coming." Marcy looked uncomfortable in her chair and she wouldn't make eye contact with anyone. "As you know, we're in a boom or bust business, and even though we've had a busy year, things have slowed down considerably over the past few weeks. While we're hopeful business will pick up soon, management tells me they don't anticipate any big changes until after the new year. This means we have to cut expenses, and I'm sorry to say it includes putting some of our staff on temporary furlough. I want to assure all of you that no one has been terminated, and you still have your health insurance and retirement accounts. However, you may need to apply for unemployment benefits to help you through the interim."

A stunned silence filled the room while a couple of hands went up. "So how did they decide who would be furloughed?" one man asked.

"It's determined solely by seniority," said Marcy. "It has nothing to do with anyone's job performance. Sarah, my assistant, is handing out envelopes with more information."

"Do you know when we'll be back?" asked another man.

"No, I'm afraid I don't, although we're hoping things will pick up after the holidays. All I can tell you is watch your email. As soon as I know anything, I'll pass the information on to you. In the meantime, if I can be of any assistance, please feel free to reach out to me."

The meeting broke up when Sarah handed out the last envelope. CeCe had a concerned look on her face when Jenna returned.

"Uh-oh. What happened?"

"I just got furloughed."

"What?" CeCe looked stunned. "There has to be a mistake somewhere. After doing such a remarkable job on the Shelton Inn, why on earth would they let you go?"

"We weren't fired," said Jenna. "We were put on an unpaid leave. Nothing new has come in, so they furloughed those of us with the lowest seniority to cut costs."

"But this isn't right."

Priscilla Wong, another interior designer, spoke up. "Sorry to break into the conversation," she said, "but I couldn't help but overhear. Whenever works slows down, those with the least sonority are the first ones they let go. Believe me, it's nothing personal."

"Then I'd say you have pretty good job security," said CeCe.

"There's no need to get the claws out," Priscilla said sternly. "I'm over fifty. If things were to get really bad, they could force me into early retirement. They've done it before. I also stopped by the Shelton Inn the other day, Jenna, and I don't think you have anything to worry about. You're going to be here for a long, long time."

"Thanks, Priscilla. I hope so too."

"Why don't I at least take you to lunch?" said CeCe. "Nothing fancy. We'll go across the street to Megan's."

"CeCe, you really don't have to—"

"It's my treat."

Jenna looked at her watch. It was only ten twenty-five. "I really would like to take a rain check, if you don't mind. We're at least an hour away from lunchtime, and I seem to have lost my appetite. I have some emails I need to answer, then I need to set up an auto response. After that I guess I'm done. For now."

"Why don't you forward you email to me instead of sending out an automated response? That way, if it's anything urgent, I can take care of it for you."

"Good idea. Thank you, CeCe." Jenna returned to her desk and opened the envelope. Inside was a letter from Robert Lacy, the firm's senior partner. In it he said the firm had experienced some unexpected expenses, which, along with the normal holiday slowdown, had left them temporarily short on cash. He was also hoping to have everyone back by the end of January. Jenna put the letter in her bag and grabbed her sweater, but she was still in a mild state of shock when the elevator arrived. Two other furloughed employees waited inside. Jenna remained silent as the two men continued their conversation.

"I still can't believe this," one of them said.

"Me neither," said the other, "but Jeff told me it's happened before. Not recently, but he also said everyone was back within sixty days."

"Maybe so, but I'm sending out resumes, just in case."

"Me too. This isn't the only game in town."

The elevator stopped at the parking garage level and everyone hurried out. Jenna sat behind the wheel of her Camry for several minutes. Always a hard worker, she had never been fired from a job before, and she recalled how her former employers always tried to convince her to stay. She had also put in many long hours on the Shelton Inn, sometimes working nights and weekends on her computer at home.

"And this is the thanks I get," she said out loud. "Maybe I need to rethink things." She put the car in gear and quickly exited the garage.

⚜TWENTY-TWO⚜

JENNA WENT through a Wendy's drive through and ordered an extra-large combo. She set it on the kitchen counter when she arrived home and changed into a well-worn pair of sweats. Sitting down at the table, she opened the fast-food bag, unsure if she was hungry or not. The burger smelled good, so she took a small bite. It was surprisingly tasty, so she eagerly dug in, washing it down with a regular Dr. Pepper. Her phone beeped as she gathered up the empty wrappers. Bill had sent a text. The seller had accepted his offer. The sale would close the day before Thanksgiving. He would move in on Black Friday. She took a deep breath before typing her response.

"Congratulations. If you need a good interior designer, I know one who's available and suddenly has more than enough free time."

He immediately replied. *"What happened?"*

"I just got laid-off or furloughed or whatever you want to call it." Her phone rang an instant later.

"Okay," said Bill. "What happened? From the top."

"Let's just say it's been a really lousy Monday morning. As soon as we arrived, we were told to report to a staff meeting, where they gave us the bad news. Things happened. They had to cut expenses. At least the sacrificial lambs were determined by seniority and instead of job performance, but it still sucks."

"I can certainly understand why you'd be upset," said Bill, "but it's not the end of the world. You still have a job."

"It sure doesn't feel like it to me. I get my last paycheck this coming Friday."

"Do you have anything in savings?"

"I put a little in each payday, so I should have enough for a couple of house payments. Maybe a few groceries if I eat beans and rice, but I don't enough to cover all my other bills for the next two months."

"Don't panic," said Bill. "I know it's easier said than done, but I've been there a time or two myself. Might be a good idea to call your credit card companies and see if they'll let you skip a payment. Stephanie's husband, Josh, is also a financial planner. If you'd like, I can get you his phone number, and you can set up a meeting with him. No doubt he can give much better advice than I can."

"Thanks, I'd appreciate it."

"In the meantime, I'm at loose ends myself, and both of us could use a little time out. My studio won't be ready until next week, and you mentioned something yesterday about your parents being in Hawaii."

"Dad had a layover, so Mom flew with him. Unfortunately, I no longer have my travel benefits. They ended when I turned twenty-three."

"Actually, I was thinking we could go somewhere closer. Like Estes Park or Steamboat Springs. It hasn't started snowing in the mountains yet, so the ski resorts aren't open, and we could probably find a good rate."

"I don't know."

"When was the last time you had a vacation?" he asked.

"Two years ago. However, my vacation pay isn't available at the moment."

"Don't worry, it's my treat. We'll take the Explorer. I'll see if I can find an Airbnb with a decent kitchen, and we'll buy some groceries along the way. Granted, it might not be as scenic as it was when you were there with Stacy, but we can still go for hikes, or we could even go fishing if you'd like."

"Stacy and I hiked around Lake Estes while we were there, but she didn't have any fishing gear, and I didn't want to give her any ideas."

"Oh, c'mon. Where's your sense of adventure?"

"Don't ask."

"It's been years since I've taken Connor fishing, and I just remembered all my fishing gear is somewhere in storage right now. We planned on using it in Florida."

"We can go fishing next time, but for now I'm sure we can find other things to do."

"We certainly can," said Bill. "I'll bring my camera and sketchbook, and you may as well bring your sketchbook too."

"Alright. So, when do you want to go?"

"Let me see what I can find online, and we'll go from there."

A new text message from Bill arrived an hour later. *"Pack your bags. I'm picking you up first thing in the morning. We'll be in Estes Park for the next three days, only this time you won't be sleeping in a tent."*

* * *

Jenna was in better spirits when Bill arrived the following morning. She greeted him with a kiss and handed him a grocery bag.

"What's this?" he asked.

"A frozen lasagna I'd stashed in the back of my freezer."

"Put it away. You're out of work so I'm taking you to breakfast. Then we'll grab some groceries."

"Are you sure you don't want me bring anything?"

"Just a sketchbook. I want to see how good your drawing skills are."

"It's in my bag, and I just remembered the most important thing." She stepped away for a moment, returning with her dominos set.

"Still think you can beat me?" he asked.

"I let you win last time."

"Sure, you did." Bill chuckled as he picked up her bag and they were soon on their way. The midmorning sun was shining when they arrived in Estes Park. The fall foliage had peaked, but the aspens still had a smattering of gold leaves. Bill turned onto a quiet sideroad, and a single-story wood cabin with green trim came into view.

"Cute place," she said.

"I thought you might like it."

They eagerly hopped out of the Explorer, and as they approached the front door, Bill looked up something on his phone.

"Here's hoping the combination they gave me works." He entered the numbers into the lockbox, and, to his relief, it opened. As he unlocked the door, he motioned for Jenna to go inside. The main room had a cozy looking sofa and love seat with a built-in brick fireplace and plenty of firewood. A small kitchen stood off to the side with four stools placed in front of a breakfast bar. Down the hallway were two bedrooms and a single bathroom. The larger bedroom contained a queen-sized bed, while the other had a pair of twins. Inside the utility room was a washer and dryer with plenty of room for skis or fishing gear.

Jenna went out to the back deck. "Take a look at this view," she said. The Big Thompson River flowed behind the house. She walked down a short incline to the large, flat boulders placed along the riverbank and gazed at the fir-covered mountains. "It's so beautiful," she said.

"It sure is," said Bill. "So, let's unload the car. Then we'll grab our sketchbooks and find ourselves a nice scenic hiking trail."

They hurried back inside, and once the last grocery bag was emptied, they took a short drive to Rocky Mountain National Park. As they sketched, they reminisced about the times when Jenna was a student and Bill had taken the class around the campus to draw the scenery.

"It wasn't an easy time for me," he said. "I felt very conflicted. It's when I first realized teaching was one of my life's callings, but had it not been for Mary Beth's life insurance policy, I wouldn't have had the opportunity to get my master's degree."

"What were you doing before?"

"I worked for a custom body shop. We'd strip down old cars and turn them into hot rods. Most of our clientele were collectors. A few were even used in movies and TV shows."

"Sounds like an interesting job."

"It was, and it was a fun job too, but the pay wasn't great. I was also finishing up my bachelor's degree, so I was taking classes at night. Back then, Mary Beth was the main breadwinner." Bill sighed and tried to focus on his sketchbook, but he was having trouble concentrating.

"You okay?" asked Jenna.

"Yeah, but now that the sun's dipping down, I can feel the temperature dropping."

"I noticed it too."

"Then I guess it's time to head back to the cabin. We'll light a fire in the fireplace and pop the frozen pizzas in the oven."

Jenna stood and dropped her sketchbook into her backpack. "Sounds good. I'm starting to get hungry. Then, after dinner, we'll break out the dominos."

"Winner take all?"

"Is there any other way to play?"

* * *

Jenna was sleeping soundly when Bill woke up the following morning. As he watched her, he felt the same conflicting emotions he had felt the day before. While remaining firm in his conviction to never marry again, he was also allowing himself to become too attached to her. The day would come when he would have to set her free, and the longer he waited, the more difficult it would be for both of them. For the moment, however, Jenna was in a vulnerable place. It would have to wait until she returned to work. He let out a deep sigh as she began stirring and opened her eyes.

"Good morning," she said.

"Good morning. How'd you sleep?"

"I slept well. I dreamed we were making wild, passionate love."

Bill smiled despite himself. "It wasn't a dream. It really happened, and I must have worn you out."

"Then I guess all the fresh air and sunshine must be affecting you. So, what's for breakfast?"

He wrapped his arms around her and gave her a squeeze. "Well, at the moment it's you. Then, after I'm done, I'll microwave some frozen pancakes."

Jenna laughed as he ran his fingers through her hair. Ninety minutes later they were back in the Explorer. Bill drove to several scenic spots on the other side of Estes Lake, but the hours passed too quickly. He sighed as he closed his sketchbook for the last time.

"I'm glad we made the trip," he said. "I now have plenty of new material to work with, and I'm eager to start some new projects. I'm also counting the days until my studio is ready."

"And I need to find some temporary work once we get back," said Jenna. "Before we left, I posted my resume on LinkedIn, and someone's taken an interest."

"Care to tell me about it?"

"It's a small interior design firm in Littleton, so it's close to home. One of the partners is on maternity leave, and they're getting a little backlogged."

"Maybe it'll be a better job than the one you have now."

"We'll see, although I'd rather stay with Salisbury. I love working with architects." She stood and dusted herself off. "On the other hand, I would have loved to stayed here longer."

"Me too, but we can always come back."

Returning to the cabin, Bill headed straight to the refrigerator while Jenna went out to the back deck. He heard a strange sound as he grabbed a couple of beers. No doubt there were wild animals close by. He heard it again when he picked up the pretzel bag. Looking at the side door, he didn't see Jenna on the deck. Perhaps she had wandered down to the riverbank. His heart suddenly dropped. He heard the sound again, and his blood ran cold. It wasn't an animal. Someone was calling for help.

"Jenna!" He called out her name as he raced out the side door. Somehow, Jenna had fallen into the river. The water may have only been a few feet deep, but it was icy cold. She was trying to get out, but was having trouble climbing over the large boulders. Bill saw the fear in her eyes when he reached down and grabbed her hand.

"Hang on! I'm going to pull you up. Try to climb while I'm pulling you. On the count of three, okay?"

"Okay." Her response sounded breathy.

"All right. One. Two. Three!" Saying a silent prayer, he reached under her shoulders and pulled her up as she climbed. As she scrambled over the boulder, her forward inertia pushed him backwards, but he managed to keep his balance.

"Are you hurting anywhere?" he asked.

Her teeth were chattering as she tried to speak. "I don't know. I'm so cold." Her hair and clothes were soaking wet, and a cool breeze was blowing, making her feel even colder.

"Let's get you inside." He rushed her down the hallway and into the bathroom. Jenna was shivering as he grabbed some extra towels.

"We need to get you out of these wet clothes."

Jenna's hands were shaking as she tried to remove her sweater.

"It's okay," he said. "I've got you." He undressed her and dried her off as quickly as he could, but her face looked pale, and she was covered with goose bumps.

"Hang on," he said. "We'll get you warmed up in a minute." He scooped her up and carried her into the bedroom. Turning down the bedcovers he placed her in the bed and threw extra blankets on top of her, but she was still shivering. He stripped down to his shorts and climbed in next to her. Her skin felt cold as he wrapped himself around her, trying to warm her with his body heat.

"Try taking some slow, deep breaths. There you go. That's a little better."

After holding her for several minutes, he felt her body slowly relax. "Are you feeling better?" he asked.

"A little."

"Good. We'll just hang out here for now."

She had finally stopped shivering, and she began talking a few minutes later. "I was standing by the river, enjoying the view, when I spotted a bald eagle. I watched it as it flew overhead, and as I turned around, I somehow lost my balance. Next thing I knew, I was in the water. It felt like a thousand needles were going through my body all at once. I was trying to get out, but I was having trouble breathing. It took everything I had to call for help, but I was afraid you wouldn't hear me."

"It's okay. I got to you in time. I've already lost one woman I loved, and I'll be damned if I'm going to lose another."

He regretted his words the moment they slipped out of his mouth. No doubt he was reacting to the shock of what had happened. He looked at Jenna, but she didn't appear to be listening, much to his relief.

"Sorry," she finally said. "I guess I'm not all here right now. What were you saying?"

"I was asking how you were feeling."

"I'm okay, although I'm a little discombobulated at the moment."

"Probably to be expected," he said, reassuringly, "and I think you're going to be okay."

"I'm also feeling a tad too warm."

"Now there's a good sign. Do you want me to take off one of the blankets?"

"Please."

He hopped up and tossed one of the extra blankets on the chair. "How that?" he asked.

"Much better, thanks."

He got back in bed and once again wrapped himself around her. This time her skin felt warmer. She moved her arm from underneath the covers and took a closer look.

"Looks like I'm okay. I don't see any big bruises coming up."

Bill took a closer look. "I can see a few tiny little scratches, but no serious injuries. Do you want me to take you to the emergency room? Just in case?"

"No, I think I'm okay. I fell backwards, but thankfully the river was pretty shallow. I was only underwater a few seconds before I got back on my feet. I tried to climb out, but the boulders were too big and I couldn't get a grip."

"Thank goodness you're okay. So, can I get you anything?"

"Maybe a cup of hot tea."

"Coming right up. Are you feeling hungry?"

"Not really. Go ahead and heat up the chicken enchiladas for yourself. I may have some later. If not, we'll have what's left for breakfast."

Bill hopped out of bed and grabbed his robe.

"Would you mind getting mine as well? I need to put my wet clothes in the washer. I also need to shampoo all the muck out of my hair."

"I can put your clothes in the washer for you."

"It's okay, Bill," she said with a slight grin. "I can take care of my own laundry."

"I'll get your robe. Then I'm going to light a fire in the fireplace. Once it's going, I'll come get you and you can take care of your laundry. Then, after you're out of the shower, I'm parking you on the sofa. I want you to take it easy tonight."

❧TWENTY-THREE❧

CECE SIGHED AS she gazed at Jenna's empty desk. It felt strange not having her office buddy close by. Taking a sip of her morning coffee, she turned her attention back to her computer and weeded her way through her email. As she scrolled down the list something unexpected caught her eye. One of Jenna's forwarded messages had come from Ken's personal Gmail account. The subject line read, "You Really Need to Stop Ghosting Me."

Obviously, it was a personal message, but why had Ken had sent it to Jenna's business account? Perhaps he sent it by mistake. As CeCe hovered her mouse over the forward button, she began having second thoughts. While Jenna never elaborated on exactly what had happened between her and Ken, she had made it abundantly clear that she had moved on. CeCe had also told him, many times, to stop bothering her. In all the years she had known him, she had never heard of him stalking anyone, although he could be extremely stubborn when he wanted to be. Perhaps it might be a good idea, for Jenna's sake, to give the email a cursory glance. If there was nothing negative in his message, she would mark it unread and forward it. Taking a deep breath, she clicked on the link. Her heart sank as she read it.

What's going on? All of a sudden, my text messages aren't being delivered, and when I sent you an email, it bounced. I already told you I'm not interested in rekindling any past romance, but I would very much for us to remain friends. From what I hear, you're not seeing anyone at the moment, and I already told you Jeri and I are nowhere close to making a commitment. There's no reason why we can't stay in touch. I'd like to meet you somewhere lunch, just to say hi and catch up on things. So let me know when and where you'd like to meet, and we'll go Dutch.

The message seemed harmless enough, but she still felt uneasy about forwarding it. She quickly grabbed her phone and sent Ken a text message.

"I guess I forget to tell you. Jenna is out of the office for the next few weeks, and she's forwarded her email on to me. I'm afraid she won't see your message until sometime in January."

Ken immediately texted back. *"What happened?"*

"The firm is experiencing a temporary cash flow problem, so they furloughed a few employees, including Jenna. She'll be back after the holidays."

"Unless she finds a job somewhere else."

CeCe raised her brow as she read his message. She hadn't considered the possibility of Jenna looking for work elsewhere. Her response to Ken was short and to the point.

"Please don't send personal messages here. The server archives all our email."

He responded a moment later. *"I figured as much, so please delete it. Would it be okay if I stopped by after work and brought some pizza?"*

"We'd love it. See you tonight." CeCe felt relieved as she deleted Ken's message. Hopefully, no one else would ever see it.

* * *

Ken sighed as he set his phone down. He knew he was taking a chance when he emailed Jenna's work account. While disappointed she wasn't there to read it, sending it had been worth the risk. CeCe had given him valuable information. As he thought it over, he realized he had a golden opportunity exact his revenge. No doubt CeCe would buy his story about wanting to help Jenna out and not expecting anything in return. Always gullible, she never seemed to catch on. His timing was also impeccable. Jeri had a class that night. He wouldn't have to make up an excuse about why he didn't invite her along.

* * *

CeCe eyed the two extra-large pizza boxes Ken carried inside. "Looks like you brought quite a haul," she said.

"I got our favorites plus an order of wings," he said. "Sausage and pepperoni for me, and Hawaiian pizza for you and John, although I still can't understand how anyone could possibly eat pineapple on a pizza."

"I keep telling you to try it. John wasn't sure at first either, but now he loves it."

"I'll have to take your word for it." Ken followed CeCe into the kitchen and set the boxes on the counter while CeCe grabbed some plates and napkins. John came in and took three cans of Coors Light from the refrigerator.

"So, how's it going, Ken?" he asked.

"It's going great, but how about you guys? I had no idea Salisbury and Norton was short on cash."

"It's nothing to be concerned about," said CeCe. "A couple of big projects went over budget, which isn't unusual, and clients are sometimes slow to pay, but we're hardly going bankrupt. However, they decided to furlough some of the staff just in case something unexpected came up. As I told you this morning, Jenna should be back in January. Early February at the very latest."

"So, I'm told," said Ken. "However, I'm a little confused about why she got furloughed in the first place, especially after doing such an amazing job on The Shelton Inn."

"I was just as shocked as you are. So was she, but it was done by seniority. She was also in between projects, which may have been a factor as well." CeCe opened the pizza boxes and told Ken to help himself. He eagerly loaded his plate and sat down at the kitchen table.

"But I still feel really bad for her," said Ken. "I'm also a little worried about her. You may recall me going with her last year when she bought her new car. I don't know if I should be saying this or not, but they didn't give her as much as she wanted for her trade, so she had to pull some money out of her savings account in order to get the payments she wanted. Later on, she said it would take some time to build her savings back up."

John looked at his wife. "Are you staying in touch with her?"

"Yes, but it's only been a few days since she was furloughed."

"Then she needs to apply for unemployment benefits."

"Which would only be about half her salary," said Ken.

"I know, but I can help her get a short-term loan so she can keep up with her bills." He turned back to his wife. "Please call her in the morning and give her my number."

Ken gritted his teeth as he sat down at the table. John was interfering with his plans.

"The reason I stopped by tonight is because I want to help her out as well." He reached for his wallet and took out a VISA gift card. "This is for her, so she can buy groceries and put some gas in her car."

"It really wasn't necessary, Ken," said CeCe. "The holidays are coming up. Maybe you should hang onto it and give it to a family member for Christmas."

"I'll worry about my holiday shopping later, and I promise I'll find something nice for Jeri too, but right now I'm more concerned about Jenna. I honestly want to help her out. So, please, as a favor to me, see to it she gets it. Tell it's from a concerned friend who wishes to remain anonymous."

"I don't know, Ken. How much it worth?"

"Two hundred fifty dollars."

CeCe looked shocked. "Are you serious? That's a lot of money, and I'm not sure such a large amount is even appropriate. Fifty or seventy-five dollars maybe, but certainly not two-fifty. I think you should use it to buy a Christmas gift for Jeri."

"Okay, so maybe I'm being overly generous, but Jenna is still very special to me. I just don't want her to know I'm helping her out, which is why I want you to tell her it's from a friend who wishes to remain anonymous."

"Alright, but she's still going to want to know who gave it her."

"If she asks about me, you'll have to tell her a little white lie."

CeCe reluctantly took the cards. "Okay, I suppose I could tell her it's from Oscar. He really appreciated her all hard work on the Shelton Inn."

"Perfect. There you go." Ken turned his attention to John. "I'm also relieved you can help her get a loan, if she needs it."

"I'm just doing my job," said John. "So, how's Jeri? Did she fill out an application with us?"

"I think she may have, but I'm not entirely sure. I'll ask her the next time I see her."

Once again, CeCe looked surprised. "You mean you're not talking to her every day? You've been together for almost a year."

"Actually, it's only been about nine months," said Ken.

"Which is almost a year. I figured by now you'd either be living together, or perhaps thinking about getting engaged."

"Nope, not even close. I know you really like her. I like her too, but I'm still not sure if she's the one or not." He needed to change the subject before John became suspicious. Picking up a slice of pizza, looked John in the eye.

"So, do you think the Nuggets will make it to the playoffs this year?"

"It's too early to say," said John, "but so far they seem to be off to a good start." They speculated about the rest of the season until John finally excused himself and opened the refrigerator.

"You want another beer, Ken?"

"I'm good, thanks."

"You know the Nuggets are playing tonight, so I'm going to turn on the pregame show. You're welcome to stay and watch if you'd like."

"Thanks. I'll be there in a minute."

John stepped out and CeCe waited until they could hear the tv in the other room. "Okay," she quietly said. "I get it that you still have a thing for Jenna, but it's over. You also told me you were getting ready to end it with her."

"Because I was really scared at the time."

"Scared of what?"

"When you first introduced us, I thought if it worked out, great. If not, we'd wish each other well and move on. But the more I got to know her, the more I liked her. Then I got scared. What if she didn't feel the same about me? No one wants to be rejected, especially when you've really fallen for them. So, I decided to rein myself in and take things a little slower. Then I got an invitation to my cousin's wedding, and it was okay to bring a guest. Weddings, as you know, are romantic, so I thought maybe, on the way home, I'd tell her how I really felt and see if she might be willing to make a commitment someday. But thanks to my aunt Theresa, I never got the chance."

"What did you aunt do?"

He gave her a sad look. "She gave Jenna a lot of grief about ordering the pasta instead of the chicken the rest of us were having. I still can't believe she got all worked up over something so trivial, but she did. My uncle Walter finally had to intervene."

"Reminds me of one of my great-aunts," said CeCe. "She was a busybody who was always telling the rest of us what to do."

"Then you know the type. So, the minute the meal was over, Jenna tells everyone she has a headache and she's going home. Later on, she sends me a text telling me she's moving on. I tried to get her to change her mind, but she said no. Thankfully, Jeri came along soon after. Don't get me wrong. I honestly care about Jeri, but I still have unfinished business with Jenna. Until it's resolved I can't make a commitment to Jeri, or anyone else for that matter. So, I tried reaching out to Jenna. I just want to spend some time with her, on her terms, so I can work through those unresolved feelings and get some closure."

CeCe patted his forearm. "I'm sorry, Ken. I had no idea you cared about her this much."

"I do. I'm just not the type of guy who shows his emotions. It's really hard for me to open up to women. So, is Jenna seeing anyone?"

"I know she and her friend Bill are really close, but so far as I know they're just friends."

"Are you sure? She may not be telling you everything."

"Well, I've noticed she looks really happy whenever his name comes up. I also met him the one time."

"Yes, I know," said Ken. "So how did they act when they were together?"

"I really can't say. He was busy trying to sell his art. Jenna was introducing people to him, but I didn't really see them talking very much to one another. John and I were only there for a short time."

"I know. I was just wondering. So, please, as a favor to me, give her the gift card, and let me know how she reacts. And if you get the chance, please tell her I wish her well, and I'm not trying to get her back. Just tell her I wish things had ended on better terms."

"Okay, I'll try, but if she doesn't want to talk about it, I'll have to let it go."

"I understand. At least you would have tried, and please keep me up to date about Bill."

"Why?"

"Because I worry about her," said Ken. "You know those artist types. They're not known to be dependable, and I don't want her getting hurt."

"You are aware that Bill is also a college professor, so I have a hunch he's dependable."

"Even so, I don't want to see her getting hurt, and I know I can always count on you. In the meantime, I'll help you with the cleanup, and then we'll go watch the game."

⤳TWENTY-FOUR⤵

JENNA SLEPT peacefullY through the night, seemingly unscathed by her fall in the river, but it had left Bill badly shaken. Every time he closed his eyes, he saw her struggling to get out, and he barely managed to get a couple hours of sleep. At least the sun was finally up. As he tried once again to make himself comfortable, Jenna began stirring and greeted him with a smile.

"Good morning."

He gently stroked her arm. "Good morning to you as well. So, how did you sleep?"

"Like a rock. Falling in the water must have really drained my energy. So what time is it?"

Bill checked his watch. "It's seven fifty-two."

"Then I guess it's time to think about getting up." She looked at him more closely. "Are you all right? Your eyes look a little bloodshot and you have circles underneath them."

"I didn't sleep very well."

"I'm sorry. You should have woken me up. I would have gotten you a cup of warm milk."

"It's okay. I didn't want to disturb you. I also wanted to keep watch on you, in case something happened."

"Bill, I'm fine. If it were a near drowning, I'd be at risk for complications, but it wasn't."

"How do you know?"

"I learned about water safety at summer camp when I was a kid. I also know it upset you as well, which is why you should have woken me up. We're supposed to watch out for one another. So can I get you anything?"

"Not at the moment. I'll make some coffee before I hop in the shower. Then, soon as I get dressed, I'll heat up the breakfast biscuits."

"No," she said firmly. "I'll make the coffee and heat up the breakfast biscuits while you take a shower."

"Okay, I won't argue with you. Then, after breakfast, we need to get ready to go. We have to be out of here by eleven o'clock."

"I know, but I'd feel a whole lot better if we could stay an extra day so you could get some rest."

"I'll be fine, but would you mind driving? I don't feel up to it today."

"I'd be happy to, and you can take a nap on the way home." Jenna grabbed her robe and excused herself to make the coffee. Bill joined her in the kitchen a few minutes later, freshly showered and shaved, but he still felt exhausted. He poured himself some coffee while Jenna heated up the biscuits. They lingered over their meal until they finally checked the time. It was after nine o'clock. Bill tidied up the kitchen while Jenna packed her bag.

* * *

Jenna's phone rang while she was packing. Salisbury and Norton was calling. Hoping for good news, she eagerly accepted the call, but her hopes waned once she heard CeCe's voice.

"Hope I'm not catching you at a bad time," she said.

"Not at all," said Jenna. "So, what's up?"

"I found an envelope on my desk this morning. Inside was a VISA gift card along with a note instructing me to give it to you. It had been left at the front desk by a concerned client who wishes to remain anonymous."

"Do you know who it was?"

"No."

"Then it must be from the Sheltons. Do you know how much it's for?"

"No, I don't."

"Let's wait and see if I need it first. I have an interview next week for a temporary job with another interior design firm."

"You're not leaving us, are you?"

"No," said Jenna. "I'd be filling in for someone who's on maternity leave. I'm also hoping Salisbury will be ready for me to come back once she returns. Assuming I get the job."

"I hope you get it too, but there's no guarantee, and the gift card could help you buy gas and groceries in case it doesn't work out."

"I know, but—"

Bill called out from the other room. "Are you about ready?"

"I'm sorry," said CeCe. "I didn't know you had company."

"It's okay," said Jenna. "So, about the gift card, I really appreciate the offer, but let's wait and see what happens first."

Bill stepped into the room. "Oh, sorry. I didn't know you were on the phone."

"You're fine," said Jenna. "I'll be done in a minute."

"Sounds like you're busy," said CeCe, "so I won't keep you. Why don't you drop by later? We'll go have lunch Megan's. My treat."

"I appreciate the offer, but I'm not in Denver right now. I'll let you know if I get the temporary job or not." Jenna ended the call and turned her attention to Bill.

"That was CeCe."

"So, I gathered."

"Apparently Oscar Shelton heard I was furloughed, so he dropped off a gift card for me."

"Which was certainly thoughtful of him. Have you finished packing?"

Jenna nodded toward her bag. "As soon as I toss in my hairbrush, I'm ready to go."

* * *

A surprised CeCe carefully set the receiver back in its cradle. Not only were Jenna and Bill more than friends, they had taken a romantic getaway.

"Wow, Jenna," she said under her breath. "You really are discreet, aren't you?" She grabbed her mobile phone and pounded out a message to Ken.

"We need to talk. As soon as possible." She sent the message and anxiously waited for a response, but none came. Ken was either in a meeting, or busy with a client. She turned her attention back to her work, but she was having a hard time concentrating. Finally, her phone beeped.

"I was away from my desk. What happened?"

"I have news about Jenna, but I need to deliver it in person."

"What happened? Is she okay?"

"She's fine, but we need to talk. Free for lunch?"

It took a moment for him to respond. *"Yes. Can you meet me at O'Malley's Grill?"*

"Sure. What time?"

"Any time after the lunch rush. Would one o'clock work for you?"

"See you at one."

* * *

Ken was anxiously waiting when CeCe arrived. "Sorry for the delay," she said. "There was a little fender bender along the way, and you know how everyone has to slow down and gawk."

"You're fine," said Ken. "You're only a couple of minutes late, and I went ahead and ordered you an iced tea."

"Thanks."

"You're welcome. Today's special is the grilled chicken sandwich combo, and you can have onion rings if you prefer."

"Then I'll have onion rings."

They placed their order and Ken wasted no time. "So, what happened with Jenna?"

"I called her first thing this morning. I was worried it might go to voicemail, but she answered."

"I see. So, what did she have to say?"

"She has an interview coming up for a temporary job with another interior design firm."

"What firm, and where?"

"I don't know. She didn't tell me."

"Then you should have asked. You're supposed to be keeping an eye on her."

"It's only an interview," CeCe said firmly. "Who's to say she'll get the job? I also told her about the gift card. She thinks it's from Oscar Shelton, but she wants to see if she gets the job first."

Ken took a deep breath. He didn't want to appear too frustrated. "Okay, it's a little setback, but we can deal with it. What do you think about dropping it in the mail? I know it's kind of old school, but you could include a note saying Oscar insisted she take it."

"I hadn't thought of that."

"Good. Problem solved."

"Not exactly."

Once again, he was taken aback. "What do you mean by, not exactly?"

"While we were talking, I heard someone else in the room."

"Any idea who?"

"Her friend, Bill," said CeCe.

"Are you sure?"

"Positive. I remember his voice."

"Okay," said Ken. "So, what were they saying?"

"First, I heard him in the background, I but couldn't make out what he was saying. Then I heard him again about a minute later. He was apologizing for not knowing she was on the phone."

"But you keep saying they're just good friends, so maybe he stopped by with some Egg McMuffins or something. I've been known to do that."

CeCe squirmed in her seat. "She wasn't home. She said she was out of town. Where, I don't know. She didn't say and I didn't ask. She just said she'd call me later. I'm sorry, Ken, but she's definitely moved on. I know you're disappointed, but my mother always said things have a way of working out for the best. You've found someone who's a much better match for you, and I could tell by the look in her eyes that she really does love you."

"I know she does, and I care deeply about her as well. However, Jenna is standing between me and her."

Once again, CeCe's voice was firm. "Only if you allow it. I don't mean to sound insensitive, but a lot of us have people from our past. Remember Alec?"

"I remember Alec quite well. He couldn't keep it zipped, even after you got engaged. You deserved better."

"I know I did, but I was still devasted when I found out he had another woman on the side. Don't get me wrong. I love John very much, but Alec had a certain quality which no one else has had, before or since."

"He was a player, CeCe, and a player can't be a player without his captivating charm."

"Which is the point I'm trying to make about Jenna. She may not be a player, but she sure can keep as secret, as I discovered today."

"She's discreet."

"To a fault. So, what else is she hiding?"

"I don't think she's hiding anything," said Ken. "She simply likes her privacy, and she's not a gossip, which are some of the things I like about her."

"Jeri didn't strike me as a gossip either. You need to move on. Jenna has found someone else, and so have you. I know you want to help her out, so if she doesn't get the job, I'll try to offer her the gift card one more time, but I'm not going to push if she says no. I already said you should use it to get something nice for Jeri. I know you're not ready to give her a ring, but you could certainly get her a nice pendent or a pair of earrings. Do you know what her birthstone is?"

"Ruby."

"Red is a beautiful color, and it's perfect for Christmas. You should be able to find her something nice for two-hundred fifty dollars."

"We'll see," said Ken.

CeCe quickly changed the subject. Ken nodded as she babbled on, but he really wasn't listening. He was too busy thinking about his next move.

ᏍᎧTWENTY-FIVEᏍᎧ

BILL MANAGED To get a little rest on the way back to Denver, but he declined Jenna's offer for lunch once they arrived. He was too tired to eat and anxious to return to the hotel, so he gave her a quick goodbye kiss and promised to call her later. Arriving at the hotel, he grabbed his bag and hurried inside. The elevator doors opened as he approached. He was surprised to see the young couple who stepped out.

"Hey, Dad," said Conner. "Fancy meeting you here."

"I could say the same. Did you stop by to see me?"

"We knocked on your door, but you were out."

"I've been out of town for the past couple of days, and I just got back."

"I see," said Connor. "Kelsey arrived last night. I didn't want her staying here by herself, nor did I want to wear out my welcome with Caleb, so we'll be here until our apartment is ready. And where have you been?"

"I took a short trip up to Estes Park."

"Sounds like fun. Do you need help with your bag?"

"No, but thanks for the offer."

"Are you sure? I don't mean to sound rude, but you look beat."

"I'm fine. I just didn't sleep well last night."

"In that case let me help you."

"I'm good," said Bill. "You kids have somewhere to go, and I don't want to keep you."

"We'll least walk you to your door," said Kelsey. "It'll only take a couple of minutes."

Bill didn't argue as Connor took his bag, but the elevator doors had closed. Another car arrived a minute later and they hurried inside.

"Third floor," said Bill.

"I know, Dad. And just so you know, Kelsey and I are on the second floor, on the other side of the building."

"We're in room two-fourteen," said Kelsey.

The elevator doors opened. Bill led them down the hallway to his suite.

"I see you have the same set up as us," said Connor. "Queen bed with a kitchenette."

"So, how's the job search going?" asked Bill.

"I finally heard back from the hospital, and I interviewed with them yesterday. It went really well. The job is similar to what I was doing in Florida. I have a second interview on Monday, but they said it's just a formality."

"Good to know, and I'm proud of you, but let's not celebrate until it's official."

"I agree."

"Anything new from the attorney?" asked Bill.

"Not yet."

"I'm sure you'll hear something soon," said Bill, "and by the way Kelsey, you look different." He gave her a closer look. "You got a new haircut, didn't you?"

Her dark curly hair barely touched the top of her shoulders. "I sure did. With a big move coming up, I wanted something less maintenance."

"And it makes her look really hot too," said Connor. "So, what happened in Estes Park that caused you to lose sleep?"

"We were staying in a little cabin which backed up to the Big Thompson River. Jenna somehow took a tumble and ended up in the water. She's fine, but it scared the living hell out of me."

"I'll bet, and I'm glad she's okay."

"Me too," said Bill. "We'll talk more about it later. Right now, the old man needs to get some rest."

"Not a problem. We were on our way to find Kelsey a good winter coat."

"She'll definitely be needing one."

"This winter will certainly be different," said Kelsey. "I've never been in snow in my life."

Bill looked at Connor. "You'll need to take her out to an empty parking lot and teach her how to drive on icy roads." Bill stifled another yawn and Connor took his cue.

"I will, but for now we're out of here. Get some rest, and if you're up to it let's do dinner tonight."

"We'll do it tomorrow night. I plan on going to bed early tonight."

* * *

Jenna met with other interior design firm the following week and called her mother when she returned home. During the conversation, she found out her father had switched places with another pilot who wanted to stay home and take his children trick-or-treating.

"I have an idea," said Claire. "Since we're both home alone, why don't we go have dinner somewhere? It's been a long time since we've had a mother and daughter night out."

"I don't know, Mom. Right now, I have to watch my spending."

"I'm your mother, so it's my treat. I really enjoyed our lunch at Sam's Place, and I can't think of a better excuse than Halloween to go back. I'll pick you up in thirty minutes."

It was Jenna's first time being back at the hotel since the day she had lunch at Sam's Place with her parents. Halloween decorations had been placed around the lobby, along with a Happy Halloween banner behind the front desk. Sam's was also festive with fall centerpieces on each table and lighted Halloween decorations at the bar. The restaurant was busy when they arrived. Claire introduced herself to the hostess, saying she had reserved at table for two.

"Right this way, Mrs. Winters." She led them to a table near the bar. Claire gazed at the decorations once they were seated.

"I'll always remember the way my grandmother used to talk about Halloween," she said. "They don't celebrate it in England, so she never understood the significance. She thought the whole thing was, in her words, 'rather silly.'"

"Sounds like she was never fully Americanized," said Jenna.

"Not entirely, and she never lost her English accent either, but she did love Colorado. She said it reminded her of the mountains in Scotland and Wales. I was fifteen when we took our famous family trip to England to meet our uncles, aunts, and cousins."

"I know. You used to talk about it when I was a kid."

"It was a life-changing experience. After we got home, I decided I was going to be a flight attendant so I could go back and visit, which I often did. It's also how I met your father."

"And I'm sure you remember how I used to talk about becoming a flight attendant when I was a kid."

"You did," said Claire, "but later on you found the right career for you. So how did the interview go?"

"I'm not sure. Turns out they're interior decorators who work with people who are either buying new homes or remodeling."

"Which you do as well."

"I do, and I'll be helping Bill with the house he's buying. However, they were completely overwhelmed when I showed them my work. Apparently, I was more than they were bargaining for, so I may be overqualified."

"I know, but it's only a temporary job."

"We'll have to wait and see."

"And speaking of Bill," said Claire, "I'll be forever in his debt for rescuing you from the river. It still makes me shudder when I think about it."

"Mom, I'm okay. I wasn't hurt."

"But you still could have drowned."

"I was having trouble getting out because of the boulders they'd placed along the shoreline, but I'm fine. Had Bill not been there I would have found another way to get out."

"Mothers always worry about their children, even when they're adults. Someday, when you're a mother, you'll understand."

"I suppose, but right now my prospects aren't looking so good. Stacy sent me a text the other day saying she's met someone new, and if that wasn't enough, Ken's trying to worm his way back in."

Claire looked concerned. "Really? What's he doing now?"

"He keeps sending me emails and text messages, saying he wants us to be friends and suggesting we meet for lunch somewhere."

"I see. So, what did you tell him?"

"I said no. I kept reminding him he has another girlfriend, but he says they haven't made any kind of commitment, and they're still free to date other people."

"Which may be well and good, but you've already told him no. He needs to respect your boundaries."

"I know," said Jenna. "He also claims he's having second thoughts about me."

"Which is a load of bunk and you know it. I'm more inclined to believe your mutual friend CeCe has told him about your friendship with Bill, so now he's trying to make trouble. There are men out there who do that sort of thing."

"Which is what I think as well, so I finally blocked him from my phone and email. I haven't heard so much as a peep from him since."

"For now," said Claire, "but once you go back to work you know CeCe will start telling him about you. I really think you should use this time off to look for another job."

"I just said I'm waiting to hear back from the other design firm."

"I'm not talking about the other firm. I'm talking about looking for a permanent position someplace else. Or perhaps even going out on your own. If it's something you'd like to do, you know your father and I would help you."

"I don't know, Mom. I'll have to think about it. In the meantime, I have an appointment with an artist friend of Bill's who's also a financial planner. He says he can help me plan a budget to help get me through until I go back to work."

A server wearing a black cape with a witch's hat and blue lipstick arrived with hot bread and two glasses of ice water. Once she took their drink orders, Claire picked up where she left off.

"So why don't you ask Bill's friend if he can come up with a plan to help you branch out on your own? You've got your unemployment, and somehow, I doubt you'll be back at Salisbury the day after New Year's. Call me the eternal optimist, but I think the reason this happened is because there's a better opportunity out there for you. You just need to find it. And speaking of Bill, how's he doing?"

"He's doing well," said Jenna. "Tomorrow morning Connor and his girlfriend move into their new apartment. He just got an offer for an administrative position at Southern Memorial Hospital. Bill says it's similar to the job he had in Florida, but with better pay."

"See? Things happened because he had a better opportunity here."

"Maybe, but he sure went through a lot of grief to get there, and since he's just starting there's no guarantee it'll work out. In the meantime, he and Kelsey plan on cooking Thanksgiving dinner at their new apartment, and they invited Bill and me to join them. He thinks it's just as good a time as any for Connor and me to meet."

"Well, isn't that interesting?"

Their drink orders soon arrived, much to Jenna's relief. "So, are you and Dad still spending Thanksgiving in Boston?" she asked.

"We are. Your father has a morning flight from Denver to Boston on Thanksgiving Day, and I was able to get a ticket. We'll join the rest of the flight crew for the Thanksgiving buffet at the hotel, so it'll be like old times. I also reserved a seat for you, but I wasn't going to pay for it until after we talked."

"I appreciate the offer, and had I not had other plans I would have loved to have come along. How long will you be in Boston?"

"Just overnight. Your dad has a flight to Vancouver, Canada the following day, and we'll have a brief layover there. We fly back to Denver late Sunday night."

"You two have quite the life," said Jenna. "Sometimes I wish I'd followed through and become a flight attendant too."

"You still could, if you wanted to. You're certainly good at working with people. I thought about going back myself after you started college, but I would've started over from scratch. It would have taken some time for me to get enough seniority to fly with your father, and I didn't want us becoming roommates who hardly saw one another. I also believe if you were to set up shop as an independent interior designer there would be people out there like the Sheltons, who would either work with you, or perhaps give you good referrals."

"I'm sure they would," said Jenna. "In fact, CeCe called me the other day. Apparently, word got to Oscar about me being furloughed, so he dropped off a gift card for me."

"Which proves there are people out there who are willing to help you. I've also told you before I don't trust CeCe. She's too close to Ken for my comfort, and I still say she's a troublemaker."

"It's okay, Mom. I don't discuss my personal life with her. In fact, I made a point, not too long ago, of telling her my private life is none of her concern."

Claire looked her daughter in the eye. "I know the type, Jenna. I worked with flight attendants who were gossips. CeCe is one of those who'll take an innocent comment out of context and put her own spin on it. I think you'd be wise to look for a job elsewhere and leave her be."

❧TWENTY-SIX❧

BILL PARKED HIS Explorer in the loading zone and looked at Jenna, seated in the passenger seat. "You know, if someone had told me last July I'd be back in a few months, I would've said they were crazy, but here I am."

"For whatever reason, it wasn't meant to be," said Jenna, "and I for one, am glad you're back."

"Me too, so let's get started."

They hurried inside the building, walking past the co-op art gallery in what had once been the lobby. Turning down a hallway, Bill stopped and unlocked his studio door. "Well, what do you know? It's toasty warm in here." He took a closer look at the shiny new furnace, mounted on the wall. "At long last, I can finally work in here in the winter. The building was built in the nineteen-sixties. You would've thought it had central heat."

"Actually, it did at one time," said Jenna. "Your old furnace is too modern for the nineteen-sixties, and whoever mounted it did a sloppy job. You also have a closed off ceiling vent."

"Good eye."

"It's why they pay me the big bucks." Her demeanor quickly changed. "At least, they used to pay me the big bucks. So, now that you have heat, will you still be doing wood reliefs?"

"Absolutely. I found a good deal on a used shed. It looks sort of like a miniature cottage. The guy said it was his ex-wife's she shed."

"How cute."

He gave her a look. "I'm just buying the shed. She kept all the furnishings, but it'll be perfect for woodworking. And speaking of work, we need to unload."

It took several trips to get everything out of the U-Haul trailer. After setting the last box in the corner, Bill cleared a space and opened the blinds, revealing a concrete filled swimming pool with three large ceramic kilns on top of it.

"The one thing this place has going for it is plenty of natural lighting, and I'm greatly relieved Sally didn't rent it to someone else. I'm also checking out of my hotel room first thing tomorrow morning and camping out here until the house sale closes."

"Does she allow that?"

"Not exactly." He rolled out an air mattress and plugged in the pump. "However, the building was originally a hotel, so we all have showers and toilets, and people sometimes sack out in their studios if they're working late. I kept an air mattress and sleeping bag here for years. Beats the heck out of sleeping on the concrete floor. We also have an unwritten rule. Don't tell Sally."

"Smart thinking."

He looked at her more closely. "You've been quieter than usual today. Is everything okay?"

"Not really."

"So, what happened?"

"I got an email early this morning. The design firm I interviewed with went with another candidate. I was really counting on getting the job."

"I'm sorry, Jenna. I was hoping you'd get it too. Did you meet with Josh? He can help you plan a budget."

"I met with him last week. He gave me some really good suggestions to get me through until things get better." She let out a small chuckle.

"What's so funny?" he asked.

"He was very professional. He was even wearing a shirt and tie, but as we were talking, I kept seeing the photo you took of him and his wife in the back of my mind; the one you used for the wood relief. It felt a little funny."

"It shouldn't have. As I recall, you took a life drawing class in college, so it's not like you've never seen a nude model before."

"I know, but they were all strangers. I never knew their names, and I never saw them outside of class."

"They were people like Josh and Stephanie, who do art modeling on the side because it pays well and it's a nice income supplement. I've been known to do it myself."

"Really?"

"I do it to help other artists. I also did it when I was in grad school because I had a son to support. However, I only modeled at the community colleges, and not the university where I was a teaching assistant. It's a really easy job when you stop and think about it. All you have to do is hold a pose, and most jobs only take an hour or two. It's something you may want to consider until you find other work."

Jenna's face turned pink. "I don't know if I could handle being naked in front of a stranger. Would it bother you if another man saw me?"

"Not at all. You could also limit yourself to women artists if you prefer, and not all art modeling is nude modeling. The models are oftentimes clothed. I would also refer you to people I know and trust."

"I'll have to think it over. My mother also wants me to look for a job with another design firm."

"Not a bad idea. You may find something that pays better."

"Maybe, but my retirement account is through Salisbury and Norton."

"Which Josh can help you roll if you were to find a job elsewhere."

"I see. I also need to pick up the gift card from CeCe."

"If it were me, I'd get it today. In the meantime, I need to return the trailer before three, so I'll drop you off at your place on the way."

"Thanks. I'll head straight to the grocery store as soon as I pick it up."

* * *

The front receptionist looked up as Jenna stepped into the lobby. "I thought it was you," she said. "For a moment there, I wasn't sure. I've never seen you in blue jeans before."

"I was helping a friend move," said Jenna. "So, how's it going, Paige?"

"Same old same old, although Mr. Lacy just had a big meeting with someone last Thursday. I'm hoping a new project is coming in."

"Which would be really nice, because sitting at home eating beans and rice isn't exactly a vacation."

"No, it wouldn't be," said Paige.

"I stopped by because CeCe said Oscar Shelton dropped something off for me the other day, and I'm here to pick it up."

Paige looked puzzled. "That's odd. The Sheltons haven't been here since their new hotel opened."

"Are you sure?"

"Positive, but let me check the logbook just in case they stopped by while I was at lunch." Paige clicked on her mouse and looked through the entries. "Sorry, Jenna. They haven't been here some time."

"Could a courier have dropped it off?"

"If a courier service delivered it, there'd be an entry, and I don't see anything here."

"I could have sworn CeCe said it had been dropped off here, so I guess one of us got confused. He must have sent it through the mail." Jenna started rummaging through her purse. "As soon as I find my badge, I'll run up there."

"If you can't find it, I can give you a guest badge."

"Thanks, I found it." Jenna grabbed her lanyard and hopped in the elevator. CeCe greeted her with a bright smile when she walked up to her desk.

"Well, howdy stranger," said CeCe. "What a nice surprise."

"I was out taking care of other business and figured as long as I was in the neighborhood I'd stop by."

"Well, I'm glad you did, because I have something for you."

"I know. I stopped at the front desk first, but Paige didn't have it. I guess Oscar must have mailed it."

CeCe quickly turned her attention to her desk drawer. "He did, and I'm sorry I opened it by mistake. It was mixed in with my mail. I didn't realize it was for you until I saw the note."

"No need to apologize."

CeCe handed her the card, and Jenna gave her a strange look. "So, what happened to the envelope?"

"It went into the recycling bin. I wasn't sure if you wanted it or not, and I've been waiting to hear back from you."

"Then I'm sorry for the mix up. Between Halloween, and helping Bill move back into his art studio, I've apparently lost track of the time."

"How is Bill these days?"

"He's doing well. His old studio was still available, so he's leased it for another year. I was helping him move his stuff back in."

"Then I'm glad he was able to get it back. Is he working on anything new?"

"Not yet, but he's anxious to get back to work. No doubt he'll start his next project very soon."

"That's great. My client loved the piece I got for her, and she may want more. Is everything else going okay?"

"It's as good as it can be, for now. I, too, am anxious to get back to work. Has anything new come through the door?"

"Not yet," said CeCe, "but if I hear anything, I promise you'll be the first to know."

"Thanks, I appreciate it, and I won't keep you any longer. Have a Happy Thanksgiving."

Jenna's next stop was the grocery store. She shopped carefully, mostly buying things on sale and stocking up on frozen foods and canned goods. She also found a Thank You card to send to Oscar. After putting the groceries away, she wrote him a short note, telling him how much she appreciated his help and wishing him and his family a Happy Thanksgiving. She would drop it off at the post office the following morning.

✥TWENTY-SEVEN✥

JENNA RAISED HER brow when she checked her caller ID. Once again, Salisbury and Norton was calling. Hoping for good news, she eagerly accepted the call, only to hear Chad's angry voice.

"What the hell is going on?" he bluntly asked. "I just got off the phone with Oscar Shelton. He told me he just got a card in the mail from you, thanking him for the gift card he sent you. He has no idea what you're talking about, because he never sent you a gift card. So would you care to explain?"

Jenna struggled to keep her voice calm. "CeCe called me a couple weeks ago. She said Oscar heard about my being furloughed and wanted to help out, so he sent it to her in the mail. I honestly thought he was returning the favor for my helping him avoid a family brawl. Unfortunately, the temporary job I was hoping for fell through. I needed the money to buy groceries, and I wanted to thank him personally for the card."

"CeCe told you this?"

"Yes. She said the gift card was from Oscar."

"Jenna, no one has spoken to Oscar since his new hotel opened. He was completely unaware of you being furloughed. So why would CeCe make up such a story?"

"I don't know. You'll have to ask her."

"Don't worry. I intend to."

"Is there anything else?"

His voice softened. "No, and I'm sorry if I came off a little short with you. We've been doing business with the Sheltons for years. They're one of our best clients, so I'm sure you can appreciate the fact that this could potentially undermine our future dealings with them. As soon as we're done, I'm going to have a serious talk with Ms. Wood."

129

"You're not going to fire her, are you?" asked Jenna.

"I don't make those decisions."

"I would also like to know who really gave me the gift card, because this is really creeping me out."

"It would creep me out as well, so don't worry. I'll find out who it was, and I'll let you know. Now, onto better things. It's not official yet, but the other day the higher ups met with a group of investors who want to build a new, upscale restaurant in Cherry Creek. However, we don't have the job just yet. They're still working on the contract, but once it comes through, I'm hoping they'll assign it to me. If they do, I'm bringing you onboard."

"Thank you," said Jenna. "Under the circumstances, this means a lot, and I'm glad you still trust me."

"You didn't do anything wrong. Someone intentionally misled you."

"I'm also still out on furlough, and there may be someone else available who isn't. I don't want to upset anyone."

"Don't worry. I'll make sure it's not an issue. You worked with me on my last few projects, so everyone knows we're a team, but right now we're only speaking hypothetically. There's no guarantee I'll be the project architect."

"I know there isn't, but I'm still keeping my fingers crossed. I'm tired of eating hot dogs and chicken noodle soup."

"Well, in that case, why don't I take you to lunch one day next week?"

"You got it," said Jenna. "In the meantime, please tell Oscar I'm sorry for the mix-up."

"Of course. I'll be following up with him later today."

* * *

CeCe returned from lunch and found a note on her desk. Chad Runyon needed to discuss an urgent matter with her and was waiting in his office. Rumors were swirling about a new project coming in. Perhaps they were giving it to Chad, and with Jenna being out on furlough, CeCe wondered if he might include her in the design team. She had never worked with Chad before, and she was excited about the prospect. She hurried to the elevator, but Chad had a solemn look on his face when she arrived at his office. Marcy Morgan was also with him.

"Would you mind taking a seat, Ms. Wood?" asked Chad. "And would you please close the door behind you."

"Of course." CeCe felt a knot in her stomach when she took her seat.

"I'm going to get straight to the point," said Chad. "I got a rather interesting phone call this morning from Oscar Shelton, regarding a letter he received from Jenna Winters, thanking him for the gift card he'd given her. However, Oscar tells me he never sent Jenna a gift card, while Jenna tells me you gave it to her on his behalf. So, would you mind telling me what's going on?"

CeCe's blood turned to ice. She needed to come up with a good cover story, and she had to do it fast.

"I was totally shocked when Jenna got furloughed. Her desk is only a few feet away from mine, and I've gotten to know her well enough to consider her a friend. She was worried about paying her bills, which I'm sure you can understand, and my husband and I wanted to help her out. So, John, my husband, bought her a gift card, but we were concerned about her not accepting it if she knew it came from us. So, I told her the person who gave it to her wanted to remain anonymous."

"Did you say anything to suggest it came from Oscar Shelton?" asked Marcy.

CeCe's heart skipped a beat. "No. At least I don't think I did. Jenna, of course, wanted to know who gave it to her. I kept saying they wished to remain anonymous, but as we were talking, she said something about Oscar, so I decided to play along. Please understand, I never actually came out and said it was from Oscar. I simply said something to the effect that he could have possibly sent it, but I didn't know for certain. I certainly meant no harm, and I've never mentioned anything about it to anyone else."

"Okay, Ms. Wood," said Chad, "then I hope you can understand my surprise when Oscar called me this morning. The conversation was awkward, as you can imagine."

"I'm sure it was, and I'm so sorry. Would you like for me to call him and explain what happened?"

"Absolutely not," Chad sternly said. "You've already caused enough trouble. I'll call him myself when we're done here."

"I have no issue with you trying to help a coworker," said Marcy. "In fact, we encourage our employees to be supportive of one another. However, you crossed the line when you went along with Ms. Winters' assumption about the card coming from Mr. Shelton. You should have been honest with her from the start and told her it was from you and your husband. We depend on our staff being able to trust one another."

"I'm sorry. I guess I wasn't thinking. I was only trying to help."

"Which I will note in my report."

"Wait a minute," said CeCe. "Are you writing me up?"

"Yes, ma'am."

CeCe's heart sank. "Will I be fired over this?"

"Intentionally misleading a coworker about a client would certainly be grounds for termination," said Marcy, "but because you weren't acting maliciously, I'm going to recommend a reprimand instead. If Mr. Lacy decides to keep you onboard there will be a written report in your employee file because of the seriousness of the matter. Your actions resulted in the integrity of our firm being questioned by a valued client. We expect our staff to be honest with one another and to never say anything about a client which they know to be false, regardless of the circumstances."

"Like I said, I never meant to cause any harm. I was only trying to help Jenna."

"Which I'm also noting in my report," said Marcy. "In the meantime, do you have any questions for me?"

"Am I going be fired?" CeCe asked again. She clasped her hands together to keep them from trembling.

"I don't know. I'll meet with Mr. Lacy as soon as we're done. I'll let you know what he decides."

"Jenna's not in any trouble, is she?"

"No, she's not in any trouble. Based on what you've told me, and on what she said to Chad, she had every reason to believe the gift card came from Mr. Shelton. We've already told her he's not the person who gave it to her."

"In the meantime," said Chad, "Jenna still doesn't know where the card came from, and it's making her feel uneasy. I can certainly understand why she would feel this way, so I suggest you call her and explain what happened."

"Don't worry. I will. Is there anything else?"

"Not at this time," said Marcy.

"Gary is out of the office today," said Chad, "so you can use the phone in his office to call Jenna. Once you're done, you're free to go."

"I'm afraid I don't have her phone number with me. It's on my personal phone, which in my purse, underneath my desk."

"Then allow me." Chad jotted Jenna's number on a piece of scrap paper. "There you go, and she's expecting your call."

CeCe quickly excused herself and stepped into a dark office a few doors down. Her mind was reeling as she sat down behind the desk. "Well, here goes nothing," she said with a sigh. Picking up the receiver, she prayed the call would go to voicemail, and she could leave an apology message. Her hopes were dashed when Jenna answered after the third ring.

"I want to apologize for what happened." CeCe's voice sounded strained. "I didn't want you to know who the card was from, because I knew you needed the money, and I didn't want you to turn it down."

Jenna's voice sounded cold. "So, you led me to believe it was from Oscar Shelton."

"I honestly meant no harm. I had no idea you would thank him for it."

"Of course, I would have thanked him for it. He's a good-hearted man who's also very important client."

"I know. I heard all about it from Chad."

"As well you should have. So, who was it really from?"

CeCe took a deep breath and sighed into the phone. "It was from Ken."

"Are you freaking kidding me?"

"Jenna, please, calm down. It's not what you think. Ken really does care about you, and he honestly wants to help you, but he was afraid you'd say no, so he insisted I not tell you it was from him."

"Damn straight I would have said no."

"Jenna, really, it's okay. There are no strings attached. He's not expecting anything in return. He does, however, feel bad about the way the things ended between you two, and he'd like to make it up to you."

"How thoughtful," Jenna said sarcastically. "So please allow me to tell you the real story of me and Ken. When you first introduced us, I honestly liked him. He was nice looking and charming, but as I got to know him better, I started seeing things I didn't like."

"Such as?"

"He was too controlling. There were times when he was too critical as well. One minute he'd complement me on the sweater I was wearing. Then he'd turnaround say it would have looked much better if it were red instead of blue. Or he'd ask me which restaurant I would like to go to. Then he'd say he knew a better place, which was where we always ended up. It got worse later on. Whenever we discussed anything which really mattered to me, he'd vehemently disagree with everything I said. Then I'd get a big lecture about why I was wrong and he was right. It finally got to the point where I could no longer be myself around him."

"Ken can sometimes be a little too direct," said CeCe, "but he means well."

"No, he did not mean well at all. He had no respect for my boundaries, and I got tired of constantly having to defend myself. I was ready to call it quits when he got the invitation to his cousin's wedding. He begged me to go with him. He said if he went on his own his aunt would start in about him being over thirty and why hadn't he gotten married yet, and he didn't want the headache. So I went, even though I didn't want to, only to have his bitch of an aunt jump all over me for ordering the pasta instead of the freaking chicken the rest of them were having. Turns out his entire family are all arrogant, condescending, jerks."

"I understand. He's told me all about what happened at the wedding, and he feels terrible about what his aunt said to you. He just wants to have some closure. That's all."

Jenna's voice remained firm. "We already have closure. I sent him a text message as soon as I got home, and we wished each other well. Then he disappeared, only to conveniently reappear the minute Bill came on the scene. I know what he's up to. He's got his undies in a wad because I'm seeing someone else, albeit as a friend, so now he wants to make trouble, and what better way to do it than to put me in a position where I would owe him something. The other day I needed groceries and had to use the gift card to pay for them. So, here's what I'm going to do. I'm going to return the card to you, so you can give it back to Ken, along with a copy of the receipt for the groceries. Tell him I will pay him the remaining balance, with interest, as soon as I'm back to work."

"Jenna, please. I've been telling him not to bother you for some time now, but he kept reassuring me that he means no harm and only wants the best for you. He also promised me there were no strings attached to the gift card. I'll return it if you really want me to, but the groceries were a gift."

"Thanks, but no. I don't want anything from him, and I'm going to pay him back. Every penny, plus interest, like I said before. If I don't, he'll hold it over my head and use it against me. It's over, and I've moved on. He needs to move on as well."

"Okay, you made your point, and I'm really sorry it ended badly. I'll return the gift card. I'd also like to make things up to you by treating you to lunch."

"I appreciate the offer, but no. I don't want anything else about me getting back to Ken. I also want to enjoy the holidays, in peace, without Ken sticking his nose in my business."

"Okay," said CeCe. "I understand."

"I hope you do, because I meant it when I said my private life is private. Whoever I'm seeing or not seeing is none of Ken's damn business, and you can tell him I said it word for word. I appreciate you calling me, but I have other matters to attend to, and I'll make arrangements for someone to drop off the gift card."

"Of course." CeCe waited for a response, but none came. Jenna had already disconnected. She rushed back to her desk and grabbed her phone, pounding out a strong text message for Ken.

"I may be getting fired because of you. I'm done being your go-between. If you want to talk to Jenna, find a way to do it yourself."

She slammed the phone down on her desk and hurried off to the ladies' room to pull herself back together. A message from Ken was waiting when she returned.

"Sorry. I didn't mean to cause any trouble. Call me when you get off work."

ᦞTWENTY-EIGHTᦞ

JENNA STARTED AT her phone in stunned disbelief. Ken had taken advantage of her vulnerability, and CeCe had been his willing accomplice. Her mother was right. She needed to look for a job elsewhere.

"This is madness," she said outload. "I need to sort it all out." She began typing a message to Stacy.

"You won't believe what happened. Ken gave me the gift card, not Oscar."

Stacy replied a few minutes later. *"Seriously?"*

Jenna sighed as she responded. *"He's managed to worm his way back in. What the hell does he want from me?"*

"Gotta get back to work, but I can stop by later and we'll talk."

"I was hoping you would. See you when you get here."

Stacy arrived a few hours later with some Chinese take-out. "I grabbed us some dinner," she said. "Orange chicken and beef with broccoli for you, and kung pao chicken and teriyaki chicken for me."

"Thanks," said Jenna. "I'm starving."

"I also got us some spring rolls, along with a Dr. Pepper for you and iced tea for me."

"You thought of everything. I'll have to return the favor to you later."

"No rush, so let's sit down and you can tell me what happened."

Jenna grabbed some extra napkins and they sat down at the table. "I don't know where to begin."

"You can start with dumping him after the wedding," said Stacy.

"Okay, I will. When I came to work the Monday after the wedding, I thought it would be best to give CeCe as little information as possible. I simply told her it had run its course and the time had come

135

for Ken and I to go our separate ways. I tried to make it sound as upbeat as I could, and I even made a point of saying we'd had some fun times together. I also thanked her for introducing us, but it sure didn't stop her from colluding with him later on."

"I take it this is where the gift card comes in."

"Yep," said Jenna. "I used it to buy some groceries, and I wrote Oscar a thank you note. He, of course, had no idea what I was talking about, so he calls Chad, and that's when her story fell completely apart. You know, CeCe really is in the wrong line of work. She needs to go to Hollywood, because she's one hell of an actress."

"Obviously. You know I've never met her, but based on everything you've told me about her, I thought she sounded a little flakey. Your mother definitely pegged her, but even she underestimated her. CeCe is either dumber than dirt, or Ken has manipulated her as well."

"I think it's a little of both."

"I also agree with your mom. You need to look for another job."

"I'm trying." Jenna picked through her food as she spoke. "Unfortunately, we're getting into the holiday season. I doubt anyone will be hiring until after the first of the year."

"Maybe, maybe not. You never know, so it wouldn't hurt to put more resumes out there. I also think they should have fired CeCe and brought you back in."

"I couldn't agree more, but apparently they didn't, which makes me question their loyalty to me."

"Company politics suck, don't they?" said Stacy. "So, what can I do to help? Would you like me to drop off the gift card for you? It's close to where I work."

"Thanks, but I've got it covered. Chad offered to take me to lunch one day next week, so I'll give it to him. Trust me, he'll make sure CeCe gets it. She sounded really contrite on the phone too. No doubt Chad chewed her out really good."

"She certainly had it coming," said Stacy. "So, you said something the other day about helping Bill set up his new house."

"I am. He's also paying me for my services, although I'm giving him a discount, just like I did for you when you bought your condo."

"Which should help."

"It will," said Jenna. "I have to pay off my credit cards. Those outrageously high interest rates are a killer, so it will be some time before I can pay Ken back."

"I agree. Maybe you can help Bill with something else. Like helping him move into his new studio."

"I already did," said Jenna, "but all he needed was for me to help him unload a few boxes, which only took a few minutes. The rest he has to do himself. He also took me lunch on the way home. However, he did mention something else, but I'm not sure about it."

"Okay. So, what did he mention?"

Jenna set her fork down and looked her friend in the eye. "Something came up about art modeling. You know, like posing for a painting or something. He said it can pay really well."

"What kind of modeling are we talking about?" asked Stacy. "Nude modeling?"

"Sometimes, but not always." Jenna took a deep breath and sighed. "Bill has been, shall we say, rather fascinated, with my tattoo. So much so that he would like to have me model for one of his pieces. He says he'll pay me the same fee he pays his other models, which means it should be enough to help restock the cupboards. He's also willing to refer me to other artists he knows and trusts."

"Well, there you go. He's vetting the people you'd be working with, and it's not like he's never seen you naked before. It's a legit job and it pays well."

Jenna gave her friend a pleading look. "I don't know if I could do it."

"Sure, you can."

"No, I don't think so."

"Why not?"

"I don't want other people seeing me naked, even if it's a statue and not really me."

"Well, I suppose he could make the face look different."

"He already said he would create a generic face," said Jenna, "but I'd still know it was me. So would you, and so would Ken, if he ever saw it."

Stacy rolled her eyes. "Oh, c'mon, Jenna. Remember our infamous night at the tattoo parlor? You had to pull your pants down to your knees so he could ink the rose onto your hip."

"He also gave me a towel so I could cover myself. Then he stepped out of the room until I was ready."

"I know, but he still saw your naked backside while he was working."

"Only from the side. He didn't get a full view."

"Even so," said Stacy, "it didn't seem to bother you at all. Then he got to see mine, in all its glory. It wasn't anything sexual. He was just doing his job. And by the way, Alan loves my tattoo."

Jenna smiled in spite of herself. "Which would be a good thing. It'd be kind of awkward if he didn't."

Stacy chuckled as she picked up her spring roll. "Indeed. However, the point I'm making is he was seeing our bare tushes for professional reasons only. So, if I were in your shoes, and I needed money to keep the lights on, I'd do whatever I had to, even if it meant posing in the buff for an artist, be it Bill, or someone he knows. It's not like you'd be prancing around a strip club in front of a bunch of ogling men. You'd be helping an artist do their job."

"I don't know."

"So would you rather starve?"

"No."

"Then you'll have to do what you have to do until something better comes along."

"We'll see." Jenna turned her attention back to her meal. "So, how is Alan doing these days?"

"He's wonderful." A dreamy look came over Stacy's face. "He's not like anyone I've met before. He's someone I can truly be myself with. He accepts me as I am, and I do the same with him. We're not talking commitment just yet, but lately we've been talking a lot about our dreams and aspirations, and where we want to be a year from now, five years from now, and so on. We're both on the same page."

"Are you thinking that he could be the one?"

"He may very well be. We're seeing each other exclusively. Neither of us is interested in seeing anyone else. He's also starting to introduce me to some of his friends."

"What about his family?" asked Jenna

"They live in Phoenix, but they plan on visiting over the holidays, and he wants me to meet them while they're here. I'm also bringing him to my mom's place for Thanksgiving."

"Then it sounds like it's getting serious."

"I suppose. We'd also like to have you join us one night for a burger at O'Malley's Grill. Bill too, if he'd like."

"I'll ask him," said Jenna, "but even if he can't make it, you know I'll be there."

❧TWENTY-NINE❧

CECE RUSHED DOWN to the parking garage at precisely at five o'clock. Safely inside her car, she placed a call to Ken. "I'm somewhere private," she said. "What about you?"

"I'm in my office, and the door is closed. So, what the hell happened?"

"Jenna sent Oscar a thank you note for the gift card. Oscar then called Chad, and all hell broke loose. First, I got a how come and a what for from Chad and the witch from HR. Then I got a serious talking to from the big boss himself. Let's just say I've had better days at the dentist's office."

"But they didn't fire you," said Ken.

"No, they didn't, but I sure got reprimanded, along with a strong warning. If I so much as sneeze at the wrong time, I'm out the door, which means it's now a become hostile work environment."

"It may feel that way for now, but trust me, it'll blow over."

CeCe reached into her purse for a tissue. "Not when it's been written up in your employee file. As soon as I get home, I'm writing my letter of resignation, and I'm handing it to them first thing tomorrow morning. It'll be good news for Jenna. No doubt they'll bring her back to finish my project."

Ken's voice turned harsh. "You'll do no such thing."

Her stomach dropped and she felt her body tensing up. "I already told you. I'm done doing your dirty work. You'll have to find someone else. Better yet, why don't you do the right thing and let her go? She's moved on, and so should you."

"Sorry CeCe. I didn't mean to come down so hard on you. We all experience really bad days at the office, but they're not firing you proves you're an asset they don't want to lose. So rather than write them a letter of resignation, why don't you write them a letter of apology instead, emphasizing the fact that you were only trying to help a coworker and never intended any harm. By the way, you didn't tell them I'm the one who actually gave her the card, did you?"

"Of course not. I told them it was from me and John."

"Perfect. You did the right thing. So, write the apology letter, and ask them if they would mind putting it to your file. Be sure to keep a copy for yourself as well, even if they do accept it. That way you're covered in case they ever do fire you. You could present it as evidence in a wrongful termination suit."

"Which is the last thing I would ever do," said CeCe. "Getting grilled by Chad was bad enough. There's no way I could handle being cross examined on the witness stand. I'm going to look for a job elsewhere."

"No. Please, I'm begging you. Don't. If you resign, I'll feel guilty as hell, and I don't want to be the reason you quit your job. Think about your retirement account. You know they're investing it wisely, and you don't need to pay someone out of pocket to manage it for you."

"Did you forget something, Ken? I'm married to a banker, and lately we've been talking about starting a family."

"You and John? Having kids? You're kidding, right? You're two active people who are always on the go and don't want to be tied down. Somehow, I can't see either one of you changing diapers. You're the poster couple for happily married without children."

"Maybe for now, but who are you to say we'd never want a family? People change, you know."

"Some do, some don't, and I'll believe it when I see it. What I'm trying to say is you've worked really hard to get where you are, and they didn't fire you. So do your job, and I'll back off about Jenna. I promise. You are now, officially, off the hook, and we won't discuss her anymore."

Finally, CeCe felt better. "Do you really mean it?"

"Of course I mean it. I've never lied to you, and I never will. I've always played it straight with you."

"I know you have."

"So don't worry about losing your job, and thank you again for seeing to it she got the gift card.

"Actually, Ken, she won't have it much longer."

His tone suddenly changed. "What do you mean, she won't have it much longer?"

"She asked me where it came from, and circumstances being what they were, I wasn't about to lie to her again, so I told her the truth. The card came from you, and she doesn't want it anymore. She's going to return it, and she'll pay you back for the groceries she bought with it."

"Oh, so she did use it?"

"She did," said CeCe. "So, as soon as I get it back, I'll send it onto you, and you can use the rest to get something nice for Jeri. I'll let you know when she reimburses me for what she spent, and I'll pass it onto you as well."

"I already got something nice for Jeri."

"Then get something nice for yourself."

"I will, and once again CeCe, I'm really sorry this happened. I promise I'll make it up to you."

CeCe sighed as she disconnected the call started up the engine. Deep down something told her Ken wasn't through with Jenna. Hopefully, she was wrong, but even if she wasn't, it was no longer her concern.

❧THIRTY❧

JENNA NERVOUSLY stepped out of the bathroom, wearing a short-sleeve v-neck dress which had been slightly altered. One of the side seams had been partially taken out to expose her rose tattoo.

"How do I look?" she asked.

"You look good." Bill gave her a closer look. "The dress fits you perfectly, and it looks brand new. You'd never know it came from a thrift store."

"You can find good bargains at thrift stores, but somehow, I can't picture you shopping for dresses."

He gave her a sheepish grin. "I brought Kelsey with me. She's the one who picked it out."

"Kelsey?"

"My daughter-in-law to be."

"Really? Are they getting married?"

"While they're not yet officially engaged just yet, I've offered Connor his mother's wedding set, which he gladly accepted, so I expect to hear an announcement sometime soon. I also plan on giving him the rest of his mother's jewelry once they're married."

"Then I'm happy to for both of them, and please tell her thank you for picking out the perfect dress." She gave him a flirtatious look. "So, how did you know my dress size?"

"It's not what you think. Remember the night at the cabin, when I got your clothes out of the dryer and helped you fold them?"

"How could I forget?"

"I noticed the label in your jeans, and made a mental note. Turns out you and Kelsey wear the same size."

"We seem to have similar tastes too."

"I'm glad you like it. Kelsey says if you want it, you can keep it, but if you don't, she'll be more than happy to take it off your hands."

"She can keep it. I have a similar dress at home, although it's burgundy, not blue."

Bill handed her a bouquet of silk roses. "I know. I've seen you in it a few times. So, are you ready?"

"I think so."

"As I said before, the final piece will have a different face."

Her face had a slight blush. "I'm know, but if Stacy sees it, she'll know it's me."

"Then I'll let you decide if you want her to see it or not." Bill pointed to the photography lights. "I need you to stand over there."

Jenna took her place in front of the lights, taking Bill's direction as he told her where he wanted her to stand.

"This is for a wood relief titled Rose-Colored Dreams, and you'll be walking past some rose bushes in the final piece. I want you to hold the roses in front of you, and put your front leg forward, as if you were walking, so we can see the tattoo."

Jenna did as she was told, but Bill frowned and shook his head.

"Anything wrong?" she asked.

"I'm not seeing the entire tattoo. I need to find something to pin back part of the dress."

"You're in luck. I brought along a box of safety pins. They're in my tote bag."

"You stay here. I'll go get them." Bill ran into the bathroom, returning a moment later with a small box. He removed one of the pins and walked up to Jenna.

"Be really careful where you stick that thing," she teasingly said.

He teased her back. "Jenna Winters, I'm shocked you would even think such a thing. Now I need you to hold really still."

Jenna held her breath as she felt him pull the fabric back and carefully pin it into place. He brushed her hip once he finished.

"You naughty girl," he said playfully. "You're not wearing any underwear."

"No, I'm not. Panties would cover the tattoo, although I'm still wearing a bra."

"Interesting, but we need to get back to work. So front leg forward, as if you were walking, and turn your head toward towards me. Perfect. Are you okay with the lights?"

"I'm fine. They're not shining in my eyes."

"Okay. I need you to hold your position while I'll get my camera."

Jenna held her breath while Bill snapped photos from different angles. He soon announced they were done.

"That's it?" she asked.

"Yep. You can relax now." He took the silk roses and handed her an envelope. Jenna raised her brow once she opened it.

"Are you serious? It's more than enough to stock up on groceries."

"It's like I told you before. Art modeling can pay really well. I still do it on the side for rainy-day money." He handed her a card from his work table. "Rhonda Barrett is a painter who's up on the third floor. She's a good lady and I've known her for years. Her favorite subject matter is fantasy and mythology, and she's currently working on a series of nudes inspired by ancient Roman deities. I posed for her just before I left for Florida. It paid for my meals along the way."

"Were you...?" she awkwardly asked.

"Well, if it means anything, I was wearing a silk laurel wreath. Rhonda prefers to work from sketches instead of photos, so I was posing as Bacchus, the Roman god of winemaking."

"You mean you weren't Apollo?"

"Very funny. I was about to say she's highly professional and easy to work with. She also pays a generous fee, especially for nude work. I have a photo of the study painting she sent me the other day. Would you like to see it?"

"Sure."

Bill grabbed his phone and punched a few buttons before handing it to Jenna. An image of a nude man tending a lush country vineyard with a Roman aqueduct in the background filled the screen.

"I can see some resemblance," she said. "While he definitely has your hair, his face has higher check bones and more chiseled features."

"He is the Roman god after all, while yours truly is a humble artist and teacher. My point is she uses the model as a reference. She's not doing life-like portraits. I also know you're going through some lean times, and I don't want you missing meals or shivering in a cold house, so please call her if you run short on cash. You'd also be helping her out as well. She has an opening coming up in March, and she needs to get the rest of the series done. In the meantime, are you ready for Thanksgiving?"

"I think so, although I'm feeling a little anxious about meeting Connor and Kelsey."

"You'll like Connor. We have the same quirky sense of humor, and while he's not the creative type, Kelsey is. Along with sewing, she knits and crochets. She and her sister sell their wares online."

"My mother does needlepoint," said Jenna. "I tried it a few times, but I was all thumbs. I really enjoy interior design and I miss doing it. It's another reason why I'm anxious to get back to work."

"I'm moving into my new home soon."

"I know, and I can't wait to get started on it."

"I also know someone's birthday is coming up."

"I know, but I was planning on keeping it low key this year."

"Now, now," he said, "turning thirty isn't the end of the world. Quite the contrary. It's when your life starts to get interesting."

"It's interesting enough already. I just want to get back to work."

"I know you do. And speaking of, did you return the gift card?"

"Yes," said Jenna. "Chad took me to lunch last Thursday, so I gave it to him. Something tells me he gave CeCe another talking to when he gave it to her."

"I would certainly hope so. I also agree with Stacy and your parents. They should have fired her and brought you back on board."

"I feel the same. Unfortunately, I can't change office politics, which is why I'm still sending out resumes. With any luck, I'll find a position somewhere else, and I'll never have to deal with her again. Or Ken for that matter." It was time to change the subject.

"So can I see the photos?"

"Of course." Bill touched the menu bar and they looked at the photos together. "They look great," he said. "You take direction well, and you look very natural. This will be a beautiful piece when it's done."

"When will you start working on it?"

"Right after the holidays. I need some time to fix up the house and get the shed ready. In the meantime, I've decided my first bronze with be the piece Salisbury passed on."

"The bighorn sheep?"

"Yes, although it'll be smaller than originally planned."

"It's a lovely piece and I'm glad you're doing it. So, for now, if you'll excuse me, I need to change back into my jeans. I'm feeling a draft where I normally don't feel one."

"You are?" He gave her a playful look as he brushed her backside. "I have a better idea."

"Not now," she said.

"Aw, c'mon."

"I need to buy some groceries. My cupboards are practically empty, and I don't like going shopping after dark."

"Come to think of it, I need to go to the store myself, so why don't I go with you? I'll even throw in some hot dogs and a can of chili, if you're up for chili dogs and dominos. I still can't believe you beat me the last time."

"Well. I did, and you're on. Just give me a couple of minutes to change." Jenna hurried off to the bathroom, feeling happier than she had felt in a long time. Giving his late wife's jewelry to Connor meant Bill was finally moving on.

❧THIRTY-ONE❧

KEN RAN UP A flight of concrete stairs and hurried along the balcony. A winter storm was coming in and the winds were picking up. He stopped at the third door and gave it a firm knock. It opened a moment later. Jeri greeted him with an uneasy smile.

"I'm glad you could make it," she said.

He brushed a few tiny snowflakes off his jacket. "You said you needed to talk, and I wanted to get here before it really starts snowing."

"I know, and it won't take long. So please, have a seat, and can I get you anything?"

He made himself comfortable on the sofa. "I'm good," he said. "So, what's so urgent?"

She sat down in the chair across from him and gave him a serious look. "As you know, I'll complete my MBA in a few weeks, and while I was hoping to get a promotion at work, my boss has informed me it won't be happening. He said I'm free to stay on as office manager for as long as I like, but he has all the outside sales force he needs for the time being. So, I've been sending out resumes and applying for positions online, and I finally have an offer. It's an entry level management position with a major food manufacturing company, with plenty of room for advancement. It's the perfect fit for me, and if it works out, I could have a job for life."

"Then I'm happy for you. So, when would you start?"

"The first of the year. However, there's more to it."

"Okay, so what are you trying to tell me?"

"It's not in Colorado. I'd be moving to Boston."

He tried to conceal his surprise. "I see. So, have you accepted?"

"No, I haven't. I wanted to talk to you about it first."

"I understand. So, if you were to accept, when would you leave?"

"Immediately."

Once again, Ken was caught off guard. He had planned on ending the relationship after the holidays were over.

"Why so soon?" he asked. "It's not like you'd be starting next week. You haven't even finished your last class yet."

"I'm pretty much done with school, and I can finish up what's left online. However, if I were to move to Boston, I would want to spend some time with my family before heading east, which means I would go back to Las Vegas for a few weeks. And even if I don't take the job, I still I promised my mother I'd be home for Thanksgiving. You already told me you're taking a ski vacation with your family."

"Our Thanksgivings in Steamboat Springs have been a family tradition for years, and I'm happy to know you'll be spending the holiday with your family as well. So, are you going to accept the job or not?"

She shrugged her shoulders. "As I said, I haven't decided yet. So far, every time I've asked you about where things were going with us, you said you weren't ready to make a commitment. Then you'd change the subject."

"I did not," he said firmly. "What I said was it was too soon to have the discussion."

"We've been seeing one another for nearly a year, which is a long time for casual dating, and I want to know where I stand."

He gave her a hard look. "If there were a problem, I'd let you know. What I'd like to know is why were you looking for an out of state job."

"I already told you. I posted my resume on all the major job-hunting websites. They contacted me. I never approached them"

"So, when did you talk to them?"

"My first interview was three days ago, then they followed up with me earlier today. Now, in case you're wondering, I didn't take any out-of-town trips without telling you. We did video conference calls, and I most certainly never expected them to offer me the job. But to be completely honest, it's too good of an opportunity for me to pass up."

"Are you at least trying to find a job in Colorado?"

She was becoming defensive. "Of course, I was trying to find a job in Colorado. I've been looking for some time now, but the right one hasn't come along yet." She started blinking back tears. "If you had told me you were in it for the long-term, I would have thanked them for their interest and declined the interview, but so far, whenever I brought up any job prospects, you acted like you weren't interested. You kept telling me to do what I thought is best for me."

"Because I wasn't expecting you to consider a job out of state," he said sternly. "The fact that you even interviewed with them without telling me beforehand, speaks volumes. If you love me as much as you say you do, you would have declined the interview and kept looking until you found a job here."

"Wow," she said. "You're making it impossible for me to win, aren't you? You never once wanted to discuss where we were going or whether or not we had a future together. Now you're angry with me over a job offer I haven't even accepted, and you still won't tell me if you're willing to make a commitment or not."

"I never said I wouldn't marry you someday."

"Ken, I've been honest and upfront about my feelings for you from the get go. So, do I have a future with you or not? If I do, then would you be willing to move to Boston? I know it would be a big move, and you certainly wouldn't have to leave right away, but accountants are always in demand, so you know you'd find a good job once you got there. And if I don't have a future with you, then would you at least be honest enough to tell me? I have a right to know where I stand, because I don't want to waste my time with someone who isn't willing to make a commitment to me."

He would have to end it with her, but at least he would have the final say. "Okay, Jeri, I'm going to be brutally honest with you. I like you. I like you a lot. I've sincerely enjoyed your company, and we've had a lot of fun together. However, I just don't hear the violins playing. I honestly wish I did, but I don't. Sorry."

Her face flushed with anger. "So, how long you were going to string me along? A few more weeks? Another six months? Or were you planning on keeping me hanging indefinitely?"

"You know, I honestly couldn't tell you. All I can say is I've been perfectly happy with the status quo, and I saw no reason to change it."

Her eyes narrowed into slits. "You've been leading me on the entire time, haven't you? You thought all you had to do was to keep telling me you weren't ready to make a commitment, yet, because you were really waiting for something better to come along, weren't you?"

"I never made any promises."

"And I never made any promises either."

She hopped up and ran down the hallway. Ken braced himself in anticipation of the expected emotional outburst. Jeri returned a few seconds later, and she appeared oddly calm.

"Here's your toothbrush and razor. I'll put them in a plastic bag for you, and then you can be on your way."

"Don't worry about it." He stood and grabbed his jacket. "I have a toothbrush and razor at home. Maybe you could keep them as a souvenir. Something to remember me by once you get to Boston."

"Nah." She stepped into the kitchen and dropped them in the wastebasket. "I do, however, want to thank you for letting me know you think I should accept the job. It's going to be one of the best decisions I ever made. So now, if you'll excuse me, I have to reply to a very important email, and time is of the essence. Oh, by the way, did I mention there are plenty of single men in Boston? I can't wait to start meeting them. Hopefully, the next one won't turn out to be a self-centered—"

"Whatever, Jeri. So, if you're done, I'll be on my way, and it's your loss."

"Yeah, and I'll miss you like I'd miss having a toothache. Just don't let the door hit you on the way out."

"Whatever." Ken had barely closed the door behind him when he heard the latch turn. While disappointed she hadn't tearfully begged him to not to leave, he at least got to have the last word. The snow began falling in earnest as he drove out of the parking lot.

* * *

CeCe looked surprised when she answered the door. "Where's Jeri?" she asked.

"She couldn't make it." Ken handed CeCe the pizza boxes and quickly stepped inside. "I see you have a fire in the fireplace."

"It's that time of year. So, what happened to Jeri?"

"We're not seeing one another anymore."

"What?" CeCe set the pizza boxes on the counter with a thump. "So, when did this happen?"

"A few days ago. She accepted a job with a company in Boston."

"Are you serious?"

"I'm afraid so."

"So, you just let her go?"

John had a concerned look on his face as he came into the kitchen. "If everything okay in here?"

"Ken tells me he and Jeri broke up. She just took a job out of state."

"Sorry to hear it," said John.

"We had a long discussion about it, and we both agreed she probably wouldn't find this good of an opportunity again, so we wished one another well."

CeCe remained unconvinced. "Ken, I've known you over ten years, so trust me when I tell you she was the perfect match for you. You're both career oriented. You're both into sports. You have the same sense of humor, and you had a lot of other common interests as well. I kept telling you she was a keeper, and you'd be a fool if you let her get away from you."

"We talked about my going to Boston with her, but it simply wouldn't have been a good move for me. I've worked very hard to build up a good clientele, and I didn't want to have to start over."

"So, you're saying there are no accounting firms in Boston? Sheesh. Good accountants are always in demand, and who knows? You may have found a better job than the one you have here. I really think you should let her know you've changed your mind. John and I would miss having you around, but you'd be better off in Boston, and you know we'd come visit you."

John set some plates on the counter while CeCe and Ken were talking. "The pizzas are ready, whenever you are," he said

Everyone helped themselves, and as they sat down at the table the conversation turned to other topics. Ken looked forward to hitting the slopes in Steamboat Springs while John and CeCe would enjoy a quiet Thanksgiving at home.

"Some of us have to work on Black Friday," said John, "and CeCe likes to get up early and hit the sales."

"Although these days I'm doing more of my holiday shopping online," said CeCe. "I also make my famous turkey chili on Black Friday."

"Which is something I look forward to every year," said Ken.

"So, getting back Jeri," said CeCe. "Will she be going with you to Steamboat Springs?"

"No. She promised her mother she'd be home for Thanksgiving, so she's busy moving out of her apartment as we speak. She wants to spend time with her family before the big move."

"So why don't you hop a plane to Las Vegas while she's there? I'm sure she'd love to see you, and maybe you could go with her to Boston. You haven't had a real vacation in years, and you just might like it there. There's probably more of art and culture in Boston than there is here. There's a lot of history there as well."

"Jeri and I were never into art and culture. We had a hard enough time trying to figure out the meaning of the famous sculpture at Shelton Inn."

"It's an abstract piece," said CeCe. "It's up to the viewer to decide what it means."

"Which is what we thought. And speaking of the Shelton Inn, is Jenna back to work yet?"

CeCe's demeanor instantly changed. "No, she isn't back yet. I don't expect to see her until sometime in January."

"It's okay. I was just wondering, and I guess it's a good thing I didn't use the gift card to buy something lavish for Jeri."

"You could certainly use it to cover part of your travel expenses to Boston. I still think letting her go would be a big mistake."

"I'm afraid it just wasn't meant to be. I mean I liked her and all, but she just wasn't the one." He quickly turned his attention to John. "So, how are things going at the bank these days?"

"Busy. A lot of people are applying for mortgages. They want to lock in the best rates while they can."

"I hear you. I've been advising some of my own clients to do the same. So, did Jenna ever come to see you?"

"I can't tell you if she did or not because of client confidentiality."

"I understand. I was just wondering how she's doing."

"So far as I know, she's doing fine," said CeCe. "However, I'm still looking for work elsewhere. People are avoiding me because word has gotten out about the gift card fiasco. I'm even hearing whispers about how they should have fired me and brought her back. The only reason I still have a job is because the project I'm working on has already had several costly delays, and having to bring someone else in to take over for me could complicate matters further. Unfortunately, there isn't much left for me do, and I have a feeling they won't be sending any new work my way anytime soon."

"Yeah, but work always slows down over the holidays," said Ken.

"Sometimes, but not always," said CeCe.

"The point my wife is making is it's turned into a hostile work environment for her," said John, "which is also creating stress for us at home. We've been talking about cancelling our ski weekends this year, and maybe scaling back on our holiday celebration in order to give her the option of setting up shop on her own."

"Really?" Ken said, raising his brow.

"I'm keeping my options open," CeCe said firmly. "We'll have to see what transpires over the next few weeks."

✥THIRTY-TWO✥

BILL REACHED INTO his coat pocket as their server cleared their empty plates away. Jenna's face lit up when he presented her with a small, gift-wrapped box.

"Happy Birthday," he said.

"Can I open it now?"

"Of course you can open it now."

She tore off the wrapping paper and slowly opened the box. Inside was silk scarf with an abstract design and an indigo border. She smiled as she held it up.

"I love it," she said. "The pastel colors are beautiful, and the pattern reminds me of some of my glassware. It'll go perfect with the pink sweater my parents gave me."

"I'm glad you like it. So, how does it feel to be thirty?"

"I'm not sure. It's been such a busy day I haven't had much time to think about it." As Jenna was speaking their server, along with several others, arrived with a sparkling candle on a big slice of cake. She looked at Bill as they sang "Happy Birthday" to her.

"Okay, you got me," she said, "but you know I'll get you back on your birthday."

"Which won't be until next August."

"I know, and I'm sorry I missed it this year."

"It wasn't much of a celebration. The house I wanted to buy had failed its inspection a few days before. I was trying to cancel the contract, and let's just say the sellers weren't being cooperative. By the time we finally got everything settled, the problem with Connor had started up."

"How's he doing?" asked Jenna.

"Much better. So far, he likes his new job, and he and Kelsey are settled in their new apartment. She had a really good job interview the day before yesterday, and we're hoping she'll get an offer. So, are you looking forward to meeting them?"

"I think so. Hopefully, they'll like me."

"You have nothing to worry about," said Bill. "Connor likes just about everyone, and Kelsey is really looking forward to meeting you."

"I look forward to meeting her as well. So, what would you like me to bring? I can't show up at someone's home for Thanksgiving dinner empty handed."

"It's okay, Jenna. They understand. Kelsey is still looking for a job, so dinner is on Connor and me."

"I know, but my mother taught me to always bring something, So, how about a package of dinner rolls?"

"If it makes you feel better, you can bring the rolls, but it really isn't necessary.

* * *

Jenna slept in on Thanksgiving morning and enjoyed her coffee in front of the Macy's Thanksgiving Day Parade. Her phone beeped as she watched the floats go by. Her mother had sent a text message. She was enjoying her coffee in the airport lounge while her father was out on the tarmac doing his preflight inspection. Once the parade was over, Jenna tidied up the kitchen and took a shower. Bill would pick her up at one o'clock. He had told her to wear something casual, so she grabbed a pair of nearly new dark blue jeans. They would go perfectly with her new pink sweater and birthday scarf.

Bill greeted her with a bright smile as he came inside. "You look fabulous," he said.

"Thanks. A really good friend gave me a beautiful scarf for my birthday, but enough about me. How's the move coming along?"

"So far so good. I got the kitchen cabinets done. Turned out all they needed was a little sanding and a new coat of stain. The new flooring goes in tomorrow, and Saturday we get the rest of my stuff."

"I know. I'll be there helping you set everything up."

"Which I very much appreciate, and it'll be nice not having to camp out in my studio."

"Did Sally ever find out?"

"If she did, she never mentioned it."

"I think she has a crush on you," Jenna said, jokingly.

"Somehow, I doubt it. Meanwhile Connor is expecting us, so we need to get going." Jenna grabbed the dinner rolls and they hurried out to Bill's Explorer.

* * *

"It looks like Connor isn't the only one who invited guests over for Thanksgiving," said Bill. They were driving around the parking lot in search of an empty space, but the lot was completely full. "Hopefully, I can find a space in the other visitor's lot."

He drove to the other side of the complex, finally finding an open spot behind another building. "Good thing you're wearing flats. It's going to be a bit of a walk from here to Connor's apartment."

"At least the weather's good," said Jenna. "Hiking on a snowy sidewalk wouldn't have been fun."

"No, it wouldn't, and let's hope it holds out for tomorrow and Saturday." He handed her a bottle of chardonnay and grabbed a pair of grocery bags. They hurried past a big courtyard and two other buildings. Turning a corner, Bill approached a door on the ground floor and rang the bell. Connor greeted his dad with a smile, but he looked a little surprised when he saw Jenna. Bill quickly introduced her as a very dear friend. Kelsey greeted her with a warm hug, but Connor seemed more reserved, giving her a smile and a handshake.

"The turkey should be ready in another thirty minutes or so," said Connor. "In the meantime, we have some snack mix on the coffee table, and we've got the game on. We also have plenty of beer and soda in the refrigerator, so please help yourselves."

"Are you sure you don't need any help?" asked Jenna.

"Positive. Thanks for the offer, but we've got it all figured out."

Bill motioned to Jenna to take a seat on the sofa while he got their drinks. She gave him a concerned look as he sat down next to her. "You okay?" she asked.

"I'm fine," he said, keeping his voice low, "but this is their first-time doing Thanksgiving."

Connor spoke up from the kitchen. "We've got it covered, Dad. Kelsey happens to be a very good cook, and you taught me well."

"I know. I'm just saying I'm here if you need anything."

"What I need is for you to keep your eye on the game, and let me know what's happening."

Thirty minutes later Connor took the turkey from the oven and announced it was done.

"Good timing," said Bill. "There's eight and a half minutes left to go in the fourth quarter, and our team has the ball, which should get the turkey plenty of time to rest."

Kelsey looked at Connor. "Go watch the game. I can take care of the mashed potatoes and gravy."

"You're sure?" he asked.

"Yes, I'm sure. You're in my way, so scoot."

"Yes, ma'am." Connor grabbed a beer while Jenna hopped up from the sofa and offered him her seat.

"I'll keep Kelsey company so you and your dad can hang out."

Kelsey looked relieved when Jenna came in to join her. They chatted as they worked.

"I still need to find more winter clothes," said Kelsey, "but I dread the thought of going to the mall on Black Friday."

"Not to worry," said Jenna. "I know of a few consignment stores which probably won't be as busy, as long as you don't mind buying slightly used."

"Not at all. The job I was hoping for fell through, so I really need to watch my budget."

"Sorry, to hear it. Been there myself."

"So, I hear," said Kelsey. "Hopefully, you'll be back at work soon."

"Me too, but for now I have plenty of free time, and since you're still new in town, I'd be happy to take you if you'd like."

"Thanks, I'd love it. By the way, I heard all about Dad's sculpture and the hotel you helped design. We haven't had a chance to see it yet, but we're hoping to make it there soon."

"Thanks. So, what kind of job are you looking for?"

"I have a business degree," said Kelsey, "and my last job was with a law firm. I was working as a legal secretary."

"Sounds interesting."

"It was."

"Is that how you met Connor?"

"No. We actually met at a mutual friend's birthday party, but when everything started unraveling, I was able to help him find a good lawyer." She turned her attention back to the stove. "Okay. The mashed potatoes are done. Now I need to make the gravy, but I'm not exactly sure how to go about it. I planned on using gravy from a jar, but we forgot to buy it."

"I've got you." Jenna quickly grabbed the turkey baster. "If you'll bring me a pan for the drippings, along with some corn starch and milk, I'll show you how it's done. If you don't have corn starch, flour will work."

The gravy was soon ready and Kelsey began setting the table. The game ended as they brought out the last serving dishes. Taking their seats, Connor uncorked the chardonnay and filled their wine glasses.

"It smells wonderful," said Bill. "Looks like you kids did alright."

"You'll have to thank Jenna for the gravy," said Kelsey. "I wasn't sure how to make it." They quickly filled their plates and enjoyed their feast as they reminisced about other family Thanksgivings. Afterwards, Connor excused himself while Kelsey and Jenna brought out the pumpkin pie. Connor returned a minute later with an envelope in his hand.

"I got another letter from my attorney," said Connor. "While my old boss still refuses to admit any wrong doing, they're offering me a generous cash settlement."

"How much?" asked Bill.

"It's all right here." He handed his father the envelope and Bill quickly looked it over.

"So, they're offering you thirty-five grand, plus court costs and attorney fees," said Bill. "Not bad, but they still caused you a lot of damage."

"I know they did. However, I was able to find a new job fairly quickly, and with better pay. My attorney and I had a long discussion about it. We could still take them to court, and I could possibly end up with a much bigger settlement. However, there's no guarantee we'd win, and even if we did, there's no guarantee they'd pay. Then there's the other matter. Even if Angela were to be convicted of embezzlement, there were no witnesses at the meeting I had with her, so it would be her word against mine."

"She's not the injured party," Bill firmly said. "You are."

"I know, Dad, but if she were to take the stand my attorney would have to discredit her, which could get really ugly. And even though she was clearly in the wrong, I don't want to lose my case because she started balling and it made us look like we were bullying her. I just want to put it all behind me and move forward."

Bill looked at Kelsey. "What about you?"

"We've talked it over, and I think he should take the settlement. I've seen people with stronger cases than his take it to court and end up losing. Connor's already been through enough."

"He has indeed." Bill looked at his son. "You need to do what you think is best for you. If you want to take the settlement, I'll support you. If you want to take it to trial, I'll support you as well. It's entirely up to you."

"It's not going to trial," said Connor, "because I'm taking the settlement. We'll put the money into our future house fund."

* * *

"So, what did you think?" asked Bill as they drove out of the parking lot.

"I like Kelsey. You know how you can sometimes meet people and you feel like you've known them your entire life? She's one of those people. She's like the younger sister I never had but always wanted."

"I noticed the two of you hit it off right away and I'm glad you liked her. So, what about Connor?"

"He looks a lot like you, and you have similar mannerisms as well, but I really didn't get to talk to him very much."

"He was busy being a good host and making sure everything came together, and he did an outstanding job. His mother was good at that sort of thing."

"So would you like to spend the night?" she asked.

"As tempting as it sounds, I'll have to take a raincheck. The floor installers arrive tomorrow morning, eight o'clock sharp."

"I know. I'll be stopping by later to check their progress, but your studio isn't in the best part of town, and I don't want you walking around there this late at night."

"Not to worry my dear. I brought my air mattress home. So, if you're free tomorrow night, we can grab a burger and see where we go from there."

"You got a deal."

Bill was anxious to get home once he dropped Jenna off. As expected, Connor had sent him a text message, thanking him for coming. Bill smiled as he texted back.

"You're welcome. You and Kelsey did a great job. So, what did you think of Jenna?"

Connor didn't respond. No doubt he was busy helping with the cleanup. Bill went to change into his sweats. A reply from Connor was waiting when he returned, but he frowned as he read the message.

"She's certainly charming and likable, but I was expecting someone closer to your age."

Bill quickly typed a response. *"You may recall my telling you she was one of my students when I was in grad school. However, we're just friends. I have no intention of marrying her, or anyone else for that matter."* He set the phone aside with a sigh and headed off to bed.

⟡THIRTY-THREE⟡

BILL'S MOVE HAD gone smoother than expected. His furniture, along with the remaining boxes from the storage unit, were now in his new home. Jenna stayed after Connor and Kelsey left to help him hang pictures and organize the kitchen and master bedroom. Afterwards, he took her to dinner at a nearby steakhouse. When they returned, he made love to her his new bedroom. His next task was to set up his woodshop, along with the photography studio in the basement. A few unopened boxes remained afterwards, but none contained any essential items. He would unpack them at his leisure.

Chad called Jenna two weeks later. Salisbury and Norton would host its annual employee holiday party on Friday afternoon, and he wanted her to be there.

"It sounds like you know something I don't," she said. "So, what's up? Do you know who won Employee of the Year?"

"You know they keep that information under wraps. I did, however, find out that we got the prospective project I was telling you about."

"The new restaurant in Cherry Creek?"

"Yep, and while it's not official just yet, the big boss told me, in so many words, it's a done deal and it'll be my project."

It took Jenna a moment to find her voice. "Are you serious?"

"Have I ever lied to you?"

"Of course not. So, when do we start?"

"Right after the holidays, although I don't have the exact date just yet. Hopefully, I'll know more by Friday, which is another reason why I want you to come to the party."

"You don't know how relieved I am to hear this. So will the party be at the usual time?"

"Yes," said Chad. "Three o'clock, in the mezzanine, and I'd like to take you to lunch beforehand so we can discuss the project. Can you be here by one o'clock?"

"You bet I'll be there. One o'clock sharp."

* * *

Jenna greeted her coworkers with a smile as she and Chad came into the mezzanine. CeCe was across the room, chatting with other employees. Chad excused himself to talk to another architect while Paige greeted her with a hug.

"It's good to see you," she said.

"It's good to see you too," said Jenna, "and if all goes according to plan, you'll be seeing a lot more of me. Very soon."

"So I hear, and I'm really looking forward to having you back. In the meantime, have a Merry Christmas."

"You too."

As Paige stepped away Jenna went up to the refreshment table to get something to drink. Opening a can of Dr. Pepper, she heard a familiar voice.

"Well, look who's here," said CeCe. "I'm glad you came."

Jenna's response was cool but polite. "I really wasn't planning on coming this year, but Chad insisted."

"I'm glad he did. I hear you're going to be working on a new project."

"We are, but I don't know exactly when. Please tell Ken I'll have the rest of his money for him soon."

"It was a gift. You don't need to pay him back. I also meant it when I said I'm not his go-between anymore."

"I understand. I'm just saying I intend to pay him back, with interest. He'll get the money after the first of the year."

"You'll have to do whatever you think is best," said CeCe, "but if you need to talk to him, you'll have to contact him yourself."

"I blocked his number."

CeCe gave her an odd look. "Then I guess you'll have to unblock him. Trust me, he's not going to bite you. But anyway, Merry Christmas, and I'll see you when you get back."

As CeCe stepped away, Chad motioned to Jenna to join him.

"I noticed you looked uncomfortable while you were talking to her," he said under his breath.

"I was. As anxious as I am to be back, I'm not looking forward to being around her."

"I understand. Rumor has it she's been sending out resumes."

"What about the big project she was working on?"

"It's done. They finished up right before Thanksgiving. She's taking her vacation Christmas week, and with any luck she won't be back. If it were up to me, she would have been out the door weeks ago. However, she appears to have friends in high places, which explains why she's still here."

"You gotta love office politics," said Jenna, "but don't worry, I can handle her."

Robert Lacy began tapping on his glass. Once he had everyone's attention, he thanked them for their hard work over the past year and told them to expect a busy year ahead. "And now for the moment you've all been waiting for." He motioned to a nearby table, where a cloth covered several small items.

"You know, it seems like every year it gets harder for us to decide on the employee of the year. Each and every one of you did an outstanding job, and you can all give yourselves a big pat on the back. This year, however, we had someone who truly went above and beyond the call of duty. So, without any further ado, I would like to congratulate Chad Runyan for The Shelton Inn at The Denver Tech Center."

Everyone began clapping as Robert's assistant removed the cloth and presented him with an engraved plaque. Chad had a big smile as he held it up while other employees snapped photos of him and Robert with their phones.

"I want to thank Robert and the other senior partners," said Chad. "I know I had some stiff competition because like the man said, each and every one of you did an outstanding job this year, and next year will be even better."

"But wait, there's more," said Robert. His assistant scooped up three small gift boxes from the table. "We have something for the rest of your team as well, so congratulations to Mitch Harper, Jim Langly, and Jenna Winters."

Jenna and the two other architects came up to accept their gifts. Inside each box was a personally engraved brass pen set. Jenna brushed her fingers across her name. "I don't know what to say. They're absolutely beautiful, but it feels strange getting this while I'm on furlough."

"Not for much longer." Once again, Chad lowered his voice. "And if our friend is wise, she'll move onto greener pastures, which means you'll have seniority over whoever replaces her." As Jenna admired her pen set, Chad stepped away so CeCe could congratulate her.

"I'm so happy for you," she said. "If anyone deserved an award this year, it's you."

Jenna looked into CeCe's eyes and realized the compliment was genuine. "Then I guess it must have been because of all your pep talks."

"Nah. You really did an outstanding job. John and I have been back there several times since you've been gone, and we plan on going to Sam's Place for dinner on New Year's Eve."

"Will you be staying at the hotel overnight?"

"We thought about it, but we opted for an early dinner instead, followed by a nice quiet evening at home."

"Which is the best way to do it," said Jenna. "There are so many crazies on the road on New Year's Eve."

"There sure are. What about you?"

"I'm not sure. We haven't made any plans yet."

"I take it you're still seeing Bill."

"Yes. We're still good friends. He's been busy settling into his new house and getting back to creating his art."

"I hear he's in a new gallery."

"He is," said Jenna. "He's now at Anthony Sorenson Fine Art, and he'll have his next opening sometime in May. He also mentioned something the other day about a gallery in Taos which has expressed an interest as well."

"Good for him. Please let him know I'm still sending people his way, and congrats again on the award."

❧THIRTY-FOUR❧

KEN MANAGED TO grab the last open table, but it was on the far side of the room, making it difficult to see the front door. He sipped his beer as he watched the crowd. It was a busier than usual Friday night, thanks to the upcoming holidays. The door opened and several more people came inside. This time he spotted Greg, who was busy brushing the snowflakes off his jacket. Ken raised his hand, but it took a moment for him to catch Greg's eye. A server approached his table as Greg hung his jacket over the back of the other chair and sat down.

"I'll have whatever he's having," said Greg.

"Coors draft, and make it two." Ken turned his attention to Greg. "Is it starting to snow already?"

"Just flurries for now, but the wind is really picking up. They're still saying the brunt of the storm won't be here until after midnight. So, is there anything interesting happening around here?"

"Not a thing." Ken set his empty beer mug off to the side. "So far, every decent looking woman I've seen is either with a guy, or with a big group of friends."

"'Tis the season, I suppose. Bummer things didn't work out with Jeri."

"Stuff happens. She got a job offer she couldn't refuse, and I told her to go for it."

"I remember you telling me. Are you staying in touch with her?"

"Nope. We've both moved on."

"Oh, well," said Greg. "There's plenty more where she came from. So, tell me. What was she like?"

"What do you mean?"

"You know. What was she like?"

"Oh, gotcha. Actually, she wasn't bad." Ken gave him a knowing smile. "Not bad at all. She liked to please, and she was always very appreciative in return, if you know what I mean."

"Or so you say."

"No complaints so far." Ken's demeanor suddenly changed. "She was fun alright, but she just wasn't Jenna. "

Someone dropped off their beer and Greg eagerly took a swig. "Didn't you say things were winding down with her?"

"They were. However, I planned on going a few more rounds with her before I let her go. But then, thanks to my aunt—"

"I remember," said Greg, "but at least Jeri came along around the same time."

"She did, and I honestly liked her, but she just wasn't Jenna. She had style all her own."

Greg looked intrigued. "Did she now?"

"Yep." Ken looked around to make sure no one could overhear. "She's a good-looking woman to begin with, and she's even more amazing with her clothes off."

"Really? Tell me more."

"For starters, she's a natural blonde."

"Interesting...don't really see it as often as you'd think," said Greg.

"She also has perfect proportions and would make any centerfold jealous. Her boobs were just the right size too. Big, but not too big. They fit my hand just right, and I loved giving them a good squeeze. Then, when I went down to the playground, she didn't hold anything back."

"Kept the neighbors up, did she?"

Ken gave his friend a leering grin. "Let's just say I was grateful my common wall was at the garage, and not the bedroom. She was one hell of a performer, and she put on a damn good show."

"Nympho, huh?"

"Actually, no. You know she'd been married before."

"Really? I did not know that."

"She was," said Ken. "She said they were both really young at the time, and they waited until their honeymoon. She said they both felt shy, being as they were both inexperienced, so they learned how to give one another nonverbal cues."

"Sure sounds like it. Did she say what happened with the husband?"

"Not really. She just said they were both too young and should have waited until they finished college. So, fast forward about ten years. CeCe wants to fix me up with one of her coworkers. I wasn't sure at first, but CeCe's a good friend, so I went along with it and met Jenna for coffee. It was obvious from the start that she was a really bright woman, but I could also tell she was the type who wants to get to know you before she puts out. I figured she'd be worth the wait, and it paid off. But then, a few months later, the new car smell started wearing off. However, I wasn't quite finished with her yet. You know the rest of the story."

Greg looked puzzled. "Wait a minute. Didn't you say she's seeing someone else?"

"She is, for now, but he's not a keeper. He's quite a bit older than she is, and, according to CeCe, they're just good friends."

"With benefits."

"So I'm told, but again, according to CeCe, he's a widower with no intention of ever remarrying."

"Tough break for him," said Greg. "It must have been quite a loss."

"Apparently it was, but here's the thing. Jenna got furloughed from her job a few weeks ago, so I bought her a gift card to help her out. CeCe was supposed to give it to her anonymously. Later on, when she was back at work, I'd come clean, and try to win her back. But then CeCe being CeCe; she screwed up and Jenna found out it came from me. So now she's trying to figure out a way to get the money to pay me back, and I have to admit it's been fun imagining her doing whatever she has to do to get the money. Then, once she has it, I'm telling her to keep it. If she wants to pay me back, she'll have to do it on my terms, if you know what I mean. Then, once I'm completely satisfied, I'm kicking her out to the curb."

Greg suddenly looked uncomfortable. "Wait a minute. It's one thing to take her out for a drink, and then one thing leads to another, but it almost sounds like you're trying to force yourself on her."

Ken gave Greg a stern look as he picked up his beer. "I'm not forcing her to do anything she doesn't want to do. I'm just saying we've been intimate before, I'm not seeing anyone else at the moment, and she and what's his name are just friends. I'm simply telling her to keep the money. There are other ways she can pay me back if she wants to."

"If she agrees, great. But what happens if she doesn't?"

"I'd be disappointed, but I'm not taking the money back. If she feels guilty about it later on, then there's a way she can make it up to me."

"I still don't know about this," said Greg. "Date rape really is a thing."

Ken's voice turned snappy. "I already said I won't force her to do anything she doesn't want to do. I'm simply offering her an opportunity to keep the money, because she really does need it. If she refuses my offer, I'll respect her wishes. So why are you all of a sudden looking at me like I've got two heads or something?"

Greg looked him in the eye. "I guess I must be missing something, like why you insisted on giving it to her anonymously. Why not have CeCe tell her upfront it was from you, no strings attached?"

"Because I knew she would never accept it."

"And if she refused, it would have been on her, not you."

"I wanted her to have it because I knew she really needed it."

"You're sure about that?"

"Of course I'm sure," Ken said firmly. "So why are you questioning my motives?"

"Look, I'm all for getting lucky, just like the next guy, but not under these kinds of circumstances. She's in a really vulnerable position right now, and you're trying to take advantage of her vulnerability by insisting she do something she may not want to do."

"Oh, c'mon, Greg. Chill."

"She wants to pay you back. So why not take the money and just say thank you? She's not the only game in town."

"Maybe not, but I still have unfinished business with her."

"Like what?"

Ken was becoming agitated. "I already told you. It wasn't time for her to leave yet. I wanted to do her a few more times. In fact, I planned on humping her brains out when I took her home from my cousin's wedding. Instead, she makes up some cock and bull story about having a headache and leaves. She humiliated me in front of my entire family."

"Did they say anything after she left?"

"My aunt had a huge grin on her face, like she'd just won the lottery or something, while Joey, my cousin, said something under his breath about there being no nookie for me that night. Fortunately, the rest of them didn't hear it."

"I know all about what happened with your aunt," said Greg. "We've all had a woman dump us when we least expected it. Most of the time it was because they found another guy, but at least it wasn't the case this time. You even admitted to me it had run its course. All I can say is sometimes you're the dumper. Other times you're the one getting dumped. You can't have it your way all the time."

"Whatever. The point is, I'm not accepting the money. If she wants to pay me back, she'll have to do it on my terms or else, take it or leave it, because it's non-negotiable."

Greg stood from his chair and put on his jacket.

"Where are you going?" asked Ken.

"Away from here." Greg took out his wallet and dropped a few bills on the table. "I don't want any part of this. I have two younger sisters. If some guy tried something like this on one of them, he'd be a dead man walking. This should be more than enough to cover my beer and my share of the tip."

"You're overreacting," said Ken.

"Am I? You're the one who's talking about pressuring someone into having sex with you against their will." He gave Ken an angry look. "My old man may not have been the best dad on the planet, but he made sure I understood that when a woman said no it meant no. You want end up in jail? Fine, but don't expect me to come bail you out."

Ken seethed in anger as he watched Greg go out the door. His server stopped by a few minutes later.

"My buddy had to leave, but he took care of it."

"Are you sure?" she asked. "It's way more than enough."

"He said for you to keep the change, and Merry Christmas. I'll have one more, and then you can close out my tab as well."

"Thanks, and you have a Merry Christmas too."

⤦THIRTY-FIVE⤨

SEVERAL OF JENNA'S coworkers stopped by to congratulate her before they left the party. Chad also gave her a big hug.

"Have yourself a happy holiday season," he said, "and enjoy your time off. Trust me, you'll be busy come the first of the year." He gave her a final hug and hurried off to the elevator while Priscilla came over to congratulate her.

"Sorry I didn't stop by sooner," she said. "Sometimes people latch onto you and it's hard to get away, but before I go, I really want to say job well done, and you certainly earned the recognition. My husband and I finally made it to Sam's Place, and you did a heck of a good job."

"Thanks, Priscilla."

"It's like I told you before. You're going to be here for many years, so enjoy your time off while you can. Meantime, if you don't mind waiting, I'll grab my coat and we can ride down to the parking garage together."

The two women hopped into the elevator and wished each other a Merry Christmas when they stepped out. Jenna shivered under her coat. A winter storm was coming in, with heavy snows expected around midnight. She checked her phone as she waited for her car to warm up. As expected, Bill was meeting Connor as soon as he got off work, and they were going Christmas shopping. Knowing Kelsey would be on her own, Jenna sent her a text, asking if she wanted to do a girl's night out. Kelsey gladly accepted the offer.

* * *

Kelsey was all smiles when she opened the door. "Thanks for the invite. I appreciate the offer."

167

"Don't thank me yet," said Jenna. "You don't know what I have in store for you."

"What do you mean?"

"Grab your coat. You're about to find out."

Kelsey looked unsure as they stepped outside. "Hey, it's snowing out here."

"It is, and we're going to play in the snow. Sort of." Jenna reached for her key fob and pressed the remote. "Hop in."

Kelsey jumped into the passenger seat and buckled her seatbelt. "So, what did you mean about playing in the snow?" she asked.

Jenna started up the engine and adjusted the rearview mirror. "I'll show you in a little bit. First, I want to hear how the job interview went."

"It went well. As bummed as I was about not getting the job I was hoping for, I think this firm would be a much better fit. They seemed to be impressed with me, and I even got to talk to the big boss."

"There's a good sign."

"They practice civil law, but not criminal law. The last firm I worked for did both. I worked mostly on the civil side, but sometimes they needed extra help with a criminal case. Granted, we're all innocent until proven guilty in a court of law, but most of the clientele were real scumbags. This time I'd be working with people who've been seriously injured in accidents, or people like Connor, who've otherwise been wronged through no fault of their own."

"Sounds like a better job to me as well. Any idea when they'll get back with you?"

"They want to make their decision before Christmas, and said to expect to hear from them no later than Tuesday. All I can say is the big boss gave me a big smile when he shook my hand. Something tells me he didn't do this with the other candidates."

"Which is certainly encouraging." Jenna turned up the windshield wipers and put the car in gear. A few minutes later she turned into a parking lot in front of an eight-story office building. "Welcome to Salisbury and Norton. This is where I work. Everyone's gone home for the day, and as you can see, the visitor's parking lot is completely empty. The snow is also starting to accumulate, so, if you'll pardon the pun, I'm going to give you a crash course how to handle winter driving conditions."

"Okay," said Kelsey.

"Right now, I want you to hang on, and I hope you're strapped in real tight, because I'm about to show you what not to do." Jenna punched the accelerator and slammed on the brakes, throwing the car into a skid. Once it stopped, she looked at a wide-eyed Kelsey. "Are you okay?"

"I'm fine," said Kelsey. "I'm just shocked at how quickly it happened, especially when you weren't going very fast and there isn't much snow on the ground."

"It doesn't take much. Now I'm going to show you how to do this the right way." After a quick demonstration, she put the car into park. "Now we're going to trade places. You need to get a feel for this, especially if you get the new job. So, are you ready?"

Kelsey took a deep breath. "I guess I'm as ready as I'll ever be." She cautiously opened the passenger door and switched seats with Jenna. Once behind the wheel, she carefully adjusted the seat.

"Okay," said Jenna. "I want you to start driving across the parking lot. Not too fast. That's good. Now stop."

Kelsey hit the brakes. The car started sliding and skidded to a stop. "Oh my god. I hope I didn't damage your car."

"It's fine," said Jenna. "You weren't going fast enough to do any damage. Now we're going to try again. This time do it the way I told you. Light on the brakes, and don't jerk the wheel."

Kelsey drove forward and tapped the brakes again. The back wheels slid, but she kept the car under control. Following Jenna's instructions, she turned the car around and drove forward again. Each time, the car slid less.

"Okay," said Kelsey. "It's starting to feel better."

"You're getting the hang of it, just keep it slow. When you're out in traffic you'll need to keep plenty of space between you and the car in front of you. It's all about defensive driving and watching out for the other guy. The main thing is to watch your speed, and don't let other drivers intimidate you, because skidding out of control and hitting a utility pole, or another car, isn't fun."

"No, it wouldn't be."

"So, let's do a few more practice runs, and then we'll trade places again. I don't know about you, but when we're done, I think we really should go do a girls' night out."

"I'm game if you are."

After making a few more perfect stops, Jenna got back behind the wheel. "There's a little Italian place not too far from here. It's called Vito and Giana's. It's kind of a hole in the wall, but their food is amazing and they have the best pizza in town. It's also a popular place, so we'll probably have to wait for a table."

"No worries. I don't know how late Connor will be, so I'll sending him a text to let him know." Kelsey hit the send button and Connor soon replied.

"You're not going to believe this. Connor and his dad are already there. He said they just got seated a few minutes ago."

"Have they ordered yet?"

"No, not yet, although they've decided they want pizza instead of pasta."

"Sounds good. Tell him his dad knows what I like."

"Will do."

The dining room was full when they arrived, and a few of the people waiting gave them strange looks when they told the hostess they were meeting someone who was already seated. Bill and Connor greeted them with and hugs and kisses. As they took their seats, they found two glasses of merlot waiting for them.

"So, what have you guys been up to?" asked Connor.

"Making doughnuts in the snow," said Jenna.

"Come again?"

"She gave me a lesson on how to drive in the snow," said Kelsey.

"Salisbury had its annual office Christmas party earlier this afternoon, and it was snowing when I left, so I went and got her and took her back to the visitor's parking lot."

"Good for you," said Bill. "So, how'd she do?"

"She did well," said Jenna. As she and Kelsey talked about their adventure, Kelsey also told them about her job interview. They all raised their glasses when Jenna said she was named one of the employees of the year.

"You certainly earned it," said Bill, "and we're all very proud of you."

"But it still felt weird, getting it while I'm on furlough."

"But not for much longer, so let's both enjoy our free time while we still have it, because come the first of the year, I'll have to get ready to start teaching again."

They turned their attention back to their pizzas, but only a few slices remained. Their server soon dropped off their tab, and Connor and Bill argued over who would pay.

"I'm the dad, and dads always pay," Bill said firmly. "You did the heavy lifting when I was moving."

"Then we'll have to have you over for Christmas dinner."

"Holy cow," said Jenna. "I completely forgot. My dad will be home for Christmas this year, so my mother has invited all of us over for Christmas dinner, including Connor and Kelsey, and she's not taking no for an answer."

"Then I guess we'll be there," said Bill, "and please let her know we'll be bringing side dishes. So, if everyone's ready, we'll head out." He looked at Jenna. "We took Connor's Jeep, so I need you to take me back to their place so I can get the Explorer."

It was still snowing lightly when they walked out to the parking lot. Connor gave Jenna a big hug after they walked her to her car. "Thank you so much for giving Kelsey a driving lesson. I've been meaning to get it myself, but other stuff keeps popping up."

"It was my pleasure," said Jenna. "She's a quick study, and she's getting the hang of it."

"And she'll get one more lesson today because I'm letting her drive home." They stood by as Kelsey got behind the wheel, and waved goodbye as she drove out of the parking lot.

"I want to thank you as well," said Bill. "You made a good impression on Connor too. So, if you're up to it, why don't I come over to your place? We can hang out in front of your fireplace and keep each other warm."

"Sounds kike a plan to me."

✎THIRTY-SIX✎

BILL'S NEW HOME was taking shape. The shed had arrived and was ready to go. His next task was to finish setting up the photography studio in the basement. He would be doing a photo session with Josh and Stephanie right after the New Year, and he needed to clear away the few remaining boxes. Most were odds and ends, while the biggest one contained his summer clothing. One small, lonely box remained after he finished unpacking; an unopened Priority Mail shipping box. Mary Beth's employer had sent it to him shortly after her death. Knowing it contained her personal belongings from her office, he had placed it in the basement with her other belongings, where it remained untouched for over a decade. He had planned on opening it once he was settled in Florida.

"Well, here goes nothing," he said out loud. He cut through the tape and carefully opened the box. Inside was a framed school photo of Connor, along with her executive pen set. No doubt Connor would appreciate having his mother's pen set on his desk. He set it off to the side and took out the remaining item, a large resealable manilla envelope with the words, "personal and confidential" written in Mary Beth's handwriting. Inside the envelope were at least a dozen letters, all hand addressed to Mary Beth in neat block letters, but they had been sent to a private mail box instead of her office. All had come from the same sender, a man named Jason Bradford, who lived in an apartment in Wheat Ridge.

Bill furrowed his brows as he reached for his phone and looked up the name Jason Bradford. There were no Jason Bradfords currently residing in Wheat Ridge. No doubt he had moved on. There were, however, several other Jason Bradfords living in Colorado. Two were in the greater Denver area, but without more information, Bill had no way of knowing which one may have been corresponding with his late wife. He was getting a bad feeling, and he wanted to solve the mystery as quickly as possible.

He looked up the address where the letters had been sent. It was a UPS store, located in a strip mall within a quarter mile of Mary Beth's office. So why had Mary Beth rented a private mailbox? Did Jason not want her secretary opening his mail? Or was Mary Beth trying to hide something from her boss? Neither theory made sense, and his bad feeling was getting worse.

Bill took a closer look at the envelopes. All had been carefully opened with a letter opener, and the letters were still tucked inside. He looked at the postmarks. They had all been mailed within a seven-month period, with the last one being sent a short time before Mary Beth's death. Taking a deep breath, he sat down on the floor and began reading the letters. As he read, a dark story began to unfold.

Jason Bradford, or Jake as he preferred to be called, had been one of Mary Beth's clients. She had represented him in the dissolution of a business partnership, and it had been a long and difficult case. During this time, Jake worked out of his apartment as a free-lance consultant. He and Mary Beth had also become good friends. The case was eventually settled out of court. Mary Beth then rented the mailbox so she and Jake could remain in contact without leaving a paper trail.

Once Jake's case had officially closed, he and Mary Beth began having lunchtime rendezvous at his apartment. The bile rose in Bill's stomach as he read Jake's graphic descriptions of the most intimate details of their lovemaking and talked about how much she turned him on. He even mentioned the small birthmark on her upper left thigh. He also shared his sexual fantasies with her. He would end each letter by confirming the date and time for their next encounter.

Bill set each letter aside in stunned disbelief and forced himself to read the next one. As the affair continued, Jake wanted Mary Beth to file for divorce, but she had concerns about Bill finding out about them and claiming she was an unfit mother. The possibility of losing custody of Connor was a risk she was unwilling to take. Jake, however, kept applying the pressure until Mary Beth finally agreed to meet with a divorce attorney, but she ended the relationship before the papers were filed. Jake didn't want Connor to be included in the package, and Mary Beth refused to give up her son.

In his final letter, Jake begged her to reconsider as he professed his undying love for her and tried to convince her he would do his best to be a good stepfather to Connor. Bill would never know if she responded to him or not, because she died less than a week later.

As Bill set the last letter aside, a long-forgotten memory flashed through his mind. There was an out-of-place man at Mary Beth's funeral. He was seated near the back of the church, away from the other mourners. He appeared to be in his thirties, with sandy blond hair and a blond mustache, and he wore an expensive suit. He was also extremely distraught. Bill had never seen this man before and had no idea who he was. He planned on talking to him after the service, but the man made a hasty exit before it concluded.

"Oh my god," he said out loud. "That was Jason Bradford. He was there. At the funeral."

Jumping to his feet, he felt his body sway as he struggled to maintain his balance. He ran up the stairs, desperately hoping to make it to the bathroom in time. Flinging the door open, he dropped to his knees in front of the commode as everything he had eaten over the past few hours worked its way back up. Lying on the bathroom floor, he tried to make sense of it all, but there was only one inescapable conclusion. Mary Beth, the woman he had loved with all his heart and soul, had betrayed him. He wondered how many times had he made love to her, completely unaware of her having had sex with Jake a few hours before. The thought threw him into a jealous rage.

Bill felt completely numb when he returned to the basement and carefully packed up the letters, placing the large envelope, along with the other items, back in the box. Once it was safely put away, he went upstairs and packed a bag. Before leaving, he sent two text messages; one to Jenna, the other to Connor. Dropping the phone into his coat pocket, he grabbed his bag and hopped in the Explorer. As the garage door closed, he put the truck into gear and drove away.

✥THIRTY-SEVEN✥

JENNA TOOK A deep breath as she ran the numbers. While hoping to be back to work by mid-January, her official starting date had yet to be confirmed. She was also uncertain of when she would receive her first paycheck. Until then, she had bills to pay.

The mortgage and utility bills were her top priority, but once they were paid there wasn't much left. So far, she had managed to defer a car payment, but the next one would be due in early January. The minimum payments on her credit cards were also increasing, as she was using them to buy groceries. While her mother occasionally brought her groceries, Jenna had never told her parents how dire her situation was. Her phone beeped as she went over the numbers again. A text message from Bill had arrived. Her face lit up as she began reading, but her smile quickly faded.

"The time has come for us to say adieu. You won't be seeing me again. I know you and Kelsey are friends, and while I can't tell you who to associate with, I would appreciate it very much if you would avoid visiting her at her apartment. Invite her to your place instead."

Her heart skipped a beat and she quickly typed a response. *"What the bloody hell? Is this your idea of a sick, twisted joke?"* She hit the send button, but the message couldn't be delivered. Bill had blocked her number.

"Okay, Jenna, don't panic," she said out loud. After taking a few moments to gather her thoughts, she typed another text message, this time to Stacy.

"Have you got a few minutes? Something truly bizarre is happening, and I need to talk to someone."

Stacy quickly responded. *"I'm about due for a break. I'll text you in a few minutes."*

"Stacy, this is really bad. Can you call me instead?"

"Of course. I'll be with you shortly. Go get a glass of water and try to stay calm." As promised, Jenna's phone rang a few minutes later, and she tearfully accepted Stacy's call.

"Okay," said Stacy. "What happened?"

"It's Bill. He's suddenly turned into someone I don't know. I got a text message from him a little while ago, and it's like he's has some sort of mental breakdown."

"What exactly did he say?"

"Let me read it to you." Stacy went silent after Jenna read the message. "Are you still there?" Jenna finally asked.

"Yeah, I'm still here. I can't believe what I'm hearing either. Did the two of you have words about something?"

"No. Things have been going well between us. He's moved into his new home. He's looking forward to getting back to work, and Kelsey just found a job with a law firm."

"Good for her. I'm looking forward to meeting her."

"She looks forward to meeting you as well," said Jenna. "So what the hell is going on with Bill?"

"I'm not sure, but I'm wondering if perhaps someone got to him and maligned you."

"Oh my god. Ken! Ken could very well be behind this."

"Are you sure?" asked Stacy.

"Positive. Salisbury and Norton had their holiday party last week. CeCe of course was there, and we talked for a few minutes. She asked about Bill. I told her he was doing well, and we were still seeing each other. She also claims she's no longer Ken's go-between, but after the gift card incident I take everything she says with a huge grain of salt. So, how much do you want to bet Ken's behind this?"

"He could be, but we don't know for certain."

"One thing I do know for sure is I need to pay him back for the gift card as soon as possible. I planned on doing it after I went back to work, but now I've changed my mind. I'll see to it he gets his money before the end of the year."

"How? You're broke."

"I don't know. I'll think of something. In the meantime, what about Bill?"

"Jenna, I wish I had an answer, but I don't. I also need to get back to work, but we'll talk some more later. Are you going to be okay?"

"I don't know, but thanks for calling."

"Anytime. I'm here if you need me."

Jenna received another text message a few minutes later. This time from Kelsey, asking if she had heard from Bill. Not wanting to say too much, she kept her response brief.

"Yes. He sent me a message a little while ago."

"Did he seem okay to you?"

"No, he did not."

Jenna waited for a response, but none came. She wondered if something had happened to Bill. Perhaps he had fallen ill, or been injured in some kind of accident. Kelsey replied a few minutes later.

"Would you mind if we stopped by after work? Something's happened and we're trying to figure out what's wrong."

"Of course. I'm trying to figure it out as well. See you this evening."

* * *

Connor looked shaken when Jenna invited them inside. "I suppose I should be a good hostess and offer you something to drink."

"As much as I would love a really stiff drink right now," said Connor, "I think I'd better stick with ice water."

"Me too," said Kelsey.

Jenna filled two waterglasses and joined them in the living room. "So, guys, what happened?"

"Earlier today I got a weird message today from my dad," said Connor. "I guess it came around the same time as yours. He said he was leaving town but didn't say where he was going. He would be gone until after first of the year, and under no circumstances am I to contact him while he's away. That was it. He didn't even mention the holidays. This isn't like him."

"No, it isn't." Jenna. "However, he didn't mention anything about leaving town to me. He simply said we were done, I would never see him again, and while I could see the two of you if I wished, I'm not to visit you at your apartment."

"Well, you can disregard that part of the message," said Connor. "My father doesn't tell us who we can invite into our home, and you're welcome anytime."

"Thank you, and my family is still expecting you and Kelsey for Christmas dinner."

"We'll be there. I know you said things were okay between you, but did Dad say anything to make you think he was upset about something."

"No, not a thing. In fact, we had plans to go to dinner tonight. He said he was looking forward to it."

"Has he mentioned anything lately about not feeling well?"

"No, he has not. When we spoke on the phone last night, he said he planned on unpacking the rest of the moving boxes sometime today. He also said he planned on putting his Christmas tree up this weekend, and he was going to ask if you guys wanted to come over and help decorate it. It was out last conversation."

Connor looked confused. "This doesn't make any sense."

"My friend Stacy thinks my old boyfriend may have something to do with this."

"Really? Why would she think that?"

Jenna took a deep breath and sighed. "Last year, I was seeing someone a coworker had fixed me up with. His name was Ken. At first, he seemed like a nice guy, but over time he become too controlling and had to have everything his way."

"I see," said Connor. "Sounds like a narcissistic control freak"

"He was,"

"So, who ended it?"

"I did. At first, he didn't take it seriously, but once he realized I meant it, we wished each other well. Later on, I found out CeCe, his friend and my coworker, was giving him all kinds of personal information about me without my knowledge. So, after I was furloughed, she gives me a gift card, and leads me to believe it came from a well-meaning client."

"Only it didn't," said Connor. "It came from Ken, didn't it?"

"It sure did. Unfortunately, by the time I realized it, I'd already used to it buy groceries. He now has me in a position where I owe him something, and he must have said something to your father."

"Did your relationship with him by chance overlap with when you started seeing my dad?"

"No," Jenna said firmly. "I ended it with Ken in early January. I contacted your dad about doing the sculpture in March."

Connor looked concerned. "Has he ever contacted you directly?"

"He hasn't stalked me, if that's what you're worried about. He did, however, make a few overtures about us staying friends, but I said no. Unfortunately, I still owe him for the gift card, and I plan on paying him back before the end of the year."

"Good idea. The sooner you can pay him back, the better. If you need help, please let us know. We can float you a loan if you need it."

"Thanks for the offer, but I'm still doing odd jobs whenever I can, and I'll be back to work next month."

"I'm happy to hear it," said Kelsey, "but please let me know if he continues causing you any trouble. My new boss can help you take out a restraining order."

"Thanks, Kelsey, but I'm really hoping it won't be necessary."

Connor declined Jenna's offer to stay for dinner, suggesting they take a raincheck. As she walked them to the door, she reminded them again about Christmas.

"We'll be there, I promise," said Connor, "so please let us know what you want us to bring, and with any luck, Dad will be there too."

* * *

Connor said little as he and Kelsey drove home. Once they arrived, Kelsey started preparing dinner.

"Fix whatever you want for yourself," said Connor. "I'm not hungry right now."

"You need to eat. We don't need you getting sick on top of everything else."

Connor put his coat back on. "I'm fine. I'm going to take a walk. I need to sort this out. I won't be gone long, and I'll have my phone with me."

Kelsey was heating a can of beef stew when he returned. Connor tried to eat, but most of it remained in the bowl. Afterwards he helped her with the cleanup and joined her in front of the TV, but he couldn't concentrate.

"I keep thinking about the day my mom died," he said. "It was a Saturday, and it was a beautiful spring day. I was really looking forward to the end of the school year. One of my mom's friends called her, wanting to know if she'd like to go to the mall with her. Mom said she would. I was still a kid back then, and my jeans were getting a little tight on me, so she was going to buy me a couple of new pairs while she was out. Her friend stopped by to pick her up, and she kissed Dad and me goodbye. After they left, I went to hang out with a couple of friends and came home around four o'clock. Mom wasn't back yet, so Dad tried calling her, but the call went straight to voicemail. We figured she and her friend must have had a long lunch or something, and she'd silenced her phone so they could talk. A few minutes later the cops showed up at the door. Mom and her friend never made it to the mall. A fourteen-year-old-kid was out joyriding in his dad's pickup truck. He lost control and slammed head on into my mom and her friend. Both of them were dead, and the kid was critically injured."

"Oh my god. I'm so sorry." Kelsey wrapped her arms around him and hugged him.

"It was so unexpected... It was a living nightmare." Connor's eyes grew misty and he blinked away a tear. "One minute she was there. The next minute she was gone forever. Back then my dad's brother, my uncle Dave, was working for Curtis Avionics."

"The big defense contractor?"

"Yeah," said Connor. "They're headquartered in Wichita, but at the time they had a facility here in Denver. So, after my mom died, my uncle Dave got a transfer. He and his family were in Denver for about four years. Curtis closed it down when I was in high school, and Uncle Dave and his family went back to Kansas. My dad and my uncle have always been close, and his being here made a big difference."

"Maybe you should call your uncle. Perhaps he could call your dad and find out what's going on."

"I thought about it, but I don't want to upset him. I'm hoping Dad will come to his senses and either come home, or at least send me a message."

"Hopefully, he will, but if we don't hear from him by tomorrow, you'll have to call your uncle. He needs to know what happened. We'll also see if we can file a missing person's report."

"Good idea."

"Meantime it's getting late. Are you coming to bed?"

"I'll be there in a little while." Connor kissed her goodnight and tried to make himself comfortable on the sofa after she closed the bedroom door. His phone rang two hours later. Fearing the worst, he rushed to grab it. To his surprise, his grandmother was calling.

"Hey, Grandma. What are you doing up this late?"

"You dad showed up a little while ago."

"Thank God. We've been worried sick. Is he all right?"

"No, he isn't all right," she solemnly said. "When he got here, he was rambling on about your mother, but none of it made sense. It was like he was in some sort of trance, so I called your uncle. As soon as he got here, your dad calmed down and started acting more like himself."

"All right. So, what happened?"

"We're not sure. He said it's an unresolved issue with your mother, but he won't say what it was."

"They had their disagreements from time to time, but they always worked through it."

"Keep in mind, Connor, that parents keep these kinds of problems away from their children. All I can tell you is whatever it was, it has left him seriously traumatized. The three of us have talked it over. We all agree he needs professional help."

"Wait a minute," said Connor. "You're not going to have him committed, are you?"

"No. He's not a danger to himself or others. However, your uncle and his ex-wife worked with a marriage and family counselor before they parted ways, and your uncle saw her for a time after they divorced. He's going to call her in the morning and make an appointment for your dad."

"So, he's going to be staying with you through the holidays?"

"Yes, he is. Go ahead and continue with your own holiday plans. If things go as we're hoping, he'll be back the first part of January so he can get back to work. He'll also get in touch with you later on, when he's ready, but right now he isn't himself, and he's asked that you not contact him until then."

"I know he isn't himself right now, and I'm glad you called. As I said, we've been worried sick."

"I know you have. I'm worried too, but I'm praying he'll soon be his old self. So, what about you and Kelsey? Do you need anything?"

"We're fine, thanks for asking. Kelsey and I are planning to spend Christmas with friends."

"I'm glad, so Merry Christmas and enjoy your holiday. Maybe next year we can spend it all together."

"I'd like that, Grandma."

✣THIRTY-EIGHT✣

JENNA LOOKED THROUGH the peephole and greeted her friend with a relieved smile. "I'm so glad you're here, but the pizza really wasn't necessary."

Stacy followed Jenna into the kitchen. "You gotta eat sometime. I'm also sorry I wasn't able to make it last night."

"No worries. Connor and Kelsey stopped by. They were as baffled as I was. Connor sent me a text early this morning. Bill showed up at his mother's house in Wichita late last night, and they're getting him professional help. Hopefully, he'll be back in a few weeks. He has classes to teach."

"I hope so too, but it doesn't mean he'll contact you."

"I know."

"But if he does, will you take him back?"

"I hope we can work things out, but I guess it remains to be seen." Jenna took two plates from the cupboard and offered Stacy a drink.

"I'll have a Dr. Pepper too, if you've got them. Otherwise, ice water is fine."

"I happen to have an unopened two-liter bottle of Dr. Pepper in the fridge." She poured a glass for Stacy and one for herself, and took her seat at the table.

"So, how's Alan doing these days?"

"Wonderful, as always," said Stacy. "His parents are flying here from Phoenix on the twenty-third, and they're staying through the twenty-eighth. I'm really looking forward to meeting them."

"I remember you telling me. Will you be introducing his parents to your parents?"

"Yep. We're all meeting for lunch, at Sam's Place, the day after Christmas."

Jenna suddenly felt sad. "You know, life can be funny at times. For a while there I thought of The Shelton Inn as the jewel in my crown. Now I'm not sure if I could ever set foot in there again."

"I'm so sorry. I completely forgot about the sculpture in the lobby. I haven't been there yet, and figured it would be the perfect opportunity."

"It's okay. Life goes on, and I'm sure I'll create something stunning for the new restaurant I'll be working on, whenever it may be. Hopefully, right after the first of the year."

"At least you're going back to work, so you'll have something to look forward to."

"Work yes," said Jenna. "CeCe, not so much, which is another reason why I need to pay Ken back, as soon as possible."

"I'd be happy to help, and don't worry. You don't need to pay me back until you're caught up on your other bills."

"Thanks for the offer, but no. Connor also offered to help, but I turned him down as well. I can handle this."

Stacy's face suddenly lit up. "Wait, a minute. I have an idea. Why don't you do a Go Fund Me? Then everyone can pitch in a few dollars, and you won't have to pay anyone back."

"And what if Ken finds out? We still have mutual friends on social media. If they saw it word would get back to him, and I don't want him offering anymore of his so-called help. So, I'm doing something else instead."

"Which is?"

Jenna looked Stacy in the eye. "Remember that conversation we had awhile back? About art modeling?'

"I sure do."

"A few weeks ago, I posed for Bill for one of his wood reliefs, and no I wasn't naked. I was wearing a dress." A sad look came over her face. "Although I wonder if he'll even do it now."

"If he does, he does. If he doesn't, he's a fool."

"No comment," said Jenna. "Anyway, he paid me for the gig."

"As well he should."

"It was a more than I was expecting. Then he gave me the name of another artist in the same building. A painter, who's doing a series about ancient Roman mythology."

"Would you be nude or clothed?"

"Nude," said Jenna. "He said if I needed extra money to give her a call. Then he showed me a work in progress of a painting he'd posed for. Granted, she'd created a different face, but everything he has was right there, for the whole world to see."

Stacy tried to suppress a laugh. "Ever see a picture of Michelangelo's famous marble statue of David? It's an anatomically correct nude, and people come from all over the world to see it. So, who's the artist? And which Roman god did he pose for?"

"The artist's name is Rhonda Barrett. The painting is of Bacchus."

Stacy grabbed her phone and did a quick Google search. "Interesting. According to this article, he's the god of wine. And fertility."

"Don't go there," Jenna said sternly.

"I'm just saying this could be a good sign, and the artist is a woman. So, are you going to contact her?"

"Already did. I emailed her this morning. She's working against a deadline for a show this coming spring, and she'll pay me extra if I can come in before the first of the year. She needs a female model for two paintings, Diana, the goddess of hunting and nature, among other things, and Venus."

A big smile broke out across Stacy's face. "Venus, huh? The goddess of love, and the god of fertility. Say what you will, but I think it's yet another sign that Bill will be coming back."

"We'll see," said Jenna. "As for the paintings, she'll do the same with me as she did with him. The faces will be different, so I won't be recognizable. To paraphrase Bill, they're Roman gods, while we're just common, everyday people. She also wanted to know what I looked like, so I sent her a few snapshots. She said the job is mine if I want it. It'll pay enough for me to pay Ken back and, hopefully, help get me through the rest of the month."

"If it were me," said Stacy, "I would take her up on her offer. No one will know it's you."

"I know, and I'd also be helping out a fellow artist."

"And who knows? You might need the services of another artist for a project someday, maybe for something like a mural. Sounds like a win-win to me."

✂THIRTY-NINE✂

CHRISTMAS WOULD not be as merry for Jenna. She was still didn't know when she would return to work, nor was she sure of what to do with the winter scarf she had purchased for Bill. It would have to be returned, but she couldn't bring herself to take it back to the store. It would have to wait until after the holidays. She had also decided to skip the tree and decorations, until Connor and Kelsey unexpectedly showed up on a Saturday morning with a tree.

"I appreciate the thought, guys, I really do," she said, "but I decided this would be the Year of Scrooge. Or, Ms. Scrooge."

"Oh, please," said Kelsey. "Christmas hasn't been cancelled, and you could use some holiday cheer." She pointed out a spot next to the fireplace. "I think it would look great over there. What do you think, Connor?"

He looked at Jenna. "It works for me, but your opinion is the one that counts, so what say you?"

"It's okay, I guess."

Kelsey held the tree in place while Connor attached it to the stand. "I so love the smell of fresh cut pine," she said. "It smells like Christmas." She looked down at Connor. "Have you about got it?"

"I think so." He stepped back and gave it a look. "It's not tilting, and as soon as I pour some water into the stand it'll be good to go."

"Okay, I'll admit it's beautiful tree," said Jenna, "but you really didn't have to."

Kelsey's voice was stern. "I already told you. We're doing Christmas this year, no matter what."

"I also wanted to you to know that my grandmother called last night," said Connor. "She said Dad's doing a lot better, but he still won't tell anyone what happened. He says it's a private matter between my mother and himself, and not to be discussed with the rest of the family out of consideration for her. I'm grateful he's honoring her memory."

"Why wouldn't he?" asked Jenna.

"I don't know."

"It's okay, Connor. I would have never replaced your mother, because she can't be replaced."

"I know. I was also hoping it would work out for you guys as well. I don't want him to be alone for the rest of his life either. Unfortunately, he can be stubborn as hell when he wants to be, and he's still maintaining radio silence with me as well."

"He'll contact you when he's ready."

"Kelsey, and my grandmother, keep saying the same thing, but the waiting is unbearable. Dad and I were always close. After I went off to college, and then to Florida, he'd text me a few times a week to just ask how I was doing and to make sure everything was okay."

Jenna gave him a hug. "I'm sorry, Connor, but it'll work out. He'll be back. That I'm certain of. In the meantime, you have me and Kelsey."

"I know, and I'm grateful for you both."

"And while I hate to break up the moment," said Kelsey, "I have to ask if you have Christmas ornaments."

"They're down in the basement," said Jenna. "Follow me." They hurried downstairs, returning with several storage boxes. Jenna made hot cocoa as Connor and Kelsey worked on the tree. Once they were finished, Connor plugged in the lights.

"Good job, you guys," said Jenna. "It's a beautiful tree, and I'm glad you stopped by. Also please make a note on your calendars that I will be picking you up at five o'clock on Christmas night."

"We'll be ready," said Kelsey. "So, what side dishes should we bring?"

"My mother's doing roast beef and Yorkshire pudding."

Kelsey looked puzzled. "Forgive me for sounding rude, but what is it?"

"It's my family's traditional Christmas dinner. Yorkshire pudding isn't what you think. It's not a sweetened dairy product. It's more like a popover."

"Sounds good to me," said Connor. "I've always loved biscuits and gravy."

* * *

Jenna unlocked the Camry and looked at Connor and Kelsey. "You guys will have to decide who sits in the back."

"I can sit in the back." Connor opened the passenger door for Kelsey. Once she was seated, he ran to the driver's side to open the door for Jenna. He then slid into the back seat as Jenna started up the engine. "Now you get to chauffer me," he said.

"Or so you think." Kelsey gave him a look and carefully handed him a covered dish. "You're now officially in charge of the green bean casserole."

"Don't worry. My parents live fairly close," said Jenna. "We'll pop it in the oven as soon as we get there."

"Now in case you're wondering," said Connor. "I didn't hear from my father today, but my grandmother called me this morning. She wanted to wish everyone a Merry Christmas, and she's happy Kelsey and I are having Christmas dinner with you and your family. She also said something about Dad not being sure about how to approach me."

"I don't think he has anything to worry about," said Jenna. "We all know he wasn't himself when he sent those messages."

"I know, but it's still going to be awkward for him when he does reach out. I'm also hoping he'll reach out to you as well."

"Me too, but it all remains to be seen. Until then I'm not getting my hopes up. In the meantime, I'm taking care of the Ken problem, once and for all."

"How?" asked Kelsey.

"I have a little freelance job lined up for tomorrow. I'm helping another artist in your dad's building with a project. She'll pay me when I'm done. Then I'm going straight to the bank to get a certified check, which I will mail to Ken."

"A little old school, but still a good way to handle it," said Kelsey. "Guaranteed funds, and you'll have a copy of the cancelled check as proof of payment. Be sure to send to it to him certified mail. Then you'll have proof he got it."

"Good idea. I was going to put a regular stamp on it, but you're right. I'll need documentation to prove he actually received it in case he tries to pull something later on. I'll also take a picture of it with my phone. Then it's bye-bye Kenny boy, once and for all."

"What about CeCe?" asked Connor.

"I'll let her know I paid him back. Then I'll remind her about how no longer being his go-between works both ways, and whatever I do from here on out is none of his damn business. It's been nearly a year since I gave him his walking papers. He needs to get a freaking life."

"Hopefully, he will," said Connor, "but if he bothers you again, we'll have to see if Kelsey's boss can help you get a restraining order."

❧FORTY❧

JENNA CHANGED INTO her street clothes and stuffed her bathrobe into her tote bag. Rhonda was seated at her desk, next to the window. The afternoon sun lit up her silver hair.

"I want to thank you once again for coming in on short notice," she said, "and for taking time away from your holiday."

"It was my pleasure," said Jenna. "I was furloughed from my job in October, and I've been doing odd jobs ever since."

"I'm sorry to hear you were furloughed. Where were you working?"

"Salisbury and Norton Architects. I'm one of their interior designers. I designed the lobby and atrium for the Shelton Inn Denver Tech Center."

Rhonda seemed genuinely impressed. "You did? I've heard about that place. I take it you're the one who commissioned Bill for the sculpture."

"I did. I took a drawing course from him my freshman year of college, and I considered him a friend."

"I consider him a friend as well. I was one of his professors."

"You were? I had no idea."

"Bill has a genuine gift," said Rhonda. "I wrote a letter of recommendation when he applied for his teaching job at Foothills College. I also referred him to Sally. I was one of the first artists to lease a studio here, and now that I've officially retired from the university, I'm full-time painter. I hope you'll keep me in mind for other projects."

"You know I will," said Jenna.

"Bill told me he showed you a study painting of Bacchus. Would you like to see the finished version?"

"I'd love to."

187

Rhonda carefully removed it from the rack and presented it to Jenna.

"It's beautiful," said Jenna. "Such vivid colors, and such close attention to detail. I love how the face turned out. Did you use another model for it?"

"No. I only use live models for the full bodies as people come in different shapes and body types, but after decades of teaching life drawing, I'm pretty good at creating the facial features I want out of my head. And speaking of Bill, I noticed he hasn't been around lately. Has anything happened to him?"

"He's visiting family in Kansas, and so far as I know, he'll be back after New Year's."

"I see. As for the painting, it goes to the framers next week, and I'd be honored to have you at my gallery opening."

"Thank you. I'd be honored to come."

"Then I'll add your name to my email list, and is paying you by check okay?"

"Of course."

Rhonda returned to her desk and made out a check. "Thank you once again. I was at my wits end trying to find the right model for those last two paintings. I know you've never done anything like this before, but you did an outstanding job, and I'm extremely grateful for your help. So Happy New Year, and I look forward to seeing you at my opening."

They shook hands and Jenna hurried out to her car. There were too many memories of Bill inside the building, and not looking sad in front of Rhonda had taken most of her energy. She checked the time as she fired up the engine. Hopefully, she would make it to the bank before the cutoff time. Two other customers were in line ahead of her when she arrived, but to her relief she didn't have to wait long for a teller.

"I need to deposit this in my checking account." She endorsed Rhonda's check and slipped it underneath the window. "Then I need to get a certified check."

"How much?" asked the young man behind the glass.

Jenna wrote the amount on a slip of paper.

"I can make the deposit for you," he said, "but you don't have enough funds in your account to cover the certified check."

"But I'm making a deposit, and the check I'm giving you is from your bank as well."

"I understand, and don't worry. It'll process tonight, so check your phone app tomorrow morning. The funds should be available first thing and then we'll be happy to certify your check."

"Okay, fine." She waited for her receipt and hurried out the door. As she drove home, she recalled one of her last conversations with Ken. He talked about how he had outgrown his condo and planned on buying a house once the snow melted. She wondered if he was still at the same address. If he had moved, CeCe would know. She sent her a text message when she arrived home, but CeCe's response wasn't what she expected.

"*Sorry, but I can't be involved in any business between you and Ken, no matter how trivial, and you know the reason why. Thank you for understanding and Happy New Year. I look forward to having you back.*"

While disappointed with CeCe's response, Jenna was also grateful in knowing CeCe had finally learned her lesson. Taking a deep breath, she unblocked Ken's phone number. Once he confirmed his address, she would block him again.

"Okay, Jenna," she said out loud. "Let's keep this short, sweet, and to the point." She gathered her thoughts and began typing.

"*I have the funds for the gift card and will mail you a certified check. Are you at the same address?*"

He responded an hour later. "*I moved to a new place last fall. Busy right now. Will send you the address tomorrow.*"

"Same old Ken," said Jenna. She looked at her watch and made a mental note. By this time tomorrow, he would be nothing more than a bad memory.

* * *

Jenna poured herself a cup of morning coffee and checked her banking app. Rhonda's check had cleared. The funds were in her account. An hour later Ken's certified check was in her hands. She felt her body relax as she slipped behind the wheel. Ken would soon be out of her life for good. Reaching for her phone, she sent him a quick message.

"*I have your check. As soon as you send me your address, I'll take it to the post office.*"

She hurried home and waited for his response, but none came. As the hours passed, she wondered if something had gone wrong. It was nearly five o'clock when he finally responded.

"*Hectic day. Sorry I couldn't get back to you sooner. I'll stop by and pick up the check on my way home. See you in a bit.*"

"Oh, no you're not," she said out loud. She quickly typed a response. "*I'd rather send it certified mail and give you the tracking number.*" She hit the send button and waited for a response, but once again, none came. No doubt Ken was already on his way. She put the check in an envelope and waited by the door. When he arrived, she would hand it to him and send him on his way. As she waited, she sent a text message to Kelsey, who quickly responded.

"*Do you want Connor and me to stop by?*"

"*I'm good. I'll text you as soon as he leaves.*" Jenna nervously paced back and forth until she heard a car door slam. Her doorbell rang an instant later and she quickly stepped outside.

"Here you go, and you certainly didn't have to go this far out of your way. I would have been happy to mail it." She tried to give it to Ken, but his hands remained in his coat pockets.

"Later," he said. "As long as I'm in the neighborhood, I'd like for us to have a talk. Don't worry. We'll go someplace where there are plenty of people around."

"Thanks, but really isn't a good time. The house is a mess, and I have friends coming over later this evening."

"I insist," he firmly said, "and I'm not taking no for an answer. Don't worry. I promise not to take too much of your time. I only want to talk to you for a few minutes."

"Can't we just talk out here?"

"No. It's too cold, and I rather we go someplace where we can have a cup of coffee."

She knew it was useless to argue. "Okay, but you heard me. I've invited friends over and I can't stay out very long."

"I understand. You'll be home in less than hour. I promise."

Ken's black Blazer waited at the curb. Jenna anxiously hopped in the passenger seat as he fired up the engine. "There's a Village Inn just down the road," she said. "I need to pick up a pie while we're there. I'm spending New Year's Eve with friends."

"Anyone I know?" he asked.

"Nope."

"Then I'd like to take you someplace nicer, if you don't mind. We can stop at Village Inn on the way back."

"Whatever, but I still can't make it a late night. So, how's Jeri?"

"I have no idea. She moved to Boston. We went our separate ways last fall."

"Sorry to hear it," said Jenna. "CeCe spoke very highly of her. So have you met anyone new?"

"I haven't had time. So, how's your friend? The one who did the sculpture."

"He's fine."

"Is he coming over tonight?"

His questions were making her uncomfortable. "He has another commitment tonight. Some of my other friends are stopping by."

"Really? So, you're not seeing him exclusively then?"

"Bill and I are good friends, but if you really must know, the person coming over this evening is a female friend. She's bringing her significant other with her."

"I see."

Ken went silent, but Jenna became concerned a few minutes later. "So, where exactly are you taking me? You're going awfully far out of your way for a cup of coffee."

"Relax. We're almost there."

Jenna was getting a bad feeling. She wanted to text Kelsey, but she didn't want Ken asking more questions. As she looked around, she finally realized where they were going.

"Are you taking me to the Shelton Inn?"

"Yes."

"Why?"

"I was there a few months ago," he said, "and I really was impressed. I'd love it if you could show me around and tell me how you came up with your ideas."

"You've never shown any interest in my work before."

"I know, but now that I've actually seen it, I'm really captivated by what you do."

Jenna knew he was stalling, and she wondered what he was really up to. She felt even more uneasy as they drove into the parking lot. Once inside the hotel, he guided her through the lobby and stopped at the sculpture.

"What's wrong?" he asked. "You seem upset about something."

"I already told you. I need to get home. I have friends coming over this evening."

"Relax. We won't be here long. So, tell me about this sculpture. Did your clients like it? Because I don't understand the significance of it."

"The clients loved it. It's an abstract piece, suggesting water, although some people may see it differently."

"Yeah, CeCe said the same thing." He led her into the atrium. "Now this truly is magnificent."

"Thank you. I wanted people to get a sense of the great outdoors." They strolled around the atrium for a few minutes before Ken escorted her to Sam's Place.

"I thought we'd have our coffee here, and it looks like they have a few tables open." A hostess led them to a table near the back. Ken told her he wanted to order two glasses of the house merlot.

"I'll let your server know. Enjoy your evening."

"I think we can do something a little nicer than plain old coffee," he said. "So please, sit down. We'll only be here long enough to enjoy a glass of wine."

Jenna's concern turned to anger as she took her seat. "Look, I don't know what kind of a game you think you're playing, but it won't work. It's been over between us for some time." She reached into her purse and dropped the envelope in front of him.

"Here's your money, in guaranteed funds. It's every cent I owe you, plus interest."

"Which I very much appreciate." He took the check from the envelope and gave it a closer look before setting it aside. "I know you're still on furlough, and I'm sure you worked really hard to get this, but it wasn't necessary, because I don't want it."

"What? Okay, fine. I can't force you to cash it, but I have a bank receipt and I also took a picture of it, which means I can prove I paid you back. So now, if you'll excuse me, I'll be on my way." She started to leave, but Ken grabbed her arm and gave it a hard squeeze.

"Not so fast," he said sternly. "You need to sit back down, because there's another way you can pay me back."

Jenna realized she was in serious danger as she slowly sat back down, but she wouldn't allow Ken to see her fear.

"Look. You've got your money. What else do you want from me?"

"I brought you here so you can pay me back, but it won't be with money." He lowered his voice and looked her in the eye. "You see, I wasn't quite ready to end it when you broke up with me, but I'd just met Jeri, so I had to put you on the back burner until later."

"And what is that supposed to mean?"

His face softened. "It's okay. I'm not going to hurt you. I'm simply reminding you that there was a time, not so long ago, when we genuinely cared about one another, and I still care about you. You're still very special to me, and you always will be."

Their server arrived with their wine. Jenna waited until after he left. "Okay, Ken, I appreciate you telling me this. When I first met you, I was attracted to you as well, but as I got to know you, I realized it would never work between us. I planned on ending it after the holidays, but then you got the invitation to your cousin's wedding, so I went with you as a courtesy. I planned on ending it on the way home. But then—"

"I know, and I'm truly sorry about my aunt. I talked to her about it later, and she realizes she overreacted."

"Well, better late than never I suppose. However, my point is our relationship had already run its course. I would have ended it anyway, even if your aunt had been on her very best behavior that night. Now I'm paying back the money I owe you so we can both have closure."

Ken's eyes suddenly turned dark. Jenna felt a shiver go down her spine. "You're going to pay me back alright," he said through clenched teeth, "but it'll be on my terms."

Jenna glared back at him. "So, what are you saying?"

"Sorry," he said in a calmer voice. "It's been a long, stressful day, and I didn't mean to take it out on you. What I'm trying to say is neither one of us is seeing anyone else at the moment, and I've genuinely missed making love to you. It was a part of our relationship which was truly unforgettable. So, I've reserved a room here at the hotel for the night. We're going to enjoy our wine, and then I'm taking you up to the room. Once we're there, we're going to make mad, passionate love, just like we did before. I'll take you home first thing in the morning."

Jenna felt the air escaping from her lungs. It took her a moment to find her voice. "There is no way in hell I'm having sex with you. In fact, I'm leaving. Right now."

"Oh no you're not."

She grabbed her phone. "Oh yes, I am."

His eyes turned dark once again as he yanked the phone away from her. "If you don't want to cooperate, I won't force you, but surely you remember the times you spent the night at my place, don't you?"

"Actually, it's a part of my life I'm desperately trying to forget."

"You are? Then I'm sorry to hear it, but don't worry. I saved it for posterity."

"What?"

He gave her a leering grin. "I had nanny cams in my bedroom. They're so small they're hardly noticeable, so I guess you never knew they were there. One was on top of the dresser mirror. The other was in a fake electrical outlet, and I've got some really interesting videos of you."

"You're lying."

"Would you care take a look?" He punched a few buttons on his phone and showed her a photo of a nude woman with long blonde hair, but she was looking away from the camera.

"Sorry, Ken, but this isn't me."

"I'll admit your rose tattoo is hard to see in the shadows but don't worry. I'll do some photo editing before I post it online."

"It still isn't me."

"You know, it really doesn't matter if it's you or someone else, because I have plenty of others which clearly show your face. So, you can either do as I say, or you can become the next big Internet porn star. If it were me, I'd do the first and join me upstairs. Then, when I've had my fill, I'll consider the debt paid in full and delete all the footage. If you want to leave, I won't stop you, but be forewarned. There will be serious consequences if you do."

Jenna struggled to remain calm. "I think I'm going to be sick, so if you're excuse me, I need to go to the ladies' room. Now."

"Of course, but your phone stays with me, and don't even think about asking anyone to help you. If you do, you'll regret it. We'll talk more when you get back."

Jenna grabbed her purse and hurried out to the atrium. She tested a nearby employee corridor door. To her relief, it was unlocked, so she stepped inside. A set of cross corridor doors, leading to Sam's kitchen, were on the left. Her body was shaking as she took a few deep breaths and continued down the hallway toward the employee locker rooms. Hopefully, her watch was still synced to her phone. Stopping once again, she quickly scrolled through the apps, tapping on a name to quickly place a call.

"C'mon, Kelsey. Pick up. Pick up."

Kelsey answered an instant later. "What happened?"

"Nothing good," said Jenna. "I'm in serious trouble."

"What's going on?"

"Ken showed up and insisted on taking me to Sam's Place. He's reserved a room at the hotel, and he's trying to force me into going upstairs with him."

"How?"

"He says he had hidden cameras in his bedroom, which I was completely unaware of at the time, and while he was talking, I saw a look of pure evil in his eyes. I've never seen that look before and it scared the living hell out of me."

"Are you kidding me?"

"No, Kelsey, I'm not. I'm completely freaked out right now."

"So am I. So where are you?"

"He thinks I'm in the ladies' room, but I'm actually in an employee corridor. The stupid son of a bitch didn't realize I also designed the restricted areas of the hotel, and I know where all the hidden exits are. We're a few hours away from the next shift change, so I'll be safe until you get here."

"We're on our way," said Connor. "Kelsey put the phone on speaker while you were talking. She'll fill me in on the rest while we're driving, and we're leaving right now."

"You have no idea how grateful I am. When you get here turn into the main entrance and then turn left. Drive around to the back of the hotel. You'll see a metal door marked 'Employees only.' The door is locked on the outside. You have to have a special code to get in, and there are security cameras too, so stay in the car and text me. I'll come out and then we'll leave."

"Okay. I'm handing the phone back to Kelsey. We'll be in her blue Honda Civic."

Kelsey came back on the line. "Do you want to hang up? Or would you rather I stayed on the line?"

"Please, stay on the line. I'm absolutely terrified at the moment, and he may send someone to look for me. If he does, I'll have to make a run for it."

"What if someone accidentally finds you?"

"My Salisbury lanyard is in my purse. I'll make up some story about someone calling and saying there's a problem with corridor, and I'm here to check it out."

Kelsey kept Jenna up to date on their progress as they made their way to the hotel. "Okay," she finally said, "we're turning in to the entrance now."

"Thank goodness. Now turn left."

"We did. We're heading around the back right now."

Jenna hurried toward the exit and heard the car engine. As she ran out the door, Kelsey rolled down the passenger window.

"The back door is unlocked."

Jenna jumped into the backseat. Her voice was shaking as she tried to speak. "Thank God you're here. I've never been so scared in my life."

"Where's your coat?"

"At Sam's. Ken has my phone too. Both of them can be replaced. I just want to get the hell out of here."

Connor drove up to the front entrance and parked at the curb. "What are you doing?" asked Jenna.

He quickly unfastened his seat belt. "Wait here. If I'm not back in five minutes, call the police."

"Wait!" shouted Kelsey, but she was too late. Connor was already out of the car and rushing to the front door.

* * *

Connor kept his wits about him as he walked through the hotel lobby. He slowed his pace as he passed his father's sculpture, but he would have to come back another day to give it a closer look. He hurried into the atrium and spotted the entrance to Sam's Place.

"How many," asked the hostess.

"Actually, I'm here to see a friend." Connor quickly scanned the dining room. A lone, dark-haired man was seated near the back. Across from him was an empty chair, with a woman's coat draped over it.

"I found him. I'll only be a minute. I just need to return something to him." He hurried to the table and sat down.

"If you're waiting for Jenna, she's left the building," said Connor.

"And who are you?" asked Ken.

"Her guardian angel. I see she gave you your check, so she's paid you in full. I just need her phone and her coat, and I'll be on my way."

Ken reluctantly handed her phone to Connor. "Her coat's on the chair."

"I know, but before I go, I need to let you know that uploading revenge porn is illegal in Colorado. So, if I were you, I'd think really carefully before I posted anything online, unless of course you don't mind being up to your eyeballs with court dates and legal bills. Oh, and I would delete everything I had of her off my devices as well, because you certainly wouldn't want it being used as evidence against you in a court of law. Think of the scandal, and how much it could damage your reputation. Jenna also told me to tell you goodbye and to have a good life, and under no circumstances are you to ever contact her again."

Connor grabbed Jenna's coat and hurried out. The two women were anxiously waiting when he got back in the car. "So how long was I gone?" he asked.

"Not long," said Kelsey.

"Here's your phone and your coat."

"Thanks. So did he say anything to you?" she asked.

"Not much. I simply told him what Kelsey said about revenge porn, and warned him about posting anything of you online. He didn't argue or cause a scene. For all he knows, I'm the new man in your life. We're going to make a quick stop at your place so you can pack a bag, because you're staying with us until the restraining order is served."

* * *

Connor carried Jenna's bag inside the apartment. "I'm afraid we don't have a guest bed, but the sofa is pretty comfortable. Kelsey will get you some sheets and blankets. So, are you okay?"

"I'm pretty shaken, but I'm feeling a little better. For a while there I really thought I was going to be forced into doing something against my will, and I still feel half sick to my stomach."

Kelsey came in with an armful of bed linens. "Sorry they don't match, and you'll have to use a sofa pillow."

"It's okay," said Jenna, "they'll do."

"I've got some tomato soup and I'm making us grilled cheese sandwiches."

"I'll join you in a couple of minutes. First, I need to go pull myself back together."

"Take your time." said Connor.

Later that night, after they had gone to bed, Connor grabbed his phone from the nightstand and typed a text message.

"Sorry to break protocol, but earlier this evening Jenna's ex-boyfriend tried to rape her. She's okay. Kelsey and I got to her in time. She's staying with us until she can get a restraining order against him."

❦FORTY-ONE❧

KELSEY TIP-TOED into the kitchen and quietly reached for a coffee mug, but Jenna was already awake.

"Mind if I join you?" she asked.

"Not at all," said Kelsey. "Did you sleep well?"

"Not really. The whole episode kept playing back in my mind."

"I'm so sorry. Connor didn't sleep well either. He woke me up a couple of times tossing and turning, so I'm letting him sleep in. I also sent a text message to my boss. He would be more than happy to help you get your restraining order, and you have me as a witness."

"I know, but it'll cost money I don't have right now."

"I already told him. He said not to worry. He'll give you a discount and you can work out a payment plan later, but right now we need to get rolling. These things take time, so sooner we can get your paperwork filed the better. I'm taking you to the office with me, and I'll bring you back when we're done."

"It's okay," said Jenna. "I have my Uber app. You don't have to give me a ride home."

They heard water running. Connor was in the shower. He soon joined them in the kitchen, freshly shaved and wearing a clean shirt and tie.

"Guess it's my turn now. I won't be long." Jenna grabbed her bag and hurried down the hallway.

* * *

"Is she alright?" asked Connor.

"She said she didn't sleep well, which really isn't surprising. While she's getting ready, I'll heat up some oatmeal, then I need to get dressed."

197

"Need any help?"

"I can dress myself."

"You're sure about that?"

"It's not the time, my love," she said. "I also need to make the oatmeal. Then you need to get to the office."

The doorbell rang as Connor filled his mug. "Oh, crap. Do you think Ken could have somehow found out she's here?"

"I don't see how. I didn't see any suspicious vehicles parked on her street when we left."

"Neither did I, but he could have downloaded some sort of malware on her phone, so stay here until I find out who it is." Connor looked through the peephole and quickly opened the door.

"Oh, my god. I don't believe this. I've been worried sick." Connor embraced his father and they held each other for a moment. "So, what the hell happened?" he asked. "And how did you get here?"

"I left Wichita as soon as I got your message."

"So, you drove all night?"

"I did, and I'll explain the rest later. Right now, I need to know if she's alright."

Connor invited his father inside and poured him a much-needed cup of coffee. "I'm afraid I don't know all the details. She owed him some money, and wanted to pay him back."

"I know how it all came about," said Bill. "Ken, along with one of her coworkers, duped her into thinking Oscar Shelton had given her a gift card, when it actually came from Ken."

"She told us about it," said Kelsey. "I already knew he was a real piece of...well, you know, but I had no idea he was this devious."

"He is," said Bill. "So, what the hell happened last night?"

"She got the money to pay him back," said Kelsey. "So, she called him to get his mailing address, but he insisted in picking it up in person, and he wouldn't accept the money unless she agreed to go with him."

"Which is how she ended up at Sam's Place," said Connor. "That's when he told her he'd reserved a room and demanded she have sex with him. If she didn't, he threatened to post a video he'd surreptitiously recorded of her in his bedroom online. It was recorded before you came along, Dad."

"I know," said Bill. "So why is this guy still walking around?"

"Good question," said Connor. "She managed to get away from him and called Kelsey, and we got there as quickly we could. Once she was safely in the car, I went inside and had a little chat with him."

"What the hell were you thinking?" Bill sounded angry. "You don't know what else he's capable of."

"It's okay, Dad. We didn't raise our voices or cause a scene. I simply told him that what he planned on doing was illegal, and there'd be a heavy price to pay if he followed through with it. I think he got the message, at least for now. Kelsey's taking Jenna to the office with her this morning so she can meet with her boss. He's going to help her take out a restraining order against him. She'll be staying with us until he's served."

A voice spoke up from the hallway. "I think they've pretty much covered everything."

They all looked at Jenna as she set her bag next to the sofa. "I'm not hungry, so I'll skip the oatmeal, but I can help with the clean-up."

"Thanks," said Kelsey, "but I really think you should eat something."

"I'm fine. I ate last night."

"Dad's here," said Connor.

"Yeah, I thought he looked familiar. I know I'm not supposed to be here, but as you just heard, it was kind of an emergency."

"Okay," said Bill. "I want both of you to delete the text messages I sent you. I wasn't myself at the time, and I honestly don't remember sending them. I also want you to know they blew me away when I read them later on."

"So, what happened, Dad?"

"It's like your grandmother said. All marriages have their challenges. Your mother meant the world to me, but somehow, I came up short."

"How do you know?"

Bill took a deep breath, hoping Connor would buy his story. "I was down in the basement, finishing my unpacking, when I came across a box containing your mother's personal belongings from her office. I'd never opened it, so I figured the time had come. There was a pen set I'd like for you to have."

"I remember it," said Connor, "and I'd love to have it. Thanks for offering it to me."

"You're welcome. The other thing I found, along with one of your old school pictures, was a private journal she kept hidden in her desk. I had no idea she kept a journal, but there it was. So, I started looking through it."

"You okay, Dad?"

"I'm fine, but what I found out, Connor, was that she was very unhappy in the marriage. Don't get me wrong, she loved you dearly, but somewhere along the line she'd fallen out of love with me and she didn't want to be with me anymore. She even met with a divorce attorney, but later on she changed her mind because she didn't want you growing up in a broken home. I had no idea she felt this way, because for whatever reason, she put up a brave front and never told me, and now I feel like I've failed her."

"I'm sorry, Dad. I had no idea."

"As well you shouldn't have. Anyway, after I finished reading it, I went into total shock. It was like I was stuck in the back of my head, watching myself from a distance, and I must have been on autopilot. As I said, I honestly don't remember sending either one of those text messages, and I barely remember the drive to Wichita. It wasn't until your uncle showed up and started talking to me that I finally snapped out of it, and I've been living in the real world ever since. What I'm trying to do now is make sense of it all. I'm also trying really hard to stop blaming myself for not being a mind reader." He focused his attention on Jenna.

"Connor sent me a text message late last night, telling me what happened. As soon as I read it, I packed my bag and drove straight here, because there's no way in hell I'm letting him get away with this. At least this time I remember the drive. I was listening to a fascinating conversation about UFOs on *Coast-to-Coast AM*."

"Are they real?" asked Connor.

"Apparently so, although I've never seen one myself."

"What about your therapy?" asked Jenna.

"We'll be video conferencing the rest of it, and don't worry. I've gotten all the crazy out of my system. But for now, Connor needs to get to work. I'll follow you to Kelsey's office. Once you're done, I'm taking you to my place so we can talk."

"I'm not making any promises about staying there."

"I understand, but we still have some important matters to discuss."

ᏉFORTY-TWOᏇ

KELSEY'S BOSS, Peter Davis, was a senior partner with the firm. He had been practicing law for nearly four decades.

"Don't worry, Ms. Winters," he said. "I've dealt with plenty of cases like this before. These clowns always think they can get away with it, but in the end, it costs them a whole lot of money. I can certainly help get you a permanent order of protection against him, although it'll take a few steps. We'll start with a temporary order. You could also sue him for civil damages if you wish."

"All I want is to get this creep out of my life, once and for all," said Jenna. "I also want him to delete anything he has of me off his devices."

"A reasonable request, and we can certainly ask him to do so. A strongly-worded letter, stating we intend to sue, oftentimes does the trick. Especially when the defendant is a professional who doesn't want his reputation to suffer or lose clientele as a result."

"Connor pointed this out to him as well," said Kelsey. "He said Ken looked genuinely scared when he left."

"Something tells me he'll be happy to comply," said Pete. "I'll get started on this right away, and I'll keep you posted. With any luck, this will be over and done with within a few weeks."

Bill extended his hand as they got up to leave. "Thank you for meeting with us on such short notice."

"It was my pleasure, and don't worry, Ms. Winters. We'll take care of it."

* * *

Jenna felt relieved as they drove out of the parking lot. "I think you're in good hands," said Bill. "Ken is going to be dealt with, once and for all. I also want to thank you for including Kelsey and Connor in your Christmas plans. I'm sorry I wasn't able to be there."

"It was a nice evening, and my folks were impressed with both of them. It was also fun watching them experience roast beef and Yorkshire pudding for the first time. Kelsey wasn't sure at first, but once she tried it, she thought it was okay. Connor, on the other hand, wasn't a bit shy. He poured some gravy on top of his pudding and chowed it down."

"He's always loved bread and gravy. I used to make my mother's hot turkey sandwiches when he was a kid, and he couldn't get enough of them." Bill tried to stifle a yawn.

"Are you okay to drive?" asked Jenna. "You've been up all night."

"It's starting to catch up with me, but I can get us home. It's not much further."

"I know, but I'm happy to take the wheel if you want me to."

"Thanks, but I've got it."

Jenna felt apprehensive when Bill pressed the remote to open the garage door. After carrying their bags into the living room, he asked her to accompany him down to the basement. She sensed a change in his mood as they went down the stairs.

"Here we are. The scene of the crime." He stepped into the utility room, returning with a Priority Mailbox, and set the contents on the table.

"The version of the story I told you this morning wasn't quite accurate," he said. "Connor is to never know what really happened. Mary Beth is still his mother. I don't want him traumatized or to have his memories of her tarnished. I'm going to step outside while you take a look at what's inside the manilla envelope. In the meantime, you still haven't eaten anything, so I'm going to heat up some soup."

"Thanks. I'll join you upstairs when I'm done."

As Bill went upstairs Jenna grabbed the envelope and dumped out the contents. Once she finished reading the letters, she put them back in their envelopes and hurried upstairs. Bill was busy in the kitchen.

"What are you doing?" he asked.

"Looking for a match."

"There's some by the fireplace. Wait a minute. Are you going to burn the letters?"

"Yes."

"Why?" he asked.

"To set you free from Mary Beth. I'm sorry she cheated on you, and believe me, I know how it feels. Arthur cheated on me as well, remember? You need to cut whatever ties you had with her, once and for all, and we're going to start with these letters. Do you have any of her other belongings?"

"I gave all her clothes to charity before I went to Florida," said Bill. "However, I'm saving her jewelry for Connor to give to Kelsey once they're married."

"I understand, but maybe Connor should decide when he wants to give it to her."

"Fair enough, but I'd rather he not keep it in the apartment."

"Then you'll have rent a safe deposit box at the bank. Is there anything else of hers which needs to be taken care of?"

"Connor's baby book, and a few family photo albums."

"Then I guess you'll have to have to decide if you want to keep them or offer them to Connor. Arthur and I had no children, so it's something I didn't have to deal with."

"I know you didn't. I also want you to know that whatever feelings I may have had for Mary Beth are now dead, but I'm still very grateful to have Connor. I wouldn't trade him for anything, although I had my moment of doubt regarding him."

"How so?" asked Jenna.

"After reading the letters, I wasn't sure if he was really mine or not."

"Even if he wasn't biologically yours, you still raised him, and you were his dad in every way that counts."

"I know I was. Then, when I was in Wichita, I remembered something. Back when Connor was in high school, he did a genealogy project for one of his classes. We both sent DNA samples to one of those ancestry websites. The results confirmed we were father and son. Turns out I'm part Irish, part German, part Italian, and part English. Connor is as well, but he's also part Greek on his mother's side. And to think of how you laughed at me the time I told you I was your Italian stallion."

"It was the way you said it. It sounded pretty funny." Jenna dumped the letters into the fireplace and dropped the manilla envelope on top of them. Bill struck a match and lit the corners of the envelopes. As the flames consumed the letters, he wrapped his arms around her and held her tight.

"Thank you for doing this. It needed to be done."

"I'm glad. Hopefully, she can now rest in peace."

"So, do you want to stay here? Or would you rather go back to Connor and Kelsey's apartment?"

"I think I'll stay here, if it's okay with you."

He looked her into her eyes. "Thank you for not giving up on me. There are no words to describe how incredibly sorry I am for hurting you. I completely blindsided you. And Connor."

"Mary Beth also blindsided you. I'm not going to lie. The messages you sent us were hurtful, but we also knew something was terribly wrong. Then your mother called Connor, and she kept us in the loop. At that point all we could do was pray for you, and it must have worked."

"Thank you." He held her once again. "Thank you for everything you did. I was so afraid you wouldn't take me back. So, let's get you fed. Then we both need to get some rest." He brought her into the kitchen and gave her a bowl of chicken vegetable soup, along with one for himself. After they finished their meal, he took her to the bedroom.

"As much as I would like to make love to you, I simply don't have the energy at the moment."

"Neither do I."

"So, let's take a nap, and we'll see how we feel when we wake up." He turned down and coverlet and watched her as she undressed. "Looking good, Venus."

Jenna's face turned red. "What? How did you know?"

"Rhonda sent me a text message after you left. Did you do it to get the money to pay Ken?"

"Yes. I wanted to pay him back, as quickly as possible."

Jenna crawled into bed. Bill joined her a minute later. Cuddling underneath the blankets, they both fell into an exhausted sleep.

✤FORTY-THREE✤

JENNA WAS SLEEPING soundly when Bill woke up. Reaching for his bathrobe, he climbed out of bed and peered through the blinds. It was late in the afternoon. As he stepped back from the window, Jenna began stirring and sat up. He sat down next to her.

"How are you feeling?" he asked.

"Physically, I feel much better. Emotionally, not so much. I'm still creeped out over Ken. Funny how you think you know someone. Then you find out you didn't."

"Tell me about it."

She squeezed his hand. "I honestly think she was a good woman deep-down. In the end, she chose you and Connor over him."

"Maybe so, but she was also living a lie. She should have told me she wasn't happy. We could have at least tried to work things out. Instead, she chose to live a double-life."

"Unfortunately, when it comes to infidelity, people don't think logically. They think with their emotions. Sex outside of marriage is the ultimate forbidden fruit, and there are some who simply can't resist. Arthur certainly couldn't. For a long time, I kept thinking it was my fault, because I somehow wasn't meeting his needs. Stacy finally set me straight and told me it had nothing to do with me. He was doing the deed with his boss so he could advance his career."

"Shameless harlot that he was," said Bill.

Jenna burst out laughing. "I guess so. Seriously though, the reason doesn't really matter, because there's never any excuse for cheating. After I found out he begged me not to leave him, but he'd gone too far. I could never trust him again. Hopefully, he's learned his lesson."

"I hope he has too. I don't know if I ever told you this, but I was barely twenty-one when I first met Mary Beth. I was working at the auto body shop, and one of their customers wasn't happy for some reason, so he decided to sue. I was one of the people who worked on his car, and Mary Beth was the attorney representing the shop. I guess opposites really do attract, because we were drawn to one another from the get go. The case was soon settled out of court, so I asked her out. She accepted, and we quickly became an item. We simply couldn't get enough of one another. We were married a few months later. She was going on thirty and anxious to start a family because of her age, and Connor was born the following year. So, was I nothing more than a baby daddy?"

"Unfortunately, she's not here to tell her side of the story, although I truly believe she did love you for a time. I also think the two of you were too different from one another for it to have lasted over the long term. Sooner or later, you would have gone your separate ways, and now that she's gone, you need to go on with your life."

"I know," said Bill. "I just wish I hadn't wasted all those years grieving her, and swearing I would never marry again, when I could have found someone else and been happy." He wrapped his arms around her and held her close. "I'll always be eternally grateful we reconnected. So, before I allow myself to become too distracted, let's get cleaned up, because I'm taking you to dinner. Someplace special. Maybe the place in Cherry Creek where I took you the night before I left for Florida."

"You mean you're going to wear your suit? For little ole me?"

He shot her a look. "Not quite. It's a little too cold outside, so I'm wearing my black turtleneck sweater and a pair of dress pants. Then when we get home, I have surprise for you."

"You do?" she said flirtatiously. "So, what is it?"

"If I told you, it wouldn't be a surprise."

"I'm afraid I don't have a dressy outfit with me. All I have are the black slacks and red sweater I wore to the attorney's office this morning. Everything else is jeans and casual tops."

"It'll do nicely, so let's get ready."

* * *

"Funny how much things can change so much in such a short period of time," said Jenna. "The last time we were here everything was so different. You were leaving for Florida the following morning, and I was doing my best to put on a brave face."

"It was also hotter than hell that night," said Bill. "I was sweltering in that suit, but now we can look forward to happier days. New Year's Eve is coming up. Got any plans?"

"So far, I'm free on New Year's Eve. However, Kelsey sent me a text message while you were in the shower. I have a court hearing scheduled at ten o'clock tomorrow morning for the restraining order. She's offering to take me."

"Have you responded?"

"Not yet. I wanted to discuss it with you first."

"Tell her we'll meet her at the courthouse."

"You're coming with me?"

"Of course, I'm coming with you," he said. "Things are different now. So, what would you like to do for New Year's Eve?"

"I'm not sure. My parents will be in Hawaii. Dad has an early flight to Maui that morning, and Mom's going with him. Once they get there, he has a three-day layover."

"Do they know about your hearing?"

"No, they don't. I want to wait until the restraining order is in place before I tell them about what happened with Ken. My mother has been concerned about him for some time now. I don't want to put a damper on their New Year's Eve plans, or worse, have her cancel so she can stay here with me. My father turns sixty-five next October. He'll then be forced into mandatory retirement. I want them to enjoy their flight benefits while they can."

"I didn't realize your father had you when he was in his mid-thirties."

"My mother is his second wife. There were no children from his prior marriage."

"Interesting," he said. "So, what about your mother?"

"She was single when they met."

"I seem to recall an old Frank Sinatra song about love being better the second time around, so I guess there must be something to it."

"Must be. It's been their song since before I was born."

"So, about that surprise," said Bill. "I've decided not to give it to you when we get home."

Jenna looked stunned. "What do mean? Did I say something to upset you?"

"It's okay." He gave her hand a squeeze. "I decided to give it to you now, while we relax and enjoy our wine. Hopefully, you'll like it. If not, then I guess I'll be out of luck."

"I'm sure I'll like it if it's coming from you."

"Hopefully, you will, but first I want you to know that I bought it for you while I was in Kansas."

"It's okay, Bill. I got you something for Christmas as well, but it's at my house."

"We can get it tomorrow," he said. "So, do you recall what I said to you the night we were here before? It was right before I left your house."

"I'm not sure," said Jenna. "It's was such as emotional night for me. I was doing my best to keep from crying in front of you."

"I understand, but try to relax for a moment and concentrate. Maybe you'll remember."

"Okay." Jenna took a deep breath and closed her eyes. "We were waiting for your Uber ride. Once it arrived, we said our goodbyes. Then you said something else. It was rather unexpected."

"Do you remember what it was?"

"Of course, I remember. You said if you were to have ever married again..." A surprised look came over her face. "Oh my god! I don't believe this. Are you asking me to—"

"As a matter of fact, I am." He reached into his pocket and placed a black velvet box on the table. Inside was a diamond solitaire ring.

"After I got my master's degree, I kept thinking about you. There were so many times when I thought about looking you up, but I always figured you either had a boyfriend, or a spouse or significant other, so I didn't. You have no idea how happy I was when you contacted me about the sculpture. I also meant it when I told you if I ever remarried, it would have been you. So, the time has come for me to let go of all my previous hang-ups and do what I should have done years ago." He stopped to clear his throat.

"Jenna Winters, I've been in love with you for over ten years, even though I've spent most of them trying to deny it. I would be honored to have you for my wife, so will you marry me?"

"Yes, I'll marry you." She stopped to wipe a few tears away with her napkin.

"Well, that's certainly a relief. It would have been really embarrassing if you'd said no. So, let's see if it fits."

He slipped the ring on her finger. It fit perfectly.

"I still can't believe this," Jenna said as she admired it. "So how were you able to get this? You've been out of work for some time."

"There was a nice sum of money left over from my late wife's insurance policy after Connor finished college, so I opened up an investment account. It's how I'm able to get by teaching part-time instead of full-time at the college." He gave her a mischievous look. "I also do odd jobs for extra cash, so just call me Bacchus." He raised his glass. "So, here's to the god of winemaking, and the goddess of love."

They took a sip, and their server stopped by to see if they were ready to order.

"In a minute," said Jenna, "but first I need someone to take a picture of the two of us so I can send to my parents. Would you mind taking it?'

"Not at all," he said.

She handed him her phone. Bill wrapped his arm around her shoulder as she placed her left hand to show off her ring. Once he finished, Bill ordered raw oysters for their appetizer. Jenna started laughing after their server left.

"What's so funny?" asked Bill. "We're going to celebrate when we get home, although we can't make it too late of a night. We have to be at the courthouse in time for your hearing."

"I know." Jenna quickly sent her mother message. Her phone rang while they were ordering their main course. As expected, her mother was calling.

"Does this mean what I think it means?" asked Claire.

"It does," said Jenna.

"You have no idea how happy your father and I are, but please, whatever you do, don't go running off to the justice of the peace again."

"No worries, Mom. Once was enough. I want a real wedding this time."

"Then we need to get busy and start making plans."

"We will," said Jenna, "as soon as Bill and I set a date and figure out what we want. In the meantime, please tell Dad I love him, and if I don't see you before, have a Happy New Year in Hawaii. We'll talk more when you get back."

* * *

Bill lit a fire in the fireplace and joined Jenna on the sofa. "I'm afraid I'm clueless when it comes to planning weddings," he said. "All I need to know is where and when I need to show up."

"Don't worry. Mom and I can handle the details. I just need to know who you'd like to invite."

"Well, let's see. Obviously, I want my family there. What about you?"

"My parents, of course," said Jenna, "and Stacy and her significant other. I suppose it all depends on how big of a wedding we want. It's a second marriage for both of us, so I think we should keep it simple and limit it to immediate family and close friends, and perhaps a few coworkers."

"I totally agree," said Bill. "I'd like to have Rhonda and her husband there. We go back many years."

"I know you do. I'd like to include Chad and his wife as well, but definitely not CeCe."

"Absolutely not," Bill said firmly. "I have no problem with her buying my art, but she's hardly been a friend to you. She's the one who created this whole nightmare in the first place."

"According to Chad, she's on vacation this week, and he's hoping she won't come back."

"Which makes two of us, so I'm doing a quick mental head count. It looks like we'll have about twelve to fifteen people there. I think we should rent a ballroom at the Shelton Inn, and have Sam's cater the reception. It's the most meaningful location I can think of. One of my former coworkers from the body shop is now a Methodist minister. He can perform the ceremony."

"Then I think we have the guest list covered," said Jenna.

"I would also like for you to move in with me. This house is bigger than yours, and you can bring your furniture here and redo it any way you'd like. I've got my shed and the basement for doing my art. The rest I can do at my studio, now that I finally have a working furnace."

"Sounds good to me. My house is kind of small. We'll decide together on what furniture to keep and what to get rid of. Then I can put my house up for sale."

"You could, but I have a better idea. Would you be willing to sell it to Connor and Kelsey? He plans on marrying her someday, and he's been putting money away for a down payment on a house, but first he wants to be sure his job works out."

"We can certainly talk to him and Kelsey about it. I love the idea of keeping it in the family."

A strange look came over Bill's face. "I suppose you want to have kids."

"It would be nice," said Jenna, "although I'm not in any big rush. If it happens, it happens. However, for the next few months, I'm going to be busy designing the interior for a new restaurant. So, what about a June wedding? Or even July? It should be completed by then."

"It might not work me. I'll be teaching this summer."

"Okay, so what about spring break?"

"It's a busy travel season," said Bill. "Flights are booked, and hotels are full, which might be an issue for my mom and my brother." He thought it over for a moment. "Here's a thought. What about President's Day weekend? We could have the ceremony on Friday night, and stay at the hotel through Sunday, sort of like a mini honeymoon. We'll take our real honeymoon later in the year. Perhaps in August, before the fall semester starts. I'd love to go back to Florida for a visit. There are nice places in the Keys where we could stay, and we'd be booking it well in advance. We could even get married in August if you'd like."

"August in Denver can be pretty warm," said Jenna. "I don't want to be sweating in my wedding dress, but I love the idea of the beach, so I'm definitely up for a summer honeymoon in Florida. It'll give me plenty of time to shop for a bathing suit."

He brushed a strand of hair away from her face. "Hmm...I forgot about you not having a bathing suit."

"It's like I told you before. I live in Denver, and I don't have a pool."

"I have a better idea."

"What's that?" she asked.

"We'll find a place with a nude beach and have our honeymoon there. Then you won't need to worry about a bathing suit."

Her face turned slightly pink. "I only posed for those paintings because I needed the money, and with the understanding they wouldn't look like me when she was done."

"And you know Rhonda is good for her word."

"She is. She also showed me the completed Bacchus. It looked amazing."

"I know," said Bill. "She sent me a photo of it. So, what about Venus?"

"You'll have to wait to see the painting. I was also Diana, and she's supposed to be a virgin."

"Is she? Well, I have a cure for that, and it's coming up right now."

❧FORTY-FOUR❧

CECE OPENED HER front door and smiled. "Happy almost New Year, Ken. I'm so glad you decided to come after all." She looked at him more closely. "Are you okay?" she asked. "You look upset about something."

"I've been better." He came inside and followed her to the kitchen. Setting the pizza boxes on the counter, CeCe offered him a Coors, which he gladly accepted

"So, what happened?"

"It's kind of a long story," he said. "a few days ago, Jenna sent me a text message, out of the blue. She had my money and wanted my address so she could mail it to me. I thought I'd save her the cost of a stamp, so last night I stopped by her place after work to pick it up."

"I see. So did she say something to upset you?"

"No," said Ken. "Once I got there, I told her I wanted to talk, you know, just to clear the air and set things straight, so I offered to take her out for coffee, someplace public, where we could talk. At first, she refused. I really had to convince her I would only take a few minutes of her time, then I'd take her straight home. For the life of me, I don't understand why this woman thinks I'm the boogeyman."

"Oh, c'mon Ken. She's never put you down. At least not around me. She simply told me she'd moved on and didn't want to create any misunderstandings between you and Jeri."

"Which I appreciate, but Jeri left town months ago."

"I know, but Jenna didn't know that."

"Which is exactly why I told her. She said she was sorry to hear we'd gone our separate ways. I also wanted to take her someplace nicer than a cheap diner for a cup of coffee, so I took her to Sam's Place. Once we got there, I told her, she didn't have to pay me back. I wanted her to keep the money because I knew she needed it, and I kept reassuring her it was a gift with no strings attached. So, she excuses herself to go to the restroom and doesn't come back. I was getting really worried that something might have happened to her. So about twenty minutes later some guy who I've never seen before comes in. He told me Jenna had left, and I'm to leave her alone, or else."

"Are you serious?"

"I'm afraid so," said Ken. "All I was trying to do was pick up a check she insisted on me taking, as well try make up for the way things ended, and she responds by sending in some guy to do her dirty work."

"Did he say who he was?"

"No. Apparently, she's found someone else. At least he's a younger guy this time, but he's one arrogant son of a bitch." Ken opened his beer and looked around the room.

"So, where's John?"

"He's running a little late, but he should be here in about fifteen minutes or so."

"Hard to believe it's almost New Year's Eve. We'll be closing up shop early on New Year's Eve, and I imagine he will be as well. So, how are things going with you?"

"At the moment everything is great. I took my vacation this week, and I've really been enjoying the holidays."

"I'm glad, so what are your New Year's resolutions?"

"To eat more pizza." CeCe opened the lid and took some plates from the cupboard. "John said to help ourselves if he were running late."

"I will in a minute. I want to drink the rest of my beer first. It's been a hectic week at the office, and Jenna's little stunt didn't help either. I gather she's still on furlough."

"She is, but not for much longer. Chad just got a new project, starting the first of the year, and he asked for her personally, in spite of the fact that I was available. Apparently, he's still holding a grudge over the gift card incident. I did, however, see Jenna at the company holiday party. Chad Runyan was named Employee of the year for the Shelton Inn. Jenna and the rest of the crew were mentioned as well. They each got a little gift from the boss."

"I'm glad she got a mention, but you don't look too pleased about it."

"I'm getting really tired of all the office politics," said CeCe. "While the rest of the world was oohing and aweing over the Shelton Inn, I was working with Justin on a new medical center. It may not have been as glamourous of a project, but it'll serve a lot of people, and it's certainly a bigger asset to the community than a hotel and restaurant. Everyone agreed the interiors were beautiful, and I put a lot of thought into them. I even included one of Bill's smaller pieces in the main lobby, but did I get any thanks or recognition from anyone? Oh, hell no. They were all too busy kissing Chad's rear end, along with the rest of his team's."

"I'm sorry, CeCe, and I agree. You're not getting the recognition you deserve, and it's wrong."

"Thank you. I appreciate your support."

"So did Jenna say anything to you about what she's been up to while she was there?"

"She said she had the money to pay you back," said CeCe. "So, I reminded her I'm no longer your go-between, and she would have to call you herself. I'm sorry, Ken. I guess this is partly my fault too. Had I known what she was really up to, I would have said sure, I'll see that he gets it. I have no idea what's going on with her. All I can tell you is I've never seen this side of her before. I also know Chad wants me out the door, and she's taking his side so she can move up the company ladder at my expense. I've spent the past week debating if I even want to go back there or not."

"No," Ken said emphatically. "Whatever you do, don't quit, because if you leave, they win. You've apologized for the misunderstanding with Oscar Shelton. They need to let it go and move on. Jenna needs to change her attitude as well."

"I'll know more once she's back to work, and believe me, if she bad mouths you in any way, I'll put a stop to it. I am curious about one thing though."

"Which is?"

"I asked her about Bill, said CeCe. "She said he was busy working on a project, and there was no mention of them going their separate ways. Seems kind of odd for her to have a new man in her life two weeks later."

"Perhaps the younger guy was waiting in the wings."

"I suppose. All I can tell you is once we're all back at work I'm going to see what I can do to knock her off her high horse. Meantime I just heard the garage door open, which means John has arrived."

❧FORTY-FIVE❧

AS EXPECTED, Kelsey was waiting in the courthouse lobby when Bill and Jenna arrived. "I've got your paperwork," she said. "All you have to do is sign it, tell the judge what happened, and ask the court to make the order permanent. It's a reasonable request, so the judge should grant it. So, if you're ready, we need to get to the courtroom."

Kelsey led them to the elevator, and they took their seats in the gallery. The judge soon arrived and began calling cases. Most were routine matters which only took a few minutes of her time. Finally, Jenna's case was called. Kelsey joined her as they approached the bench.

"I'm afraid it's a complicated story," said Jenna.

"They usually are, Ms. Winters. So can you tell me what happened?"

"Of course." As Jenna recalled the events the judge asked her a few questions. Kelsey then corroborated the story.

"Okay, Ms. Winters, I think I see what's happening. The court will grant your request for a fourteen-day restraining order. You'll need to have him served, and I'm also scheduling a hearing for two weeks from today to determine if a permanent order of protection will be necessary."

"Thank you, Your Honor," said Jenna. The judge hit her gavel and called the next case as they left the courtroom.

"We'll take care of having him served," said Kelsey. "So, are you guys doing exciting for New Year's Eve?"

"We're ordering in and watching the festivities on TV," said Bill. "Are you and Connor going out?"

"Nope. We're staying in as well. Connor says New Year's Eve is amateur night." She gave them each a hug and hurried away.

"She didn't notice the ring," said Jenna.

"At the moment she has more important things on her mind," said Bill, "and I'm relieved she didn't. I want Connor to hear it from both of us, so I'm thinking we could have them over for dinner New Year's night."

"Good idea," said Jenna. "In meantime, we have other business to attend to." They exited the building and hurried out to the red Explorer. Their next stop was Jenna's house. As they came inside, they realized the Christmas tree was drying out.

"I guess it's served its purpose," said Jenna, "so we'll have to take it down while we're here."

"If you'll bring me the boxes for the ornaments, I can start working on it while you pack your bags."

As Bill tended to the tree, Jenna rummaged through her closet, this time packing outfits suitable for the office. Bill was nearly finished when she returned to the living room. She took the boxes back down to the basement while he loaded her bags in the Explorer and took the tree to the curb. She was vacuuming up the dead needles when he returned, and they were soon ready to leave.

"I'm sure going to miss this place," she said.

"How long were you here?"

"Four years. CeCe's husband got me the mortgage. Back then I really thought she was someone I could rely on. Who knew, right? I'll call Chad as soon as we get home. With any luck, I'll be back to work before the next hearing."

Chad was flabbergasted when Jenna told him about what Ken had done. "I'm incredibly grateful you were able to away from him," he said. "Had someone from the hotel called about you being in the corridor, I would have verified your story. So, what happens next?"

"Kelsey said she'd take care of the paperwork and get him served. It should happen sometime between now and New Year's Day."

"Well now, wouldn't that be a fine way to start the New Year? However, at the moment I'm more concerned about CeCe. It's yet another reason why they should have fired her, because I don't want her being a problem for you once you get back, which by the way, will be a week from Monday. Someone will be sending you an email later today."

"Oh, thank goodness," said Jenna. "It's about time. You don't know how happy I am to hear it."

"I'm also making a note on my calendar about your hearing, and not to expect you until after lunch. As for CeCe, I'm not a legal expert by any means, but I would think a restraining order would prevent someone from contacting you indirectly through a third party, so I'll let Marcy know. She can advise CeCe not to harass you, and I'll see if we can move your desk to a different part of the room."

"Thank you, Chad. The more distance you can put between us, the better I'll feel."

* * *

Ken wrapped his pillow over his head, but whoever was at the door kept knocking. He laid perfectly still. To his relief, the knocking stopped. As he began stirring, the doorbell rang.

"You son of a bitch," he said outload. "Don't you know it's New Year's morning?" Throwing on his robe, he stormed to the front door, shouting obscenities at the man who stood on the other side. The man, however, seemed undaunted.

"You've been served." He calmly dropped a paper at Ken's feet and walked away. Ken picked up the paper and went inside. Jenna had taken out a restraining order against him, and a hearing had been scheduled.

"If you think you can get away with this," he said, "you have another thought coming. It's your word against mine, and I'm going to deny everything. You're the one who contacted me, remember? You insisted on paying back money I'd given to you as a gift, and now you're slandering me. What do they call it? Entrapment? Yeah, that's it. You can't prove any of it, so I'm making a case for slander and entrapment. Happy New Year to you too, bitch, because you're about to get what's coming to you."

❧FORTY-SIX❧

BILL PREPARED HOT turkey sandwiches for New Year's dinner, much to Connor's delight. Afterwards, he opened his Christmas gifts.

"Circumstances being what they were," he said, "I wouldn't have blamed any of you if you'd returned them, but I'm glad you didn't."

"You weren't yourself, Dad," said Connor. "Trust me, the Christmas gifts were the last thing on our minds. Besides, having you being back is the best gift any of us could have asked for."

"Thank you, son, and thanks for the sweater too."

"You're welcome, but you'll have to thank Kelsey for the sweater. She's the one who picked it out. You know how I hate shopping."

"Thank you, Kelsey. You did a good job."

Jenna handed him another package. "This one's from me, but I'm afraid it's not as elegant as what you gave me."

"Really?" asked Connor. "What did he give you?"

"She'll show you later." Bill turned his attention back to Jenna. "You also know I'll love whatever it is, because it came from you." He ripped open the paper and found a red knit scarf. "It's perfect, and goes nicely with my new sweater. He gave her a thank you kiss and stood from his chair. "So now, if you ladies will excuse us, I need to take Connor down to the basement."

Connor suddenly looked worried. "Okay, Dad. This is bringing back some not-so-happy childhood memories, because nothing good ever happened whenever you took me down to the basement."

"It's okay, son," Bill said with a chuckle. "You're not in trouble this time, but there is something I need to discuss with you." He looked at Jenna and Kelsey. "Don't worry. We'll be back in a few minutes." He motioned to Connor to follow him downstairs, where he had placed several items on a small folding table.

"This stuff all belonged to your mother," said Bill. "She would have wanted you to have it, so feel free to take whatever you'd like."

"I remember this." Connor eagerly picked up the pen set and gave it a closer look. "Thank you for passing it on to me. I'll have to see about getting a new inscription so it'll have my name on it."

"You're welcome." Bill picked up a small plastic bag. "You may recall your mother not being big on flashy jewelry, but she had a few nice pieces, which I would like to pass on to you, in case you should ever have a daughter someday." He emptied the bag on the table and pointed out a few items.

"The antique garnet broach belonged to her grandmother. Your grandparents gave her the gold bracelet when she graduated from college, and the diamond earrings when she finished law school. Then I gave her the opal pendent and earrings one year for Christmas."

"I remember," said Conner. "It'll go in the safe deposit box, along with the wedding set. And just so you know, I plan on having the diamond reset before I give it to Kelsey so she can have her own wedding set, assuming of course she accepts."

"I don't see why she wouldn't."

"I don't either, although we're not quite there yet. First, I want to make sure my job works out. I've only been with the hospital for a few weeks."

"So, how's it going?"

"It's going great. I like their corporate culture and I have an interesting job. They have a really good health plan and parental leave, if and when I ever need it. They also have a better retirement plan than my old job."

"The move back to Colorado is getting better and better. And look, I also have your old baby book; in case you wanted it."

"Hmm...I don't know about that."

"Your mother was sentimental about certain things, and I think you should have it. It's part of our family history. Don't worry. I have an old photo album with plenty of your baby pictures. I'm also keeping the framed photo of you that was on your mother's desk."

"What about her journal?"

His question caught Bill off guard. It took him a moment to gather his thoughts. "It's no longer here. You have to understand, Connor, that she wrote about some highly personal and private issues she had with me, and they'll stay with me. What matters is she loved you, very much, regardless of how she felt about me. If it means anything to you, I have a lot of unanswered questions myself, but she's not here to tell us her side of the story, so we have to let it go and let her rest in peace."

"Did you throw it away?"

"No. I didn't want anyone else seeing it, so I burned it, and when I did, I felt as though I had somehow set her free. So, let's head back upstairs and help with the cleanup."

Connor packed up his items and they hurried upstairs, where they found a surprised Kelsey.

"Is something wrong?" asked Connor.

"No," she said.

"I handed her a pan to dry," said Jenna, "and she saw the ring."

"What ring?" The realization slowly dawned on Connor. "Wait a minute…are you saying?"

Bill wrapped his arm around Jenna's shoulder and told Connor and Kelsey to take a seat in the living room.

"As you know, son, I first met this lady back when I was in grad school. I was drawn to her from the start, but the timing wasn't right. I thought I'd get over her, but I didn't, and as the years passed, I deeply regretted not following through and pursuing her. Then she contacted me about doing the sculpture, and you know the rest of the story. Now that I'm back, I finally asked her marry me, and in spite everything, she said yes." He looked at Connor more closely.

"Are you okay?" he asked.

"I'm fine. I'm just a really surprised. While I certainly never expected you to be alone for the rest of your life, I really didn't think you'd ever remarry."

"Well, son, I didn't think I'd ever remarry either, and for a long time I didn't want to, which is why I kept sabotaging myself."

"I was also married once before," said Jenna. "I was very young at the time, and it didn't last long. Afterwards I went off to college and became one of your dad's students. I had the biggest crush on him, which I never got over either, but at the time I figured it was just a post-divorce thing so I never said anything to him."

"Even if she had," said Bill, "the timing still wasn't right. She was strictly off-limits because of the teacher-student relationship. I also had you to raise, and you weren't ready for me to get serious with anyone, so I had to put my own wants and needs aside until you became an adult. Now that you have, she and I can finally have a future together."

"And I certainly don't want to be the bad guy who says no."

"You'd better not," said Kelsey.

"So, what else can I say, other than congratulations, and I'm genuinely happy for both of you." He gave Jenna and his father a big hug.

"I'm happy for both of you as well." Kelsey too gave them a big hug. "So, when's the big day?"

"President's Day weekend," said Bill. "We're also keeping it small. Just family and a few close friends, and we'll be having it at the Shelton Inn. If it wasn't for her contacting me about the sculpture, we would have never reconnected."

❧FORTY-SEVEN❧

JENNA'S PARENTS WERE back from Hawaii, and she and Bill joined them for a post-holiday dinner. They hadn't met Bill before, and Jenna felt anxious as they were getting ready.

"Does this look okay?" she asked. "I want to look festive but not overdressed." She was wearing her pink birthday sweater, along with the scarf Bill gave her.

"You look fine," said Bill. "I especially like the scarf you're wearing."

"I thought you might like it. You look great in your new sweater too."

"Thanks, but are you sure I don't need to wear my suit?"

"I'm positive. Notice how I'm wearing jeans with my sweater. Dad always goes casual whenever he's home. No doubt he'll be in his blue jeans as well."

* * *

Jenna rang the doorbell, and her parents quickly answered. As expected, her father was wearing blue jeans with a crew neck sweater. Jenna made the introductions once they came inside. Her mother asked to see the ring while Nick offered them something to drink.

"I'll have a Coors, if you've got one," said Bill.

"I certainly do," said Nick. "What about you, Jenna?"

"I'm fine, for now."

The two men sat down in front of the TV while Jenna joined her mother in the kitchen "Something sure smells good," she said.

"I'm roasting Cornish game hens," said Claire, "and I'm making wild rice to go with them."

"Sounds wonderful. Can I help you with anything?"

"You could make the salad if you'd like."

"Of course." Jenna opened the refrigerator and began setting the fresh vegetables on the counter.

"Any news about when you'll be going back to work?" asked Claire.

"As a matter of fact, there is. I'll be back a week from Monday, and it can't come soon enough. Bill's back at the college this coming Monday, so next week I'll be spending some time at my place trying to figure out what to move to Bill's place. Maybe you could help me."

"I'd love to. So, what about your house?"

"I plan on selling it, unless you and Dad would like to downsize."

"No thanks," said Claire. "I know we keep talking about it, but then we can't decide what to keep and what to get rid of. I'm also glad you're moving in with Bill. That way Ken won't know where you are."

"No, he won't."

"What's the matter?" asked Claire. "All of a sudden you seem upset."

Jenna took a deep breath. "I had another incident with Ken."

"When was this?"

"A few nights after Christmas. You remember what happened with the gift card?"

"How could I forget?" said Claire. "I kept telling you I had a bad feeling about CeCe, and she turned out to be worse than I thought."

"She sure did, but she wasn't involved with this. At least I hope she wasn't."

"Alright, so what happened?"

Not wanting to upset her mother, Jenna downplayed the details. "I wanted to pay Ken back before the end of the year."

"Good thinking," said Claire. "So, I take it you paid him."

"I did. I wanted to mail it, but he insisted on picking it up in person. Then he insisted on taking me out for coffee, but he took me to the Sam's Place instead of Starbuck's. Once we were seated, he said he wanted to buy me dinner and make an evening of it. For some reason he's under the delusion I want him back. I said no thanks and called Kelsey. She and Connor came and picked me up, and I've not heard from him since."

"I'm glad they were able to help you, but I still have a bad feeling about CeCe. No doubt word of your engagement will get back to him once you're back at work."

"Don't worry, Mom. It's all good," Jenna said reassuringly. "We're making some changes. From what I understand, she's been told, in no uncertain terms, that if anything happens, she's out the door. Chad also tells me they're moving my desk to the other side of the room, so she won't be in such close proximity anymore."

The kitchen timer went off as Jenna finished making the salad. Claire took the hens out of the oven and tossed a bag of frozen carrots into the microwave. As she and Jenna put the side dishes on the table Nick and Bill came into the kitchen.

"Do you need any help with anything?" asked Bill.

"I think we've got it," said Claire, "so go ahead and sit down. Did you want some Dr. Pepper, Jenna?"

"I think I'll have a glass of ice water instead. I'm trying to cut down on the soda."

Jenna took her seat, and over the meal they discussed their wedding plans. "I know it's not the big, flashy wedding you always wanted me to have," said Jenna, "but it's a second marriage for both of us. Besides, I'm in my thirties, and I want you and Dad to hang onto your money for his retirement."

"You needn't worry about his retirement," said Claire. "He has a good retirement plan with the airline, but you're right about having a nice wedding without it being a big, lavish affair. We can also go shopping for a dress. Maybe we can find a nice cocktail dress in white or ivory, which would be perfect for a small wedding."

"Then we'll go one day next week."

"I'm looking forward to it," said Claire.

"I'm glad we got everything settled," said Bill. "Just let me know when I need to rent the monkey suit and what time to show up."

"Me too," said Nick.

The conversation shifted to his art and the upcoming semester. "Between the moving from Colorado to Florida and back I'm running behind, and Sorenson's is planning a show for me this summer."

"You certainly did the right thing bringing your son back here," said Nick. "I would have done the same, and I'm glad it all worked out for him. He's a remarkable young man. You did a good job with him."

"Thanks. Being a single dad had its challenges. My brother and his wife did what they could to help, but nothing could bring back his mother, and her absence was certainly felt."

"No doubt. Flying is much safer than it was a generation ago, but I still used to worry about what might happen to Claire and Jenna if the unthinkable were to happen to me."

"So did your family emergency get resolved?" asked Claire.

"Yes, it did." Bill's expression turned serious. "Being as I'm about to become part of the family, you need to hear the real story, and I think it's best you hear from me. What I'm about to say is never to leave the room, because Connor is never to know about it."

"Of course," said Nick. "So, what happened?"

"A few weeks ago, I came across a box containing my late wife's personal belongings from her office, and when I opened it; well, let's just say it was my own version of Pandora's box. I found a cache of love letters from the man she was having an affair with. Talk about being blindsided. I never suspected a thing, and I needed some time away from everyone and everything so I could sort it all out."

"I'm sorry, Bill," said Nick.

"It's okay, although there's a part of me that would still like to hunt her lover down and give him his just desserts. He knew she was married, and but it sure didn't stop him from getting involved with her, and neither of them felt any remorse for what they had done. She's the one who finally ended it, and she was killed in a car crash a short time later. Maybe it was karma, or maybe it was just a tragic coincidence. What I can tell you is had I known about it at the time, I would have divorced her and fought for custody of Connor, but I certainly would have never wished her harm."

Nick looked at Claire, who gave him a nod. He then looked Bill in the eye and took a deep breath.

"Well, as long as we're being honest with one another, there was a time, before Jenna came along, when I was that guy, and I never felt remorseful either. I was married at the time, not to Claire, but to someone else who I'd married for all the wrong reasons. So, I made up for my mistake by skirt-chasing. Now, just so you know, I never knew any female attorneys, but there were plenty of stewardesses out there who liked to play around. Some were single, others were not, but I honestly didn't care, because my wife was my insurance policy. If anyone got too serious, all I had to do was tell her I was married, and just like that, all my troubles went away."

"In other words, my father was a skank," said Jenna.

"Which I freely admit, but at the time I was proud of it. So, along comes a flight attendant named Claire Evans. She's single, unattached, and absolutely gorgeous, so of course I went after her."

"Did you know he was married?" asked Bill.

"I thought he was single when I first met him," said Claire. "I didn't find out about the wife until much later, and over time I forgave him."

"For which I'll always be eternally grateful," said Nick. "So, Claire and I really hit it off, but she wasn't like any of the others. I was falling hard for her and she was falling hard for me as well, which frankly scared the living hell out of me, and I was trying to find the courage to end it with her. Then one fateful day, she tells me she's pregnant,and I watched my entire life flash before my eyes. I told her not to worry. I'd help cover the cost of taking care of it. I also told her we could do a layover in Europe if she was worried about her family finding out"

"Which didn't go over well with me," said Claire. "I'd already decided I was going to keep my baby, with or without him."

"A point which she made quite clear," said Nick, "although I was still trying to convince her to change her mind. Two weeks later we were flying from San Francisco to Honolulu. Halfway across the Pacific Ocean, we get a call from the cabin crew. A drunk passenger has flipped out. He's ranting and raving and running up and down the aisles threatening other passengers, but we're over the damn ocean. There's no place for me to land that isn't a few hours away. There's nothing I can do other than follow airline protocol, which was to lock the cockpit door and divert to the nearest airport, which happened to be Hilo, Meanwhile the flight attendants are trying to subdue the guy, but it's only making matters worse. He punches out a male flight attendant, then he shoves Claire into a lavatory door and knocks the wind out of her. That's when Bobby, the male flight attendant, along with a few other passengers, managed to tackle him and tie him up with zip ties, seat belt extensions, and whatever else they could get their hands on. There was also some concern about Claire possibly having a concussion. So, one of the flight attendants stayed in the back of the plane with her while I spent the next few hours locked in the cockpit, not knowing if she or the baby were okay or not. That's when I did some serious soul searching. By the time we landed in Hilo, I had a whole new outlook on life. We got her to the hospital, and other than some bruises and a big lump on the back of her head, she and the baby were okay."

"I was stiff and sore for a few days," said Claire, "and I was also pretty shaken up. It was a traumatic experience."

"For both of us," said Nick. "As soon as we got home, I told my wife I wanted a divorce. I also told Claire I was married. She didn't take it very well, and we had some serious issues to resolve. My ex-wife also made things as difficult as she could, mostly out of spite, and it ended up costing me some serious money. Claire and I were married the day after my divorce was final, and we had Jenna two months later. The two of them are the best thing that ever happened to me, and I will never be that guy again."

Bill looked at Jenna. "Did you know you were almost born out of wedlock?"

"Not until I became an adult," said Jenna. "I was going through my divorce from Arthur and dealing with the all stuff that comes with it, and Dad slipped up one day and said he'd experienced some similar things when he got divorced. I of course asked him what was he talking about, so he and Mom told me the whole story. Afterwards, I felt a lot closer to my dad. Neither of us ever want to experience it again."

Claire began clearing the table and Jenna helped carry the dirty dishes to the kitchen. They returned a few minutes later with slices of fresh strawberry pie, but Claire looked concerned when they sat back down.

"Is something wrong with your dessert?" she asked Jenna. "You love strawberry pie, so why aren't you eating it?"

"There's nothing wrong with it," said Jenna. "I just want to make sure I look good in my wedding dress."

"You'll be fine," said Bill. "We'll take an extra walk around the block tomorrow night, so enjoy it."

"In that case, I think I will."

Claire spoke up as Jenna dug into her pie. "I don't know if this is polite for me to ask or not, but will there be any grandchildren in our future?"

"You'll be getting a step-grandson," said Jenna.

"I know. He's a charming young man, and you certainly did a good job with him, Bill, but Jenna has always been serious about her career. She's never once mentioned anything about wanting to have children. At least, not to me."

"We've already discussed it," said Jenna. "Granted, I'm not planning on starting a family right away, although it would be nice if we had child someday, assuming Bill wants another one."

"I honestly wouldn't mind," said Bill. "I love being a dad, and if she ever is expecting, I promise you she will be well taken care of."

"Which I appreciate," said Nick.

"First things first," said Jenna. "Let's get through the wedding. Then we can talk about having a baby."

ꙮFORTY-EIGHTꙮ

JENNA AND HER mother found the perfect wedding dress. The ivory-colored floor length gown had a form-fitting bodice with lace sleeves and a v-neckline. It would go perfectly with her beige pumps.

"What about a veil?" asked Claire.

"I was thinking about a hat," said Jenna.

"No. A hat wouldn't work with this dress. I was thinking about making you a veil. Something simple, yet elegant."

"Wow, Mom. I don't know what to say, other than thank you. So, what do you have in mind?"

"I have a few ideas, but first I need to know what you plan to do with your hair."

"Something quick and simple. Friday will still be a work day, so I may have to get my hair done during my lunch hour,"

"Somehow, I have a feeling they'll let you have the day off, especially with Chad and his wife being invited to the wedding."

"I have a hunch you're right," said Jenna, "and I plan on having my hair put into a fancy bun, with ringlets around my face."

Claire smiled in approval. "Which would look stunning with your dress, and I already have an idea for the veil. We'll make a run to the fabric store this afternoon so I can buy some tuille, but first I want to get some lunch."

"Me too," said Jenna. "I'm starving."

* * *

Paige greeted Jenna with a warm smile as she came into the building. "Howdy, stranger. It's good seeing you back."

"It's good to be back. So did anything interesting happen while I was away?"

"Not really, although it looks like a few more projects are coming our way, so the rest of the furloughed people will be soon back as well."

"Then it sounds like we're off to a good year."

"We are indeed. Let's hope it continues."

Jenna hurried to the elevator. A few other employees were waiting, but CeCe wasn't among them. Butterflies roiled in her stomach as they stepped inside and she went straight to Chad's office. He was busy at his computer when she tapped on his door, but the rest of the design team hadn't arrived yet. His face lit up as she stepped inside, and he greeted her with a big hug.

"Welcome back," he said. "How were your holidays?"

"Interesting."

Chad raised his brow as Jenna showed him her engagement ring. "Well, what do you know, and congratulations. So have you set a date yet?"

"We have. It'll be President's Day weekend, and you and your wife are on the guest list. Don't worry about a gift. Bill and I already have more than enough stuff."

"Thank you for the invite, and I'm flattered you're including us. So, what about CeCe? Will she and her husband be there as well?"

"No." Jenna's voice was firm. "The less she knows, the better. I don't want Ken showing up and causing problems."

"I understand. We also moved your desk, as promised, but don't worry, you'll be able to find it, because there's a big balloon bouquet on it. You'll be next to Priscilla."

"Thanks, Chad. I appreciate it, and there's one more thing."

"What is it?"

"Between Bill's work schedule and our new project, we're postponing our honeymoon until August."

"Which should work just fine," said Chad. "The construction should be complete by then, and even if it isn't, we'll make sure someone's available to pinch hit."

"Thanks, Chad. I appreciate it."

"You're welcome, congratulations again on your engagement. So, at the risk of turning into a killjoy, is your court hearing still on?"

"Yes, but it shouldn't take long. I expect to be back by lunchtime at the latest."

"Don't worry about it. You're on the judge's time, not ours. Hopefully, she can get you some relief."

"I hope so too. My attorney also wrote him a strongly worded letter letting him know we haven't ruled out filing a lawsuit. If he's smart, he'll back off and let me live my life in peace."

"Hopefully, he will," said Chad. "I don't know what's wrong with people these days. Everyone seems to think they should have everything their way, all of the time, but it's not how life works. Meantime the client should be here in about fifteen minutes, so go grab whatever you need and we'll meet in the conference room."

Jenna hurried to her desk. As she admired the balloons, Priscilla greeted her with a warm smile.

"Welcome back. I think you'll like this neighborhood a little better."

"I'm sure I will," said Jenna. "It's good to be back and Chad's not wasting any time. I just stopped by long enough to take off my coat and grab a bottle of water. Then I'm off to a client meeting."

"Then I won't keep you."

Jenna lowered her voice. "So has you-know-who said anything about my being back?"

"Not a word. She knows better."

"Good to know. I'll you see you in a bit." Jenna grabbed her tablet and hurried out. Mitch and Jim were waiting in the conference room when she arrived. They too greeted her with warm smiles. Chad soon arrived with the client, a middle-aged Asian man wearing an expensive suit.

"I'd like to introduce you to our client, Dylan Lee," said Chad. "He's an executive chef who, along with a group of investors, wants to build an upscale restaurant in Cherry Creek."

"Will they be here as well?" asked Mitch.

"No," said Chad. "They're all silent partners."

"You'll be working exclusively with me," said Dylan, "but don't worry. I promise I won't be bringing any sharp knives to the meetings."

Chad introduced Dylan to his team. He gave Jenna a warm smile as he extended his hand. "Arthur said to tell you hello."

"How did you know about Arthur?" asked a surprised Jenna.

"I've known him for years, and he's mentioned you a few times in passing, but it was never anything unkind."

"I see. So how did he know I'd be working with you?"

"You have mutual friends on Facebook, and one of them shared your posts about the Shelton Inn. Arthur was most impressed with your work, so when I started talking about opening my own restaurant, he showed the photos to me. I must say I was quite impressed as well."

Chad began the meeting, and Dylan talked in detail about his restaurant. "It won't be your typical mom and pop Asian restaurant," he said. "We'll be serving high-end gourmet meals to a well-to-do clientele. Peking Duck is my signature dish, and I'll be creating other dishes with lobster, crab legs and Kobe beef."

"It sounds delicious," said Mitch. "My stomach is already starting to growl."

"Then I'll have to bring something for you to try at our next meeting." Dylan went on to describe his vision for the restaurant as the others took notes.

"As for the interior," he said, "I want a spacious, elegant dining room with a full-service bar. I also need a state-of-the-art kitchen with good traffic flow so people won't be bumping into one another."

"I can do that," said Jenna. "So, what do you have in mind for the dining room?"

"I want soft lighting, a hardwood floor, and dark wood paneling on the walls. Something well made that looks like mahogany."

"I have the perfect product. We used it in a lighter color in the lobby at the Shelton Inn, and it looks like real maple. So, what else?"

"Sturdy, well-made tables, and chairs with red cushions."

"Which I know how to find."

"Excellent. I look forward to working with you, Ms. Winters." Dylan turned his attention to the other architects and answered their questions. Chad soon escorted him to the elevator, and the rest of the team rendezvoused in his office.

"He sure wasn't what I was expecting," said Jim.

"He's not your stereotypical temperamental chef," said Chad, "but he's not afraid to take command when he's in the kitchen either. He also tells me that on his days off he enjoys pizza and burgers with his kids and watching old B-rated horror movies."

"Tell you what," said Mitch. "After all this I'm definitely hungry for some Chinese food."

"Then we'll make a run to Panda Express for lunch," said Chad, "but right now we need to get to work."

Jenna felt much calmer when she took the elevator down to her floor. CeCe looked unhappy as their other co-workers gave her a warm welcome. Taking her seat, she fired up her computer and checked her email. A stack of correspondence was waiting in her inbox. As she sorted through her messages Priscilla stepped away to get a fresh cup of coffee.

"Can I get you anything?" she asked.

"I'm fine," said Jenna. "I brought my water bottle with me."

Priscilla stepped away, and as Jenna read through her messages, she heard approaching footsteps. Thinking it was Priscilla, she kept reading, until someone interrupted her.

"I need to talk to you." There was a hint of anger in CeCe's voice.

"About what?" asked Jenna.

"About Ken." CeCe lowered her voice, but her tone remained angry. "What the hell are you thinking, dragging him into court like this? He didn't do anything wrong and you knew from the get-go the money was a gift. You were never under any obligation to pay him back, but you insisted, and all he wanted to do was buy you a cup of coffee and talk to you for a few minutes so he could have closure and move on."

"He told you this?"

"Yes, he did, and he has no reason to lie."

"Well, I'm afraid what he told you isn't exactly what happened, and I have witnesses to back me. You're also aware that the temporary order I have against him is still in effect."

"Yes, I'm aware of it, and no, he didn't ask me to talk to you. I'm speaking to you of my own accord because he's a very dear friend, and I'm trying to understand why you stabbed him in the back. All he wanted was to help you through a difficult time, and this was the thanks he got."

Priscilla returned while CeCe was talking. "Is there anything we can do for you, Ms. Wood?" she sternly asked.

"No," said CeCe. "I was just asking Jenna a question."

"I see. So does your question have anything to do with company business?"

"I just needed to ask her something. I also wanted to let her know I turned off the automatic forwarding for her email."

"Thank you," said Jenna. "I appreciate you taking care of my email while I was away, and I take it there were no urgent messages."

"No, not really. It was mostly vendors asking if you needed anything, along with the usual holiday greetings."

"Then thank you again."

CeCe was about to take her leave when Jenna brushed a strand of hair away from her face. A surprised look came over CeCe's face and she abruptly stopped in her tracks.

"What's this?" she asked, pointing to the ring.

"It's my Christmas gift from Bill."

"You mean…you're getting married? I thought the two of you were just good friends."

"We are good friends. In fact, he's my best friend. Now, in case you're wondering, it's going to be a very small wedding. Just our immediate families and a few close friends."

"I see," CeCe said, somewhat awkwardly. "Well, in that case, congratulations."

"Thank you."

As CeCe hurried away, Priscilla gave Jenna a concerned look. "If she harasses you in any way, be sure to let Marcy know. She's not exactly popular around here and we all think she should have been fired weeks ago. We also know she'll mess up sooner or later. All I can say is the sooner she's gone, the happier the rest of us will be."

* * *

CeCe grabbed her purse and went to the ladies' room. Stepping into a stall, she grabbed her phone and began typing.

"She's back alright. She's also wearing a diamond engagement ring. I'm sorry, Ken, but she's moved on for good. It's time for you to move on as well. I still think you should reach out to Jeri and see about moving to Boston."

She waited for a response, but none came. She was about to leave when the phone vibrated in her hand. Ken had sent a reply.

"So, who's the lucky guy?"

"Her friend, Bill."

"Interesting. I wonder what happened to the younger guy."

"I don't know, and I didn't ask."

"Did she say anything else?"

CeCe took a deep breath and continued typing. *"Just that it'll be a small wedding. That was it. If I start asking questions, she'll get suspicious and I'm out the door."*

"Then you don't know when it'll be."

"No, I don't, and somehow I doubt she'll tell me."

"I understand. I just wish you could come to my hearing. I could use some support."

"I'll be there in spirit. We'll talk more later."

She hurried back to her desk. To her relief, no one seemed to notice she was gone.

৯FORTY-NINE৵

JENNA LOOKED IN the mirror and inspected her outfit once again. She was wearing her navy-blue pantsuit, but she wondered if it she should wear any jewelry with it.

"You look fine," said Bill. "Very professional, but not overdressed. Are you sure you don't need me to come to the hearing?"

"I'll be fine. You need to be at the college today so you can meet whoever registered late for your classes. Kelsey and Connor will be there. So will my attorney. We'll tell the judge what happened, and my attorney will present the additional evidence I was telling you about. He also should have gotten the letter my attorney sent him about filing a claim against him, but so far, he hasn't responded. If he's smart, he'll back off."

"I know, but he's not acting logically. He's harboring some sort of grudge against you, and I'd sure like to know what it is."

"According to CeCe, he was upset because I left the wedding early. Apparently, it embarrassed him, but oh well. If they'd kept his aunt on her leash, I could have ended it with him in a more dignified way."

* * *

Kelsey and Connor, along with Peter Davis, were waiting in the courthouse lobby when Jenna arrived. After riding up the elevator together, Pete asked them to take a seat on one of the benches in the hallway.

"While this should be an open and shut matter," he said, "I want to warn you that judges can sometimes act unexpectedly. I'll present your case, including the new evidence, as well as present Connor and Kelsey as witnesses. She may or may not ask the two of you any questions. If she does, answer them truthfully, but only tell her what she asks for.

233

Don't volunteer any information unless it's relevant. Otherwise, it may complicate things." He focused his gaze on Jenna.

"They should have a pen and paper on the plaintiff's table. If not, I have some with me. If Ken says anything you object to while he's speaking to the judge, write it down for me."

"Of course," said Jenna.

"So, if we're ready, let's go inside. We have a few minutes before court goes into session. Hopefully, they'll call our case soon."

They followed him into the courtroom and found an empty bench near the back of the gallery. Ken was already inside, seated near the front, but there was no one else sitting with him. Pete whispered softly into Jenna's ear.

"Looks like he may not have an attorney. This may help us."

Jenna nodded, but she still felt nervous. Five minutes later the bailiff entered the room and ordered everyone to rise. The judge took her seat and began calling cases. The first two only took a few minutes of her time. The next case also involved an order of protection. The plaintiff was a mother of three whose ex-husband had been leaving her threatening voicemails and text messages. After presenting her evidence to the judge, she was granted a one-hundred-twenty-day order of protection. Jenna hoped it would be a good sign.

Jenna's case was called next. She nervously followed her attorney to the plaintiff's table while Ken calmly took his seat at the defendant's table. Once they were seated, Pete presented her case to the judge. Afterwards, the judge turned her attention to Ken.

"These are all vicious lies, Your Honor," he said. "None of this ever happened. Last fall, after we'd ended our relationship, I learned through a mutual friend that Ms. Winters had been furloughed from her job. I still considered her as a friend, and I wanted to help her out, but I did so anonymously." As he told the rest of his story, Jenna jotted a quick note to her attorney. Ken was exaggerating and taking things out of proportion. He gave her a slight nod as Ken continued.

"Ms. Winters then told me she wasn't feeling well, so she excused herself and went to the ladies' room. I waited for her to come back, but she was taking a really long time, and I was worried she might be seriously ill." He pointed to Connor, seated in the gallery. "Then the gentleman over there appeared, completely out of the blue. He told me Jenna had left, and then he started threatening me."

"I see," said the judge. "So, did he cause a scene? And were there any witnesses?"

"No," said Ken. "He spoke in a normal tone of voice, but he refused to tell me who was. He claimed he was her, quote, 'guardian angel,' and he was there to get her belongings. I didn't say anything else. He grabbed her phone and her coat and he left. Once he was gone, I waited for a few minutes, just to be sure it was safe for me to leave. Then I asked for the check and left."

"I see." The judge turned her attention to Connor, asking him to approach the bench and to state his name for out court.

"My name is Connor David Haskell, Your Honor. I'm a friend of Ms. Winters."

Ken looked stunned. "Are you related to Bill Haskell?" he asked.

"I'll asked the questions," the judge sternly said.

"My apologies, Your Honor," said Ken.

The judge turned her attention back to Connor. "My father is Ms. Winters' significant other, but he was called away on a family emergency, so Kelsey, my girlfriend, and I were keeping an eye on her while he was gone. Jenna called Kelsey, saying it was an emergency and to please come pick her up. So, we dropped everything and got to The Shelton Inn as quickly as we could."

The judge asked Connor a few more questions. Once she was satisfied with his answers, she turned her attention back to Ken.

"Mr. Haskell was absolutely correct when he informed you that revenge porn is illegal in Colorado."

"I understand, Your Honor," said Ken. "However, I have no compromising photos of Ms. Winters and I never have. We used to pull practical jokes on one another, and the photo in question came from an adult website. I figured she'd get a good laugh out of it, but she obviously didn't, so I immediately apologized and deleted the photo. I most certainly never threatened to post any indecent photos of her online, because no such photos of her exist. It's yet another of the vicious lies she's spreading about me."

The judge looked unimpressed as she turned her attention back to Jenna's lawyer. "Do you have anything further to present to the court?"

"Yes, Your Honor, I do." He picked up a sheet of paper and handed it to the bailiff. "I have a written statement from The Shelton Inn, along with a copy of the receipt, verifying that Mr. Frank did indeed reserve a room that night on their website, and paid for it with his credit card."

The color quickly drained from Ken's face as the bailiff handed the documents to the judge. After looking them over, she gave Ken a stern look.

"Would you care to explain, Mr. Frank?"

"I have no comment, Your Honor."

Her voice remained firm. "I see. You are aware, sir, that perjury is a serious offense."

"I understand, Your Honor."

"Is there anything else you would like to tell the court before I hand down my decision?"

"No, Your Honor, there is not."

"Very well then." She turned her attention back to Jenna and her attorney. "The court hereby grants Ms. Winters' request to extend the Order of Protection for an additional one-hundred and twenty days. I'm also scheduling another hearing in May to determine if another extension is warranted." She banged her gavel and called the next case as

Ken quickly left the courtroom. As Jenna and the others stepped out to the corridor, Kelsey gave her a congratulatory hug.

"It looks like you took care of him. Somehow, I doubt he'll give you any more trouble."

"I hope you're right," said Jenna, "but I still have a bad feeling about CeCe. Even though they moved my desk away from hers, she's still a trouble maker, and she's made it abundantly clear that she's on Ken's side."

"If she becomes a problem," said Pete, "I'd be more than happy to write her a cease-and-desist letter."

"Let's wait and see what happens first. As I said before, all she has to do is sneeze and she's out the door. And in spite of everything that's happened, I still feel very sad about it. While we never hung out after hours, she was still a good office buddy. Speaking of which, I need to get to work."

"So do I," said Connor. "Be sure to let Dad know what happened."

"You know I will. I'll send him a text as soon as I get in my car."

"Would you like for me to walk with you?"

"I would. Thanks, Connor."

"Let's set up a meeting for either next week or the week after," said Pete. "I'd like to follow through and file a claim against him. That way I can have a computer forensics expert inspect his devices to see if he did indeed take any surreptitious photos of you."

Pete shook Jenna's hand while Connor gave Kelsey a quick goodbye kiss and walked outside with Jenna.

"You know you really should follow his advice and file a lawsuit," he said.

"I'd would prefer not to, if it's at all possible. I just want him out of my life."

"I understand how you feel. It wasn't so long ago when I was in a similar predicament."

"I remember. So did they pay you the money?"

"As a matter of fact, they did," he said. "It's now the new house fund. And speaking of new houses, I'll see you on Saturday. I'm helping with the big furniture swap."

✑FIFTY✒

CECE'S PHONE vibrated. Glancing around the room, she wanted to be sure no one was watching. To her relief, everyone appeared to be busy, so she quickly opened her desk drawer. Ken had sent her a text message, and the news wasn't good.

"Jenna brought a lawyer, and the judge believed her lies. When I tried to tell my side of the story, I was warned about committing perjury."

CeCe quicky typed a reply. *"I'm so sorry. I was really hoping you'd win. Can't talk now, but John's feeling a little better, so you're welcome to stop by this evening."*

* * *

Ken arrived with several grocery bags. CeCe led him to the kitchen and he set them on the counter.

"I figured we may as well take a break from the pizzas with John being sick and all, so I stopped by King Soopers and got us a lemon chicken with all the fixings. I also got John a pint of chicken vegetable soup. So, how's he doing?"

"He's feeling a lot better," said CeCe, "but he's still not well enough to go back to work. This year's flu is really bad."

"So, I hear, and what about you? Are you okay?"

"So far, so good. John insisted I sleep in the guestroom until he's fully recovered." She put his soup on a bed tray, along with a dinner roll and a few extra napkins. "I'll go take this to him. Feel free to make yourself at home until I get back."

"Of course. I'll put the rest of the food out while you take care of him."

"Thanks. I'll be back in a couple minutes." CeCe stepped out while Ken unpacked the grocery bags and carved the chicken. She looked surprised when she returned.

"That's quite a spread, Ken."

"Their deli has a lot to pick and choose from, and I guess my eyes were bigger than my appetite. You should have enough left to last a day or two. You've had enough to deal with lately, and you don't need to worry about cooking."

"I appreciate you thinking of me, and you're right. I have had a lot to deal with lately. Too much, as a matter of fact, and if things weren't unpleasant enough, Jenna just started working on the fancy new restaurant I was telling you about while I'm stuck with all the little pissant jobs no one else wants, like figuring out how many toilets we can fit into a public bathroom."

"Seriously?" he asked.

"Okay, maybe it was a slight exaggeration, but it's still pretty close to the mark. They're giving me all the, if you'll pardon the expression, crap jobs. I know what they're doing. They're trying to get me to leave, and it's working. Trust me, I'm ready to walk out the door for good."

"No, not yet. I still need you to be my eyes and ears."

"Oh c'mon, Ken. Enough already. Jenna has moved on. She and Bill are engaged to be married. It's time for you to move on as well."

"But they're not married yet. Have they set a date?"

"I don't know, but even if they have, no one's going to volunteer any information to me."

"I know they won't, but I also know you have a remarkably good sense of hearing."

"I do," said CeCe. "However, they've moved her desk. She's now across the room from me. She's next to Priscilla, who's always harbored a grudge against me for some reason."

"A minor setback, but it's not that big of a room, and voices carry. You can always get up and stretch your legs."

"If I did, they'd catch onto it in a hurry," said CeCe. "It's like I keep telling you. It's become a hostile work environment, which is why I'm still sending out resumes."

"Any luck?" he asked.

"I've had a few emails, but so far, no actual interviews. We're just getting out of the holiday season, so I'm hoping things will start picking up. So, moving on. What exactly happened at the hearing?"

"It wasn't good," said Ken. "Let's fix our plates and I'll fill you in." He helped himself to a chicken leg while CeCe grabbed a couple cans of Coors from the refrigerator. Once they took their seats, Ken told her what had happened.

"As I said, Jenna has a lawyer, so he did all the talking. She also brought along two witnesses, and I now know who the individual was who threatened me at Sam's Place."

"Well, don't leave me in suspense," said CeCe. "Who was he?"

"Bill Haskell's son, Connor. He said his father had been called away on a family emergency, yet I vividly recall Jenna telling me Bill had a prior commitment that night."

"Did she say where?"

"No," said Ken.

"Then maybe his prior commitment had something to do with the out-of-town family matter. So, was there anything else?"

"There was. Her attorney presented the receipt for the room I'd reserved that night."

CeCe immediately snapped to. "What are you doing here? You're supposed to be in bed."

John had come into the kitchen, wearing his pajamas and robe. His face looked slightly pale, and he had several day's growth of beard.

"I told you. I'm feeling better, and the soup is delicious. I just wanted another roll, and the fruit salad looks really good too. Do you mind if I have a little?"

"Help yourself," said Ken.

"I'll get it," said CeCe.

"No, stay where you are," said John. "I can get it."

"I don't want you having a relapse," said CeCe.

"It's okay." John spooned some salad onto a small plate. "I may not be ready to go back to work just yet, but I'm perfectly capable of getting some food. I'm also trying to decide if I want to keep the beard or not. So, what do you think, Ken?"

"I think it looks good on you."

"I think it does too, so I'm probably going to keep it. Enjoy your dinner, folks, and I'll talk to you later, Ken."

CeCe waited for John to close the bedroom door before she spoke up. "So where were we? Okay, now I remember. You were saying something about them finding out you'd reserved a room that night, and I'm curious as well. So why would you do something like that if you were only taking her there for coffee?"

"I guess I was being overly optimistic. I was really hoping that if we started reminiscing about old times, she'd finally realized she'd made a mistake and take me back, and we could start the celebration that night. Instead, she got all huffy and left. The last thing I wanted to do was upset her, so I tried to apologize to her, but she refused to listen."

"I understand. However, my advice to you is to wish her well and let her go. She's marrying Bill, and there are other women out there."

"I know," said Ken, "and it's not that I'm not looking, because I am. However, having someone take out a restraining order against you doesn't look good either, and I'm trying to protect my own reputation. There are clients out there who do background checks on those they do business with, and this could hurt my bottom line."

"Which is certainly understandable," said CeCe. "However, restraining orders don't last forever, and it's not uncommon to get one when someone's going through a bad break up or a messy divorce. And, if you're really that concerned, you could take out a restraining against her as well."

"I suppose I could, but for now, I really need you to be my eyes and ears. So, would you mind keeping a close watch on her and keeping me informed about what she's up to? If she's saying bad things about me then you bet, I'll take out a restraining order against her as well."

CeCe squirmed in her seat. "I don't know, Ken. I'm already on thin ice as it is."

"I know you are. I certainly don't need to know what her wedding dress looks like, or how many bridesmaids she has, but I have a right to know if she's spreading more lies about me. I already mentioned you having a sharp sense of hearing, and I noticed how you apparently waited until you heard John close the bedroom door before you began talking again. At least it's what I think you did, because I sure didn't hear it."

"I did, and you're right, so okay. If I overhear Jenna, or anyone else, saying anything derogatory about you, I will let you know. The minute I hear it."

Ken sighed in relief and gave her a smile. "Thanks, CeCe. I appreciate it. You're a true friend, and I'm grateful knowing you'll always have my back."

❧FIFTY-ONE❧

BILL AND CONNOR moved Jenna's furniture the following Saturday. Kelsey helped her make up the bed while the two men carefully loaded Bill's old bedroom and dining furniture into the U-Haul truck. Once it was secured, they took a much-needed break on the sectional sofa. Jenna offered them soft drinks, and as they relaxed, she asked Connor and Kelsey if they would be interested in renting her house.

"We really appreciate the kind offer," said Connor, "but our apartment lease won't be up until November. If you let us know when you you're having your garage sale, we'll be happy to help out."

"Thanks, and I'll let you know. It'll be sometime this spring, after the snow melts off."

"In the meantime, Kelsey and I are still contributing as much as we can to our house fund. We're hoping to be in a position to start looking for a place of our own in about another year."

"Good to know," said Bill, "but don't wait too long. You never know when interest rates will go up. Your stepmother and I are also willing to help out if you need it."

"Thanks, Dad. We'll let you know if we do. And didn't you mention something the other day about a gallery in Taos?"

"I did," said Bill. "It's not a done deal yet, but they're very interested. I'll be meeting with them over spring break."

Jenna looked at her watch as the two men were talking. "I didn't realize it had gotten so late. As soon as you're ready, Kelsey, we need to get going. I told Stacy we'd meet her for lunch at one thirty, and she's really looking forward to meeting you."

"I look forward to meeting her as well," said Kelsey.

241

"Then, after lunch, we'll help her find a maid of honor dress, along with something nice for you."

Kelsey's face lit up. "You know I'm always up for looking at new dresses, and I may as well look for some new shirts for Connor while we're there. Some of his stuff is looking a little threadbare, and he hates shopping."

"They're not threadbare," said Connor. "They're just getting comfortable."

"You tell her, son," said Bill.

The two women laughed as Jenna grabbed her coat and keys. "I promise I'll have her home in time for dinner."

"It's all good" said Connor, "so take your time. We don't have any big dinner plans for this evening, and I'll probably be beat after moving all the furniture around."

"You ladies have fun," said Bill. "Connor and I are going to take their stuff to the apartment, then we'll grab a burger after we drop off the rental truck."

Jenna and Kelsey said their goodbyes and hurried out. Once they were gone, Connor's mood turned serious,

"Dad, is there anything else going on I should know about?"

"Why do you ask?"

"You seem to be in a big rush to get married. Granted, most of our friends are still single, but the ones who are married were engaged for several months the wedding."

"We didn't want to wait that long."

"Why not? You've known each other years, so what difference would a few more months have made?"

"As you get older, son, you start to realize life is short, and you don't want to waste time on things if you don't have to, but not to worry. We'll still have our father and son times. Maybe not as often as we did before, but we'll still have them."

"I know we will, and please understand, I'm not jealous of Jenna. Mom's been gone a long time, and I genuinely like Jenna, although I consider her more of a friend than a mother figure."

"Which is perfectly understandable, considering the age differences. And while no one will ever take your mother's place, you also need to understand that even if I didn't know what I know now, sooner or later, your mother and I would have gone our separate ways, although we would have always cared about one another. At the time we were married, we were both caught up in the moment and not thinking that much ahead, but rest assured, having you was the best thing that ever happened to both of us."

"I know, but there hasn't been a day since she left when I haven't thought of her and wished she were still here."

"She was your mother," said Bill. "It's perfectly natural for you to feel that way. I feel the same about your grandfather. I'd give anything to have him back, even if it were only for a day."

"Me too," said Connor.

"I know you would, but getting back to Jenna. I want you to understand that my relationship with her is very different from what I had with your mother. Jenna and I are soulmates, but it doesn't mean I loved your mother any less. We shared a bond with you, and she will always be special to me."

"Thanks for letting me know. I appreciate it"

"You're welcome. It's time for you to focus more on your own life and stop worrying so much about your old man. So, let's go unload your furniture, and then we'll grab some lunch. I don't know about you, but I'm starving."

* * *

The next few weeks were a whirlwind of wedding plans and dress fittings. Jenna was grateful for her mother's help. She was also busy creating the interior for Dylan's new restaurant. Like the Sheltons, he knew what he wanted, and she found him easy to work with. The day before her wedding, Priscilla, along with a few other co-workers, took her to lunch and presented her with an envelope once they were seated at their table.

"Be careful when you open this," said Priscilla.

"Why? Is there a stuffed snake in there that'll jump out at me?"

"No, there isn't," she said, "but I'll give you a hint. It's something you can use to keep your new hubby happy after the honeymoon, if you know what I mean."

"How intriguing." Jenna opened the envelope. Inside was a wedding card with their hand-signed well wishes, along with a fifty-dollar Amazon gift card.

"Thank you, all of you," said Jenna. "I'll certainly put the gift card to good use for something sexy, but you really didn't have to do this."

"Between CeCe's shenanigans, and you being furloughed, you've had an incredibly hard year," said Priscilla, "and we're all happy to finally see things going so much better for you. So, enjoy your special day."

* * *

Jenna stayed with her parents that night. Wanting to make the evening special, they went to dinner at a neighborhood restaurant they had frequented when she was a child. Upon returning home, they gathered around the fireplace and reminisced about old times until Nick finally stifled a yawn.

"Uh-oh," he said. "We've lost all track of time, and it's almost one o'clock in the morning. We need to put the bride-to-be to bed, and then we need to get to bed ourselves. We have a really big day ahead of us tomorrow. Or should I say, later today."

"Don't worry, Dad. Chad already knows I'm taking the day off, so we can sleep in. We'll have plenty of time to get things ready."

"We also needed some quality time together, just the three of us," said Claire. "Because after tomorrow, our lives will be very different."

"They will indeed," said Jenna. "I also wanted to make up for what happened the last time. I blindsided both of you, and I'm truly sorry for what I did. Trust me, if one of my future kids even thinks about trying to do anything even remotely close to—"

"It's alright, Jenna." Claire patted her daughter's arm. "We forgave you a long time ago, and you've certainly come a long way since then. This time you're marrying the right man for the right reasons, and your father and I couldn't be happier. So, let's call it a night. We can finish this conversation in the morning."

Jenna felt content as she went upstairs to her old bedroom. A queen-sized bed had replaced her old twin bed, but the night stand and dresser she grew up with were still there. As she settled underneath the covers, she thought about all the times when she had come home from college and went to bed thinking about Bill, and wondering what may have become of him. Now they would be spending the rest of their lives together.

* * *

The sun was shining brightly when Jenna woke up the following morning. She quickly rolled out of bed and made her way downstairs to the kitchen. It was a few minutes past nine, but her parents weren't up yet, so she brewed a fresh pot of coffee. Her mother joined her as she poured herself a cup.

"I'll have one too, if you don't mind," said Claire.

"You got it." Jenna poured a cup for her mother and sat down with her at the table.

"So, if you're ready," said Claire, "I'd like for you to try on your veil. Are you still planning on wearing your hair in a bun?"

"Yes."

Claire had a glimmer in her eye. "Then stay here. I'll be right back." She rushed out of the room, returning a moment later with the veil. The ivory colored tuille fabric had been gathered underneath two white silk roses.

"It's beautiful," said Jenna.

"There's a hair clip underneath the roses, so we can secure it just above your bun. Then you'll be all ready."

Jenna embraced her mother and squeezed her tight. "Thanks, Mom. I love it, and it goes perfectly with my dress."

"In the meantime, you reserved a room at the hotel, didn't you?"

"Of course I did."

"Alright, so here's the plan. We'll check into the hotel later this afternoon. I've also made us dinner reservations at Sam's. We'll order something light, perhaps a big salad. No doubt you'll be feeling nervous by then, and we don't want you burping during the ceremony."

"No, we certainly wouldn't," Jenna said with a laugh.

"Or, if you'd prefer, we can order room service."

"No, I'd rather be downstairs. I'd also like to have Stacy join us, if it's okay with you. She is the maid of honor, you know."

"Of course it's okay," said Claire. "I haven't seen her in a long time. So how is she these days?"

"She's doing well. She's still seeing Alan, and it looks like it's getting serious. He'll be there tonight as well."

"Yes, I saw his name on the guest list. Then, after dinner, we'll wait for your father's text message. As soon we hear from him, we'll get you in your gown and veil."

"So, Dad will be bringing Bill?"

"Yes. He'll pick Bill up in your car, which we'll leave at the hotel. We'll go home in the Mercedes."

"Sounds like you have everything planned out."

"Down to the last detail," said Claire. "So, go ahead and try on the veil. If anything needs to be adjusted, I should have enough time to get it done, but first we need to take care of breakfast."

As expected, the veil was perfect, and Jenna couldn't wait to see it with her dress. Nick came downstairs while the two women were making scrambled eggs. After breakfast they went over Claire's checklist one last time, and she made a few last-minute notes.

"I think we've covered everything," said Jenna. "If not, we'll have to wing it, but right now we need to get the hair salon."

"What about lunch?"

"There's a Japanese restaurant two doors down from the salon," said Jenna. "They have really good bento boxes, and we'll get there after the lunch rush."

It was late in the afternoon when Jenna and her mother returned. Jenna had a new French manicure, and her hair had been carefully tucked into a bun, with ringlets framing her face.

"Well, don't you two look beautiful," said Nick. "I see your mother got her hair done as well."

"Classic bobs never go out of style," said Claire. "So did you pick up your tuxedo?"

"I did. Bill and his brother have theirs as well."

"I forgot about his brother," said Claire.

"You'll be meeting the rest of his family tonight," said Jenna, "but if you'll excuse me, I need to get my bag. Oh, and I forgot to ask. What are you wearing, Mom?"

"The mauve cocktail dress I loaned you last year."

"Perfect," said Jenna. "I got a lot of compliments the night I wore it."

Claire hurried off to load their dresses in the car while Nick offered to get Jenna's bag.

"I can get it, Dad," she said.

"No, I will get it. Wait here. I'll be right back." He hurried upstairs, returning a moment later with Jenna's suitcase. "Before you go, I want to tell you something."

"What is it?"

Nick set the bag down and gave her a warm embrace. "Before I give you away, I want you to know that no matter where your life takes you, you will always be my baby girl, and I love you very much."

"I love you too, Dad."

Jenna had an unexpected surprise when she arrived at the hotel. Her room had been upgraded to a suite.

"Complements of Mr. Shelton himself," said the desk clerk.

"Are you sure?" she asked.

"I spoke to him personally. He said to put you in the bridal suite, and it's on the house. He said it was his way of thanking you for the work you did on the hotel. I had no idea you were the one who designed the lobby and atrium. It's truly spectacular."

"Thank you, and please, tell him thank you as well."

"What's the room number?" asked Claire.

"Five-twenty," said Jenna.

"Good. I'll meet you up there in a few minutes."

"Where are you going?"

"I want to check the ballroom to make sure everything is ready and they have enough chairs. I'll be up soon."

Jenna felt anxious as she stepped into the elevator and hurried to a door at the end of the hall. Once inside her suite, she found a bottle of champagne on ice from the Sheltons, along with bouquet of long-stemmed roses from Connor and Kelsey. The bridal bouquets had been placed next to the vase. She went into the sleeping area and gazed out the window at the Denver skyline. Her mother arrived a few minutes later.

"What a beautiful room," said Claire. "You did an amazing job."

"Thanks, although I never imagined I would ever use it."

"Life sometimes has as a way of going full circle. Had it not been for this hotel, you would have never reconnected with Bill." She picked up the champagne bottle and gave it a closer look. "Dom Perignon. Good choice, Mr. Shelton."

✑FIFTY-TWO✑

JENNA WATCHED HER reflection in the mirror as her mother clipped on her veil. "There you go," said Claire. "So, what do you think?"

"I think she's gorgeous," said Stacy, "but something's missing. You need something old, borrowed and blue, and I have just the thing." She reached inside her purse and handed Jenna a small drawstring bag.

"Wow," said Jenna. "You're letting me borrow your sapphire pendant? Are you sure?"

"Of course, I'm sure. It'll go perfect with your dress. You can give it back to me later."

"Thank you, Stacy," said Claire. She put the pendant around Jenna's neck, being careful not to disturb the veil. As they admired it someone knocked at the door.

"Stacy, can you get that?" asked Claire.

"Sure." Stacy opened the door. Nick waited on the other side.

"Is it safe for me to come in?" he asked.

"Of course, it is," said Jenna.

"You look absolutely beautiful." He gave Jenna a quick kiss on the check. "So, are you ready?"

"I guess I'm as ready as I'll ever be. I take it Bill has arrived."

"He has. He also hates wearing a tuxedo almost as much as I do. You know, the more I get to know him, the more I like him."

"That's good, Dad," said Jenna, "since he's about to become your son-in-law."

"So, what about David and his mother?" asked Claire.

"They're here," said Nick. "So are Connor and Kelsey and the rest of the guests. They're all waiting for the bride to make her entrance, so we need to head downstairs."

"In a moment," said Claire. "First, I want to take some pictures."

"But they're waiting," said Nick.

"Then they'll have to wait a couple minutes longer." Claire grabbed her phone and began taking photos. One of Jenna with her father, another of Jenna and Stacy.

"I'd be happy to take a few shots of both of you with Jenna," said Stacy. Claire eagerly handed Stacy her phone. Afterwards, she picked up the two bridal bouquets and gave the one with peach-colored roses to Stacy.

"Look at that," she said. "They match your dress perfectly, and this one is for you, Jenna."

"Of course," Her hands were trembling as she took the white rose bouquet. "There. I think I've got it. Guess I must be having a little stage fright."

Stacy tried to reassure her. "Don't worry. If you faint during the ceremony, I'll catch you."

"Somehow I knew I could always count on you."

"It's what I do, and I couldn't be happier for both of you."

Nick offered Jenna his arm and escorted her to the elevator. As they rode it down, it stopped on the third floor. An older couple stepped inside to join them. They offered their congratulations as they continued down to the lobby and strolled into the atrium.

"So, this must be the famous sculpture," said Stacy.

"The one and only," said Jenna.

Stacy brushed it with her hand as they walked by. "Maybe it'll bring me good luck as well."

Connor's friend, Caleb, was waiting at the other end of the atrium. He had volunteered to photograph the wedding, and he, too, wanted to get a few shots of the bridal party before the ceremony.

"I think that's enough for now." He led them to the ballroom and opened the door. Stepping inside, he escorted Claire to her seat and gave the keyboard player a nod. She began playing, "Here Comes the Bride" as Bill, his brother David, and the minister waited in front of the wedding arch. Stacy made her way up to the arch as Nick and Jenna slowly walked behind her.

Bill gave Jenna's hand a squeeze as Nick gave her away and welcomed Bill into their family. Worried she might drop the ring, Jenna felt greatly relieved once she slipped it on Bill's finger. A few minutes later the minister introduced Mr. and Mrs. Willis Haskell to their guests. As they applauded, the keyboard player began playing, "The Wedding March." Jenna took Bill's arm and they walked to the back of the room, taking their place next to the wedding cake.

"Let's do whatever we have to do as quickly as possible," Bill said under his breath. "Then we can get the hell out of here. This tuxedo is killing me."

Jenna gave him a knowing look while their guests formed a receiving line. As they greeted them, Bill's mother, Kitty, gave Jenna a warm embrace.

"I'm so glad the two of you found one another again," she said. "Bill often spoke of you over the years, and he deeply regretted the circumstances being what they were at the time you first met."

"I felt the same," said Jenna, "but back then, I don't think either one of us were ready."

"I don't think you were either, but I'm so glad it worked out this time around. He really does need you, even if he won't admit it."

As Kitty stepped aside, Bill introduced Jenna to his brother, David.

"I can definitely see a family resemblance," said Jenna.

"Yeah, but I'm the better looking one." David gave her a warm embrace. "Welcome to the family, sis."

Kelsey and Connor offered their congratulations, and Jenna introduced Chad and his wife to Bill.

"Nice to finally meet you in person," said Bill. "I also want to thank you again for referring me to Sorenson's Gallery."

"It was my pleasure," said Chad. "We're looking forward to your opening in May."

After greeting the rest of their guests, it was time to cut the cake. Caleb took a few more photos, and Kitty approached them as Caleb stepped away.

"Claire and I can take it from here," she said. "You kids need to run along. We'll save you some cake for later."

"Thanks, Mom," said Jenna, "but before we go, I need to toss my bouquet."

As expected, Stacy and Kelsey were the only two single women in attendance. Jenna tossed the flowers into the air, and they landed squarely in Stacy's hands, much to Alan's surprise.

"Let's get out of here before he passes out," said Bill.

"Good idea," said Jenna, "but first I need to tell my mother goodbye. I'll only be a minute."

Claire gave Jenna a big hug as she told her goodnight. "As soon as the other guests leave, your father and I will be joining David and Kitty at Sam's for a nightcap."

"I'm glad you guys are getting along," said Jenna. She then gave her father a quick goodbye.

"I love you, Baby Girl."

"I love you too, Dad, and we'll see you soon." She quickly rejoined Bill, and they discreetly slipped out the door.

"It's been a hectic day, and I'm ready to unwind," said Bill. "Hopefully, they delivered my bag to the room. I really need to get out of this tux."

"I'm sure they did. I noticed a bellman in the hallway when we were leaving. Did you get a room key?"

"I did. It's in my coat pocket."

They quickly hopped into the elevator. Bill took off his tie and unbuttoned the top of his shirt as they rode up to the top floor. He felt relieved once the doors opened.

"Come with me," said Jenna.

"You know I'll follow you anywhere."

"Down, boy."

"Hey, I'm just saying."

Jenna stopped at the end of the hall and waited as Bill unlocked the door.

"Not so fast," he said.

"Why?"

"You're about to find out." He swooped her off her feet and carried her into the room, gently setting her down on the sofa. Taking off his coat, he sat down next to her.

"So, how are you feeling?" he asked.

"Relieved. I love my mother dearly, but she was driving me crazy. So, now that the wedding's over, she can spend more time traveling and doing things with Dad, and less time worrying about me."

"Jenna, can I let you in on a little secret?"

"Sure. What is it?"

"Once you become a parent, you never stop worrying, as you may find out some day. I still worry about Connor. He stopped by last night, and we had a long talk."

"Is anything wrong?"

"No, nothing's wrong, although he's still trying to get used to the idea of me getting married again. For a long time, it was just him and me against the world, and I kept telling him I would never remarry. So, he naturally assumed he would always have me to himself, even after he had a family of his own."

"Are you saying he jealous?"

"Not at all. He thinks the world of you, and he's genuinely happy we found one another. He just didn't think we'd ever take it this far, but don't worry, he'll be okay. He just needs a little time to sort through it." As Bill glanced around the room, something caught his eye. He went to take a closer look.

"Well, what have we here? It looks like a bottle of Dom Perignon."

"It is. Compliments of Oscar Shelton."

"So, what else do we have?" He wandered into the sleeping area. "What the hell? Jenna, did you know about this?"

She rushed into the bedroom. "Know about what?" she asked.

"This." Bill pointed at the recessed ceiling over the bed.

"Oh, that. It was Oscar's idea. He wanted to make the bridal suite special. He told me about how he'd once stayed in a hotel room in Las Vegas with a mirror over the bed, and he had a glimmer in his eye when he described it. I got the distinct impression he was traveling with someone other than his wife, but of course I didn't let on. I decided to go with mirror tiles. I thought they'd look a little more romantic, and Oscar agreed."

Bill too had a glimmer in his eye. "I think they're going to be a whole lot of fun, as long as they are no hidden cameras behingd them."

"No. I assure you there are no hidden cameras."

"I see. So, let's find out other little secrets the room has." He wandered into the bathroom and flicked on the lights. The spacious bathroom featured a walk-in shower big enough for two, along with a large, garden bathtub with jets.

"I wanted the bathroom to be romantic too," said Jenna. "So, I made the closet a little smaller. That way I could make the bathroom bigger and create a unique bridal suite."

"You've certainly thought of everything."

"The Sheltons were pleased, but I never thought for a moment I'd ever use it myself."

"They wanted a sculpture for the lobby, so here we are. If we should have a son someday, we may want to name him Oscar." He gave her an affectionate kiss and removed her veil, setting it off to the side, along with his glasses. She started to remove a hairpin, but Bill told her no.

"Your hair looks incredibly sexy, so we'll worry about it later. First, I'm going to draw us a nice warm bath so we can relax for a little while."

"Sounds wonderful."

"So, let's get you out of this gown."

She couldn't resist teasing him. "You naughty boy. I may have to go downstairs and tell your mother on you."

"If you did, she'd be on my side." He unzipped her gown and removed his shirt, revealing a white cotton undershirt. "It feels good to be out of that stuff. I felt like I was wearing starched cardboard. So, if you'll hand me your gown, I'll go hang it up."

He gave her breast a squeeze as she stepped out of her gown. Once the items were safely hung in the closet, he peeled off the rest of his clothing and stashed it in a laundry bag.

"This feels so much better," he said. "By the way, did I mention that we'll be spending most of the weekend naked?"

"We are? So, what happens when we get hungry?"

"We call room service. When it arrives, we'll put on our bathrobes. As soon as they leave, we'll take them off, so as of now, you're officially overdressed." He unhooked her bra and helped her out of her undergarments.

"You are so beautiful." He wrapped his arms around her and squeezed her bare backside. "I'll always be grateful we found one another again."

"Me too."

He led her into the bathroom turned on the bathtub faucet. As they waited for it to fill up, Jenna grabbed a few packets from the sink.

"Here's some bath salts, along with a bar of soap."

"Thank you, my dear." He kissed her passionately and gently squeezed her breasts. "These feel nice. They also feel like they're getting bigger."

"Really?"

"I noticed you've put on a couple of pounds, but don't worry. It's in all the right places, so it looks good." He gently nibbled on her nipples as he squeezed her backside. Finally, Jenna spoke up.

"Bill? The bathwater?"

"Oh, right. You're driving me to distraction, but it looks like it's about ready." He checked the temperature and turned the faucet off. "Nice and warm, but not too hot. After you my dear." He extended his hand and helped her into the tub. Once she was settled in the water, he climbed in to join her.

"This feels heavenly," she said. "I couldn't wait to get out of my shoes. My feet were starting to swell."

"Would you like for me to give them a little foot rub?"

"I'd love it. Thanks."

He turned on the jets and began rubbing her feet as she leaned back in the tub and relaxed in the foamy water. "It smells like lilac, and I love lilac."

"I'm glad you like it, but don't get too comfortable."

"Why not?"

"Because we have some very important things to do later on." He too leaned back and relaxed until the water started turning cold. Once they were dry, he took her by the hand and led her to the bed. Turning down the covers, he motioned for her to lie down and waited until she was comfortable before taking his seat at the foot of the bed.

"I can't believe we finally made it," he said.

"I know. It all feels like a dream. I'm afraid someone's going to come along and wake me up."

He began massaging her legs. "If it is a dream, then we're both having the same dream at the same time." He began rubbing her abdomen, working his way to her breasts, squeezing them as he kissed her passionately. Jenna softly moaned in contentment. He then kissed his way back down to her breasts, sucking and nibbling on her nipples as she moaned a little louder.

"Do you like it?" he softly asked.

"Um-hum."

"Good, because there's more coming." He licked and nibbled on her breasts again, and slowly kissed his way down to her bikini line.

"So, what have we here? I think you should let me take a closer look." He pushed her knees away and slipped a finger inside as he massaged her with his thumb. She moaned with pleasure.

"So, you like it?'

She replied with another groan, and as her moans became intense, he laid down next to her.

"Well now, you've got me all excited too. So, you need give me a good squeeze." He placed her hand on him, gasping with pleasure as she pleased him in return. Her groans grew louder as he slipped a finger back inside her and massaged her again. "Oh, baby," he said breathlessly. "Keep squeezing me. Harder. Harder."

Their moans grew louder as he slipped another finger inside.

"Yes, yes," Jenna said breathlessly. He rubbed her a little longer with his thumb, and as she groaned, he mounted her and pushed his way deep inside, gasping in pleasure as she clamped herself down on him. He bit down on her breast as she wrapped herself around him. As he picked up the pace her, body writhed until she reached her climax and cried out in pure ecstasy. He reached his release an instant later, sucking her breast as he too slowly came down and laid his head on her chest.

"So how are you feeling?" he asked.

"On top of the world."

"Me too. I guess we've sealed the marriage as we are now, officially, consummated. I love you, Jenna. Now and forever."

"I love you too, Bill. Now and forever."

❧FIFTY-THREE❧

BILL WAS WORKING in the basement when Jenna arrived home. She soon came downstairs to join him. "So how was your day?" he asked.

"I'm not sure," she said. "As soon as I arrived, I found a note from Chad on my desk, wanting me to come up to his office."

"Was there a problem?"

"I suppose it depends on how you define a problem. A new project came in last Friday. They gave it to Justin Shaw, who's one of their best project architects, and he promptly brought CeCe on board. So much for her being on probation, or whatever you want to call it. She worked with him on his last project, and he's had her back all along, which explains why she wasn't fired. In fact, her job is probably more secure than mine, because she still has seniority over me."

"I'm sorry, Jenna. I sometimes have to deal with office politics at the college, and I hate it. She hasn't been bothering you, has she?"

"No, she hasn't. In fact, we pretty much ignore one another, although she did congratulate me, along with the rest of my co-workers."

"So now that she knows we're officially married, she can pass the information onto Ken."

"I'm sure she will. Hopefully he'll finally get a clue and move on. So, how was your day?"

"It went well. I only teach one class on Tuesdays and Thursdays. Then I hurried back here because I had a photo session this afternoon with Josh and Stephanie. I need to get back to the business of creating art."

"Doesn't Stephanie work at the gallery on Tuesdays?" asked Jenna.

"She does, but Tuesdays are their slowest day of week, so she was able to leave early. While they were here, we had an interesting conversation about the high cost of putting a child through college."

"I see. So, what did they have to say about it?"

"I think I may have mentioned before that they put their art modeling money into their kids' college funds, and Josh said if we were to have any kids, we should set up their college funds while they're babies. So, I've decided I'm not going to wait. I'm going to start working on it now. If we have kids, great. If we don't, we'll add it to our retirement fund."

"I see. So, how are we going to make this extra money?"

"I'm in a building full of artists," he said, "and art models are always in demand. I also think you should consider doing more of it as well. Rhonda was very pleased with the work you did for her. It wouldn't take much of your time as most jobs only last for an hour or two."

"I know, but what if a male artist wants me to model for him?"

"It shouldn't be a problem," said Bill. "Not all jobs are for nude work, and I can personally vouch for all the male artists in the building. They're highly professional, they would treat you with the utmost respect. They would also be more than happy to provide a chaperone for a nude session if I wasn't available. There may also be times when we would work together. Rhonda mentioned something at the wedding about possibly doing a Garden of Eden series. If she does, she would like to use both of us for the entire series."

"I could definitely work with her again."

"I could also use you for some of my own projects, just like I did for the woodcut. It would save me the cost of having to hire someone else."

"I could indeed. So, what do you need me to do?"

"I thought you'd never ask." He grabbed a box from the table and presented it to her. "My body paints arrived today. I'd like to test them on you, if you'd be willing."

"I see."

He handed her a piece of tracing paper. "Here's the sketch I was working on when you came in. As you can see, I've incorporated your rose tattoo into the design, and if it turns out the way I'm hoping, I'd like to use it for one of my bronzes. We can get started after dinner, if it's okay with you."

"As long as you help with the dishes."

"I'd be happy to. Oh, and I almost forgot. The gallery in Taos is still very much interested in representing me. Spring break is coming up soon, so I'm going to drive down there to meet with them in person, and I'd like for you to come along."

"On a weekend?"

"No. They do most of their business on weekends. It would be on a weekday."

"I would if I could, but at the moment I'm in the middle of a big project at work."

He suddenly felt disappointed. "I understand, and I'll only be down there for a day or two, but I'll sure miss you while I'm gone. Would you like for Connor and Kelsey to stay with you while I'm away?"

"No, I'm good. The order of protection I have against Ken is still in effect, and I haven't heard a peep out of him in weeks. CeCe doesn't talk about him anymore either. At least not whenever I'm around. Meantime, I can smell the pot roast cooking, and I'm starving."

"Me too. So, let's run upstairs."

* * *

"The things I do for you," said Jenna. Stepping underneath the photography lights, she took off her bathrobe and waited as Bill turned off the overhead lights.

"I'll always be grateful for you supporting me as an artist," he said. "Not all spouses do. Mary Beth never had much of an interest in art."

"I have a creative career myself so I get it, and I'm willing to help you as much as I can."

"And I love you dearly for it." He picked up a drawing tool and held it up so she could see it. "This is your everyday drugstore eyebrow pencil, so you know it's safe. The paint is water-based, and it washes off with soap and water. So, are you ready?"

"I'm ready."

Bill looked at his sketch and began drawing the design on Jenna's skin. She took a deep breath and held still as he drew his design.

"Okay, I've got the front done, so if you'll turn around, I can draw the back."

"You're doing both sides?"

"Yep. It's for a bronze, although I may do a woodcut version with just the front later on."

"How big will it be?"

"I haven't decided yet, but I'm thinking it'll be about the same scale as the bronze I did of Stephanie last year." He went back to work, and was soon ready to apply the paint. He started with her face. The paint felt refreshingly cool as he gently brushed it onto to her skin.

"How does it look?" she asked.

"So far so good. The colors are staying vibrant as they dry, and they blend together nicely. I'll show it to you once I finish taking the photos, but no more talking for now." He worked his way down her shoulders and chest, and from there down to her stomach. She soon felt him applying paint in an unexpected place.

"You're painting me down there?" she asked.

"Yep. It's part of a leaf, so I'm painting it dark green. I also need you to keep still."

She took a deep breath and waited patiently for him to finish. Once he was done, he began painting her legs and her backside. Finally, he put his paintbrushes down.

"We're in the home stretch," he said. "Now I need you to turn slightly to your left, no more than three or four inches, then put your weight on the other leg and bend your knee."

"Like this?" she asked.

"Yes. Now, turn your head to face me, and put your hand over the tattooed hip. Just like that. Now, place your other hand on your waist. There, you got it. Now stand still and don't move. This won't take long." He grabbed his camera and slowly walked around her, taking photos from every angle.

"Got it. You did a fantastic job, and you can relax now. So would you like to take a look?"

"Of course." He handed her the camera, and she slowly looked through the photos.

"My goodness," she said. "I really do look like a human canvas. You can tell I'm naked, but you've applied the paint in all right places, so, technically, I'm covered."

He turned on the overhead lights. Jenna gazed down at herself for a moment before reaching for her robe. "Not so fast," he said.

"Why not?"

"Because I'm taking you upstairs. Looking at you naked does certain things to me. I was having some challenges while I was working, and I need some relief."

"Of course," she said coyly. "I'm more than happy to help make you feel better."

"You look like you could use some relief yourself, and I think we should definably help one another out. Then, after were done relieving one another, we'll take a shower together. Since I'm the one who put all the paint on you, the least I can do is wash it off."

* * *

Bill looked at Jenna as they held each other in the afterglow. "Look at that," he said. "The paint stayed on you. None of it came off on me."

"As long as it washes off. I have to be at the office first thing tomorrow morning."

"I'm sure it will." He looked at her more closely. "Are you alright?"

"I'm fine. Why do you ask?"

"Because all of a sudden, you look a little pale."

"I'm fine. My stomach's doing a few flip flops, but I'll be okay in a couple of minutes."

He felt even more concerned. "So how long has your stomach been bothering you?"

"For a few weeks now. Between the Ken incident, and all the excitement planning the wedding, and worrying about the office cuckoo bird, I've had a sensitive stomach, but it's okay. I'll get a little queasy for a couple of minutes, and then it clears up."

"Oh, dear god," he said.

"What's wrong?"

He took a deep breath. "Jenna, I've noticed you've been a little, off, lately."

"It's stress. It sometimes affects my cycles."

"And you've been on the pill the entire time?"

"No," said Jenna. "After you left the infamous text message, I knew I wouldn't be with anyone for the foreseeable future, so I decided to give my body a break and go off it for a while. Then you came back. I use the rings as back up, so I started using them. Now that the wedding's over, I should start going back to normal."

"Okay, I have to ask. The day I came back, I took you back to my place after your hearing, and then we had a little celebration after you said yes. We went to your place the next morning."

"Which is when I got the rings. I was only unprotected the one time."

"It only takes one time, Jenna."

"I know it does," she said, "but I'm not pregnant."

"You're sure about that?

"Positive."

"But you just said your stomach has been bothering you."

"It's stress."

"I understand, but we need to find out what's going on," said Bill. "If it's a nervous stomach, we need to get it treated before it creates other problems. And if you're pregnant, we'll also need to get you to a doctor."

A serious look came over her face. "If I were pregnant, would it be a problem?"

"Are you kidding me?" He wrapped his arms around her and gave her a big squeeze. "No, it wouldn't be a problem. I love being dad, and I wanted to have other children after Connor was born. Unfortunately, his mother didn't. She was too wrapped up in her career."

"I am too, but at least my occupation is a little more flexible. If we had a baby, I could set myself up as a freelancer and work out of the house. That way I wouldn't be missing any soccer games or dance recitals, or any other kid stuff."

He gave her a loving kiss. "So, let's find out if we're having a baby or not. In the meantime, I need to wash the paint off you."

Jenna stopped at the drugstore on her way home the following night. An anxious Bill greeted her when she came inside. She hurried into the bathroom, and they both watched intently as the test turned positive.

"Oh, my, god," she said.

"It's okay," said Bill. "By my calculations, you should be about six to seven weeks along. I've been down this road before. I also promised your father you'll be well taken care of."

"Easy for you to say. You're not the one having it."

He gave her a reassuring hug. "You won't be going through it alone, I promise. I'll be there every step of the way, including the labor and delivery, but right now we need to get you to a doctor."

"What about my mother? She'd want to know. So would my dad."

"I know, but let's wait until you see the doctor first. We'll announce it to the rest of the family later."

✋FIFTY-FOUR✦

CECE HAD NOTICED a change in Jenna. Over the past few weeks, she had arrived late for work twice. Each time she said it was because she was having dental work done. While her face looked a little fuller, CeCe had a feeling there was more to the story. Jenna was also dressing differently. Gone were the tight, form-fitting dresses and skirts. She had replaced them with looser fitting sweaters and tops. Perhaps she was gaining weight. Some women did after they got married, but Jenna still looked slim as ever.

This morning, Jenna had once again arrived late, and she was carrying a King Soopers bag. Obviously, she had stopped at the store on her way to the office.

"Did something happen?" asked Priscilla. "For some reason I was thinking you had gotten here before me and were in a meeting."

"No, I just got here," said Jenna. "Our next client meeting is on Thursday. I'm late because I had a doctor's appointment."

"I see. So, is everything okay?"

"I'm fine." Jenna turned on her computer and stepped out, once again returning a moment later with a bottle of water instead of her usual morning coffee. CeCe stared at her computer screen as she listened in on their conversation.

"I did have a hectic weekend though," said Jenna. "We finally got the last of my furniture moved over Bill's house, and it felt both happy and sad at the same time. I have many good memories of my house, and as happy as I am to be married to Bill, getting my old place ready to sell makes me feel a little sad."

CeCe took a pad from her desk as Jenna and Pricilla were talking. If Jenna were to mention anything about Ken, she would write

260

it down and let him know. She was also curious about Jenna's medical appointment, and what might be in the bag. Hopefully, it didn't contain anything she could use against Ken.

"As my mother used to say," said Priscilla, "when one chapter of your life comes to an end, it means the next one is about to begin."

"I know, and I can't wait to start the next chapter, but right now duty calls. I need to get the rest of those estimates done so I can put together my next price quote for Mr. Lee."

"Then I won't keep you."

CeCe pushed her pad off to the side and tried to get back to work. Justin's latest project was a state of the art police station, and CeCe's contribution was nearly complete. She would soon be stuck once again with boring, busywork jobs any draft person could do. Taking a deep breath, she logged into LinkedIn. To her dismay, there were new no inquiries from any prospective employers. Logging out, she checked the other job-hunting websites. One had a new listing for an interior designer, but her excitement waned as she read the job description. A flooring company was looking for an outside sales person to bring samples to their prospective customers' homes and take measurements. It also paid a commission instead of a salary. CeCe let out another sigh. It seemed like whenever she found an interesting job listing, she was either overqualified, or the person who posted the listing didn't fully understand what an interior designer actually did.

Jenna soon excused herself and hurried off to Chad's office, leaving the shopping bag on top of her desk. She told Priscilla she would be return in about an hour. Thirty minutes later Priscilla, along with two other designers, took their lunch break. CeCe's stomach was starting to rumble as well, but Victoria, the one remaining designer, was eating lunch at her desk. CeCe needed to come up with a believable excuse to interrupt Victoria's meal and, at the same time, find out what was in Jenna's shopping bag. She opened a folder and began flipping through the papers.

"Sorry to bother you, Victoria," she said, "but would you mind if I bummed a few paper clips off of you? I seem to have run out."

"Of course. Here you go."

"No, no," said CeCe. "You're busy. I can get them."

"Thanks. I'm on a really tight deadline right now."

CeCe hurried over to Victoria's desk, giving her a quick thank you as she took the paper clips. Walking past Jenna's desk, she took a deliberate misstep, pushing the shopping bag onto the floor as she pretended to lose her balance.

"Whoa! There I go, being clumsy again."

"Are you okay?" asked Victoria.

"I think so. My mind was elsewhere and I guess I wasn't paying attention to where I was going." As CeCe dusted herself off Victoria turned her attention back to her project. CeCe scooped up bag and quickly glanced inside as she set it back on Jenna's desk. It contained a deli sandwich, an orange, and a bottle of prenatal vitamins. She glanced back at Victoria, who was still immersed in her work. So, Jenna was pregnant. It certainly explained the wardrobe change and the doctor's appointments. CeCe rushed back to her desk and quickly put on her coat.

"I think I'll grab some lunch before I make another mess," she said. "Talk to you later."

Victoria barely acknowledged CeCe as she hurried out to the elevator and rode it down to the parking garage. Safely inside her car, she placed a call to Ken.

"What's up?" he asked.

"Are you someplace where we can talk privately?"

"I'm in the break room, eating a sandwich. No one else is in here at the moment."

"Any chance of anyone coming in?" she asked.

"Maybe. Matt hasn't had his lunch yet."

"Then would you mind grabbing your stuff and going back to your office and closing the door? This really is urgent."

"Okay. Give me a minute, and this had better be good."

"Let me know when you can talk." CeCe anxiously waited for Ken to come back on the line.

"Alright, I'm in my office, and I've just closed the door. So, what's going on?"

"I hope you're sitting down, because what I'm about to say will blow you away."

"Yes, I'm sitting down. So, what the hell happened?"

"Jenna's pregnant," said CeCe.

"What?"

"Jenna's pregnant. She's going to have a baby. I'm sorry, Ken, but you need to let her go, once and for all. I've never understood this obsession you've had with getting her back. I also have a feeling that deep down, you were angry with her for some reason. For what it's worth, I've never once heard her mention your name to anyone besides me, so I highly doubt she's holding a grudge against you. What I do know is whatever issues she may have had with you in the past are no longer relevant. She just wants to be left alone, and there are other single women working here who I would love to introduce to you. Like Paige, the front receptionist. She's in her mid-twenties and she's also blonde. She's friendly, outgoing and nice looking. Then there's Sydney. She's one of the architects. She's in her thirties and she has long, dark hair. She also—"

"Okay, okay," Ken said firmly "I appreciate the thought, but no. I'm not interested in seeing anyone else at the moment. I still have unfinished business with Jenna."

"Unfinished business? What the hell are you talking about? Were you not listening to me? She's having a baby, which means she's moved on for good. She also told me the only reason she went to the wedding with you was because you begged her to, because you didn't want your family asking questions."

Ken suddenly turned angry. "Excuse me, but I don't beg a woman for anything because I don't have to. I'm the one in charge, not her, and if she doesn't suit my needs, I cut her loose."

"What do you mean? I've never heard you talk this way before."

His voice was calmer. "Sorry, CeCe. I'm trying to process this, and I guess your comment caught me off guard. What I meant to say is no, I wasn't planning on making a commitment to her, but I wasn't quite ready to end the relationship either. But then my—."

"I know all about your aunt, but you also know relationships are a two-way street. If someone isn't happy and wants to end it, you can't force them to stay with you just because you're not ready for them to leave. They have the right to go if they're not happy."

"Not with me they don't," Ken said curtly.

"What?"

"Sorry. I guess that didn't come out right either. What I meant to say is when the time comes to end a relationship, both parties need to sit down together and discuss it face-to-face. Then no one walks away thinking they did something wrong, or ends up blaming themselves for something which wasn't their fault. Unfortunately, Jenna never gave me the opportunity to tell my side of the story. It's the reason why I took her to Sam's Place the night she returned the money. All I wanted to do was to ask her why she ended it with me, in a public place, so she wouldn't feel threatened, but once again, she never gave me the chance. We'd barely taken our seats when she said she wasn't feeling well. Then she bolted off to the ladies' room."

"Granted, I don't know how far along she is, but it very well may have been because she's pregnant, and sometimes women get nauseous when they're pregnant, which means it might not have had anything to do with you at all. She must have called her friends to come get her because she wasn't feeling well, and she didn't want you to know."

"Maybe so, but she should have at least had the decency to come back to the table and tell me she wasn't feeling well. I would have been happy to take her home. So, how did you find out about her being pregnant? Did she tell you?"

"No. I found out by accident. It's a long story, and I'll fill you in on the rest later. Right now, I'm getting hungry, and I need to take my lunch break."

"I understand," said Ken, "and I appreciate you letting me know. So, would you mind keeping me in the loop?"

"I don't think it would be a good idea, Ken. She's moved on. From what I've seen of Bill, he strikes me as a very good guy, and they're about to start a family. So, what would you have to gain?"

"Nothing. I don't want anything from her, and I assure you I'm not trying to win her back. I also promise not to ever contact her again, either directly or indirectly. You have my word on it. I just want to know if she's doing okay, that's all. I don't need to know all the intimate details of her life. So why don't you call me later? When we have more time to talk."

"Of course. I'll call you tonight."

"I look forward to it. So go get yourself something to eat, and we'll talk later."

✎FIFTY-FIVE✐

KEN'S ANGER TOWARD Jenna had turned into a seething hatred. Not only had she defied him by ending their relationship, she had married another man and was carrying his child. Then came the letter from her attorney. They were threatening to take legal action against him. As far as he was concerned, she had gone too far and she would have to pay the price. He laid low, waiting for the perfect moment, and it had finally arrived. CeCe overheard her telling another co-worker Bill was in Taos, meeting with a prospective gallery. With him being away, she would be an easy target, and he would strike without warning.

He told his boss he had to leave early for a dental appointment. No one suspected a thing when he told his coworkers goodnight. Hopping into his Blazer, he fired up the engine and placed a phone call. A woman quickly answered.

"Hey, Alecia, it's Ken. I have the license plate on my truck. You're absolutely certain no one can trace it?"

"Positive," she said. "Just drop it off when you're done, and we'll make sure it disappears. No one will ever be able to prove it was you."

"I knew I could count on you."

"Do you have the rest of the money?"

"I do. Five hundred dollars. All in twenties and fifties. And thanks for being patient. I didn't want to raise suspicion at the bank."

"Not a problem," she said. "You've helped me out in the past, and I know you're trustworthy. I'll see you in about an hour."

"See you then." Ken put his phone away and grabbed a bag from the passenger floorboard. Inside was a knitted cap and a hoodie sweatshirt. Tossing his jacket in the back seat, he put on the sweatshirt,

265

concealing as much as of his face as he could before putting on the cap and tucking his hair underneath. No doubt there would be many witnesses, but none would be able positively identify him. He smiled as he looked at himself in the rearview mirror.

"Well Jenna, what can I say? You wanted me out of your life, so I've decided to make my exit memorable. You're about to get the scare of your life, and if you lose your baby, oh well. At least it isn't my kid."

He put the Blazer into gear and focused his attention on the traffic. It was nearly five o'clock when he drove into the visitors' parking lot at Salisbury and Norton Architects. Jenna and her co-workers would soon be heading home, and they would have to go through the visitors' lot as they made their way to the exit. Backing the Blazer into an empty space, he shut down the engine and waited. His patience soon paid off. One by one, employee vehicles began coming out of the parking garage. He fired up the engine and waited for the gray Camry. It soon drove by. He pulled up behind it and followed it out of the parking lot, once again smiling to himself as they headed toward the freeway. By the time Jenna realized what was happening, it would be too late.

A traffic light turned yellow as Jenna approached and she hurried through. Ken accelerated as well, but he was unable to clear the intersection before the light turned red. He held his breath, hoping no police cars were nearby. To his relief, he saw no flashing lights in his rearview mirror. He moved quickly as they merged onto the freeway. Within seconds he was in the next lane, driving beside her. Jenna realized something was amiss and picked up her speed, but he stayed even with her.

"So, Jenna, how do you like me now?" he asked out loud. "For the next few minutes, I'm going to be a thorn in your side. First, I'm going to force you off at the next exit. After that I'll play cat and mouse with you, just to mess with your head. With any luck, you'll be in a state of total panic, but don't worry. I'll disappear before the cops show up, and best part is you won't be able to prove it was me, because the license plate doesn't match mine, and everyone will think you've lost your mind."

As he continued driving next to her a nearby tractor-trailer rig laid down its horn at another motorist. The loud, unexpected sound startled him, causing him to jerk the wheel and sideswipe Jenna's car.

* * *

Jenna noticed a black Blazer behind her as she made her way to the freeway. She immediately thought of Ken, but shrugged it off. His office was several miles away from her workplace, and he lived in another part of town. A traffic light turned yellow as she approached, but she was too close to stop safely. Punching the accelerator, she hurried through. Once she was clear she checked her rearview mirror. The black

Blazer was still behind her. Whoever was driving was in a hurry to get somewhere. She thought about pulling over to let it pass, but the freeway was coming up. She was anxious to get home, and whoever it was would no doubt pass her once they were on the freeway.

As she merged into the traffic the Blazer pulled up beside her, but it didn't pass. She hit the gas, but the Blazer stayed even with her. She was about to call nine-one-one when the Blazer suddenly sideswiped her. Holding tight to the steering wheel, she managed to keep her car under control and safely pull over to the side. Her hands were shaking as she came to a stop and turned on her flashers. She reached for her phone, but it wasn't there. It had bounced out of the console. As she fought the urge to panic, another car pulled over in front of her. A black woman wearing a nurse's uniform hurried out and ran up to her while the traffic around her had slowed to a crawl.

"Are you okay?" she shouted through the window.

"I think so." Jenna pushed the button to roll the window down, but it abruptly stopped halfway down. She then tried to open the driver's side door, but it too was jammed.

"I've lost my phone and I can't get out."

"Don't worry," said the nurse. "I'm calling nine-one-one. Try not to move around until the paramedics get here and check you out."

Jenna took a deep breath and waited until the other woman disconnected the call. "Did you see who hit me?" she asked. "It was a black Chevy Blazer, but I didn't see the driver."

"The other driver lost control after hitting you. I know some other cars hit him, but I didn't have a clear view, so I'm going to see if anyone else needs help. Don't worry, the paramedics are on their way. I'll be back soon, I promise." She hurried away, only to return a short time later with a grim look on her face.

"What happened?" asked Jenna.

"It's bad. Real bad. It's a fatality."

"Was it a man or a woman?"

"It was a man."

"Did he by chance have dark hair?"

"He was wearing a ski cap, so I couldn't tell. It's a pretty grizzly scene. He lost control and rolled. He was also hit by several other vehicles, including a semi-truck going at a high rate of speed. I checked for a pulse, just to be sure, but there wasn't one. Fortunately, he didn't have any passengers with him. The semi-truck driver is pretty shaken, but otherwise seems to be okay, and thankfully no one else was seriously injured."

"Oh my god," said Jenna. "I think I know who he might be."

"You can let the officers know, but I'm pretty sure they'll have to use dental records in order to positively identify him."

They heard approaching sirens. Two highway patrol cars had arrived. An officer asked Jenna if she was okay while the other officer began closing off lanes and directing traffic away from the crash. A firetruck and an ambulance arrived a minute later.

"Are you okay?" asked one of the medics.

"I think so," said Jenna. "I know I'll be a lot happier once you can get me out of here."

"It's what we're trying to do, ma'am. Just sit tight and try to relax. We'll have you out as quickly as we can."

As they went to work Jenna watched the nurse as she talked to one of the officers. Once they were finished, she stood by and waited as the firefighters removed the driver's side door.

"Thank goodness." Jenna tried to step out of the car.

"Not so fast," said one of the medics. "We need to check you out first."

Jenna had some minor cuts and bruises, but no sign of any serious injuries. The medics, however, became concerned when she told them she was pregnant.

"We're taking you to the hospital," said the medic who was treating her. "We want to get you checked out and make sure the baby's okay. You're not bleeding, are you?"

"No, I'm not bleeding."

"Which is a good sign. So just relax, and we'll get you on a gurney."

"Which hospital?"

"Southern Memorial."

"Thank goodness. My stepson works there. I need someone to call him."

"What's his name?"

"Connor. Connor Haskell. He works in administration."

"We'll take care of it, and we'll ask him to meet you there, so just relax and enjoy the ride."

Jenna reached for the nurse's hand and thanked her as they loaded her into the ambulance. As they drove away the paramedic checked her vitals again.

"Is my baby going to be okay?" she asked.

"Hopefully. Are you feeling any cramping?"

"No. Other than being badly shaken I feel fine. Do we know who was driving the Blazer?"

"I'm not sure, but the officers will want to talk to you once you're checked out."

"Good, because I'm anxious to talk to them as well."

* * *

Jenna nervously waited for her test results to come in, but there was still no sign of Connor. She had arrived at the hospital after he had left for the day. She was also getting hungry, so someone brought her a

Sprite along with a few crackers. As she took another sip of soda, one of the nurses knocked at the door.

"You have a visitor," she said.

"Is it the highway patrol?" asked Jenna.

"No, it's me," said a familiar voice. Connor came into the room and greeted her with a reassuring hug.

"Thank goodness you're here. I was worried about how I was going to get home. My phone and keys flew out of the console, and I don't know if anyone has found them yet."

"Don't worry. I'll make sure you get home, and I'm sorry I didn't get here sooner. My phone was charging in another room and I didn't hear it ring. So, what the hell happened?"

"Someone deliberately sideswiped me on the freeway. I'm okay. Just few scratches, but you know how hospitals are. They have to run all kinds of tests."

"To make sure you don't have a traumatic head injury or any internal bleeding."

"None of the above, thank goodness," said Jenna. "The highway patrol said they would be sending someone to talk to me here, but so far no one's showed up."

There was another knock at the door. This time the doctor came in. He immediately recognized Connor.

"Well look who's here? Did you get the rest of the stuff I needed?"

"I'm working on it, but right now I'm here for Jenna."

"Sorry, you're right. Makes sense with you both being Haskells." He looked at Jenna. "All your test results are in. Everything looks good, and you're right at twelve weeks along. However, as a precaution, I want you to take the next couple days off and rest at home. You may also be a little stiff and sore for a few days." He turned his attention to back to Connor.

"Are you okay? You look like you've just seen a ghost."

"Umm...you were saying something about her being twelve weeks along?"

The doctor gave him a strange look. "Are you saying you didn't know your wife was pregnant?"

"She's not my wife, and I'm not the father. I'm the very surprised half-brother who had no clue."

"I'm married to Connor's dad," said Jenna. "My husband is away on a business trip, so I had the nurse call Connor."

"My god," said Conner. "The two of you sure know how to keep a secret. Is there anything else I should know about?"

"We did the bloodwork," said the doctor, "and we know what you're having. Do you want to know, Jenna? Or did you want it to be a surprise?"

"No, we want to know."

"It's a girl."

"Well I'll be damned. My husband was right. He had a feeling we were having a girl. Are you sure you're okay, Connor?"

"I have no idea. I'm still waiting for the shock to wear off."

"We wanted to wait until I was at least twelve weeks along before we announced it, so we planned on telling the rest of the family over the weekend."

"Sorry if I ruined the surprise," said the doctor, "but congratulations on your new little sister, Connor. Someone from the highway patrol is waiting to see you, Jenna, so I'm going to let him talk to you. Then you're free to go."

The doctor stepped out and Connor grabbed his phone. "I'm calling my dad. Right now."

"Would you mind waiting a few minutes?" asked Jenna. "I need to talk to the officer first. I know who's responsible for this, and I want some answers."

"So do I."

Connor typed a message to Kelsey while Jenna anxiously waited for the officer. He came in a few minutes later and gave Jenna a plastic bag containing her phone and key fob, along with some paperwork.

"There were several witnesses who stated the Blazer may have intentionally hit your vehicle, which we've noted in the accident report. We've tentatively identified the driver as Kenneth Timothy Frank. However, we're waiting for the coroner to confirm it."

"My god," said Jenna. "I thought it might have been him. I'm also sorry to hear he didn't make it."

"So, you knew him?"

"I did at one time. I dated him before I met my husband. He was a friend of one of my coworkers. Her name is Cecelia Wood. She's the one who introduced us."

"So, how long were you seeing one another?"

"About four months."

"So, who ended the relationship?"

"I did," said Jenna. "At the time I thought it ended amicably, and we both moved on to other people. However, he contacted me a few times later on, saying he wanted us to keep in touch, but I kept telling him no. I didn't think it was appropriate."

"Did he threaten you in any way?"

"No. At least not back then. Later on, however, he and CeCe decided to set me up in such a way that I would owe him a favor." As Jenna described the details of what happened the officer took notes.

"He was becoming more aggressive too," said Connor. "When she tried to pay back money, he insisted on taking her out for coffee so they could talk, but he took her to a hotel instead and demanded she have sex with him. Fortunately, she managed to get away from him before anything happened, and my girlfriend and I came and picked her up."

"I'm glad you were able to get away unscathed," said the officer.

"It was a close call alright," said Jenna. "I met with an attorney the following day and we took out a restraining order against him. The attorney also sent him a strongly worded letter, warning him that if he continued, we would take further action against him."

"Which may have pushed him over the edge."

Jenna's voice was firm. "I'm also expecting a child. I needed to protect her as well as myself."

"I understand," said the officer. "So did Mr. Frank know you were expecting?"

"No. The only person at my workplace who knows about the baby is my boss. He needed to know when I'd be going on maternity leave. Trust me, he has no love for CeCe, so there's no way she could have gotten this information from him."

"I'd also like to have a talk with Ms. Wood."

"You know where we work, but I'm afraid I don't have her home address or cell phone number. Her husband's name is John."

"Don't worry, we'll find her."

"Is there anything else?" asked Jenna.

"I think we've covered everything," said the officer. "You may want to talk to your attorney about filing a claim against his insurance company. He was clearly the driver at fault."

Connor grabbed his phone as the officer took his leave. "Are you ready to go?" he asked.

"As soon as they bring me my paperwork."

"Which can sometimes take a while. Then, I'm taking you home. I don't know about you, but I'm starving."

"Me too. Other than a few crackers I haven't eaten since lunch."

"And now you're eating for two. I still can't get over this. So, I'm sending Kelsey a text to see if she can grab something to go as soon as we leave. Any preferences?"

"Whatever you guys want is fine."

"Okay, and now we're going to call Dad. Hopefully he's someplace where we can talk." Connor punched a button and put the call on speaker. Bill answered on the first ring.

"Hey Connor, what's up?"

"I'm at the hospital with Jenna. She and the baby are okay, although you and I need to have a little talk about keeping secrets."

"We wanted to wait until the time was right. So, what the hell happened?"

"I was on my way home from work," said Jenna, "and I noticed someone was following me. It was Ken. He tried to run me off the road as soon as I got on the freeway. I'm okay, but my car may be totaled."

"Are you serious?"

"I'm afraid so," said Connor. "They brought her here by ambulance and checked her out, and she's okay."

"You're sure?"

"I'm fine," said Jenna. "Just bumps and bruises, but they want me to take a couple days off work, which is probably for the best, because it'll keep me from throttling CeCe."

"So, where the hell is Ken? He'd better be sitting in a jail cell somewhere."

"Actually, he's in the morgue," said Connor.

"Are you serious?" asked Bill.

"He didn't make it," said Connor. "A highway patrol officer came to talk to her. According to him, Ken crashed his truck right after he hit her and he was killed instantly. It's unfortunate that it ended this way, but at least he can't hurt her anymore."

"I feel bad for his family," said Bill, "but he brought it on himself."

"We're just waiting for the doctor to sign off on her paperwork, then I'm taking her home. Kelsey's going to bring us some takeout. So, do you need us to stay with her tonight?"

"Actually, I'm on my way as we speak."

"It's a long drive, Dad. You wouldn't get here until after midnight."

"Connor, it's okay. I left Taos right after my meeting. I should be home within the hour."

❧FIFTY-SIX❧

CECE WAS WEEPING uncontrollably when the doorbell rang. "Tell whoever it is to go away," she said between sobs. "I don't want to talk to anyone right now."

"I understand," said John, "but let me find out who it is first. I'll only be a minute." He hurried to the front door and looked through the peephole. A police officer stood on the other side. He quickly opened the door.

"Can I help you?" he asked.

"I'm sorry to disturb you," said the officer, "but is your wife at home?"

"She is, but she's not up to seeing visitors at the moment. Is there anything I can help you with?"

"No, I'm afraid I have to talk to her, but I promise I'll only take a few minutes of her time."

"You can try," said John, "but she's extremely distraught at the moment. A close friend of ours was killed in a traffic accident earlier this evening."

"I understand, and I'm sorry for your loss. However, we're still investigating the accident, and we need to ask her a few questions."

"She wasn't there when it happened."

"I know she wasn't," said the officer, "but we need to clarify a few things. I promise it will only take a few minutes."

John reluctantly led the officer to the living room. CeCe did not respond well. "What are you doing here?"

"I'm sorry to disturb you, ma'am. I understand a close friend of yours was —"

"I already know. Ken's mother called me a few minutes ago. So, what do you want?"

"Again, I'm very sorry to disturb you. We're still trying to determined what happened, and we think you may have some information which could help us."

"What kind of information?"

"It concerns Mr. Frank's relationship with one of you coworkers. A woman named Jenna Haskell. It's my understanding you introduced him to Ms. Haskell."

"I did." CeCe grabbed a fresh tissue as she tried to pull herself together. "Back then her name Jenna Winters. She got married a few weeks ago."

"I understand. So can you tell me more about her relationship with Mr. Frank?"

"What does this have to do with anything? I can assure you Jenna wouldn't have been with him."

"I'm afraid I'm not at liberty to say," said the officer. "So can you please tell me more about his relationship with Mrs. Haskell?"

"It started a year ago last fall. Jenna was single at the time and wasn't seeing anyone, and Ken had recently broken up with his girlfriend, so I arranged for them to meet for coffee one night after work. They hit it off, and they dated for a few months. He really fell for her, but she didn't feel the same, so she ended the relationship. She said there were no hard feelings. At least there were none on her end."

"I see. So, what about Mr. Frank?"

"He was disappointed. He had fallen really hard, but then he met someone else a short time later. I really hoped it would work out for him this time, but it didn't. He wanted Jenna back. I kept telling him she'd moved on, but he couldn't seem to move past her. Then, this past fall, she got furloughed. Ken wanted to help out, anonymously, but then she found out about it, so she stabbed him in the back. That was the thanks he got."

"So would you care to explain?"

"It's kind of a long story," said CeCe.

"I have plenty of time."

The officer took notes as CeCe told him about what had happened with the gift card. Afterwards, he had a few more questions.

"So, how did he react when he found out she had gotten married?"

"As I said, he was disappointed, but he thanked me for the information. I told him the time had come for him to find someone else. I even offered to introduce him to some other single women I knew, but he declined. I figured he needed some time to get over her."

"When was the last time you spoke to him?"

"The day before yesterday," said CeCe. "He asked me about Jenna, as he often did. He knew she wasn't coming back, but he stilled cared about her and he wanted to make sure she was doing alright. I told him she was fine. Then he changed the subject."

"Did he bring her name up again?"

"Not that I recall."

"Did you volunteer any information to him about Mrs. Haskell."

CeCe looked down at the floor. "Not that I recall."

"You're sure about that?"

"Yes, I'm sure. Please understand, I'm still shock. I've known Ken since we were in high school, and we were like brother and sister. I've told you everything I know, and I would very much appreciate it if you would respect my privacy during this very difficult time."

"I understand, and thank you for your time. I can see myself out."

"I'll go with you." John escorted the officer to the door and quickly returned to CeCe's side. "Are you okay?" he asked.

"Not really."

"I watched your reaction when he asked you about giving more information to Ken about Jenna. Is something else going on here?"

"I found out Jenna is pregnant."

"How?" asked John.

"I have my ways."

"Oh, boy, here we go again. So did you tell Ken?"

"I did," said CeCe, "but not for the reason you think. I was trying to convince him to move on."

"Great. They're obviously fishing for information, and I'm concerned about what would happen if they were to find out he knew about her pregnancy."

"How would they? It was a private conversation between Ken and myself, and he's no longer here."

"Maybe not, but they could still get ahold of his phone records. I also know you and Ken used to text each another a lot."

"If they do, they'll see how many times I reminded him it was over between him and Jenna."

"CeCe, I don't think you're grasping the severity of the situation. Jenna may not have been in the truck with him, but she's somehow involved, and they obviously suspect some sort of wrongdoing on his part may have led up to the accident. They may not be able to prosecute him, but if they can somehow prove you were an accessory to whatever he may have done, we could have a serious problem."

CeCe's heart skipped a beat. "Oh my god! I never encouraged him do anything illegal."

"I know you didn't, but you were involved in the gift card incident, which almost cost you your job. I kept warning you about sticking your nose into other people's business, but you never seem to listen, so now we need to take some precautions."

CeCe was starting to panic. "Oh my god! Do you think I'll be arrested?"

"I don't know," said John, "but I think we'd better find you an attorney, just in case."

Ken was laid to rest three days later. After the service his cousin, Joey, stared into space as the rest of the family brought CeCe and John up to date on the details of what had happened. While most of his family believed it was a tragic accident, his mother, and his aunt Theresa, weren't so sure. They were convinced Jenna had somehow provoked him.

CeCe returned to work the following Monday. To her relief, Jenna wasn't at her desk when she arrived. She grabbed a cup of coffee and tried to boot up her computer, but it wouldn't accept her password. Thinking she'd made a mistake, she entered it again, making sure she had typed the all the keys correctly. Once again, it rejected her password. She was getting a bad feeling, but her phone rang before she could call the IT department. Justin wanted her to come to his office as soon as possible. Her heart sank when she reached his door. Marcy, from human resources, was waiting with him.

"Would you mind taking a seat?" said Justin. "And please close the door behind you."

CeCe's hands were shaking as took her seat. "What's going on?" she asked.

"Marcy, I think you should tell her," said Justin.

Marcy turned her attention to CeCe. "I want to begin by stating for the record that we don't get involved in our employee's personal lives unless there is a very good reason for us to do so."

"So, what are you trying to tell me?" asked CeCe.

"As, you know, Jenna Haskell was involved in a traffic accident the other night on her way home from work, and while we're truly sorry for the loss of your friend, Jenna has provided us with a copy of the police report. The evidence strongly suggests that he intentionally tried to run her off the road."

"I know," said CeCe. "The police came to my home and questioned me about it. However, I wasn't there, and I knew nothing about it."

"I understand, but the authorities have been keeping her up-to-date with their investigation. They've recovered Ken's phone, and one of their experts has examined it. We now know you were sending Ken text messages about Jenna."

"He still cared about her. He just wanted to be sure she was okay."

Marcy's voice was stern. "No, ma'am. You told him a lot more than that. A few weeks ago, he received a text message from you regarding Jenna's engagement, and you gave him a lot of personal information about her. This happened around the same time she was taking out an order of protection against him."

"I didn't know about the restraining order until after the fact. Had I known, I wouldn't have given him the information."

"Even if you didn't know about the order of protection, you still knew he had a history of harassing her. You yourself were involved in the gift card incident, and you were warned back then to not to give him any more personal information about her, yet you continued to do so anyway. Your actions put her life in danger, and I have a responsibility to make sure this firm won't be held liable for anything you may have done. Therefore, we've terminated your employment, effective immediately. I need you to surrender your employee badge, and you have fifteen minutes to gather your personal belongings and vacate the building. Security will escort you to your car, and they will take your parking pass. Do you have any questions?"

"What about the project I'm working on?"

"It'll be assigned to another interior designer," said Justin. "I'm sorry, CeCe, but rules are rules."

"So, where's Jenna?" asked CeCe. "Heaven forbid I were accidentally run into her in the hallway on my way out. No doubt she would accuse me of something I didn't do."

"She's not here at the moment," said Marcy, "and that's all you need to know. In the meantime, you need pack up your personal belongings. Please let us know if you need any help taking them out to your car."

"I think I can manage." She took off her lanyard and threw it at Marcy, but it landed at Marcy's feet. "Oh well. I guess you'll have to pick it yourself, because I don't work here anymore."

CeCe stormed back into her desk and began rummaging through the drawers. Her only personal belongings were a few of John's business cards, and a silk plant sitting on top of her desk. She started to drop the cards in her purse, but thought better of it, so she dropped them on the floor. She then removed all the remaining contents from her desk, dumping them onto the floor as well.

"What the hell?" asked Priscilla.

"It's a little going away present from me," said CeCe. "You see, I don't work here anymore."

"Well, thank goodness for that, but if you throw your computer onto the pile, I'm pretty sure they'll deduct the replacement cost from your paycheck. They may even take you to court."

"Fine, have it your way. You can even call security if you want, but by the time they get here, I'll be gone." She picked up her nearly full coffee mug, but once again, Priscilla quickly intervened.

"If you throw that at anyone, I will call the police and have them charge you with assault."

"Well now, aren't you just the killjoy? It was just a little joke, but you obviously didn't get the humor. So long, bitches. Please tell Jenna I hope she rots in hell, because it's her fault Ken's dead."

CeCe slammed the mug on her desk and laughed as the contents splashed out. "Oh, well," she said. "I'd clean it up, but I don't work here anymore so someone else will have to do it." Grabbing her silk plant, she hurried to the elevator. Once she was in her car, she took her parking pass from her rearview and tossed it out the window as she drove away.

❧FIFTY-SEVEN❧

PETE CALLED JENNA a few days later. "I have good news," he said. "The authorities have examined all of Ken's electronic devices. He never had any compromising photos or videos of you. Nor did they find any hidden cameras in his home."

"Oh, thank goodness," said Jenna. "This is good news. So, where did the photo he showed me come from?"

"From an adult website, as he admitted to the judge. He then changed the background to make it appear as though it had been taken in his bedroom."

"Did he by chance share the photo with anyone else and claim it was me?"

"No, he did not. Your stepson called his bluff."

"Good to know. So, what happens now? she asked.

"His phone and laptop will be released to his family. So, did you want to hear the other good news? They've made an arrest in his case."

"Really? Who was it?"

"A woman named Alecia Gerhart," said Pete. "She's part owner of a wrecking yard, and she was also one of Ken's clients. She provided him with an altered Colorado license plate which they apparently thought couldn't be traced. It was on Ken's truck at the time of the accident."

"Typical Ken," said Jenna. "He always thought he was above reproach. Now he has to answer to a higher authority."

"Indeed, he does. We'll go ahead and continue with the claim against his insurance company, and it's looking more and more like they're going to offer you a generous out-of-court settlement. Then you can move on and enjoy your life with your new family."

* * *

Jenna and Bill decided to name their daughter Gwendolyn Ann. As they waited for her arrival, Jenna became increasingly anxious. Waking up early one morning, she took a deep breath slowly climbed out of bed, being careful not to disturb Bill. As she came into the kitchen, she noticed the floors looked dirty. She grabbed a mop and started cleaning as she waited for her coffee to brew. Bill joined her an hour later, as she was scrubbing down the countertops.

"What on earth are you doing?" he asked.

"Catching up on housework. I'm also trying to figure something out."

"Alright. So why don't you take a break, and we'll sit down and discuss it over coffee."

"Good idea." She poured a cup for him, and another for herself. "You know, I never thought I'd get used to decaf, but here I am."

"We finally found the right coffee. So, what's on your mind?"

"I'm not sure if I want to go back to work after the baby comes."

"I thought you said it had become a more positive workplace once they got rid of CeCe."

"It has," said Jenna. "We all love Lara. In fact, she's the one who organized my baby shower, and with her onboard, I should have enough seniority to never have to worry about another furlough. However, I don't feel comfortable leaving Gwen at daycare."

"I'm only at the college a few hours a week, so she can hang out with me while you're at work."

"But you have your own projects to work on."

"Connor did just fine with his baby swing and playpen. Once he started walking, we babyproofed the house and started teaching him what was off limits. Trust me, she'll learn her limits too."

"You make it sound so easy, but back to the matter at hand. I don't want to miss seeing her take her first steps, or hearing her say, 'Mommy,' for the first time." She stopped for a moment and put her hands on her belly.

"I know. We're talking about you, so settle down."

"Are you okay?" asked Bill.

"I'm fine, but she's been really active this morning. So, as I was about to say, I was wondering what you'd think about my putting a home office in the other room as working as a free-lance designer and decorator like we've discussed before. There are small architectural firms who outsource their interior design work, and there's always someone wanting do a complete home makeover."

"You know I'll support whatever decision you make, but let's take it one step at a time. Okay?"

"You're right. I'm getting too far ahead of myself this morning. Must be those maternal instincts kicking in."

"No doubt you're feeling anxious about your labor and delivery as well. Trust me, I'm every bit as anxious as you are. In the meantime, I'm going to make us some breakfast. Then I'm heading over to the college because I have a class to teach. I'll only be gone for a couple of hours, and I'll have my phone with me. Will you be okay until I get back?"

"I'll be fine," said Jenna. "My due date is still a few days away."

"They're not fixed in stone. I wish there was some way Connor, or Kelsey, or your mother, could come stay with you."

"They have to work, and Mom is in Japan with Dad. He makes his final flight today. Don't worry. I'll be fine."

Bill heated up some frozen waffles and helped with the cleanup. After he left, Jenna somehow managed to make herself comfortable on the sofa and fell asleep in front of the TV. Bill gently woke her when he returned.

"Back so soon?" she asked.

"I was gone for a good two hours. You must have been really tired."

"I was." She sat up and tried to get on her feet, but as she did, she was suddenly cried out in pain.

"Are you alright?"

"I don't know. It felt truly awful, and it wasn't like the false alarms I had before."

"Let's get you back on the sofa." Bill helped ease her down and grabbed his phone. "I'm turning on the stopwatch, then I'll get a pen and paper. Let's make note of the time, and see what happens next."

"Do you think I may be going into labor?"

"Maybe. I don't know yet, but if it is, I'm calling Connor."

"Why?" she asked.

"Because he's been a licensed EMT ever since he finished high school, and he spent his summers working in a hospital when he was college. If for some reason we don't make it to the hospital in time, he can deliver the baby. He's done it before."

"Really? Wonder why he never told me."

"I don't know," said Bill, "but I'm sending him an urgent text right now. Meantime I want you to relax and we'll see what happens."

"Easy for you to say." Jenna laid back on the sofa and tried to get comfortable, but she soon had another sharp pain.

"Breathe, breathe," said Bill. "There. That's better."

"How long?" she asked.

"Fifteen minutes." He quickly jotted down the time and sent Connor another text. Over the next few hours Jenna had more contractions. "They're getting a whole lot closer," said Bill, "so I think this may it, because Connor just said he's on his way. You need to put whatever else you need in your bag so you'll be ready to go when he gets here."

Jenna hurried off to the bedroom while Bill sent text messages to his mother and brother. Connor arrived a few minutes later.

"Is everything okay?" he asked.

"So far so good," said Bill. "I'm going to get her car out of the garage, and I want you to ride in the backseat with her."

"You got it, Dad."

Connor helped his father load Jenna into her new Accord. Once she was settled in the back seat, Connor sat down next to her.

"Are you sure you don't want me to drive?" he asked.

"I'm sure," said Bill. "I managed to drive to the hospital when your mother was getting ready to have you."

"Then you must have nerves of steel, Dad. If and when the time comes for me, I can't imagine driving Kelsey to the hospital."

"We'll worry about it later, and I'm not quite ready to be a grandfather just yet."

"It'll be here soon enough," said Connor. "I plan on giving her the ring before the holidays. Assuming she says yes."

"I don't think you have anything to worry about," said Jenna. "Uh-oh. Here we go again."

"Take a deep breath," said Connor.

"I'll be fine," she said between clinched teeth, "as soon as I'm done killing your father."

"She's definitely in labor, Dad. Hang on, Jenna. There you go."

Jenna soon relaxed. "When the time comes, I guess your kids will have an aunt who's more like a cousin."

"I guess so," said Connor. "Although I am feeling a bit of sibling rivalry at the moment. See, I knew I'd get a smile out of you if I tried hard enough."

"I'm just smiling through the pain." Jenna was having another contraction as they turned into the hospital entrance. Once again, Connor noted the time.

"We made it," he said, "although it'll probably be some time before she delivers. I'll stay with you while you get her checked in, then I'm going back to my office, so keep me posted, and let me know if you need anything."

"Will do, and thanks, Connor," said Bill.

Jenna was soon taken up to her room. It looked more like a bedroom in someone's home than a hospital room. Once she changed into a hospital gown the nurse checked her cervix.

"Not bad," she said. "You're dilated up to six centimeters."

"Is that all?"

"I'm afraid so, but don't worry. You can get up and walk around, or make a few phone calls or send some text messages so the rest of the family knows what's going on. Some women find that walking helps move things along. We can even do backrubs and foot massages if you'd like."

"But my water hasn't broken yet."

"Don't worry, we'll take care of it." The nurse turned her attention to Bill. "You may want to run down to the cafeteria and grab something to eat. She's going to be awhile."

"Good idea," said Jenna. "Go take a break."

"Are you sure?" he asked

Jenna pointed toward the door. "Go, and take your time. You may as well call you mother while you're out. She'd probably appreciate an update. As soon as you leave, I'm sending my mother a text."

Bill returned an hour later. Jenna had dilated another centimeter and they had given her an epidural, but her disposition had not improved. Her mother had returned her text message. They were about to leave Tokyo, and would be arriving at the hospital around midnight. Her labor continued over the next few hours, but she was still a long way from delivering. Connor stopped by after he got off work, and he and Bill went across the street to get a pizza. A new nurse midwife was on duty when they returned. Her name was Elizabeth.

"How's she doing?" asked Bill.

"We're definitely getting close," said Elizabeth.

Bill joined Elizabeth at the foot of the bed while Connor sat down in a chair next to Jenna.

"I was just reminiscing about when I first started college," she said. "My advisors said I needed to take a basic drawing class. It'll be fun, they said. The grad students teach them, they said, and they're much easier to work with than the professors. So, I looked at the schedule. There was a drawing class that met one o'clock in the afternoon, three days a week. The instructor's name was Haskell. So, fool that I was, I signed up. Eleven years later, and this is how I end up."

"Did she get an A?" asked Elizabeth.

"A minus," said Bill. "She was late with one assignment."

"I was down with the flu that week, you son of a bitch. I should have taken my cue back then and transferred to another class. If I had, I sure as hell wouldn't be in the predicament I'm in now, would I?"

"You passed the class, and you still did better than the rest of the students."

"Not quite. Miguel got an A. No minus."

"You're right. I forgot about Miguel. Wonder whatever became of him? He was really talented."

"I don't know, nor do I care," said Jenna. "So, ten years later I'm working as an interior designer, and the client wants custom made sculpture. My boss asked if I knew someone, but by then I'd done the right thing and lost touch with our friend here. So, I looked him up, and as luck would have it, he was still in town. Got the sculpture done. Client loved it, but I then I made the fateful mistake of allowing him to take me dinner."

"Which I couldn't do before, because of the teacher-student relationship," said Bill, "but I always liked her."

"Gotcha," said Elizabeth.

"So can I have a do-over?" asked Jenna.

"No," said Bill and Elizabeth at the same time.

Connor burst out laughing. Jenna gave him a hard look.

"Oh, laugh it up, why don't you?" Her mood suddenly changed. "Uh-oh. Something's happening. It almost feels like I've ruptured something."

The nurse quickly examined her and looked at Bill. "Good news. The baby's crowned. Would you like to take a look?"

"Oh wow," said Bill. "I can see the top of her head."

"Let's get her mother ready," said Elizabeth.

"Would you like for me to stay up here with you?" asked Connor. "Please."

"If it's okay with you, Elizabeth, I'd like to stand behind her so I can lift her shoulders and help her push. She's had a long day and she may be getting tired."

"You got it," said Elizabeth. "We'll roll the bed forward to make room for Connor, if it's okay with you, Jenna."

"Do whatever you have to do," said Jenna. "I just want to get this baby out."

The nurse soon told her to push. Connor lifted her shoulders and eased her down between pushes, but after an hour Jenna was exhausted.

"I don't think I can do this much longer."

"Sure, you can," said Connor. "You're almost there."

"How much longer?" she asked Elizabeth.

"I can't say exactly, but you're getting pretty close."

"The baby only has a couple more inches to go," said Bill. "Something tells me this kid is going to be the type who'll go hide somewhere when she gets into trouble and refuse to come out."

"I seem to recall doing that a few times when I was a kid," said Connor.

"And it never ended well, did it?"

"Nope."

Elizabeth told Jenna to push again. "Would you like for us to set up a mirror so you can watch?" she asked.

"The moment of birth is amazing to see," said Connor. "There's really nothing quite like it."

"I'll have to take your word for it," said Jenna. "I just want to get this done." She pushed a few more times as the baby's head made its way out. "Surely we must be done by now."

"We're almost there," said Elizabeth. "We need one more big push."

Jenna took a deep breath and gave one final push. Elizabeth pulled the baby out and another nurse began cleaning her up. Gwen started fussing while Bill stood in awe, completely mesmerized by his newborn daughter. The nurse handed her to her father and she looked around the room as he held her. Jenna sat up, and he handed Gwen to her mother. "We did it." He gave her a kiss. "She's absolutely perfect."

Jenna cradled the baby in her arms, but when Gwen looked at Connor she began crying again.

"Well, that figures," said Connor, "but I can tell she has a healthy set of lungs."

"And look. She's got reddish hair," said Bill. "The same color yours was when you were born. She'll probably have the same hair color we have."

"We need to cut the cord," said Elizabeth, "and then we need to let the pediatrician check her out." As they clamped off the cord, Connor looked at Jenna.

"This may look a little scary," he said, "but don't worry. She won't feel a thing."

"I'm ready," said Jenna.

"Good, because Dad's got the scissors."

"There's really nothing to it," said Bill. "I did the same thing when Connor was born, and there we go. All done. Your birth is now complete, Princess."

"I'll hang with Jenna while you check the baby out," said Connor. "Then I'm out of here. I have someone waiting for me at home, but first I'd like to take a few pictures."

Once the baby was checked out and diapered, she was wrapped in a pink blanket with a little pink cap. Bill held her in his arms while Connor snapped a few photos. Before leaving he hugged his father and his stepmother.

"Thank you for allowing me to be here," he said.

"Thank you for keeping Jenna calm," said Bill. "It made a big difference.

* * *

It was nearly midnight when someone softly tapped on Jenna's door. Her parents had arrived. Gwen was asleep in her bassinette when Bill invited them inside, but Nick went straight to Jenna's bedside and gave her a lingering hug.

"I want to see my baby girl first," he said. "So, how are you doing?"

"Much better than I was a few hours ago. So how was your last flight?"

"Routine," said Nick, "which is always the best kind."

"So did they throw you any kind of farewell party?"

"No, they didn't. It was more like a shakedown. They needed me to handover my employee ID and anything else I may have had which belonged to them. Afterwards, we shook hands, and they wished me luck."

"Tell her the rest, Nick," said Claire.

"Unbeknownst to me, the rest of the crew passed around a card around during the flight for everyone to sign, so your mother will have something nice to put in her scrapbook."

"That's enough chit-chat for now," said Claire. "I want to see the baby."

Bill gently took Gwen from her bassinet and handed her to Jenna. As they admired their granddaughter, he snapped a few pictures with his phone.

"I think I'll page the nurse and have her take the baby to the nursery," said Bill.

"No," said Jenna. "I want her to say here with us."

Bill stood his ground. "No can do. You need your rest, and she'll be sleeping in her nursery once we take her home."

"He's right," said Claire. "You need to get your rest while you can. Speaking of which, your father and I are still on Tokyo time, and it's well past our bedtime. We need to go home and get some sleep, so we'll see you sometime tomorrow."

"I'll let you know when she's released," said Bill.

"Then we'll meet you at your place."

As Nick and Claire stepped out a nurse arrived to take the baby. Once everyone was gone, Bill grabbed a blanket and a pillow and made himself comfortable on the recliner.

"So, are you still sorry you signed up for my class?"

Jenna couldn't resist teasing him. "I don't know. I'll have to think it over and get back with you later."

"Sorry about the A minus," he said with a yawn, "but I had to be fair to the other students."

"So you say."

"And what's that supposed to mean?"

"It means I'm never going to let you live it down. So, goodnight, Bill, and don't worry about anything I may have said earlier. I still love you."

"It was the hormones talking, and now you're sounding a little more like yourself again." He reached over and squeezed her hand. "Goodnight, Jenna. I still love you too, and I always will."

THE END

JENNA'S FAVORITE BROCOLLI SALAD

2 to 3 strips of cooked bacon or ¼ cup prepackaged bacon bits
1 package of broccoli florets, fresh or frozen
½ red onion, diced
¾ cup fresh raisins
¼ cup chopped cashews
1 cup Miracle Whip
½ cup brown sugar
2 tablespoons white wine vinegar

Cook bacon in a skillet over medium heat. Drain on a paper towel and let cool. Mix broccoli, red onion, raisins, and cashews in a large mixing bowl. Crumble bacon into small bits and add to broccoli mixture.

Mix brown sugar Miracle Whip, and vinegar in a small bowl. Add to the broccoli mixture in small amounts. Blend thoroughly between each addition. Chill at for least two hours before serving.

ABOUT THE AUTHOR

Marina Martindale began her career as a graphic designer and artist. After successfully submitting articles to trade publications, she realized that writing was her true life's passion. She draws her inspiration from her own real-life experiences, as well as those of the people around her. The stories, however, are fiction.

Marina currently resides in Denton, Texas. In her spare time, she enjoys music, photography and traveling. For information about other Marina Martindale contemporary romance novels please visit her website at marinamartindale.com.